HEROES
OF
ENGLANDOM

HEROES
OF
ENGLANDOM

ERIK JACOBS

Heroes of Englandom

First edition: 2019

This book is an English version of *Héroes de Englandom*,
the Spanish original edition by Erik Jacobs.

www.erikjacobsbooks.com

ISBN: 978-3-9525047-2-7
ISBN EBOOK: 978-3-9525047-3-4

To all my little and big heroes…
You make the difference.

CONTENTS

CHAPTER 1

PATRIOTS

THE THREE MOST IMPORTANT WOMEN IN MY LIFE stand a few steps in front of me, on either side of the full-length mirror I'm staring into. On my left, my mother and my younger sister, Lily, study me with critical eyes, eager to find something else that needs to be polished or straightened, but after a few seconds, they nod and smile in approval. On my right side is Zara, my best friend. She also beams at me with that knowing look on her face that I'm so familiar with. Then the three of them turn their heads in sync, directing their gaze to my reflection, smiling the whole time. They are satisfied with the last-minute tweaks they considered necessary.

When we arrived at the ceremonial building this morning, they didn't let me go directly to the auditorium to find my seat with the others. They dragged me into this hallway, on the side of the lobby, to inspect me from head to toe. They had to make sure every detail of my appearance lived up to the occasion.

"It's the most significant day of your life—you have to look spectacular," Zara had insisted earlier, and both my mother and Lily couldn't agree more.

I know they're right, though for somewhat different reasons than they think.

Starting today, I can live with less fear.

Now they're less likely to kill me.

At just nineteen years old, I am becoming an officer in the Great National Army of Englandom, the "backbone of our homeland," as any elementary school kid can recite. Today I'll be promoted to a higher caste, and with me, my immediate family moves up too. Our future, our protection, are practically guaranteed. The new caste will provide us with the strong shield I so long for.

Since the Council of Governors established the caste system, we've been members of the Commons, the largest of the castes comprised of citizens with constitutional rights. The majority of the population with pure English origin belongs to our caste, although there are some exceptions. My maternal grandfather, for example, was of Spanish ancestry, but fortunately, thanks to his patriotic distinctions during the Separatist War, he avoided being degraded when the segregation took place.

And now I'm the one, by my own merits, making my family advance in society.

"So? Am I okay now?" I ask them, anxious to get to the auditorium and finish this ceremonious step before it overwhelms me.

"Of course, Derin. You look so handsome, and very elegant!" says Lily in an enthusiastic tone, speaking for the three of them.

Although she's already fourteen years old and quite mature, everyone at home still considers her the baby of the family. It's probably due to our age difference because when she was born, I was already five, and Brian had just turned four. Sometimes he tries to annoy her by saying that he and I were planned children, but she wasn't, meaning she was a product of "carelessness." But she's too smart to be bothered by such nonsense. Physically, she's almost an exact copy of my mother: the same slender figure, the same upturned nose, the same straight, light brown hair. Their almond-shaped eyes are nearly identical, except Lily's are brown, like my father's and Brian's.

"I hope they catch you on camera during the parade and show you on the giant screens," she continues. "You know all my friends think you're hot!"

I know who she's talking about: her schoolmates, who gossip nervously around me when they come over to our house. I find it funny, though I'm uncomfortable being the center of attention.

I turn my head to the right side of the mirror, to Zara, my best friend—my only friend—to catch her reaction to Lily's comment.

"Definitely, they'll all go crazy!" she says, but she smiles at me with a gaze full of complicity. It's an expression I know well, which I playfully call "mocking malice." I know exactly what she's thinking.

For a second, we both enjoy the innocent irony of the comment from my sister, who doesn't know me as well as my friend.

Zara has been my shadow since elementary school, and we're the same age. She's the one person who knows the real me. I trust her completely.

In a way, her story is similar to mine. Her family originally comes from an island in the Caribbean, but due to her grandfather's heroic actions and loyalty to the country, she now belongs to the Commons. She has her own fears to deal with, though. Because of her dark skin and exotic features—she's beautiful—she is often the victim of racist insults and slurs. These profanities are commonplace, since the regent himself, the head of the fourteen governors, is very fond of uttering them. He even encourages them, expressing them with a detestable comic air.

"You're the crazy ones," I reply with a grin. "I do look good, but that's it, so don't exaggerate."

"Oh my. Our Derin, always so modest and harsh on himself," Zara says reproachfully, smiling but shaking her head.

"Really, *Lieutenant Dark*, it's so hard to convince you," says Lily. "But even you have to admit that you look gorgeous."

I stiffen and look sideways to make sure none of my peers are nearby. I don't want to imagine what they'd say if they heard my little sister calling me *gorgeous*. They'd never stop mocking me.

"Okay, okay," I finally give in. "I have to admit that you've made me look great, so thanks. But don't get ahead of yourself, Lily. You still have to wait a bit longer to call me lieutenant."

My mother, who hasn't intervened in our conversation, just smiles with teary eyes, nodding along to everything Zara and Lily say.

"Mom, what do you think?" I ask her. "Do you think *these* two are right?"

She broadens her smile even more and dries a tear with the handkerchief she hasn't let go of all morning.

"Of course, darling, you look lovely," she replies. "You'll shine up there. We're so proud of you."

Lovely… It seems that today I'll have to accept all kinds of pompous, feminine adjectives. I find them horribly inadequate, but I won't complain about it to my mother right now. She's very excited and emotional.

I haven't seen her so happy in a long time. She's gleaming and can't stop smiling. It's evident that she feels very proud of me, and that fills me with joy. But I also recognize in her look and her posture a kind of relief. As if a heavy weight has been lifted off her. As if she was aware of the danger that I've always shouldered, which has been considerably reduced now, though it will never disappear completely.

Somehow, perhaps from maternal intuition, she must understand that they can't hurt me now, at least not so easily.

As members of the Commons, we were citizens with rights, but we were also exposed to our country's deficiencies and dangers, such as the scarcity of almost everything, the growing restrictions of certain individual freedoms, and above all, the arbitrary punishments and executions. Sure, in comparison to what the others—the majority—suffer, we should be grateful: we can live in London and breathe clean air, we have access to good education and health, we all work and earn credits, and we've never lacked food, however basic and tasteless it may sometimes be.

But even as citizens with rights, the shadow of the ever-present risk of losing everything is always on us, one way or another. Any severe misconduct from any of us means the whole family is in danger of falling out of favor—of suffering the pain and humiliation of being degraded to the Disloyal caste, the lowest caste of society, whose members have no rights and live in gigantic ghettos outside our cities.

But as of today, I have fewer reasons to worry about that. Today, my family and I become Patriots.

Above the Commons, the members of the Patriots are the most privileged group of the population—apart from our leaders, of course. Our new rank provides us with a house in a better area—almost twice the size of our current comfortable dwelling—equipped with luxuries that, up to now, we have only been able to dream of. We get the right to have an eCar (together, we already have enough credits to buy one), and we'll have access to a range of restricted consumer products, especially more natural and tastier food than the synthetic kind our current diet is based on. There's also the possibility of getting a special permit to leave the country for a few days. But most importantly, the caste provides us with a much stronger degree of protection against punishments, the loss of our privileges, and degradation.

In the Patriots, I'll be safe. We'll all be safe now.

"Thanks, Mom," I reply. "I owe it to you … to all of you. But look at you, you look amazing. You have all the bearing of a Patriot."

"That's sweet, darling, but I've barely managed to dress up a little bit," she says, somewhat embarrassed because she must be aware that her elegance and distinction make her look striking, and she's unused to that, being a modest person.

"Can you see now where my modesty comes from?" I ask Lily and Zara, smiling. "So don't blame me." I turn to my mother again and say to her, "You have the right to be dazzling, Mom, you're a Patriot now. Indeed, you could even pass for a Patrician!"

The Patricians are the highest, the smallest, and most exclusive of the four castes in our society. You could say they're what we used to call "aristocracy," although now that term is forbidden. They're the ones who control the Government, the Army, all the institutions of the State, the economy, and in general, all the country's wealth. We can't say it out loud, but everyone knows it: the Patricians are the owners of Englandom.

"Oh, Derin, the things you say," replies my mother, looking at the simple blue dress she's wearing. "How could anyone think that I'm a Patrician, wearing *this*? No Patrician woman would ever wear anything made of Petex."

"Mom, I can assure you, your dress looks like it's made with imported fabrics, not Petex," I say bluntly, though deep down I know she's right.

Since the only abundant resource in the country is oil, which no one else in the rest of the world is interested in, the government technicians invented Petrotextile, or Petex, a synthetic textile that is highly versatile and durable. Everything in Englandom seems to be made of Petex. For our clothes, the Commons and the Patriots have some variety of textures and colors. The Disloyal must settle for coarse fabrics in muted tones, usually in shades of grey and greenish brown.

"But, anyway, it's about time," I say to my "three girls," as I usually refer to them. "You need to go find Dad and Brian. See you in a bit."

"Good luck, darling," my mother wishes me. "Enjoy your ceremony."

"Good luck, Derin!" Zara and Lily say at the same time.

Before leaving, I gaze one last time at the image in the mirror.

I recognize my own reflection, but a distant voice in my head tries to convince me that I'm looking at somebody else. I see a young man, six feet tall with a slim, athletic build, short and straight dark brown hair, and grey eyes (I try to recognize my mother's in them, but I'm not sure). As always when I stand in front of a mirror, I fixate on the scar that crosses my left eyebrow diagonally and divides it into two. As always, it brings back bad memories. I'm wearing the elegant dress uniform: black pants and leather boots, a long-sleeved scarlet coat with a high neckline, gold buttons and badges, a black leather belt with a golden buckle, white gloves, and a black peaked cap with golden embroidery.

It's the living image of the gleaming young officer on the cover of the thick book, *History of the Great National Army of Englandom*... But it's not me.

—

THE AUDITORIUM IS FILLED TO THE VERY LAST SEAT.

For a moment, I don't understand how it's possible that the place is so packed, but then I realize what's going on. They've surely "invited" additional people so that the ceremony looks better. It's possible they'll pick some images from our graduation to show during the broadcast of the grand celebration that will take place later.

Because this year, the date of our graduation from the Military Academy wasn't chosen arbitrarily. Today, we celebrate the thirtieth anniversary of the founding of our country: the Great Nation of Imperial Englandom. The country that the first governors established after winning the Separatist War.

That was the war that almost escalated into a world conflict because of the intervention of the European hegemonic bloc and other foreign forces. It culminated in the separation of Northern Ireland and the definite submission of Scotland, which disappeared as an independent nation. The governors founded Englandom on the island formerly known as Great Britain: they closed the borders, initiated segregation of the people, and undertook the task of creating a new society, the society of the castes. Anyone with foreign blood, or who hadn't demonstrated their profound loyalty to the fatherland, became a Disloyal.

I find it a bit strange to think that our country is barely thirty years old.

It's the only country I know—very few people have permits to get out, and the Government censors all information from abroad—so for me it feels like it's been this way for centuries, but I know that's not true, and I know it could be different… better.

Some older people who knew the outside world before the war—and who no longer care about being detained as traitors and executed—express a sad verdict: even though we're in the year 2055, instead of being modern, our country seems to have gone back a century. While the rest of the world advances by leaps and bounds—according to the propaganda of the regime's enemies, whose dissemination is punishable by death—we're stuck in the past, with no way forward.

For my part, I try my best to help improve the country. Although it's not easy.

But those musings are for another day. Today, everything has to stay positive.

My peers and I take up the first two rows of the auditorium. I'm in the second row, three seats from the right aisle. Those three seats are empty because I'll be the last one to go on stage. They call us according to the alphabetical order of our surnames, and since mine begins with "D," I normally should be one of the first; but as I got the best scores on the graduation tests, I'll receive a special honor at the end.

On the stage, they've placed a dark wooden podium on the left side, where Captain Alan Foster, our commander, will lead the ceremony. A little farther back, in the center, there's a long table with a white tablecloth. Four representatives of the Government and the military high command are sitting behind it.

Captain Foster begins calling the cadets.

Each one of my peers gets up when he hears his name and walks up to the stage; there, he receives the official badges and heads to the dignitaries' table to be congratulated. Then each new officer walks off the stage using the steps on the opposite side and returns to his seat.

When the last of my peers, Rob Schilling, returns from the stage and takes the empty seat to my left once more, my heart begins to pound. I hide it well, but I'm really quite shy. I hate being the center of attention. It requires tremendous physical and mental effort to conceal my nervousness. I try to calm down, but it feels like the whole audience can hear the thunder coming out of my chest. I keep looking forward, stunned.

I don't catch all the phrases the captain says, which barely reach my ears. I know that he's praising me because I vaguely pick up that he mentions "his exceptional abilities in Military Strategy" and "his outstanding performance in Territorial Control." When he says something about "his exemplary discipline, leadership, and camaraderie," I freeze. I fear that I won't be able to get up when he calls my name.

"Lieutenant Derin Dark," I hear in the distance.

My legs lift me and take me to the stage like a robot. I walk up the steps and head toward Captain Foster. I stop in front of him and execute the military salute flawlessly, bringing my right hand toward my temple with my fingers joined together. The captain shakes my hand firmly and gives the officer's badges to me.

"Congratulations, Lieutenant Dark, you deserve it. I'm very proud of you," he says with a genuine smile. Then he pins the Graduation Honors medal for being first in my class on the left side of my coat, above my chest.

"Thank you, captain," I reply earnestly, tilting my head a bit forward.

I turn to the audience, which erupts into deafening applause. I remain like this for a couple of seconds, as required by the protocol, looking straight ahead with a blank stare. I know that my family is near the center of the auditorium, but I avoid looking down. I don't want to see my mother and Lily crying; I can't allow my eyes to get wet. I must not show any weakness.

I walk to the dignitaries' table to shake their hands. Unintentionally, I raise my eyes a fraction of a second toward the huge, square crimson banner that hangs over them, with images and letters embroidered in gold: the flag of Englandom.

It consists of a garland or crown formed by fourteen lions, each bearing a sword in its claws (these symbolize the fourteen protectorates). In the center of the crown, in very large letters, is the acronym of the country: "GNIE"; below it, a bit smaller and following the curve of the garland of lions, is the full name: "GREAT NATION OF IMPERIAL ENGLANDOM"; and above the acronym, also following the curve of the garland, are the three supreme virtues: "PRIDE, JUSTICE, AND FREEDOM."

A lump forms in my throat when I read those words.

Justice and freedom? How far we truly are from achieving them!

The four representatives from the Government and Army ceremoniously express their congratulations and their best wishes that I continue to serve the country with dedication and loyalty. I feel as if each one of them has slapped me.

Why can't I just enjoy this moment like a normal person?

Upon my return to my seat, the captain indicates that the graduation ceremony is over, and reminds the audience that it's a citizen's duty to participate in the commemorative celebrations on this day. Before leaving the auditorium, the whole audience stands up, and we all sing the national anthem in a single zealous voice.

When the official photographers finish taking our pictures, I join my family in the lobby.

Lily and my mother rush toward me and hang themselves from my neck with emotional displays of affection. Zara also hugs me but doesn't say anything. I understand that her strong embrace is more than congratulations: she wishes me, without words, lots of strength and courage.

My father and my brother Brian, more composed, approach me next:

"Congratulations, son. We're very proud of you," says my father, hugging me.

"Thanks, Dad… I owe it to all of you," I answer, trying to keep my voice from breaking.

"Nonsense," he replies very seriously. "Everything is because of your own merit. It's the reward for all your efforts and sacrifices. Besides, we're the ones who are grateful. Thanks to you, our life will improve considerably."

Now he's the one whose voice breaks. He hugs me again.

My father has always supported my decision to pursue a military career, although, at times, I've questioned whether he does it out of sincere conviction or resignation. Deep down, I feel that he shares the concerns of my brother, who disapproves of my decision to become part of "the system."

Brian and my father don't hide their disapproval of our society and the Government's organization. It's not that I'm blind to all the faults and imbalances (they're obvious), or that I ignore the abuses and discrimination suffered by a large part of the population. On the contrary, I'm fully aware of what's wrong. Besides, I have a personal interest in changing certain things because I could become a victim of them myself… and my family with me. But I firmly believe that only from within, like a cog in the machinery, can we have a real positive impact.

I wish the two of them could understand me better, but I have to remind myself that they don't know my internal motivations. So, we stick to discussions about the facts that are visible to all, though only at home. It's too dangerous to criticize the Government in public or to seem unsure of one's own patriotic loyalty, especially since the attacks perpetrated by the insurgents have increased considerably.

These rebel groups, called "radkers" (or radical hackers) by the Government, constantly try to infiltrate and wreak havoc on the main infrastructures vital for the functioning of our social and economic system. They're the regime's number one enemy and are considered the country's greatest danger. As a new Army officer, the rebels are now my problem as well.

Now it's Brian's turn to congratulate me.

As he approaches me, I feel guilty at the sight of the fading purple blotch on his left temple, where I punched him.

Our relationship isn't the most brotherly. Not over a week ago we had our last confrontation, which ended in a fistfight. Even though he managed to hit me hard in the ribs too, and I still feel pain where the blow bruised me, I hit him harder. Brian is only a couple of inches shorter than me, but he's more buff. My great advantage is my military training. When he can't control his temper and decides to use his fists against me, he never wins.

Like my father, Brian has curly, copper-colored hair, and pale skin; he also has large, expressive brown eyes, a fleshy nose, and freckles on his face. Some friends say that he and I are each other's nemesis: we are opposites, not only physically, but also personali-ty-wise. Brian is messy, restless, impulsive, and very outgoing. He doesn't mince his words, saying what he thinks without consid-ering the consequences too much. Since he can't' freely express his criticisms of the system in public, I think he blows off steam by reproaching me for my "disgusting" loyalty.

Brian looks at me and smiles. Although he doesn't hug me— thank goodness, that would be too awkward—he pats me on my left arm, near my shoulder.

"Well, champ," he says, "you did it. Congratulations… Seri-ously, I'm happy for you."

I know it's not easy for him to say that.

"Hey, come on, you're not going to start crying too, right?" I say in a playful tone, to loosen up the tension of the moment.

"Didn't you see me back there?" he replies. "Everyone handed me their handkerchiefs. I couldn't hold back the tears."

"Yeah, yeah, your eyes are super swollen from all the crying."

It's a pity that we have become distant from each other. I really miss him. I hope one day we'll be able to heal the wounds.

His path is the same as my father's: teaching. I hope his anger and frustration will fade over time, at least when he becomes a teacher. He just turned eighteen, so one can expect that maturity and a university degree will help him calm down.

Though I doubt he'll change a lot… He's too impulsive and stubborn.

A good example of his defiant nature is his decision to date Mia, a girl from the Strip, the largest ghetto on the outskirts of London, where millions of Disloyal live. I'm not saying he's not in love, because I know for a fact that he's crazy about her, but it's always seemed to me that Brian has never paid particular attention to any girl who wasn't a Disloyal as if he intentionally wants to show off his rebelliousness. Mia is going to become a kindergarten teacher, as far as I know, but she won't be able to teach in London and will have to stay in the Strip.

If one day he marries her, Brian will be degraded to Disloyal, lose all his caste privileges, and have to leave the city. But for the time being, he's here and makes a great effort to be nice. I know he's trying hard not to ruin my day.

"Well, the moment for emotions and crying is over now," I say as I pat him on his left arm too. "Anyway, thank you, I appreciate it."

"Sure. As Dad said, you really deserve it. In spite of everything."

He seems to mean what he's saying; it moves me a little. He shows me a faint but genuine smile and then walks away.

However small, this is the only show of affection that can be expected between us.

CHAPTER 2

FLAGS AND DRONES

WE LEAVE THE AUDITORIUM COMPLEX TOGETHER and walk to the elevated train station, just a couple of blocks away. The dense magnetic train network—which replaced the underground tube, almost entirely destroyed during the war—and the omnipresent towers that purify the air are two of the regime's greatest achievements, at least here in London. Combustion vehicles were banned in the city years ago, so if you're not a Patriot or a Patrician and don't have an eCar or helijet, you depend on the magnetic train. The absence of combustion engines means few harmful emissions, but the pestilent and polluted air from the Strip—less than thirty-five miles away—sometimes reaches here depending on the wind's direction and strength, hence the need to clean it.

Brian will meet Mia at the station and go who knows where to watch the commemorative parade on the big public screens, while the rest of us will go right to the parade's route.

Zara and I walk side by side, a couple of steps behind the others. She nudges me gently and says in a low voice:

"So? Do you think *he* will be there too?"

She's referring to Dylan, Mia's cousin, a boy I met briefly a few days ago and who I can't get out of my head. Before I met him, I was already aware that Dylan preferred boys. By chance, I'd overheard a conversation between Brian and Mia that made the matter clear. Since then, I was intrigued about what he'd be like. When I finally met him, I was awestruck.

"Ah, who knows?" I reply, trying desperately not to sound too interested. "Besides, what difference does it make? I'm a Patriot now, an Army officer, and he's a *deel*. I'm sure he hates me and my guts."

Generally speaking, we call all Disloyal "deels," and they too have several pejorative names for each of the higher castes.

"Are you serious?" she throws back, pretending to be outraged by my comment. "You know that you're gorgeous, and today in your dress uniform, you look devastatingly handsome."

"Well, anyway…" I reply, "even if he liked me, which I doubt, you know it's out of the question. I can't risk having anything to do with a deel. It's dangerous enough that Brian is with one of them."

"Goodness, Deedee, it's not like you're going to marry him," she says in an exasperated tone.

She calls me *Deedee* sometimes, especially when we're alone. It's the nickname she came up with years ago when she read aloud the initials of my first and last names.

"Of course not, but marriage isn't the issue," I reply. Then I continue, pointing at my family. "I can't take that risk, much less now. If the Government finds out about me, then I'm done for… they'd crush me and all of them with me."

"I think you're exaggerating a bit," she says. "If you're careful and discreet enough, you could indulge yourself in a little excitement and pleasure. Others do."

"Yeah, yeah… you might be right, but I would never put my life and the future of my family at stake just to satisfy a personal desire. The price would be too high."

"Well, then we're screwed, right?"

"Yes, we're screwed," I say, shrugging my shoulders and grimacing in resignation.

We arrive at the station. Inside, under the lit-up red cube that hangs from the ceiling and marks the meeting point, we recognize

Mia. And yes… Dylan is there too: the blond guy with tousled hair holding his skateboard with one foot.

I get as nervous as when they called my name to go on stage to receive my badge… even more nervous. I feel like an insecure and clumsy child. I hate feeling like this.

Brian goes ahead of us and greets Mia with a kiss on the lips.

"Hi, baby," he says. She kisses him back and hugs him.

They met a little less than two years ago, during a visit to the Strip that my father and other teachers had organized to donate learning materials. They both say it was "love at first sight," and they've been a couple ever since.

Mia then turns to my mother and greets her with an affectionate hug.

"Emma, how elegant!" she says.

"Thank you, darling, you're too kind," replies my mother, who then turns to me and quickly adds: "But look at Derin, our new lieutenant. Doesn't he look spectacular?"

All eyes are on me now, and I feel like I'm burning up.

"Of course! Derin, you look wonderful!" says Mia in her sweet and genuine voice as she hugs me. "Congratulations, what a great achievement!"

I like her too. She's seventeen years old, with a slim figure and long, wavy dark-blond hair. She has expressive hazel eyes and delicate features, and she's a bit taller than Zara, Lily, and my mother. She and Brian make a beautiful couple. If only she weren't a Disloyal… Well, anyway, today I won't think any more about it.

"Thanks, Mia. You're very kind," I reply.

After that, she hurriedly greets my father, Lily, and Zara in the same affectionate manner. She then turns to her cousin and says:

"You remember Dylan, right?"

With a sudden impulse, I get ahead of the others and hold out my hand.

"Um… sure. Hi, Dylan, how are you?"

For a frightfully awkward second, everyone stays silent, staring at me in amazement. My action has been too unusual. It's not like me. They're used to seeing me as a rather quiet and even taciturn person. I blush.

Dylan, as surprised as the others, comes forward.

"Hi, Derin, how's it going? Um… congratulations," he says.

He shakes my hand without looking at me directly. I'm dying of shame.

"Err… thanks," I reply, praying for someone else to say something, anything.

"Hello, Dylan, how are you?" my mother says all of a sudden, sounding a bit too enthusiastic. "Don't tell me you came all this way on your skateboard."

I lock eyes with Zara, who looks at me with a compassionate expression. My mother's attempt to divert attention away from me is evident to everyone. I feel out of place. It's embarrassing. Besides, I'm now annoyed by the fact that Dylan didn't care to look me in the eye, even though I have exposed myself so disastrously.

I can barely take my eyes off him. While he greets the others, I shoot furtive glances at him and adore what I see: Dylan Blake, "the genius boy" from the Strip. He's a self-taught computer systems expert, who at seventeen has a job in the city and privileges that for most of his caste are unattainable.

It's easy to see that Mia is his cousin. They could pass as twins or at least siblings, but Dylan is much more handsome. His body is slim and defined; he's a little shorter than me (I'd guess around five feet nine); his dark-blond hair is short on the sides but longer on top, enough to show something of a wave—often, a lock falls across his forehead, which makes him look charming and carefree—and the features of his angular face are fine but masculine. His brown eyes—those eyelashes—have a deep and dreamy gaze; he has a small nose—my mother would call it a "button nose"—and his perfect lips always seem to outline a slight, almost imperceptible smile that captivates me. He's wearing a grey overall and a blue t-shirt that fits him tightly.

I have to make an effort not to gawk at him, as I fear everyone will notice. My recent clumsy moment is enough awkwardness for one day.

After a while, my parents, Lily, and Zara say goodbye and walk up to the track level to take their train. They'll try to find a good spot along the parade's route. Brian, Mia, and Dylan will meet up with some friends before leaving. Even though they are deels, both Mia and Dylan have special permits to enter the city. Dylan works in one of the Government's ministries, and Mia works part-time babysitting two small children in a home of Patriots.

While I say goodbye to them too, the loud cries of an angry man make us wince. We all turn our heads in the same direction.

Two security agents violently slap and insult a boy of about twelve or thirteen, who appears to be a deel, although he could also be a Common. He falls to the floor. Stunned, with his nose broken and his face full of blood, the poor boy tries to get up, but they hit him harder. He loses consciousness. Behind them hangs a giant Government billboard with images of the governors and phrases alluding to the thirtieth anniversary of Englandom. I immediately realize what "crime" the boy has committed: he has drawn a pig on the billboard and next to it written the word "fatgul," the pejorative term the Disloyal use to refer to the Patricians—"fat moguls"—especially the governor-regent.

They drag the unconscious boy away… to who knows where. If he's a Common, punishment will be truly severe. If he's a deel, punishment will be death, for him and his family.

The rage on Brian's face makes him look like a demon, and I have the impression that he's about to run after the agents to help the boy. Mia puts a hand on his shoulder as if trying to calm him down, and I'm ready to hold him back with all my strength, if necessary. But Brian turns around and wraps his arms around her.

I turn my head toward Dylan, and our eyes meet for a fraction of a second; he also burns with rage. There have been few moments in my life that have made me feel more ashamed and insignificant than now.

—

A WHILE LATER, I take the magnetic train with my peers and arrive downtown, at the meeting point where we have been summoned.

It's a beautiful autumn day. There's not a single cloud in the blue sky. In the sunlight, the leaves of the trees, which are already different shades of yellow and orange, appear to be made of gold paper. At the meeting point in Trafalgar Square, my peers and I have joined the new officers from the rest of the country and wait in a formation of rows, fifteen across. I'm in the front row, close to the left flank, with the other officers who have received individual honors. The parade has been going on for almost an hour now, with an impressive display of all the best that represents the nation, including our National Army's most modern and powerful weapons. In intervals of a few minutes, several squadrons of fighter planes, bombers, helijets, and drones cross the sky in the same direction as the parade.

Despite the majesty of the day, I can't help but remember the awful tragedy that took place a few years ago in this same square. Hundreds of students were peacefully demonstrating for a more flexible education law. They asked that their careers not be imposed on them, but rather that they could decide for themselves. They were all massacred most savagely, live, during a compulsory official broadcast.

We've just been told that we start marching in five minutes.

I take my teleCard out of my pocket and try to call, one after another, my father, my mother, and Zara, but no one answers. No wonder; they'll be absorbed watching the parade, and there's too much noise for them to hear the ringtone. It's so silly, but I want to make sure they know I'm about to march in front of them.

Every citizen of legal age has a teleCard because the Government gives us one when we turn fifteen. It's a high-tech device, about five inches long, thin and rectangular with rounded corners. The front is entirely covered by a digital screen, without any bezels; the back cover is metallic, in the color of the caste we belong to and engraved with our full name, as well as our citizen number. The device's system contains all our personal data and serves as our official ID. Without a teleCard, you're nobody. Besides ID, we use it to receive and pay with credits, to communicate, to receive messages from the Government, and to participate in citizens' consultations, among other things. My teleCard is olive green, the color of the Commons. In the next few days, we'll exchange our teleCards for new ones in navy blue, the color of the Patriots.

We hear the order to advance and start marching.

Our formation closes the parade, and now we're about to cross under the Admiralty Arch to get onto the Boulevard of the Patriots, which used to be called The Mall.

My adrenaline rises to maximum levels. Hundreds of thousands euphorically cheer the parade along the boulevard, which has become a magical path of gold and crimson. On both sides, colossal Englandom flags are interspersed with oversized golden torches, whose flames exceed the height of the trees. The deafening combination of the aircraft roaring in the sky, the marching music played by the bands, and the cheers of the crowd is highly stimulating.

At the end of the boulevard stands the imposing Palace of the Governors, the seat of government, which until shortly before the establishment of the GNIE was called Buckingham Palace. That's where the last king, King William, resided. He was deposed and banished from the country along with his entire family. The original palace looks like a toy beneath the steel and concrete giant that rises above it.

It's a skyscraper shaped like an elongated, glass-sheathed pyramid. At a height of about two hundred feet, there's a wide overhang: a kind of balcony, or rather an observation platform. From there, the fourteen governors—each of them head of their respective protectorate's ruling family—watch the parade. They are presided over by the governor-regent, Eugene Crowley.

I feel like we reach the end of the Boulevard of the Patriots in a flash.

We arrive at the large square in front of the palace and take our place in the designated area. From where I'm standing, I can see the two huge screens that hang from both sides of the governors' balcony.

I fix my gaze on the left-hand screen. The fourteen governors sit on red thrones that form a semicircle on some kind of stage. If not for the magnified images on the screen, it would be almost impossible to recognize them: apart from the distance, the massive volume of the building makes the people up there look like ants.

Regent Crowley stands up and walks to the front of the platform, toward a transparent podium, surely bulletproof.

The Crowleys are Englandom's most powerful Patrician family and have presided over the Council of the Governors since the establishment of the GNIE. Back then, the fourteen governors elected Alistair Crowley as the first leader of the nation. After the death of the elderly Alistair, which occurred when I was in secondary school, the Council elected Eugene to succeed his father.

He's a chubby man in his fifties with straight blond hair, almost white; he has a round face with a bright pink color, as if sunburned, yet his skin seems too smooth for his age. He's wearing a black robe with red and gold details.

During his speech, as always when we see him on television, he emphasizes certain phrases with a rehearsed, ritual quality that has become his distinguishing mark, and which provokes mockery and fear at the same time:

"… and we beat the ruthless enemy that wanted to destroy our country and our identity." He pauses briefly, looks directly at the camera—at us—and opens wide his small, bright blue eyes, lifting the corners of his lips into a grotesque smile, a strange grimace that reveals his perfectly white teeth. Then he adds, slowly enunciating each word, "This is the truth."

He then makes a long pause and continues:

"… because we have built a proud, fair, and prosperous society, free of the impurities of race and decadent foreign influences." In the same ritual as before, he adds, "This is the truth." He keeps going like this for an unbearably long time. "… and with the unconditional support of my fellow governors here today, I continue to serve our great nation humbly to guarantee peace and prosperity… This is the truth."

I can't help but smile when I remember Brian impersonating the regent this morning.

I went down to have breakfast, already wearing my dress uniform, and my father said that I looked very elegant. Brian, who was also in the kitchen, nodded and ceremoniously pronounced, "This is the truth," mocking the voice and the unmistakable grimaces of Regent Crowley. His parody of him is really quite good.

The regent keeps talking, and we all pay attention in silence.

Suddenly, I notice some restless activity around me: muttering and heads turning. At first, I don't get what's going on. After a moment, I also hear the buzzing, which is very subdued initially but soon becomes much louder.

I turn my head toward the Boulevard of the Patriots and see the source of the mechanical whirring.

A fleet of drones glides smoothly over the boulevard and toward the palace. The drones form two rows, one a few feet behind the other. Each row holds a long bar. In turn, each bar holds one end of what appears to be a giant Englandom flag, judging by the crimson color. But it's not possible to make it out completely since only the bottom side, hanging between the two bars, is visible.

I suspect this is some part of the event that wasn't communicated to the public, to surprise us with a stunt at the end of the regent's speech.

But something doesn't quite fit. Something isn't right.

What follows next happens in a matter of seconds.

The drone fleet arrives at the Palace of the Governors. The first row of drones releases the bar they were holding, while the second row continues holding on to their own bar. The crimson flag unfolds and reveals the front.

I shudder as thousands of people let out a chilling sigh of disbelief and amazement.

The flag's front isn't red, but silver-grey, and instead of the golden lion crown, we see a huge blue rose and the slogan "STOP OPPRESSION NOW!"

The symbol of the rebels.

Clad in black uniforms and helmets, several CAT agents—Counterterrorism Agency Troops—appear from nowhere and burst onto the balcony, pouncing on Crowley and the governors.

The first row of drones plummets toward the balcony as I hear the smacking sound of an anti-aircraft gun firing. Its projectiles hit the drones and make them explode into a thousand pieces. The same happens with the other drones holding the rebel flag. A cloud of grey smoke forms in front of the governors' balcony, while scraps of the flag and fragments of what had been the drones fall and scatter all over the square.

After a few seconds of shivering silence, panic breaks out.

I rush to the middle of the square, where the most considerable damage appears to be. People run everywhere in chaos. Dozens are stained with blood. Some are screaming with their hands over their heads, while others seem to be in a state of shock. But I soon realize that the damage is limited: there are no serious injuries, though several civilians bear minor ones.

Captain Foster tells us to help in any way we can, and he orders us all to meet again at the Military Academy's complex no later than tonight at eight o'clock.

The paramedics arrive to take care of the wounded; ambulance sirens are howling everywhere. Several units of the security forces, joined by CAT troops, start to clear the square and take control of the situation. They thank us for our help in escorting civilians away from the area but make it clear that we are no longer needed.

Suddenly, I think of my family, and for a moment, I fear for them, but I calm down. I'm sure they were very far from the explosions. Even so, I'm worried about a possible stampede through the crowd. I take my teleCard out of my pocket, but soon realize that the authorities have blocked the call function.

We had agreed to meet after the parade at a specific location near the lake in Saint James Park, which borders the Boulevard of the Patriots. It's a short distance from here. I head toward the park, accompanied by Chris Peterson, a classmate of mine who also agreed to meet his family there.

We're about to cross the boulevard when Chris points excitedly toward one of the big screens.

"Hey, look, Derin! They got the bastards!"

The official channel is broadcasting live images from one of the many HD security cameras scattered throughout the city. I see several CATs brutally beating up a group of youngsters with electric clubs. The camera zooms in on two anti-terrorist agents who have subdued one kid on the pavement, face down. While a CAT roughly puts handcuffs around his wrists behind his back, the other has his foot on the boy's head and pushes it roughly against the asphalt.

The camera zooms in even closer. Despite the swollen eye and the blood covering half of his face, I clearly recognize the red-haired boy lying on the ground, squirming in pain.

My heart stops. It's my brother Brian.

CHAPTER 3

LITTLE TIN SOLDIER

ABOUT SIX OR SEVEN YEARS AGO, my family had the opportunity to spend a good part of summer vacation in the Lake District. My father had rented a small cabin on the shores of Lake Windermere, which included a dock and a small motor boat. We spent hours fishing, although Brian and I were not allowed to go out on the boat without our father. That had been stipulated strictly by our mother. But the temptation was too much for two adventurous boys.

One night, as soon as we were sure our parents were asleep, we sneaked out of the cabin and went out in the boat, using the oars to get far enough away from the cabin so that the sound of the engine wouldn't wake anyone. We couldn't resist the urge to fish on our own.

We didn't catch anything, but we enjoyed the adventure. However, at some point, the conversation turned to an incident that had happened recently at our school, when some older kids had been beating up Brian, and I had joined the fight to defend him. The other guys lost the fight, and in my eyes, the whole issue was settled. But Brian was still upset because my intervention made him look like a "weakling."

I don't remember exactly what made both of us so angry that night, but we ended up fighting. Brian, who had always been very impulsive, picked up one of the oars and flailed it with quick movements near my head, trying to keep me away from him. In one of those uncontrolled motions, he miscalculated the distance and struck me over the left eye. I lost my balance from the impact and fell overboard. The blow must have left me stunned because I only remember the terrible darkness under the lake's surface and the panic that seized me when I was unable to move my arms and legs. I felt that I was drowning. I don't know how I returned to the surface, or how I got back in the boat—Brian said he pulled me out—but when I regained consciousness, he was kneeling at my side and screaming desperately at me not to die.

With the cut on my head, my face full of blood, and Brian scared to death, we returned to the cabin unnoticed. After changing our clothes, we woke our parents and came up with a ridiculous lie to explain the wound on my forehead. Incredibly, they never doubted our story.

But that traumatic childhood experience left three marks on me—one physical and two emotional: the scar that cuts my left eyebrow in two; the hydrophobia that overwhelms me in proximity to lakes, rivers, and the sea; and the deep gulf that separates me from my brother.

Now that I'm looking at Brian on the screen, mistreated and captured by the CATs, I don't see the restless nonconformist I have distanced myself from as we've become adults. Instead, I see the red-headed boy who was my best friend, the brother I always swore to protect and defend. We were like jam and bread, inseparable.

But it just can't be Brian... I think, trying to deceive myself.

Of course it's him. I only saw him for a couple of seconds, but it was him, I'm sure.

It's impossible that my brother was involved in the terrorist attack... it's absurd. There has to be another explanation. Perhaps those images have nothing to do with the attack against the regent. Maybe Brian and the other guys were doing something stupid after the attack, like shouting some anti-Government slogan. Or perhaps he was still upset by the mistreatment of the deel boy this morning at the station. He probably insulted a security agent, and things got out of control. There could be many other explanations.

But the presence of the CATs unsettles me. The anti-terrorist forces don't bother with trivial matters. That's what the security agents are for.

I wonder if my parents saw the images too.

I take a quick look at the digital screen on my teleCard, but the call function is still blocked. I speed up my pace and enter the park. I go directly to the meeting point we had agreed to, hoping to find them there.

I see Zara first… and my parents and Lily are there too.

When my mother sees me coming, she runs toward me and throws herself on me.

"Derin! Are you okay? Did anything happen to you? Where were you? We couldn't get hold of you, they've blocked calls! We didn't know if something happened to you!" she lets the phrases escape between gasps and sobs while examining me and patting me everywhere as if wanting to make sure that I'm still in one piece.

"I'm fine, Mom, don't worry," I say to her. "What about you all? Are you okay?"

The others are already surrounding me, and it's my father who continues:

"What happened, Derin?" he asks calmly. "Nobody here knows a thing. Was it an accident? We just heard a loud explosion and saw the smoke. People started screaming and running toward the lake. They're all talking nonsense."

"An accident?" I repeat, frowning at him.

"Yeah, an accident… They weren't able to control the drones properly and let them get entangled with the flag, right?" he says. "They're so inept, can't even manage to get that right. Was anybody injured?"

They have no idea what has happened.

"No, Dad," I reply, "it wasn't an accident. It was a terrorist attack."

"What?!" the four of them exclaim with expressions of disbelief.

"Yeah, the radkers. They wanted to attack the regent using drones, but the CATs blew them up," I explain.

It becomes clear to me that they didn't see the images on the screen. They didn't see Brian. I decide it's not a good idea to say anything else now, but my instinct shouts at me that I must get them out of here.

"Let's go home right now," I say urgently. "They've asked us to vacate the city. It's still dangerous."

—

DURING THE TRIP ON THE ELEVATED TRAIN, the topic of conversation in the entire car is nothing but the terrorist attack. People seem very nervous and excited. Citizens are used to constant rebel attacks, but usually, they involve sabotaging factories, attacks on transportation of essential supplies, or ambushes against military convoys outside the city. There has never been an attack as spectacular as this one, especially not so close to the Palace of the Governors. Everyone speculates on whether Regent Crowley has been killed.

I feel like I'm in a trance. I try to take part in my family's talk—they can't avoid speculating about what happened either—but inside I can't stop thinking about the images of Brian captured by the CATs.

We get off at our train stop in the 32nd district, which used to be called Harrow. It's just one stop before the station where a few hours ago we boarded the train to go to the parade.

While my parents and Lily are discussing the possibility that the Government will close all access points to the city, Zara asks me in a low voice:

"What's wrong? You're acting weird and distant."

She knows me so well.

"Nothing," I reply. "I mean, I'll tell you later, okay?"

"Yeah, whatever," she says, annoyed. She doesn't like me hiding anything from her.

We walk ten minutes until we reach our street, a long row of terraced houses with well-maintained front yards and lots of trees. A few feet from our home, we encounter Mrs. Harris, a rather prying but otherwise decent neighbor. At her side, at the end of a leash, her ugly, grumpy dog walks with her.

"Emma! What a pleasant surprise!" she exclaims in her shrill parrot voice. Just this morning, we saw her in her front garden as she wished me all the best for my graduation.

"Hello, Charlotte, how are you?" my mother replies.

"My nerves are killing me, my dear." Mrs. Harris changes her tone, now lower and more earnest, to emphasize the drama. She turns her head rapidly to look at each one of us directly in the eyes as she continues. "What do you think about *this* awful thing?" She doesn't wait for an answer but goes on with her speedy monologue: "Terrible, I can't believe it. As you know, Taylor had to stay at home, his leg is bad, but I went to see the parade, and… what can I say? My goodness! The explosion, the crowd, the panic… Oh, dear… it was terrible. I hurried back home because my heart couldn't take anymore… terrible. I already had a cuppa tea, and now I'm trying to calm down by taking a walk with Brownie. Oh, Derin, dear, what a shame that those miserable people have ruined your day this way… They're cowards. Hopefully, they'll catch them soon and make them pay for what they've done. Those despicable rebels are to blame for the fact that we've had no butter for a week! Supplies are getting worse by the day, and I do so enjoy my toast with butter and jelly… terrible."

Charlotte Harris finally ends her ranting and says goodbye.

My father opens the small iron gate in the fence that separates the sidewalk from our front yard. My mother and Lily follow him, and Zara and I enter behind them. At first, we don't notice. From the direction we're coming from, some bushes hide the small bench near the front door, but, as my father goes to unlock it, he turns his head to the left and is startled to see someone there. The rest of us catch up and see Mia and Dylan, who get up and stare at us with terrified looks, without saying a word.

Mia is visibly upset, though she tries to hide it. She's about to cry.

"Mia, darling, what's the matter with you?" my mother asks, worried, as she approaches her. Mia glances around our surroundings, at the neighboring houses and the other side of the street, and says in a barely audible voice:

"Please, let's get inside… I have something to tell you."

"But what happened, honey? Are you hurt? Where's Brian?" says my mother, now clearly frightened, placing her hand on Mia's cheek.

"Please, Mom, let's go inside. We'll talk there," I intervene in a calm but forceful voice, which indicates that I'm giving an order.

"Come on, honey, let's go in," says my father, taking her by the arm. He's realized that something is very wrong.

Once inside, with the door closed behind us, we all look expectantly at Mia.

I know what she's going to say. My heart is pounding.

"It's… Brian…" she finally releases with a sob. "They captured him… after the explosion… in the parade. The CATs took him away."

My mother brings her hand to her mouth and stifles a scream. Reacting automatically, she embraces Mia, who can no longer contain her tears.

"Let's go to the dining room, we'll talk there," I say, raising my arms from my sides and making a motion with them as if to push everyone toward the table. With my left hand, I unwittingly brush Dylan on his back, who is standing behind Mia and next to me. He turns his head quickly; he looks at me for a moment and nods.

I think it's the first time that I've had the chance to look directly into his eyes so close up. They are beautiful.

My father and the women sit down at the table. I remain standing in front of Mia and my mother, while Dylan leans against the breakfast bar in the kitchen. Mia's stuttered statement has left my family stunned and triggered a natural reaction of disbelief and confusion.

They all wait, bewildered, for the next blow to strike.

"It's true," I confirm in a clear voice.

They look at me open-mouthed.

"I didn't want to say anything until we got here," I go on. "It was too dangerous to tell you in public. After the explosion, I saw a screen that showed CAT agents capturing several young people. Brian was one of them. I'm sure it was him; they had restrained him. I don't know why and don't have any details, I only know that CATs have taken Brian." Pausing, I look into my mother's eyes, which are filled with tears. Then I turn my head toward my brother's girlfriend. "Mia, what happened?"

"I'm… I'm not sure… it all happened so quickly," she begins. "We were in Leicester Square, with some guys from the Strip and some of Brian's friends… Liam and others. The place was packed, and we didn't pay much attention to the screen in that area. Then, I don't know what happened… everyone shouted, 'Radkers!' and then the explosion. Brian and others shouted, 'They killed him! They killed him!' I didn't understand what was going on and Brian said, 'They killed Crowley!'"

She pauses to gather some strength and continues:

"Then, people started running in all directions. Brian shouted, 'Let's get out of here!' and we ran off toward the station. And then…" She lets out a sob. "… the CAT agents appeared out of nowhere and began beating up kids from the Strip who were ahead of us. Brian stopped me and shouted, 'Go back! Get out of here! If they catch you, they'll kill you!' He begged Dylan to take me away from there."

My mother holds Mia's hand tightly, and Lily, frightened, also tries to comfort her by placing her hand on her shoulder. We let Mia finish her story.

"I didn't want to leave him there… really." She starts sobbing again. "But he begged me to run away. Dylan grabbed me and pulled me out of there. Before turning onto Cranbourn Alley, I looked back and saw Brian clashing with the CATS… They were beating him badly."

Mia moves both hands over her face and breaks down in tears; she can't talk anymore.

Dylan takes over telling her story, though his voice trembles.

"We couldn't do anything… I'm so sorry." He looks at me and then lowers his eyes. "The CATS were just too many and had restrained them already. They took Brian, Liam, and others. Mia and I walked several streets down, making sure that nobody was following us and trying to go quickly without running, so as not to look suspicious. I don't know how we got to Holborn station. From there, we decided that it was best to come here."

"That was the right thing to do," I say. Dylan nods slightly and glances toward Mia and my mother.

What I've heard from Mia and Dylan doesn't reassure me, though it does reduce my worst fears that Brian might have had something to do with the terrorist attack.

"Well, we must try to remain calm," I tell them. "I'll go out immediately to find out where Brian was taken. I'm going to talk to Captain Foster; he has good contacts." I have another contact of my own, but I'd prefer not to go near *him*. "Dylan, Mia, you have to get back to the Strip right now. Come with me to Access Point 8. I hope to find the captain there before he returns to the academy. If the access point is shut down, he can help you get out."

As I'm still wearing my Army dress uniform, quite messy after the commotion of the last hours, I hurry to my room to clean up a bit and change my clothes. I wash my hands and face, and then

I put on the clean uniform that I left at home last week: dark blue pants and a jacket, white shirt, and blue tie. I make sure to remove my lieutenant badges from the dress uniform and put them on the other.

When I go down again, I approach Zara.

"I need to ask you a big favor," I say to her.

"Of course, Deedee. Whatever you want," she replies confidently, although I can't miss the anguish in her voice and her gaze.

"I need to give you something to hide," I explain. She nods.

I turn to my parents and tell them, "I don't know what's going on, or what awaits us, but it's better if Zara takes the *things* with her."

They know I'm talking about the little chest where my mother keeps her family jewels and my father's two gold watches—our only possessions of any value.

"I'm sorry to ask this of you," I say to Zara, "but it's very important. My parents will give it to you; it's a small package."

"Don't worry, whatever it is, I'll keep it safe," she replies and hugs me. She's trembling with fear.

Before leaving with Mia and Dylan, I ask my parents to keep an eye on their teleCards and any official announcements.

~

THE CITY OF LONDON is surrounded by a continuous border that in some stretches consists of a high electrified fence, in others, a concrete wall, and everywhere else, the backs of terraced buildings. It's the physical barrier that helps the Government keep the Disloyal outside the city. The same situation repeats itself in all the cities throughout the country because only the members of the citizen castes—Commons, Patriots, and Patricians—have the right to live in them.

For citizens, and the Disloyal who, like Mia and Dylan, have special permits to exit and enter the cities, each perimeter border has several highly protected access points. Every access point is a hub for the streets and highways that weren't destroyed and the entire public transportation infrastructure, including trains, that leads into the countryside.

Access Point 8 is quite close to our house since our district is on the border. The security forces of this access point are under Captain Foster's command, and ultimately, he has the final word on who enters and exits through it. Though there are also some less conventional ways to go out and come back in.

We arrive at the access point's interchange station. It's the last station in the city's train system, where you have to transfer to the train system that goes out of the city. I immediately notice that they haven't closed the access point, and the movement of people isn't restricted. I find that strange because, after what happened, I would have expected more strict control. Admittedly, I don't know the status of the other access points. What matters now is that Mia and Dylan won't have a hard time leaving.

I say goodbye to Mia with a hug. She raises her face and gets close to my ear.

"Please, find him, Derin," she begs me in a whisper. "Get him out of wherever he is. Don't let them hurt him."

"Don't worry. I'll find him. I promise."

Dylan extends his arm to shake my hand and fakes a smile. I understand that he's trying to appear as casual as possible, so as not to arouse suspicion.

"See you later, Derin," he says, smiling, but his eyes are saying: *I'm so sorry.* "I hope everything goes well."

"Yes, thanks. I hope to see you soon," I reply.

I hope to see you soon? I don't know how on earth it occurred to me to say that nonsense. Warmth builds in my cheeks.

"Yes, I hope we meet again soon," he says, now with a genuine smile and a charming look in his eyes. Then he adds, "Derin, if you need to get in touch with us, you can. Area 5D East, the second-to-last bus stop. Find Collins Street. There's an alley there called Down the River. At the end of the alley, there's a pub called Georgie's. Ask for the owner, Georgina Tebbit."

"Got it," I reply, then repeat what he has said to confirm and etch it in my mind: "Area 5D East, second-to-last bus stop, Collins Street, Down the River Alley, Georgie's pub, Georgina Tebbit."

"Exactly," he says. "Tell her you have a message for me, from the Little Tin Soldier."

He looks down and seems to blush.

"The Little Tin Soldier?" I repeat, smiling and squinting.

"Yes… don't ask."

When I was a child, I read somewhere the story of *The Steadfast Tin Soldier*. He was one of many others from a box of toy soldiers. He was missing a leg because when they poured molten metal in his mold, there wasn't enough. After an unfortunate and unlikely journey, the soldier ended up in the flames of a fireplace, next to the paper ballerina whom he had fallen madly in love with. The soldier melted because of the fire and his passion, and the only thing left of him was a small metal heart.

I don't know whether Dylan knows the children's story too, or whether he's just heard the title. I also don't know if this nickname he's chosen for me is an innocent thing, or whether it has a deeper meaning. Did he just come up with it today when he saw me in full dress uniform? Is it a kind of compliment? Or a mocking nickname? I don't know, but I don't dislike it. Actually, I find it funny. Either way, I noticed that he blushed, and I love how he looks now like a little boy caught being mischievous.

They both take out their special teleCards and walk away. I watch them go through the control booths that lead to the train tracks. There's no problem. They board the train car that goes to the Strip. A couple of minutes later, the doors close and the train leaves the city.

CHAPTER 4

DESPERATION

I HEAD DOWN ONE SIDE OF THE EXCHANGE STATION to a three-story building that houses the operation center for security forces at Access Point 8.

As I enter the lobby, I see three agents behind a long wooden counter. All three are at their desks, but staring at the television monitor hanging on the side wall. They turn their heads when they hear me come in, hesitate for a moment while they inspect me, but soon stand up and greet me. They recognize me as an Army officer and lift their right hands to their foreheads.

"Good afternoon, lieutenant," says the youngest of the three, who has approached the counter. The other two take their seats and continue to watch the official news broadcast. "How can I help you?"

"Good afternoon. I'm Lieutenant Derin Dark. Is Captain Foster here? I need to see him." I hand him my teleCard, which is in identification mode and shows my picture and personal data. The agent glances suspiciously at the green-colored back, and I promptly explain, "I'm an officer since today. I haven't gotten my new teleCard yet."

"Yes, of course, sir. Please take a seat. I'll call the captain to see if he can meet with you."

The agent returns to his desk and reaches to pick up the phone, but stops when he notices that the news broadcast has been interrupted. On the screen, the Englandom coat of arms appears over a red background, accompanied by a melody of bells that we all recognize.

An official statement.

All our teleCards—the agents' and mine—begin to vibrate and emit the same melody, which indicates that the message will be broadcast nationwide: on all televisions, public screens, and teleCards.

It's a mandatory announcement for all, citizens and Disloyal included.

Even if we decide to watch it on television, we must scan our thumbprint on the teleCard's display before the broadcast starts and once again when it has finished. This action confirms that we have viewed the message from the Government. The process is registered in the Ministry of Citizen Participation. The omission of this public requirement is penalized.

My muscles tense up, and my heart quickens.

The three agents and I hurry to press our thumbs on our devices, which in response, emit the message "Fingerprint recognized and accepted." We look impatiently at the monitor, waiting for the transmission to begin. A few seconds later, the coat of arms disappears, and the flushed face of a chubby man fills the entire screen.

Regent Crowley himself. He's alive.

I should feel relieved that he didn't die in the attack, but this worries me even more.

The regent looks directly into the camera and starts to speak. Though he must be reading from a teleprompter, he appears to look at each one of us individually. He begins by informing the public about what we all already know.

"Dear citizens. This afternoon, during the commemorative parade of the 30th anniversary of our Great Nation of Imperial Englandom, ruthless terrorists—the same ones who cowardly aim to destroy the welfare of all—have attempted a cruel attack against me, your humble servant, and the Council of the Governors," he says in a resentful tone. He then pauses and cracks his typical grotesque smile. "I want to assure all of you, fellow citizens, that these terrorists have failed." Still smiling, he continues: "Thanks to the admirable work of our anti-terrorist forces—led with the highest level of professionalism and sense of duty by Commander Nigel Crowley, my dear son—all members of the Council of Governors are unharmed."

Nigel Crowley, I repeat in my mind and push away the thought of our last encounter.

"Unfortunately," he continues, now in a more serious tone, "although these barbaric beasts didn't manage to harm the head of our country, they have wounded its soul. As a result of the attack, seven citizens have lost their lives… seven invaluable members of our society, while dozens more were injured."

What? Citizens died? But I was right there in the square, helping the wounded. I could have sworn there weren't any casualties. There weren't even serious injuries! This doesn't feel quite right. There's something odd going on here.

Regent Crowley continues his presentation. He assures everybody that the Government will take care of the families of the deceased and that the injured will receive the best medical care. He then mentions that, although investigations are still ongoing, intelligence services have made remarkable progress. A plot against the Government has been unveiled that involves people in the highest ranks. This "breaks his heart." He announces that very soon they will disclose more details, and then takes the opportunity to congratulate the CAT agents, who within minutes of the incident managed to capture many of the terrorists involved in the attack.

The terrorists involved in the attack, I repeat slowly in my mind.

What is he talking about? Does he mean the arrest of Brian and the other young people? But they had nothing to do with it! Mia and Dylan reassured me that they didn't, and I believe them, right? Yes, I have to believe them. The opposite would be insane: my brother is not a terrorist! He has nothing to do with the radkers whatsoever.

I don't know what to think anymore. It's best I focus on what I have to do next because that at least I'm sure of.

At the end of the official transmission, I scan my thumbprint again on the teleCard. The three agents behind the counter do the same. As the two older agents comment speculatively on the regent's message, the younger one picks up the phone and calls Captain Foster.

"Captain, this is Briggs. Lieutenant Derin Dark is here, he wants to see you… Yes… Yes, sir. I'll send him right up." He hangs up the phone and turns to me, pointing to the glass door to my left. "You can go up, lieutenant, through that door. Third floor, at the end of the hall. You'll find the captain in his office."

I thank him and go through the glass door. Immediately to the right, I see an elevator and some stairs and decide to walk up. Once I'm on the top floor, I continue down the long corridor toward the open door at the end. As I get closer, I see Captain Foster behind his desk. Before I can even knock on the doorframe, the captain raises his head and looks at me.

"Derin, come in, come in," he says, smiling and gesturing with his hand.

Whenever we're among civilians, or I'm alone with him, the captain spares all formalities and treats me in a friendly way. One could say that we're like uncle and nephew, although there's no blood relationship between us. Nor is he much older than I am— maybe ten or twelve years. He's a close acquaintance of my family, as his brother and my father have been good friends since they were college classmates. He was married once but tragically lost his wife a few years ago. Since then, he has seemed to only dedicate himself to his military career and his little daughter. He's a nice guy, with a tough but sophisticated demeanor. He's quite tall and thin, and he's the only high-ranking officer I've ever seen with a padlocked beard.

Captain Alan Foster has known me since I was a toddler and has supported and sponsored me from the moment I showed the interest and skills necessary for a military career. I do not doubt that he advocated for my admission into the academy. On more than one occasion—and one in particular—I've relied on his experience and advice to help me solve a problem or make an important decision. That's why I'm here now.

"Thank you, captain," I reply. I step into his office and sit in the chair he points to in front of his desk.

"What a day, right?" he says, sighing. "I've been glued to my phone ever since I got back. All security protocols had to be prepared, in case access points were closed at some point, but they never issued the order… Apparently, it was no longer necessary because the suspects had already been arrested. Did you listen to the regent's speech?" I nod, then he adds: "Strange, right? I didn't see any casualties."

The captain puts his elbows on his desk, with the palms of his hands together, like he's about to pray. He rests his chin on both thumbs and the tips of his outstretched fingers push up his nose a little. He frowns and remains pensive for a moment. Then he straightens, gives a sort of clap as if to wake up, and continues:

"So tell me, what brings you here? I'm a bit surprised. I wasn't expecting to see you until later tonight at the academy."

"Captain, may I close the door?" I ask. "I'd like to talk to you about something confidential."

"Sure, go ahead," he says with an expectant look.

After closing the door, I return to the same chair as before. I breathe in and out, then begin to tell him everything that has happened. During my story, the captain briefly interrupts me a few times to ask about a specific element or to make sure he's understood all the details.

"Since I know you have contacts at the Ministry of National Security," I explain, finishing, "I thought it was best to come to you and see if we could find out exactly what happened to Brian."

Captain Foster gets up from his chair without saying anything and goes to the window. He stands there for what seems like half an eternity, with his eyes lost beyond the glass and his hands clasped behind his back.

Finally, he lets out a short, muffled grunt and turns around.

"Derin, I don't want to get ahead of things," he says after clearing his throat. "But based on what you've told me, I think the matter is grave. And after what the regent has just announced… hmm…" Again, the muffled growl. "It's bizarre. But, as I said, let's not get ahead of ourselves. Let me make a call and see what information we can get."

Over the next twenty minutes, the captain speaks with three different people within the Ministry of National Security. The names don't sound familiar to me—but there are hundreds, if not thousands, of people who work in that ministry. Apart from some short phrases and the name of my brother mentioned a couple of times, I don't catch any of the information the captain receives from the other end of the line. I can't deduce anything from his tone of voice or his gestures either. During the whole call, he maintains a calm and uninterested tone; the only action he takes is writing notes on a pad in front of him.

After the third conversation, he hangs up the phone and reviews his notes, again and again. I know what he's doing… and it worries me. He's assessing how to tell me what's on his mind.

He finally looks up and clears his throat.

"Derin," he begins, looking me in the eyes, "I don't have good news, I'm sorry." He clears his throat again. "Brian is detained at the headquarters of the Ministry of National Security. He's being accused of belonging to illicit organizations, inciting public violence, as well as contempt and aggression against security forces, conspiracy against the Government and… participation in terrorist acts."

My heart falls out of my chest, and I freeze.

This can't be happening.

I see a vivid image of my life and my family's falling apart. We're plunging into a bottomless abyss that swallows us into its darkness.

Wake up, Derin! Wake up! I try to force myself out of this nightmare.

"Derin?" asks a distant voice that I can barely hear. I see Captain Foster in front of me and catch a glimpse of his lips moving. "Derin, do you understand what I've said?"

Of course, it's the captain speaking to me.

"Are you okay?"

I don't know why my head is nodding because I'm not okay, not at all. Then my head changes its mind and shakes in denial.

"It's not possible, captain," I hear myself saying. "It's not possible. Brian hasn't done anything like that… It's just not true."

"Derin, I'm so sorry," says the captain, genuinely distressed. "But it doesn't matter anymore what your brother has or hasn't done, do you understand? That's meaningless now. For reasons beyond my comprehension, the Government is going to charge him with the crimes I listed, and… if they decide he's guilty, you know what that means, right?"

"I know," I reply, nodding. I don't have to say it. We both know.

They're going to execute him.

This morning, just a few hours ago, I was full of pride and joy. I had taken a decisive step that would improve my life forever. It was more than a step. It was a gigantic leap that would guarantee my family's future wellbeing and put me in a privileged position of security and influence. Now everything is being ruined in the cruelest, most horrible way.

Whatever happens, they'll destroy us.

Captain Foster gets up and comes closer to me. He puts his hand on my shoulder and repeats, "You don't know how sorry I am, Derin. I'm shocked that something like this could happen to your family. It's very painful."

"What can I do, captain?" I ask in a muffled voice.

"I don't know. I'm not certain that anything can be done at all. Hmm… let's take a walk outside. I think you need fresh air."

Although I'm still dazed and confused, I know what he's saying to me: "It's better to continue our conversation on the street." It's safer to talk there. It's possible that the Government has hidden listening devices in the building that even the captain doesn't know about.

We go downstairs and walk on the sidewalk along the main street.

"Derin," the captain begins in a low but clear voice, "many things are happening in our country that we can't talk freely about… many injustices, many abuses. It's possible that your brother and the other boys had the rotten luck of being in the wrong place at the wrong time. Regardless, they will be used as scapegoats to demonstrate the power of the Government over the people. They will be sacrificed for propaganda purposes."

"That's what I fear, captain. There's no other explanation," I reply sadly.

"In the regent's statement, he spoke of a plot that involves high-ranking officials," he continues. "Whether or not that's true is irrelevant, as is whether they've actually captured the real terrorists. But the regent won't miss an opportunity like this to get rid of one or several of his most dangerous enemies, I'm certain. If that's the case, they will undoubtedly make a show of the executions. They will announce a …"

"A *Trial of the People*," I finish the sentence.

I hadn't thought of this earlier. I was too upset. But now that I understand the severity of the situation more clearly, it seems inevitable. The Government will put together another edition of its despicable propaganda show. It breaks my heart to think that this time, my brother—in fact, my whole family—will be a part of that cruel charade.

The *Trial of the People* is an elaborate television program that airs a few times a year, for several hours in the evening during two consecutive days. Watching the broadcast is mandatory. On the program, one or more "Traitors to the Fatherland" are introduced, and the Prosecutor of the Nation—the program's host—exposes the crimes in detail. At the end, all citizens use their teleCards to vote, thus deciding if the accused are guilty or not. Those found guilty are sentenced to death and executed live on television in a horrific way.

What terrifies me isn't just that the accused are part of the program, but that their families play a leading role. The public exposure and humiliation are terrible. According to caste law, the families of the guilty must bear part of the responsibility for the crimes committed, and they also receive harsh punishments, even possibly the same savage execution.

For a second, as I see the suffering my family will be exposed to, I sink into despair.

"What should I do, captain?" I have to do something, or they're going to destroy us.

"Under different circumstances," he replies in a grieved voice, looking around to make sure no one is nearby, "I'd tell you to take your family and disappear. Try to get out of the country. You can't help your brother, and you must accept that his life is now in Crowley's hands. But saving the rest of your family…"

"That's what I'll do, captain. I have no choice," I say.

"No, Derin, hold on. I said 'under different circumstances.' This is different. The attack has been too public and targeted the regent himself. Forget about running away. They're surely watching you and your family already. If you try to flee, they'll capture you all, and the punishment will be even worse. There's no escape now. I'm sorry."

"But then what can I do? Let them kill my brother and destroy us all?" I ask, feeling incredibly helpless.

I can't stand the thought of the regime destroying us, of not being able to save my family. But… maybe I have a shot at doing something.

"What if I go see Nigel?"

"Nigel Crowley?" asks the captain, frowning.

I nod to confirm that I am indeed talking about the son of the regent, head of the anti-terrorist forces. Someone I thought I'd never have to see again.

"Do it," he replies without hesitation. "Do what you must. It's your only chance."

CHAPTER 5

SHADOW FROM THE PAST

I FIRST MET NIGEL CROWLEY AT THE MILITARY ACADEMY. I was sixteen years old and had just finished my first semester as a cadet. In the second semester, I had to take lessons in Anti-Subversive Tactics, and Nigel was the instructor who taught that class.

Having the son of the regent as an instructor was an extraordinary situation for all the cadets in my class. For some, it meant a great honor; others, myself included, were suspicious of having a Patrician among us with so much power and so close to the regent, who inspired respect but also great fear.

At twenty-three, Nigel already held a senior position within the anti-terrorist forces. Nobody doubted that soon his father would put him in charge of that critical section of the Army. He was an attractive blond guy, very outgoing, and he loved being in the spotlight. It was rumored that he liked men, although no one dared to comment on this in public.

It was undoubtedly those rumors that got me interested in him. I was excited at the idea of such a powerful Patrician sharing a secret like mine. I was comforted by the thought that someone like me could have so much success, even though relations between two men are punished in our society. I had always been terrified of what would happen if they discovered that I'm attracted to men. It would be devastating for my family and me. I never forgot one occasion when, as a child, I saw security agents descend on two Common boys who were holding hands: they nearly beat them to death. It was awful, and I was afraid that something like that could happen to me too.

But suddenly, there he was, Nigel Crowley, a Patrician who didn't seem to worry too much about hiding his preferences. He did whatever the hell he wanted.

I began to see him as a kind of model of what I could become. Certain laws were harshly enforced among the Disloyal, and also among us Commons. But, apparently, members of the two higher castes could live happily without worrying too much about those laws. I promised myself then that I would at least become a Patriot. That way, I could live without fear.

Nigel Crowley gave me hope.

I suppose he must have noticed something about me that suggested I might also be interested in men. At first cautiously, but soon more daringly, he approached me and gave me hints. I thought he was trying to test me, to see if I took the bait and showed interest. He must have been convinced because one day he summoned me to his office, where he got straight to the point: he declared that he liked me a lot, that he was charmed by me, and then he kissed me. At that moment, curiosity and excitement—it was the first time I kissed another man—were greater than any fear. I let it happen without saying a word. It didn't go any further than the kiss, however. I left his office and once outside, I realized that despite the thrill of kissing a man, I didn't really feel attracted to him. I decided that it wouldn't happen again. I would avoid being alone with him.

But Nigel didn't feel the same way.

Over the next few days, he took every opportunity to approach me and ask me to meet again privately. I refused and told him that it had been a mistake, that I didn't feel attracted to him, that I was confused. I pretended that I didn't actually like boys, and I begged him to please leave me alone. But he insisted, and every time he became more aggressive, to the point of harassment. I was terrified that the others might notice something because Nigel had become reckless in his advances. Of course, he was a Patrician and the son of the regent; he could afford those things. But my case was very different. If they caught me committing "immoral acts," they would have expelled me from the academy and degrade me. I would surely be whipped and tortured before being executed.

One afternoon, when my roommate had a medical examination, and I was alone in my bedroom, Nigel came to look for me.

As expected, he insisted vehemently that I should reciprocate his interest. He argued that I was only afraid of being discovered, and he assured me that nothing would happen to me, that he would protect me, that we would have a great time together and I don't know what else. He refused to accept the fact that I didn't like him. Then, he tried to force me into kissing him, but I resisted. At that exact moment, Captain Foster came into the room to personally congratulate me on the excellent results I had scored on a test.

Everything happened quickly after that. Nigel left without uttering a word, not even looking at the captain. I told Captain Foster everything that had happened, fearing that he would condemn me and have me expelled from the academy. But it was the opposite. He assured me that he didn't care about what I did in private, or who I liked. The only things that mattered to him were my talent and my performance. He also told me that it wasn't the first time Nigel Crowley had caused a problem like this. He promised he would take care of it.

The following day, Nigel was no longer at the academy. They gave the excuse that the son of the regent had to take over a position of greater importance and could no longer dedicate time to instruction.

Captain Foster later confessed to me that he talked with Nigel about the incident in my room that day. He feared that, as a

Crowley, Nigel would probably not forgive me for rejecting him. In an attempt to protect me, he told Nigel that my version of the story was that I had provoked the "bad behavior," that I was to blame for everything. This way, the captain trusted that Nigel would leave me alone and perhaps forget the matter. He also assured him that he wouldn't file a report, out of deference to his family, especially to his father.

I haven't had any contact with Nigel since then.

But now I have to ask to meet with him to beg him for help.

It's shortly after seven in the evening when I arrive at the vast complex that houses the Ministry of National Security. It's located in front of the River Thames, just where the Palace of Westminster once stood before being reduced to ashes by incendiary bombs thrown by separatists at the end of the war.

It's a massive greyish stone building with few windows, six or seven stories high for the most part. People also call it the NBB, or New Big Ben, in reference to the old and emblematic clock tower that succumbed to fire. There's a new clock tower, integrated into the building in the same place where the previous one stood. Except this new one is twice as tall as the original. They also built a new tower in the opposite corner, where the Victoria Tower once stood. Now it's a skyscraper called the Tower of Victory.

A few steps before reaching the main entrance of the building, I suddenly stop.

Doubts haunt me.

Am I doing the right thing? Will I make things worse if I see Nigel? What will I do if he's not here? Will he let me see Brian?

I decide to enter the building. I have no other alternative, and time is running out.

I've never been here before, and I'm amazed to find myself in a grand lobby three stories high. The floor is made of reddish marble, and there's a massive chandelier with glass drops hanging from the ceiling. It reminds me of the luxury hotel I saw during the broadcast of one of the regent's birthdays. In the back, there's a semi-circular counter made of marble and wood, flanked by two access controls with metal detectors.

I approach one of the officers behind the counter and hand him my teleCard.

"Good evening," I say. "I need to see Commander Crowley. It's urgent."

Without saying anything, the officer takes my teleCard, places it on an electronic reader, and types something on his computer keyboard as he stares at the monitor in front of him. After a few seconds, he picks up my teleCard and gives it back to me.

"You don't have an appointment with Commander Crowley," he says dryly, not looking at me. "You can't see him."

"Please," I insist, "it's regarding this afternoon's attack. I know the commander isn't expecting me, but he knows who I am. The information I have is of the utmost importance. Let him know that Derin Dark needs to see him. He won't be pleased if he doesn't get this information as soon as possible."

I'm not sure what I'm doing, but I have to try to get this bureaucrat to give Nigel the message. Let him decide if he wants to see me or not.

The officer frowns and examines me from head to toe with a look of disdain. He doesn't seem to take me very seriously. He's surely used to receiving guests of much higher rank. I imagine he's considering what information a little lieutenant like me could provide that the intelligence services don't already have. But the remote possibility that I might have something important to communicate scares him. Fear of what could happen to him if this information doesn't immediately reach Nigel Crowley due to his clumsiness wins over his arrogance. He finally gives in.

"Wait over there," he says reluctantly, pointing to a long bench with a padded surface located on the side of the hall. "I'll see if he can be disturbed."

I head to the bench and sit down, somewhat relieved that at least I've managed to persuade somebody to tell Nigel that I'm here. The receptionist officer picks up the phone and makes a call, though I can't hear what he says.

The longer the wait, the more nervous I get.

Shortly after eight o'clock, I hear the mechanic whirring of the elevators behind the reception desk. A few seconds later, the hammering of heels on the marble floor echoes throughout the entire lobby. A middle-aged woman in a military skirt suit leaves the restricted area.

She comes over to me.

"Lieutenant Dark?" she asks, without smiling or waiting for an answer. "Come with me."

I get up and follow her. We go through the security control and continue to the elevators. We enter the one with its doors open, and she punches number seven. When we reach the last level, my guide advances hurriedly in silence, several steps in front of me, as if I don't even exist. I have to speed up to avoid falling behind. We cross a long corridor with offices on both sides and stop in front of another group of elevators.

Given the direction we've taken, I imagine we're in the southwest corner of the ministry, in the Tower of Victory. My hunch is confirmed when we enter the second elevator, and my companion holds her teleCard over a square plate on one side of the button panel and then presses number thirty. We arrive at what seems to be the top floor of the tower and get off the elevator.

We enter a spacious lobby with several groups of sofas and armchairs. I see some desks, where I'm guessing she and her colleagues work, although there's no one else here. We walk to the left and stop in front of a double door with a gold metal plate that says "First Commander." She knocks three times on the door, opens it, moves to the side, and tells me to go in.

Here we go, I think, my pulse accelerating.

I enter the office and hear the doors closing behind me.

At first, I think I'm alone, but I take three more steps and turn my head to the right.

In the corner of the office, which is all glass and has a perfect view of the illuminated skyscraper of the Palace of the Governors, I see Nigel Crowley.

He's sitting behind a large wooden desk that looks like it's been taken out of a museum of antique pieces. He's reviewing some documents in a folder. Only when I get very close to the desk does he close the folder, lift his gaze, and look at me.

I stop, stand straight, and execute the military salute.

"Commander!" I greet him with the firmest tone of voice I can muster.

"Derin Dark," he says, slowly emphasizing my name and giving me a faint smile that I can't decipher. "So here you are, a recently graduated officer of the Army."

I'm amazed at how much he has changed.

Over the last few years, on more than one occasion, I've seen him on television. Besides his position as First Commander of the anti-terrorist forces, he also takes up the functions of the Prosecutor of the Nation on the *Trial of the People*. The broadcast's technicians must do wonders to touch up the live images, since, on TV, Nigel looks almost the same as I remember him. But the person in front of me is very different.

He has gained a lot of weight, and his rounded face is a bright pink, like his father's. His hair has lost volume and looks discolored. He has deep, dark stripes under his sunken eyes, which are swollen and red. In general, a blend of severity and fatigue is evident on his face; he looks much older than he is. I'm sure he's abusing alcohol and drugs. He smiles, but his expression seems empty.

"I must admit, I wasn't sure you would come to see me," he continues in a relaxed tone. "In fact, until barely an hour ago, I didn't even remember who you were. But, as I've seen in this report"—he taps his fingers on the closed folder in front of him—"it seems we have a Brian Dark with us. The name caught my attention and, well, at once I got all the information I wanted." He points at his computer's monitor, smiling even wider.

"Commander. First of all, I wish to express my most sincere joy that your father is unharmed." I hope I sound genuine and convincing. "And… yes, commander, in fact, Brian is my brother. I found out he was arrested this afternoon and that he's being held here. That's why I've come to you, sir."

"But what do you suppose I can do about it?" he asks, opening the folder and flipping through the documents inside. "Everything seems perfectly clear. Let's see, what does it say here? Inciting violence, disrespect, and aggression toward authorities, illicit organizations, conspiracy… terrorism." He speaks very casually and cheerfully as if reading from a grocery shopping list. "These are serious accusations, Derin. I don't know what you expect me to do. The law is very clear."

I can't help but feel that he's making fun of me. Of course, he is.

"Please, commander." I look him straight in the eyes and speak in a pleading voice. "Brian is a good boy. Yes, he has his faults and must get back on track. But he's not a criminal, much less a terrorist. You can verify this; your intelligence agents must know that my brother doesn't have any links with terrorists, or with this afternoon's cowardly attack. Please, I beg you."

Nigel crosses his arms, leans forward on his desk, and observes me in silence for a few seconds.

"Turn around," he says, making a twirling motion with his index finger.

"Excuse me, commander?" He opens his eyes wide, straightens up, and traces a circle in the air again.

"Just turn around, as I said… turn around slowly. I want a good look at you."

Feeling like an idiot, I hesitate for a second, but then I obey and turn three hundred and sixty degrees. Maybe it was a mistake to come here after all.

"Very good," he says with a pleased expression. "Now, do me a favor, will you?" He points to the back of the office. "See that file cabinet? I dropped a pen this afternoon, and I think the bastard fell behind it. Can you please fetch it for me?"

This is a joke, right? I immediately regret coming to see him. This guy is crazy. Who knows what he's up to, but I'm at his mercy. I must do what he demands, however absurd it may seem.

I walk to the file cabinet and lie down on the floor so I can look under it and stretch my arm beneath it. I look everywhere but don't find anything. I stand up.

"I'm sorry, commander, it's not there. Could it be somewhere else?"

"Hmm, could be," Nigel replies indifferently. "Well, never mind. What were we talking about?"

He just wanted to humiliate me. Perhaps his motivations are even more perverse, but I don't have time to analyze that right now. I return to his desk.

"About my brother Brian, sir. His arrest," I say.

"Oh, yeah, that. Well, he'll get a fair trial. If he's guilty, he must admit responsibility. If he's innocent, then he'll be cleared of all charges and be released. Or do you doubt our justice system?"

He speaks as if this is a trivial matter when, in reality, Brian's life and my family's future are at stake.

Now I feel my blood boiling. I wish I could throw myself on him and beat him up on the spot, but I have to calm down. He has so much power that even a grimace would be enough for him to pick up the phone and order the immediate execution of my entire family. I must submit to his humiliations if I ever hope to convince him to help me. My fate is in his hands. He can do with me whatever he wants.

"Yes, commander," I reply cautiously. "Of course, I trust our justice system. But, sir, I'm afraid that my brother could be accused of acts committed by others. Moreover, commander," I implore him, "there's my family to think about … the damage and suffering this would cause them."

He knows exactly what I mean: the ordeal my family will be subjected to.

"Look, Derin," he says after closing the folder. "Quite frankly, I could care less about your brother's situation. I have my entire team on this case, clarifying the facts and identifying the culprits of this attack. Soon you'll learn more about the plot we've discovered. You'll be surprised."

"I understand, sir, but what about my brother?" I ask, hoping for some sign that he will help Brian … for me.

"He'll be treated most fairly, just as this great nation treats all its citizens. I will personally guarantee that. If you and your family are loyal citizens, I don't see why you should be treated unfairly."

He will personally guarantee that. I don't know if that's good or horribly bad.

"Thank you very much, commander. I really appreciate it," I reply, lowering my eyes. "Would it be possible," I continue hesitantly, "um … would it be possible to see my brother?"

I haven't even finished my sentence when he shakes his head, now with a stern look.

"Of course not, you know that," he says sharply. "He's being charged with grave crimes. We've only just started investigations. Anything else?"

It's not a question. He wants me to leave. This is all the time he's willing to give me.

I express my gratitude once again and repeat the military salute, although he only nods briefly to indicate that I can step away. When I turn around and leave, I can tell his damn eyes are fixed on my butt.

It feels good to leave the building and step out into the cool evening breeze. I hesitate between holding on to a hint of hope and feeling utterly depressed.

I was able to see Nigel Crowley, which is an achievement in and of itself. In his strange and ambiguous way, he said that Brian would receive fair treatment and implied my family wouldn't be harmed. But my instinct warns me that I shouldn't trust anything he says. How could I? I want to believe him. But I know his words can mean precisely the opposite… or nothing at all.

Has he gotten over my rejection from a few years ago? Might he even feel like he owes me something for not having betrayed him then? Does he still have an interest in me, especially after seeing me today? This is my greatest hope. With the power he holds, his influence could mean Brian's salvation.

But it's also entirely possible that he still feels humiliated and hurt, and he hasn't been able to forget it. It wouldn't be unreasonable to imagine that he's playing dirty and his real intention is to get some sick revenge on me.

I don't know what to think.

I'm hungry. I haven't had anything to eat since this morning, my head throbs, and exhaustion hits me. It's too difficult for me to analyze everything that's happened.

But I know I can't trust him. Even with the remote hope that he might decide to help me, I'm too cautious not to consider alternatives.

I decide to go to the Strip tomorrow, first thing in the morning. I have to talk to Dylan.

I smile when I remember how charming he looked this afternoon at Access Point 8, as we said our goodbyes. The way he blushed when he called me the "little tin soldier."

Could it be that he likes me?

I shake my head and try to get these thoughts out of my mind.

I'm ashamed. I don't understand how I can allow myself such things while my brother's life and my family's wellbeing are at stake.

But I just can't stop fantasizing about him.

CHAPTER 6

THE STRIP

MY ALARM CLOCK goes off at five in the morning. I wake up with the exasperating feeling that I just barely managed to fall asleep, and, for a moment, I entertain the idea of staying in bed. Then the cruel reality hits me, its stinging blow running through my entire body. I wish that when I open my eyes, I'll find out everything has been a nightmare, that none of it was real.

But this is really happening.

Last night, after informing everyone at home about Brian's whereabouts and the seriousness of his situation, I went to bed early. However, I spent most of the night awake, thinking up possible scenarios, all the bad things that could happen. I'm worn out from thinking, and I haven't reached any conclusion.

I take a shower and put on civilian clothes: a pair of jeans, athletic shoes, a grey t-shirt, and a blue zip-up hoodie. I put on an old wristwatch, which I haven't worn in years, and then I make sure to leave my teleCard in one of my desk drawers. My secret trip to the Strip won't be so secret if it's registered on the tracking device.

As I go down the stairs, I can smell toast and fresh coffee. In the kitchen, I find my mother preparing scrambled eggs on the stove. She's set the table for four.

"Good morning, Mom, did you get some rest?" She turns around, hugs me, and starts crying with choked sobs. "Don't worry, Mom, we'll find a way out of this, you'll see," I try comforting her, though my words don't sound very convincing.

Her eyes are swollen, and she looks exhausted. She's had a bad night too.

A short while later, Lily and my father join us. The four of us sit down at the table for breakfast, but there isn't much conversation. Without Brian, the mood is depressed and empty.

I don't mention it, but I'm hoping that at least a small part of what Nigel told me last night is true: that his people will treat Brian fairly.

For an instant, I'm terrified by the image of the interrogations that those accused of treason are subjected to. My stomach churns, but I soon dismiss these thoughts. I can't let fear get in my way. I must be strong for them.

I wish Zara were here. It would be great to let off steam with someone I don't need to pretend anything to. But it's best that she went home. Right now, she's also running a risk because of our friendship. If things go badly, she and her mother should avoid any contact with my family. Besides, she's risked enough already by taking the valuables my parents handed her.

After I finish breakfast, I go upstairs to brush my teeth and then hurry back into my bedroom. I grab a small figurine from my collection of superheroes, the one that looks most like a soldier. It's one of those collectible figures that are almost impossible to find nowadays. I put the figurine inside my hoodie's pocket. I feel stupid doing this. I'm not even sure why I do it. I still don't know what I'm going to use it for, but I don't care.

Downstairs I say goodbye and hug everyone, begging them not to leave the house until I get back, which I hope will be in a couple of hours. I put on a jacket, wrap a thin scarf around my neck, and leave the house.

Outside I'm greeted by a wet morning. My breath turns into whitish vapor as it touches the air. A dense fog layer conceals the sky. It's a typical morning for this season, cold and dark, just like my spirits right now. I fight the temptation to turn around and look back at the open door where my parents and Lily are watching me leave. I don't want to get depressed. From now on, there's a real possibility that every time I say goodbye, it may be the last time I see them.

I arrive at the exchange station for Access Point 8 and check the time: ten to six. I have enough time before the first train to the Strip leaves.

Several security agents are guarding the access point. Luckily, nobody's in the mood to give me a hard time. Even though I'm wearing civilian clothes, they somehow recognize that I'm someone of importance, who shouldn't be bothered without reason. Surely it's because my years in the academy have given me a bearing that makes me seem confident and determined, which no deel could pretend.

I go straight to the control booth.

Behind the glass is a young guy with disheveled hair, as if he just woke up. I make sure nobody's around before talking to him.

"Hey, good morning," I say, smiling. "Listen … um, could you do me a favor?" I lower my voice before continuing. "I need to go to the Strip … um … to *see someone* if you get my drift?"

Although nobody talks openly about this, it's common knowledge that many Commons and some Patriots travel to the Strip "irregularly" by paying bribes to avoid being registered in the system. There are many reasons to go to the Strip without being tracked. Some have relationships with deels and prefer to keep it secret; others are merely looking for a quick lay, illegal substances, or other forbidden items that are easier to find there.

The controller knows what I mean, because he leans closer to the glass, glances from side to side, and smiles at me.

"One hundred," he says.

"Do you have a good contact on the other side, at the entry checks?" I ask, raising my eyebrows. "I don't want trouble on my way back."

"What time will you return? I can get moved to the entry control booths."

"Between ten and eleven," I reply.

"No problem," he says, nodding his head. "I'll be there before ten, and at least until noon. Sound good?"

"Agreed. Fifty now and fifty on my return?"

The controller nods again. Surreptitiously, I take several bills out of my pants pocket and give him fifty pounds.

In theory, paper money is illegal, but the Government finds it impossible to control its circulation, so they've turned a blind eye. There are very few deels who work in the city and receive electronic credits, so the millions who live in the Strip have to resort to paper money—the currency used before the proclamation of Englandom—to carry out their business transactions. Besides, Commons and Patriots also need to get paper money on the black market if we want to buy anything from the Strip.

The train is already on the platform, and I get in the car reserved for citizens only. Apart from me, there's a middle-aged couple and a scruffy-looking man who seems like he's going to the Strip in search of illegal substances. We leave on time at five after six.

After forty minutes, the train approaches the entrance to the gigantic city of the Disloyal.

This city, located northeast of London, was built shortly after the establishment of the castes, to transfer the bulk of the lower-caste population here. There are similar ghettos for the Disloyal in various locations throughout the country, but no other comes close to the dimensions of the Strip. It's estimated that more inhabitants live here than in London itself. Some say ten million, others close to twenty. Nobody knows for sure. The Government's version is that there's an official census of the population, which is three million—it would not be convenient for the Disloyal to have official confirmation that they're so many—but no one doubts that the actual number is a multiple of that.

From above, the Strip is shaped like a rectangle, about six miles wide and almost twenty in length. It consists of a grid of square "areas" that are three thousand feet on each side and separated by the main streets and avenues intersecting them perpendicularly. Together these areas form rows, or "sectors," eight wide, and are divided down the middle—four on the east side and four on the west—by the Transversal Corridor. The areas' name comprises the sector number, followed by a letter—A through D—and the word East or West, depending on which side of the Transversal Corridor they are. There are twenty-eight or twenty-nine sectors, and there's a lot of space at the end to add more.

Each area, in turn, contains twenty-five blocks, five per side. It's a labyrinth of narrow streets within an endless jungle of brick and concrete.

The Strip is so immense and so full of people that I'm convinced it's the perfect place to disappear, to vanish from the face of the earth.

At least that's what I'm hoping for. That's the reason why I'm here.

Captain Foster told me that it was too late to escape with my family, but I can't rule out any options. It's clear to me that if we flee to the Strip, Brian's fate will be sealed: Nigel will have him executed. I doubt, therefore, that I can convince my parents to flee and abandon Brian to certain death. I couldn't do it either.

But maybe Lily… maybe we can save her.

The train enters the Transversal Corridor, the broad thoroughfare that extends toward the horizon without any visible end. I look out the window and—although I've been here a couple of times before—I'm astonished once again by the oppressive density of this giant, smog-covered anthill. I get off at the next station, at the end of Sector 6. The pungent smell in the air immediately invades my nose, and my eyes start to burn.

It only takes me a few seconds to get my bearings. "Area 5D East," said Dylan. It's in the lower part of the Strip, and I'm already on the eastern half, so I just have to go back along the Transversal Corridor in the opposite direction of the train.

I walk almost three thousand feet back until I reach the beginning of Sector 6, arriving at the avenue that separates it from Sector 5. I cross it and turn left at the corner.

In front of a bus stop, I look for information about routes. If possible, it's better to take a bus because I'm at the corner of 5A East and I have to get to 5D East, the last area of the sector, which is a distance of about two miles. There's no time to lose.

I have a bit of luck because, at this very moment, a bus arrives from the west and stops. I get on. There are some empty seats, but I prefer to stand near the door. I pay attention to the route diagram on a panel in front of me. I must get off at the second-to-last stop.

It takes the bus a few minutes to get there, and I'm the only one who gets off.

Collins Street, I repeat in my mind.

I'm not sure which direction to take. I now need to enter the area, and without detailed maps—which don't exist—it's easy to get lost. I notice two kids coming in my direction, a boy and a girl who look like siblings. I approach them.

"Hey, excuse me. Do you know where Collins Street is?" They look at me suspiciously and then at each other. It occurs to me that they need an incentive. I pull out a five-pound bill and add, "I'm not from here. I need to get to Down the River Alley."

"I know where it is," the boy replies, pointing to the bill. "For that much, I'll take you there myself."

He turns toward his sister, who nods, approving the transaction.

I follow them six hundred feet east. The boy then stops almost at the same moment I spot the peeling sign that says "Collins Street."

"Down the River Alley is nearby," he says, stepping into Area 5D East. His sister and I follow him.

I'm glad I've hired these guides because Collins isn't any ordinary street. It's a narrow alley that runs zigzag and, at several points along the route, forks into different directions without any signage. I'd never have found the right way on time. After about ten or fifteen minutes, the boy stops again.

"Here's Down the River," he says, pointing to the corner of the building, where a sliver of the street name painted on the wall is still visible.

I hand him the money and thank him. As the boy and his sister turn around and go back, I walk into the narrow alley.

Georgie's pub, at the end of Down the River Alley, I repeat in my head.

I continue for several more minutes and then, in the far distance, I see it: an illuminated neon sign with a red frame and letters in purple that spell "Georgie's."

My old-fashioned wristwatch marks seven forty-five. Suddenly, it occurs to me that this place may be closed. And even if it's open, there's no guarantee that I'll find Georgina Tebbit. It's possible I won't get to see Dylan or Mia either, which means the risk I've taken to make this trip will have been in vain.

I arrive at Georgie's front door and turn the handle. It's open.

I go in and immediately see a woman behind the bar. Deep in concentration, she's reviewing a pile of papers on the counter. Probably in her fifties, she's a little chubby and short. Her blond hair is swept up in a striking tower style. I can't help but notice her lipstick's bright red color, which is the same shade as the polish on her long nails.

As I take a few steps into the pub, she looks up at me.

"Sorry, darling," she says in a loud, somewhat shrill voice that is simultaneously warm and friendly. "We're not ready yet. Come in and wait if you want."

"Good morning," I reply as I approach the bar. "Actually, I'm looking for Georgina Tebbit."

"Oh, really?" she exclaims, arching her eyebrows as she scrutinizes me. "Well, you've found her, honey, she's standing right in front of you. How can I help you? Looking for something *special*?"

I'm not sure what she means by "something special," but her tone of voice and facial expressions are so funny that I can't help but smile.

"Well, yes, Ms. Tebbit, I'm looking for someone. Dylan and Mia Blake," I explain. "It's very urgent. Dylan told me to come here and ask for you … and to say that I'm the … um … the 'little tin soldier.'"

I feel myself blushing.

"Ahh, so you're the 'little soldier,'" she says, a hint of mischief in her voice. "I wasn't expecting you so soon. The Blake boy only just told me about you last night. No need to call me 'Ms.,' makes me feel old. Everyone here calls me Georgie."

"Sure, Georgie, as you wish." I reach out my hand to her. "I'm Derin. Nice to meet you."

"A pleasure, handsome," she replies, shaking my hand with both of hers. "Give me a sec, I'll try to locate the Blakes. I'll be right back."

She opens a door behind the bar and goes through, closing it behind her.

I take off my scarf and jacket and sit down on one of the barstools. I glance around, examining the pub. It's not very big, but it's cozy. The bar is located near the entrance, to the left. It consists of a long counter made of polished dark wood, with several high stools.

The floor is made of scuffed wood, and warped wooden beams support the ceiling. There are several tables with wooden chairs, both on the front wall facing the alley, and the back wall facing a canal. Here, sunlight pours in through the windows. On the canal side, there are also booths with cushioned benches. Several framed posters hang on the wall, and there's a device with lit-up, rounded edges that catches my attention. I think it's a jukebox, one of those old machines that play music from a selection they carry inside.

I'm about to get up to inspect the device when Georgie reappears.

"Good news, dear," she announces cheerfully. "I've located the Blake boy. He's coming straight away. It won't be long."

"Excellent, thanks so much."

"Want something to drink? Tea with liquor, maybe?" she asks. "You're handsome, honey, but I can tell you need something strong. I'll join you, okay?"

"Sure, thanks. I could use one."

"It'll do you good, I promise. Who isn't better after a bit of liquor?" she says, preparing the tea. Then, with an ease that shocks me, she adds: "So, tell me, what's the deal with you and Dylan? Are you a couple?"

I freeze, caught completely off-guard.

"Um… no, no, what… uh?" I stammer like a fool. "No, he and I… um, his cousin Mia is my brother's girlfriend and… um, I… no, uh…" It's so embarrassing. I grab my cup of tea and take a big sip.

Georgie's clearly enjoying my reaction. I'm sure she asked me on purpose.

"Oh, honey, London's really got you on a leash! Just look at your face!"

"No, no, it's just…" I try to mumble something, but she doesn't let me finish.

"Well, handsome, you're a catch! If he doesn't hurry up, we know what to do with you around here. You're gorgeous, honey," she answers with such a lascivious look and tone that I beg the earth to swallow me up. "Hey, speaking of the devil, here he is!"

The door opens, and I see Dylan's beautiful smile and his dreamy expression.

CHAPTER 7

PETRIFIED

I DON'T DEMAND MUCH OUT OF LIFE. I don't need lots of material things or emotional highs to be happy. I would be content with a safe and simple life, as long as it was sprinkled with moments of joy and purpose.

When I see Dylan come in, I imagine if this were our first date, our first "official" get-to-know-you. How exciting it would be, how enjoyable that sweet and innocent nervousness when you're attracted to someone and want to know more about him. And I want to know everything about Dylan.

For me, that would be a moment of pure joy.

But today isn't that moment. It can't be. I'm not here because I really like Dylan and want to get to know him better; nor am I here because I want him to understand me better and realize that I'm not the arrogant, privileged guy that he might think I am.

I'm here because I'm trying to save my family.

When I see him come in, I stand up. I don't know if it's the liquor tea or the excitement of seeing him again, but I feel the temperature rising in my cheeks and my ears. There's a strange tingling in my belly too. Dylan takes off the knitted hat he's wearing and runs his fingers through his hair, trying to fix it—though he doesn't need to; it's already perfect.

"Hi, Derin," he says, holding out his hand. "I'm glad to see you. I'm glad you came."

"Hey, Dylan." I smile back and shake his hand. A slight but exciting shiver runs through my body. "Yes, I had to come to see you, um, both of you. Where's Mia?"

"She couldn't make it, sorry. She's with my aunt today, helping out at the clinic, that'll distract her a bit. She's pretty upset about Brian. My aunt's a doctor, you see. Anyway, we decided it's best she doesn't return to London, at least for now. It's too dangerous, because of her and your brother and all that. I can't miss work. But today my shift starts at noon."

"Oh, got it," I reply. "Mia definitely shouldn't go to London now, it would be too risky. They'd probably arrest her the second she showed up. I bet they've already got her registered in the system. But you shouldn't go back to the city either."

"I have to go," he says bluntly. "I can't miss work."

I don't insist. He and his family know what's best for them.

"Should we sit down to talk?" he proposes, pointing to the booths along the back wall. I nod and follow him to the last cubicle, in the corner. We sit facing each other. Outside the window, the brown water of the canal flows past us, marking the eastern boundary of the Strip. I can't stand looking at it. The sight of any large mass of water makes me shiver.

I kick off the conversation, briefly summarizing what I've found out since yesterday afternoon. I tell him everything that I know about Brian, where they've taken him, what they've charged him with, the serious situation he's in. I mention my meeting with Nigel Crowley, without going into detail. Dylan is surprised to learn that I know him personally. I explain my fear that Nigel wants to harm my family, perhaps in a *Trial of the People*. Then I cut to the chase: I confess that I must consider the possibility of running away with them.

Dylan listens with great interest and patience. A couple of times, he looks like he's about to interrupt, but holds back until

I finish. Georgie brings us more tea, and Dylan waits until she leaves to respond to me.

"Derin, that's terrible," he begins, leaning over the table to get a bit closer. He sets his hands on the wooden surface a few inches away from mine. "I'm so sorry, for Brian, for you, for your family. And, of course, for Mia. But… there's something else you don't know yet. I think it's going to be a terrible blow for you."

I raise my eyebrows anxiously, as I have no idea what he means.

"Um, look, Derin," he continues, "I know we barely know each other and that our lives are very different and all that… but I want to trust you, and I ask that you trust me too."

"Sure, of course," I say, though I don't understand where he's heading. "What's going on? What don't I know?"

"Well, look. It may sound strange, but I know people who are very informed of everything important that happens in our country. People with contacts in all the institutions and the highest government positions, with the technological tools to monitor the most confidential conversations. I can't give you any details. Believe me, I'd like to, but I can't. It would put them in danger. But they have reliable information about what happened yesterday at the Palace of the Governors."

"Yeah?" I say, wearing a puzzled frown.

"Yes. They're absolutely certain; they know what actually happened."

"What do you mean? Do they know about the plot? And who wanted to kill Crowley and the Governors?"

"It's not a plot, Derin," he says, shaking his head. "Well, not the kind of plot you imagine, not like Crowley has presented it."

"What do you mean?"

He pauses and looks directly into my eyes before answering:

"Crowley himself is behind the attack, not the rebels or anybody else."

Dylan must be delirious; he's talking nonsense. What he's saying doesn't make sense. Why would Crowley risk killing himself? That's absurd.

"Do you get what I'm saying, Derin?" he asks as I remain silent, stunned. "It's a farce, a charade. Another ludicrous strategy to hold on to power."

"But how? What are you talking about?" I say. "Why would the regent do such a crazy thing? What's the point?"

"Crowley is a deranged psychopath," Dylan tries to explain. "His entire lineage is. When he thinks his authority and power are threatened, he resorts to drastic, violent measures."

When Dylan speaks this way, he looks so serious and confident. It amazes me. He's only seventeen years old, but he talks as though he's had extensive life experience.

"Besides," he continues. "It's not the first time he's done something like this. It's not even his most evil scheme."

"What do you mean?" I ask, trying to take it all in.

"I suppose that at school, they tell you the same official story about the war that they tell us over here, right?"

The way he says "you" and "us" unwittingly emphasizes out the differences and barriers that exist between our castes. This saddens me deeply.

"The official story?" I repeat because I'm not sure what part of the history of the war he's referring to.

"Yes, especially the events that the regime describes as 'two macabre acts perpetrated by the separatists in their desperation to overthrow the democratic government.' After those thousands of deaths, the whole country turned against the separatists and their cause and allowed the Government to end the rebellion. The civil war ended, the new nation was established, and the Crowleys took power. You know, that often-repeated story."

"You mean Blackpool and the Parliament?" I ask.

"Exactly."

Suddenly, I can see everything.

It's like a curtain has risen, revealing the sinister truth behind it. Even before he explains further, I understand. I can't believe it.

I feel like I've suddenly had an epiphany. As if the dense grey cloud of indoctrination and manipulation has dissipated and shown me the facts as they are. I see the hidden reality with total clarity. I have no doubt it's true.

Any primary school kid can recite from memory the historical events that put an end to those set on destroying our country, leading to the creation of the Great Nation of Imperial Englandom.

In school, we learn that the Irish and Scottish separatists, supported by the European bloc, provoked a bloody civil war that divided our nation, claimed hundreds of thousands of lives, and destroyed almost all the infrastructure. They explain to us that the separatists were about to be defeated, but, in an act of desperation before their imminent fall, they perpetrated two repugnant and sinister attacks that changed history.

First, during a reckless attack on the naval base at Clyde, in what was then Scotland, they extracted a small nuclear device from a submarine, which was detonated two days later in the seaside town of Blackpool. Everything within a half-mile radius of the detonation point was pulverized. Thousands of innocent lives were lost. It was the darkest moment in our history.

And a week later, while the whole country mourned in pain from such an atrocity, the separatists attacked Westminster, the seat of Parliament in London. Their sophisticated missiles obliterated the building, and hundreds of people died in that hell, including almost all members of Parliament.

The public outrage and chaos were such that the civil war came very close to turning into a global conflict, with the intervention of other world powers. To avoid a nuclear catastrophe that would have ended all life on earth, the Government led by Alistair Crowley—father of the current regent and grandfather of Nigel—signed a non-aggression treaty with the European bloc. Independence was conceded to Northern Ireland, but the separatist attempts of Scotland were ended once and for all. The agreement also guaranteed the non-intervention of the European bloc in internal affairs on the island of Great Britain.

Our army ended the rebellion, and the new country of Englandom was established. The entire territory of the island was divided into fourteen protectorates, and segregation began: the rearrangement of society into four castes. The fourteen governors, led by the first regent, took over the government of the new nation and closed the borders. The rest of the world was left to its own devices. Englandom could shine at last.

This is the official story.

In a fraction of a second, I now realize that everything is a farce.

I don't know how Dylan knows all this, but I don't doubt anything he says.

He explains that the Crowleys themselves, with the help of their henchmen, caused those horrendous attacks and blamed them on the separatists with the sole aim of manipulating public opinion in favor of them seizing absolute power. It's disgusting.

A terrible sense of hatred floods me. And worst of all, if Blackpool and the Parliament attack were perpetrated by the Crowleys, as well as the fake attack yesterday, what else are these monsters capable of?

I feel terrified. It is as if molten lead is running through my veins, paralyzing me as it becomes solid.

Brian… My parents… Lily!

"I can't believe it. It's outrageous," I say, with my head lowered and my eyes fixed on the table, on Dylan's hands.

"It's hard to fathom such evil," he replies in a gentle tone.

"But… those people you know," I say, looking up to meet his gaze. "The ones with powerful contacts… could they do something for Brian?"

"I don't know. I don't think so," he replies. "Besides the information I just gave to you, they don't have further details. They don't know yet what Crowley's real intentions are. But they're sure we'll soon find out. There's talk he's going to assassinate one or more of the governors opposed to his life-long rule."

I remember that Captain Foster mentioned something similar about the regent taking this opportunity to purge his enemies.

"What they've told me about your brother, though," he continues, "is that you should do everything you can to escape and bring the rest of your family to the Strip. I'm sorry to tell you this, but nothing can be done for Brian. He's at the mercy of the Crowleys. I'm so sorry, Derin. Mia knows this too, and she's devastated."

Somehow, I knew it, but I didn't want to accept it. Now I have no doubt. They're going to kill Brian. And if I don't do something soon, they're going to kill us all.

I look at my watch and realize it's a quarter to nine.

"I have to get back," I say, pointing to the time. "I don't know what I'm going to do, Dylan. I have to go home and talk to my parents. If we manage to leave the city, what should we do?"

"Come here directly, of course. Georgie will call us right away. She'll know how to keep you safe until one of us arrives."

We say goodbye to Georgie and leave the pub.

Dylan decides to accompany me to the train station. We walk without talking much. I think he understands how distressed I feel, and prefers not to force a conversation. When we reach the main street, we get on the bus that takes us to the Transversal Corridor. From there, Dylan knows where to catch another bus to the nearest train stop, so we move quickly.

When we arrive at the station, we go up to the platform where the trains leave for London. The information board announces that the next departure will be in four minutes.

We see the train approaching in the distance, and suddenly I remember.

"Oh, I almost forgot," I say, reaching into my hoodie's pocket to take out the soldier figurine I snagged from my bedroom this morning. "It's silly, I know," I say, a bit embarrassed, "but when I saw it, I remembered you and the 'little tin soldier.' I thought you should have it."

Dylan gazes at the figurine and grabs it. Smiling, he examines it and then looks up into my eyes, widening his smile even more.

I hear the train arriving behind me. Soon I must get on and leave him, but before I turn around, Dylan steps close and hugs me.

He catches me by surprise, and I don't know how to react.

I'm petrified, with my arms hanging down, while he wraps me in his own. I can smell his wonderful scent close to me.

"Thanks," he says. "Please, be very careful. I hope to see you soon."

He lets go so I can get on the train.

From the window, I watch him as the train pulls away. My eyes get watery. I smile at him one last time before his image disappears into the distance.

I don't know if I'll ever see him again, but I know that I want to find out if that hug meant as much to him as it does to me.

—

AT A QUARTER PAST TEN, I get back to London. At the exchange station for Access Point 8, I have no problem locating the controller from earlier in the entry control booths. I approach the glass and, after making sure there are no security agents nearby, I slip him a fifty-pound bill. The controller recognizes me immediately, takes a cautious look around, grabs the money, and nods.

I've visited the Strip and returned without leaving a trace. At least this has worked out.

The train ride has given me time to reflect on the shocking revelation from Dylan and weigh the alternatives. Everything that happens from now on will be terribly painful, that much I know. Now I'll have to take the decision with the least disastrous result.

I'm pretty sure my parents won't hear anything about escaping and leaving Brian behind. I won't either. I can't run away and abandon him, or them.

But Lily, my little sister. We can save her.

My parents will have to accept that at least we can try to prevent her from suffering everything coming our way, even if it means sending her to the Strip and separating from her, maybe forever. It's the right thing to do. And we should do it immediately because we're running against the clock.

I get a lump in my throat, thinking that I might never see Dylan again. I feel a void in my chest, where my heart should be, and this emptiness fills with an intense pain that I've never known before.

I turn the corner and go down our street.

I look ahead, toward my house, and immediately notice that something isn't right. I walk faster, agitated.

My heart skips a beat when I recognize two black vans: CAT. Counterterrorism Agency Troops.

I freeze. I can't feel my pulse. I feel like I'm falling into an abyss.

I've arrived too late. I've failed them, I think, resigned.

With an overwhelming sense of helplessness, I approach the garden fence in front of my house with my head down. Visible out of the corner of my eye, behind the black vehicles of the anti-terrorist forces, there are two white vans with the logo of the state television channel. When I turn toward my house, I find a team of technicians working on spotlights and cameras.

A CAT agent talks to one of the television technicians, who's holding a folder and wearing a communication device with a headset and microphone.

When he sees me, the CAT walks toward me.

I prepare myself for a blow from the electric club attached to his waist. I won't resist. But the agent does nothing of the sort.

"Derin Dark? Your teleCard, please," he says in an almost friendly tone.

"Uh … I don't have it with me, sorry. I think I forgot it upstairs in my room when I went out a little while ago."

"Let's go in," he replies, seeming undisturbed. He doesn't even bother to ask where I've been.

In my house, an army of government employees ransack everything and everywhere. They move furniture, raise cushions, open drawers. My parents and Lily, who are sitting at the dining table, look at me with pale faces.

"Your family is ready," says the CAT who met me outside, pointing to the three small suitcases to one side. "You have ten minutes to pack personal items to take with you: clothes, photographs, toiletries. Nothing of value, nothing electronic. I'll escort you, and your luggage will be inspected later."

They don't let me talk to my family, but their anguished expressions say it all. They're terrified.

"Where are you taking us?" I ask the CAT, not expecting an answer.

"The Ministry of National Security."

CHAPTER 8

PRISONERS

I ONLY HAVE A VAGUE IDEA OF WHAT'S HAPPENING. My brain is numb. I let a kind of mechanical automatism take over me as I fill the sports bag that I take out of the closet. When nothing else fits, and I close the zipper, I've already forgotten everything I've put inside. Before leaving my bedroom, I take one last look around me. I try to etch every detail of this place into my memory. It's where I've spent so many hours of my childhood and adolescence, where I've planned and dreamed of my future.

I'm guessing I'll never come back here again.

"Your teleCard?" the CAT agent reminds me.

"Yes, sorry, here it is," I reply, taking it out of the drawer where I left it this morning. I hand it to him. He checks the engraving on the back as well as my picture and personal data on the display, then puts it in one of his uniform's pockets.

When we go downstairs, I barely have time to hug my parents and Lily.

"Leave your bag there, with the others," the agent says. "They'll be taken separately. Now let's move it. I'll go first and then you all. We'll go straight to the first van."

The agent opens the door and steps out. My parents and Lily follow, and I bring up the rear.

The heat wave from the spotlights hits me. The camera flashes force me to place my right hand as a visor over my eyes. Everything happens very quickly, but I understand that Crowley's media spectacle has begun. We're now part of the show.

They make us climb into the back of one of the black vans. The interior is a windowless compartment, separate from the driver. My father and I sit on the left-side bench, while Lily and my mother sit opposite us. Two CAT agents also get in behind us and close the two doors. The van starts moving.

My father has his hands between his legs and his head bowed, with his eyes fixed on the floor. My mother and Lily put their arms around each other, with their heads tilted to the side and their foreheads touching. I hear them sob.

"Everything will be okay, don't worry. You'll see," I tell them.

I can't think of anything else to say. I don't have any idea of what awaits us.

My mother raises her head for a moment, looks at me, and nods, forcing a weak smile. She knows I'm just trying to encourage everyone.

The lack of visual contact with the outside distorts my sense of time and orientation. Maybe it's been half an hour, or an hour, I'm not sure. After a while, we come to a complete stop, and the van's engine is turned off.

We've arrived. Wherever they've brought us.

They open the doors of the van and tell us to get out.

We're in a large underground parking garage, I'm guessing in the basement of New Big Ben, the headquarters of the Ministry of National Security. Four CAT agents direct us through very long corridors that change directions several times until we reach a group of elevators. We go up to the fourth floor, and from there we continue through another zigzagging labyrinth. We stop in front of a door guarded by two security agents.

The CAT who confiscated my teleCard and inspected what I was putting in my sports bag points to the door and gives me a brusque nod. He wants us to go in there.

I go first, open the door, and prepare to step in, but stop abruptly.

"Brian!" I exclaim when I see him sitting at a table in the center of the room. His face is bruised and his right eye swollen.

My mother passes by me like a thunderbolt and throws herself at my brother, letting out an animal moan that releases her repressed emotions. She hugs him violently and breaks into tears. My father and Lily follow her inside.

I approach him too and, before I can say anything, Brian hugs me. I hear him sniffle to suppress tears. It's the first time he's ever held me like this.

"You okay?" I ask.

He nods. I know he's holding back his feelings, mainly because of my parents and Lily.

The CAT agent closes the door and leaves us alone, without giving any further instructions.

Brian looks me directly in the eyes—something he never does—and says:

"How are you all? How's *everybody*?" I notice the minimal change in his tone of voice. He wants to know about Mia.

"*All* well," I reply, emphasizing the word 'all' so he gets my meaning. "Don't worry."

He nods. He's understood me and knows that Mia and Dylan are safe.

"What the hell is going on? What is this?" he asks.

"We don't know yet. What happened yesterday?" I reply, eager to hear his version of events, though I know he hasn't committed any crime. All this is a farce.

"I really don't know. I don't understand a thing…" he begins. "We saw the explosion, there was chaos, everyone ran in all directions… then the CATs began beating us for no reason at all. We hadn't done anything, I swear!"

"Then what happened?" I ask, pretending for the microphones.

"Well, they hit me hard and arrested me. They did the same to Liam and the others. They brought us here and interrogated me twice," he replies, struggling to sound calm, but I know he's very nervous. "What's going on, Derin? Do they think I'm involved in that crap? It's ridiculous…"

"No, of course not," I say, trying to sound sure of myself. "It must be a misunderstanding. A mistake, you know, with all the confusion yesterday and everything. Things will clear up soon, you'll see. We all know you're innocent. Justice will prevail, and they'll let you go."

I can't allow Nigel's intelligence agents, who are surely listening in and recording our conversations, to have the slightest suspicion that I know this is a sham. My parents and Lily have said almost nothing. They're too afraid of saying something inappropriate.

But there's not much time to talk either since, after about ten minutes, an officer of the ministry comes in without even knocking on the door.

I recognize her immediately. She's Nigel's assistant, the one who last night escorted me from the lobby of this building to Nigel's office.

"I'm Lieutenant Deacon," she says, sitting down in one of the free chairs. "I'm here representing the Prosecutor of the Nation."

Chief of the anti-terrorist forces, Prosecutor of the Nation, the regent's son, heir to the throne, Nigel Crowley… damn bastard!

She opens a folder and reads aloud the formal accusation against Brian. It's the same one I already heard from Captain Foster and Nigel himself. Then she continues with the information that interests me most:

"The accused Brian Dark, along with the others accused of these crimes, will be judged by the citizens' wisdom through a special broadcast of *Trial of the People*, which will take place over the next two days starting tomorrow." *Starting tomorrow!* I'm surprised; it seems the Crowleys are in a hurry with this charade. She continues: "The immediate family of the accused—Thomas Dark, father, Emma Dark, mother, Lily Dark, sister, and Lieutenant Derin Dark, brother—will participate in the *Trial of the People*, according to that procedure established in the Compendium of Laws of the Just Society, and will remain within these facilities during the course of the program." She closes the folder and looks up. "You'll have all the best comforts during your stay, and if at the end of the trial, the accused is declared innocent, you'll be permitted to return to your home, and the Government will be very generous in compensating you for the inconvenience."

It's humiliating, the brazen way this woman says those words: "If he's declared innocent." None of the defendants on a *Trial of the People* has ever been declared innocent.

I've been stupid to hold on to the slightest hope regarding what Nigel told me last night. He said Brian would be treated fairly and that my family wouldn't be harmed. But he's thrown us into the lion's den by making us participate in the *Trial of the People*. He must be rolling on the floor with laughter.

"Now we'll take you to your rooms," the lieutenant says to wrap up.

As she leads the way, with the same hurried pace as last night, four of the ministry's security agents escort us without losing sight of us for even a second down the twists in the corridors. We take an elevator and go further up.

I expected a cell or a simple room, but I'm amazed to see where they've led us. We're on level twenty-two of the Tower of Victory, where the entire floor looks like a hotel. We've been given a luxurious corner apartment, in the same location that several levels above, Nigel has his office.

What game are you playing, you bastard? I think, furious.

There's a large living room, a dining room, and a kitchen with a bar, all with an open-plan layout and modern, elegant furniture. They've brought our bags up already.

"You'll find everything you need," says Deacon. "There are drinks, fruit, and snacks in the fridge, but they'll bring you lunch in a while. You must stay inside the apartment, you can't go out. There will be surveillance outside. Tomorrow morning, you'll be allowed to go outdoors for half an hour, and perhaps again in the afternoon before the broadcast."

She rushes through the notes in her folder, making sure she hasn't forgotten any details. She's about to leave, but she turns her head toward us before stepping out.

"You should consider yourselves lucky," she adds in a condescending tone. "Not everyone is provided with these amenities. Governor Hall has been put in a cell for common criminals."

Governor Hall? So that's the enemy Crowley wants to get rid of: Graham Hall, the governor of the protectorate of Leeds. Who would have thought? Hall has a reputation for being a fair and good-natured regional leader, and he doesn't stand out in any particular way on the council of the fourteen governors. A pretty harmless figure, you could say. I wonder what he's done to become an enemy of the regent.

It's extraordinary that he's been put in a cell while we get these luxurious accommodations.

There are two bedrooms, each with a full bathroom. My parents and Lily take the larger room, where there's a double bed and a single bed. Brian and I stay in the other one, which has two singles.

The five of us then sit on the sofas in the living room, which occupies the corner of the apartment and features floor-to-ceiling windows. The short conversation about the breath-taking view of the city is superficial and quite forced. We feel watched.

A little while later, they bring us lunch.

A handful of waiters in navy blue uniforms, embroidered with the logo of the restaurant Stevens—one of the most exclusive in the city—enter pushing two side tables on wheels and place them next to the dining table. The three levels of each wheeled table are filled with trays and platters containing enough delicacies for a dozen people to eat. There's a cream of shellfish soup with bubbles that, when they burst, draw images of fish and shells on the surface. There are juicy beef medallions—from natural meat, not the dry synthetic kind—stuffed with fresh vegetables and herbs; potato chips in the shape of planets and stars; rice and pasta in various colors; and for dessert, in addition to chocolate cakes and tropical fruit, there's a tray full of spheres of paradise. When you put these soft balls of different textures in your mouth, they dissolve and create a burst of astonishing tastes and sensations on your palate. I had never tried one before today, as only the very wealthy can afford them. It impresses me how exquisite they are. We've never dined so elegantly in my life.

All of this baffles me.

My brother Brian is accused of serious crimes and will be tried in a *Trial of the People*. In spite of his innocence—since this is entirely a set-up—the most probable thing is that he'll be declared guilty and executed… and who knows what they'll do with the rest of us.

So, what does all this mean? Why do they let us stay in a luxury apartment and provide us with exclusive dishes that almost nobody in this country can afford?

Is it possible that Nigel still feels something for me and has decided not to harm my family? After all, we have nothing to do with this. It's "simply" a perverse plan to get rid of an opponent of the Crowleys. We're here because of a very unlucky twist of fate since Brian was only by chance in the wrong place at the wrong time. They could have taken any other innocent boy to serve as a filler for this charade.

Could all this be Nigel's compensation for having to play a role in his father's sick games?

Maybe he'll have Brian declared innocent. Perhaps they'll set us all free. It's in his hands, it's up to him. Will he ask me for anything in return?

Or is all this just a cruel way to show me his power and make fun of me—like he did yesterday—before ending my life?

I don't know what to think. Anything is possible.

For the moment, I try to do my part so that we get the best possible outcome in the plot we find ourselves in. I decide to act for the microphones and the hidden cameras: I encourage my parents and my siblings to enjoy the food, assuring them that we've been blessed by Commander Nigel Crowley's kindness and that it's an example of the decency and generosity of the regime.

It's a surreal show because everyone follows my lead. In the end, we wind up enjoying the banquet.

When they come back later to clear the tables and clean the dining room, one of the guards outside the door of the apartment tells us to turn on the TV. There will be a mandatory official broadcast. Since our teleCards have been confiscated, we have no other way to find out.

We wait expectantly for over ten minutes until the transmission finally begins.

Again, it's the regent addressing the country.

He begins by using trite phrases and elements from his past speeches to remind his audience of the pain caused by the constant attacks of the radkers against our country. He repeats the same old tune about the shortage of food and essential consumer items, cuts in the energy supply, failures and breakdowns in public infrastructure systems, danger to the citizens outside protected cities… the same as usual. Then he focuses on yesterday's attack and announces that the anti-terrorist forces have captured the masterminds behind it and others involved.

He explains that members of the Patricians—"the purest and most dignified caste"—have succumbed to the temptation of power and allied with rebel groups to overthrow the Government, assassinating him and taking his place. The architects of the plot include the governor of the protectorate of Leeds, Graham Hall, and his regional head of government, Lewis Freeland. He indicates that these national traitors have also poisoned the minds of several young people of the Commons to incite them to commit crimes against the State.

Surprisingly, he thanks Lucius Hall, Governor Hall's son, for his invaluable patriotism. When he learned that his own father was the mastermind behind the conspiracy against the regent, he didn't hesitate to turn him in.

Crowley ends by announcing that the accused will be judged in a *Trial of the People*, and reminds citizens of their civic duty to participate in the trial and issue their verdict.

So that's it. It's official.

For some reason, the regent wants to get rid of Governor Hall and his head of government. He must fear them a lot to have arranged such a spectacle with an alleged terrorist attack that aimed to end his life.

I don't care if they want to kill each other. But what fills me with frustration and pain is that my family is affected, in the harshest way, by this power struggle between Patrician families. It's so infuriating and unfair that my body hurts in anger.

We spend the rest of the afternoon like caged animals: nervous, frightened, and restless. When dinnertime approaches, we ask the guards not to bring us anything. We ate so much for lunch that we're too full. If they bring us more food, it would go to waste. Besides, the kitchen and fridge are full of snacks and drinks.

We're overcome by incredible fatigue, no doubt because of the roller coaster of emotions we've been forced onto, so we go to bed early. I've never experienced a bed so soft and comfortable. It's like lying on a cloud. But, as much as I toss and turn, I can't fall asleep. I hear Brian snoring and get upset because he's fallen asleep so fast.

I immediately scold myself for such silly and inconsiderate thoughts.

He doesn't know everything that I do. He doesn't know that the whole matter of the attack isn't true, that it's only a set-up by the Crowleys. I haven't been able to tell him or my parents. I don't know yet whether I should. I don't think they'll be able to handle it. They already have enough to deal with as it is. I don't want to make things worse. I can barely stand it myself, and I'm on the verge of losing my sanity.

I get up quietly and go to the kitchen. I heat up some milk, pour it into a cup, and take it with me to the living room. I don't have to turn on the lights, because the curtains are open and enough light comes in from outside. There's a full moon.

I go the windows and gaze at the illuminated city. Private heli-jets glide through the air in all directions. Almost opposite where I'm standing, a short distance away, rises the imposing skyscraper of the Palace of the Governors. I lift my gaze and see, at the top, the gigantic cube illuminated with Englandom's coat of arms. I wonder on which level Regent Crowley lives. I wonder if Nigel also lives there.

I think of something else: if this apartment were located in the opposite corner, maybe I could see—in the distance, from this height—the lights of the Strip.

I try to imagine what Dylan is doing right now.

I remember his embrace and an uplifting feeling, a strange mixture of excitement and serenity, runs through my body. I can still smell his scent, and I don't want it to fade away. I don't want to forget it.

I wish I hadn't been petrified and had hugged him back.

What wouldn't I do to see him again and hold him in my arms!

CHAPTER 9

BEFORE THE SHOW

SOUNDS COMING FROM THE OTHER ROOM AWAKEN ME. I open my eyes and notice that the bed next to mine is empty. Brian has left the bedroom door open. I yawn so intensely that my face almost falls off, then get up. On the way to the bathroom, I glance through the doorway: they've brought breakfast. Brian and my father are already sitting at the table. With a grumble, my stomach reminds me that last night I didn't eat anything but an apple. I take a shower and get dressed before going out to meet the others.

In the dining room, my father tells us that earlier, when they brought breakfast, one of the security agents told him that we should be ready by nine thirty.

At precisely that time, two agents come into the apartment and order us to follow them.

We go down to the eighth level. As we step out of the elevator, we find ourselves in a big room flooded with light shining through large windows at the front and on both sides. There are several groups of armchairs, sofas, and tables with chairs. On one side I see a bar. Again, I have the impression of being in the lobby of a luxury hotel. There are several small groups of people talking throughout the different areas of the room. They watch us with curiosity and whisper when we walk toward the front glass doors.

Outside, we are met by a beautiful park with green spaces and tiled paths. Several trees grow here, along with lots of bushes and flowers. I hear the chirping of birds and the soothing sound of water somewhere, and then I see the fountain. Later, I notice that there's also a heliport on a raised platform, and farther behind, the new clock tower rises.

We're on the rooftop of the Ministry of National Security. I would have never imagined such a lovely spot above this dull, threatening building. Nothing of the sort is visible from the street. We couldn't see it from the apartment either since the view there overlooks the opposite direction.

They tell us we'll be here until a quarter past ten. We're allowed to move around without restrictions. They don't seem worried about losing sight of us since it's impossible to get out except via the doors we just stepped through. There's no way to escape unless you jumped over the edge and fell flat on the pavement, a hundred feet below.

My parents and Lily go ahead and inspect a fish pond, while Brian and I walk to the left, toward the fountain. The water that flows down three different levels to the pond below makes a pleasant but intense splashing sound, so we dare to speak with little fear.

Brian can't hold it in anymore and starts talking, asking between his teeth:

"Is she really okay?"

"Yeah, she's okay. Both of them went home without problems."

"How do you know? Did they send you a message? Did you talk to them?"

"I saw them myself *there*," I answer, looking straight into his eyes. "I mean, I saw him, but he assured me that she was safe too."

I don't have the courage to tell him all the details of my trip to the Strip.

"Great, that's really great. At least there's that," he says, nodding. Then he continues: "Derin, what's all this shit? Why are we here? It doesn't make sense, I've got nothing to do with the attack."

After my thoughts last night, I've decided not to say anything about what I've learned. Not to Brian or my parents. It wouldn't do any good and would complicate things even more. What they already know about the regime is bad enough.

"I don't know," I lie. "I'm not sure. I mean, it's obvious this is a serious mistake. I don't understand why they're accusing you of being involved in this."

That part's true. I don't fully understand why.

"But, if they think Governor Hall's to blame, why take me? What do they want?" he asks, desperate to understand even a hint of this madness.

"I'm afraid we're kind of a filler," I dare to say. It's better he's aware of this much now; sooner or later he would realize it himself. "Just dirty rotten luck. But Brian, remember you've got a history that's somewhat… controversial. You must be prepared. They'll rub it in your face and use it for their own purposes. Maybe to set a precedent, I don't know, or to teach other kids from our caste a lesson about what happens if you're not completely loyal to the regime."

"Bastards," he says in a whisper, almost unintelligible. "They're capable of anything, right? Do you think they'll kill me?"

"No, of course not, don't worry," I lie again, shaking my head. "I'm hoping Nigel Crowley will take pity on us. I saw him yesterday."

"Of course, you know him! I hadn't thought of that," he replies. "What did he say? Is he going to help us?"

"I don't know. It's hard to make sense of what that guy says or does."

"This is my fault, right?" He turns his head toward my parents and Lily with a sad look. "They've accused me because of my foolishness. And now they'll make them suffer. I'm so sorry…"

He's about to cry.

"Of course not! It's not your fault, or anyone else's," I say firmly, putting my hand on his shoulder. "Don't talk nonsense. This is just another one of the regime's despicable actions. You've always been right about that."

Unfortunately, I don't only say this to alleviate his sense of guilt: it's also true. In this country, you don't have to be guilty of anything. Here they can kill you whenever and however they want to. The worst part is that they murder your loved ones too. Once sentenced to death, your only hope is that they'll kill you quickly without forcing you to watch your family suffer.

We hear the roar of a helicopter. I search the sky and see it: it's a military aircraft, an old model, one that makes too much noise. It descends onto the helipad. A man in military uniform carrying a briefcase gets out of the passenger cabin and walks through the park as the helicopter takes off again.

I recognize the tall man with the beard almost immediately.
It's Captain Foster.

I shift my gaze to my parents and Lily, who are sitting on a bench near the helipad. My father stands up and walks toward the captain, waving his hand. When he reaches him, he grabs him by the arm and says something in his ear. The captain answers back.

"Brian, it's Captain Foster," I confirm. "Come on, let's go!"

When we're thirty feet away from them, the captain says good-bye to my father, nods at my mother, and advances toward us.

"Captain," I say, amazed. "What are you doing here?"

"Are you boys okay?" he asks first and foremost. Brian and I nod. "I've got an emergency meeting with all the access point chiefs and Commander Crowley," he explains. "I must go now, I can't be late."

"Captain, can you do anything for us?" I ask, hoping for any sign of encouragement.

"Did you speak with him? Could you see him?"

"Yes, last night. But you know what he's like, so ambiguous. I don't know what he'll do. Do you have any way to intervene on our behalf?"

"I don't know. I doubt it," he says with compassion. "This is very complicated. I'm so sorry, boys. I'll do what I can, but you must be prepared. This matter is solely in the hands of the regent and Commander Crowley. It's extremely serious."

I understand what he's saying. He can't take too many risks. He's got his daughter.

He says goodbye with a prolonged squeeze on my arm, as if he were saying goodbye forever. At the entrance of the tower, a CAT agent waits expectantly to escort him.

We spend the rest of the morning and midday confined to our golden cage.

For lunch, the same employees from Stevens bring us a banquet as splendid as the day before, although this time we don't manage to eat as much. The nerves hit our stomachs with increasing force.

Long hours of intense emotions await us. We must be at the TV studio for the *Trial of the People* at three. The live broadcast begins at six and lasts until nine, but the program's team needs several hours of preparation before it starts. At ten to three, Lieutenant Deacon appears with four security agents. I wonder why they didn't come earlier since the state television's complex is located in another part of the city, several miles from here. There's no way we'll make it by three unless they fly us over there.

"You don't need to take anything with you," says Deacon in her typical dry and formal tone, always consulting the notes in her folder. "The producers will give you further instructions."

We go down the elevator to level two. From there, they guide us through a labyrinth of offices to the end of a wide corridor. We arrive at a kind of rectangular lounge, quite spacious, with offices along the sides. The center office, surrounded by glass walls, draws my attention. We approach that office and, although the interior is not yet lit, I can see enough through the glass to understand what's going on inside. It's the control booth for a TV studio. I can make out rows of monitors, as well as boards with an infinite number of illuminated buttons, knobs, and handles. Past the back wall, also made of glass, I see a huge recording studio.

So, Trial of the People *is broadcast from here,* I think, somewhat surprised. I didn't expect it, though it makes sense. I suppose it's very convenient for Nigel.

Lieutenant Deacon knocks on the glass a couple of times and signals to attract attention. A young guy turns around and notices her. He takes off his headphones, gets up, and comes out of the control room.

"These are the Darks," says the lieutenant, pointing to us.

"Excellent, lieutenant," replies the TV guy. Then he turns to us. "I'm Andrew Frost, production manager assistant. Follow me, please."

We take one of the elevators to the side and go down three levels. They take us to a windowless room that contains some sofas, a large television screen, a fully-equipped bathroom, and a dressing table that extends along the entire length of the right-hand wall. Above its mirror, equally long, a row of intense lights burns. In one corner, there's also a small fridge.

Andrew Frost gives us some instructions about the preparations that will take place in the next few hours. Makeup artists and stylists are on their way. He'll be back later to go over several important points of tonight's program's script.

So far, we haven't seen or heard anything about the other defendants. Governor Hall and his head of government will inevitably appear in the program since they're the main attraction. But we don't know if, besides Brian, there will be others. Brian said they captured several boys and girls along with him, most of them deels, but also some Commons—including his friend Liam, though he hasn't seen him since they were brought to the ministry. I take it for granted that the deel kids are already dead.

The following hours are strenuous.

A squad of stylists and makeup artists transform us. My mother is dressed in a flashy purple dress with earrings and a matching pearl necklace. They give her an exaggerated hairstyle that doesn't become her at all and redraw her face with intense makeup. Her delicate features are now hard and vulgar. Lily has also been changed completely: she's wearing a dress that's too risqué for her age, with bare shoulders and a wide neckline. They've even made her put on a padded bra, which makes her breasts stand out too much. They've left her hair and face so dazzling that she seems much older than she is. She looks like a frivolous, trite girl.

"You look fantastic, honey!" says the most annoying of the stylists for the umpteenth time. "You'll win over men's hearts all over the country, as will your mother."

My blood boils. I can't stand seeing what they're doing to them.

My father has been given a light blue suit with a yellow tie, and his hair has been ruffled. He doesn't look cool and carefree, but rather disheveled and awkward. Brian is wearing dark grey pants and a grey short-sleeved shirt. They've put something in and around his eyes to make them look large and threatening, and have smeared something in his copper hair to turn it deep orange, almost fire engine red.

I'm aware that they're not leaving anything to chance in this program. Every decision they make has a very specific goal.

I consider myself lucky. They've only put on some makeup and given me one of my academy uniforms, with the official insignia.

With the bustle of styling arrangements and the constant mocking chatter of the stylists, the rest of the afternoon goes by in a flash.

At twenty to six, Andrew Frost comes to get us.

Accompanied by four security agents, he leads us to the studio, which is on the same level we are now. We enter it through a narrow tunnel from one of its back corners. We immediately hear the muted roar of a crowd. When we get out of the tunnel, we find ourselves in a large square chamber, two or three stories tall. Several mechanical devices with cameras and reflectors hang from the black ceiling. Three sides of the studio are taken up by bleachers full of spectators, fanatics for the regime who consider it an honor to be invited to the show.

They take us to the middle of the set. There, forming a semi-circle that opens toward the front, and a few feet apart from each other, they've placed five moveable compartments with low railings. In each booth, there are two rows of chairs.

There are five defendants, I think as they lead us to the second booth, counting from the right.

Andrew Frost tells Brian that he should sit alone in the front row. My parents, Lily, and I sit in the chairs in the second row, behind Brian. The four security agents stand behind our booth.

From my position, I have a clear view of the monitor in front of us, on the right side. I shudder when I see us on the screen, looking horrible and nervous. On that monitor, we'll see what they broadcast to the whole country. It has a built-in camera with a small but powerful spotlight so that millions of viewers will see us in high definition.

At any time, the director can choose to broadcast live the slightest emotion from the accused and their families.

Looking straight ahead, I notice the ring on the metal floor, in the center of the crescent formed by the booths. It's a circle about six feet in diameter.

My stomach churns. I've seen it on other broadcasts.

It's a sort of hydraulic platform that goes down to a lower level. At the beginning of the program, Nigel Crowley makes his dramatic entry on that platform, but it's also used at the end of the trial. On the second day, the defendants found guilty descend into the Chamber of Purgation, where they're executed live through a series of dreadful procedures.

Feeling nauseous, I force myself to think of something else. I don't want to throw up in front of the audience, in front of the whole country.

We're the first defendants to arrive. The other four booths are still empty, but we've only just taken our places when I sense people in the audience pointing toward the other corner of the studio, on the opposite side of where we came in.

I turn in that direction and see security agents escorting an older, bald man with glasses through another tunnel. This man walks with his head down.

I recognize him immediately. It's Governor Graham Hall.

I'm surprised he's come alone, without his family.

Behind him, another group of agents escorts a tall and robust man, who I believe is Hall's head of government, Lewis Freeland. He's accompanied by a middle-aged woman and a girl a couple of years older than me. I'm guessing they're his wife and daughter. They seem disoriented. Despite the thick makeup, their eyes look swollen and red.

They lead Governor Hall to the booth in the middle of the semicircle, parallel to the edge of the stage and next to ours on the left. He sits down in the front row. In the booth to the left of Hall, Lewis Freeland and his family take their places. The security agents remain standing behind them.

A minute later, another entourage of security agents comes out, escorting two groups through the same tunnel we used. In the first group, I see Liam Mitchell, Brian's friend, accompanied by his parents and brother. Liam's a big, muscular guy, with broad shoulders and thick arms. He has short, dark hair and although he's about the same age as Brian, he seems older because of his size and his dark beard, which has gone unshaved for several days and also makes him looks menacing. The rest of his family looks as bad as mine.

In the second group, there's a young and handsome guy. He comes out with his wife, also very young, and a set of precious twin girls about three years old. I have no idea who they are. Liam and his family sit in the first booth on the left side of the semicircle, the furthest away from us, while the other family is taken to the booth on our right, the first on this side. I'm moved by the two adorable girls, who smile at everyone without any idea of the hell they've been dragged into.

We're not allowed to talk to the other defendants, so Brian just nods his head when Liam takes his place and looks over at him.

The program's attendants give final instructions to the audience in the grandstands, while some technicians do last-minute checks on the main screen covering the entire wall behind the stage. Nigel Crowley will assume the main platform, placed diagonally on the right side of the stage, almost opposite our booth. On the other side, also diagonally, there's a smaller platform, more like a desk. That's where the Defendants' Attorney will sit.

We have no idea who the Defendants' Attorney will be. It's not that important either. The defense lawyer plays a purely symbolic role. He's there to pretend that a fair trial is being carried out, but everyone knows that the only thing that matters is what the Prosecutor of the Nation says.

My legs start to tremble. In a couple of seconds, the whole country will witness Nigel destroying the defendants and their families one by one. My family.

My mind is blank. I'm scared of what he's going to say in Brian's case. Will he keep his word? Will he be fair and leave us unharmed by this mess? Or will he be cruel and make us all suffer, despite my brother's innocence?

My mother, seated next to me, grabs my hand and squeezes it tightly. I don't want to look at her. It's enough that I can see her on the side screen.

Nearly all the studio lights are turned off, and a digital counter with bright blue numbers appears on the stage's big screen, showing thirty seconds.

The countdown begins.

… 29… 28… 27… 26…

I can't look away from the digits. Now they've turned green.

... 20 ... 19 ... 18 ... 17 ...

The huge digits change with a hypnotizing blink. After ten, the numbers turn bright red, and the entire audience joins the countdown with a deafening roar:

"Ten! ... Nine! ... Eight! ... Seven! ... Six! ... Five! ..."

My heart beats so fast and so violently that I feel like my chest is about to explode.

"... Four! ... Three! ... Two! ... One! ... Zeeero!"

Here we go.

CHAPTER 10

THE TRIAL OF THE PEOPLE

THE PROGRAM'S LOGO appears on the screen. After two seconds, it fades out and leads into an elaborate introductory sequence, which is dramatized by a musical interlude. During the introduction, those of us in the TV studio see a cone of bright light projected over the metal circle in the center of the set. We hear a click and then a mechanical whirring sound. The metal circle lowers and leaves behind an opening in the floor. The program's introductory sequence has finished, and now live images appear on the screen.

"Ladies and gentlemen… the Prosecutor of the Nation: Nii-iggel Crowwwley!" a deep masculine voice announces.

The resounding applause and cheers of the audience join the deafening fanfare of trumpets and drums. All other sounds are completely muffled beneath them, so we don't hear the mechanical whirring of the platform going up again.

In the midst of this fervent reception and with all the theatricality that his office and role deserve, Nigel Crowley slowly emerges from the bowels of the earth. With his head tilted back, his chin raised, and his arms extended at his sides with his palms upward, he looks like a prophet or demigod being received and acclaimed by his people.

I'm completely absorbed as I watch him on the circular platform, which elevates him to a height where his feet are now at our eye level.

He's dressed in a white long-sleeved robe, open at the front, which reaches down to his ankles. The silver-and-gold embroidery radiates infinite sparkles under the powerful reflector's light. Under the robe, he's wearing a bright blue suit with a high-collared jacket, as well as black patent-leather shoes. They've dyed his blond hair a more platinum color and combed back a thick strand, which sticks out strangely from the rest of the hair. His makeup is grotesque.

Watching him live, a few feet away in that ridiculous outfit, he looks like a Mardi Gras figure; but I'm puzzled when I see the images broadcast on television, which now also appear on the big screen at the back of the stage. I don't know how the technicians have managed to achieve such a radical change in Nigel's appearance. In the images, he looks slim, impressive, and almost handsome. They must have very sophisticated and expensive technology to achieve that effect; perhaps his absurd makeup serves as a guide for the computers to digitally alter his face.

At the end of his grand entrance, Nigel welcomes the studio audience and all TV viewers. While he speaks from the circular platform, the cone of light is replaced by a set of lights that illuminate him from several positions.

He warns in a dramatic tone that this *Trial of the People* has special significance, due to the terrible crimes the defendants are accused of. He reminds viewers of their duty to follow the trial and issue their verdict during tomorrow's program—or rather threatens them with the consequences if they don't.

Then he begins an extravagant summary of the terrorist attack against his father, Regent Eugene Crowley, and explains that on this first day of the trial, he will introduce each one of the defendants and their families. He will expose the crimes they're indicted for in detail, as well as the arguments and evidence that will prove their guilt.

In short, he intends to entertain the audience with the sham he and his father have concocted, I think, disgusted.

Before starting the accusations, Nigel has to take his place on the stand. The circular platform slides along the mechanical structure supporting it and hovers a couple of inches above the stage, so that Nigel can now easily step down. There, a throne-like armchair with a high back and red velvet upholstery awaits him.

At some point, the Defendants' Attorney also has entered and taken his place on the small stand on the opposite end of the stage. He's a short guy, with drooping shoulders and a tasteless appearance. His eyes are sunken and half-closed, and he wears tiny glasses. Compared to Nigel, he really looks insignificant.

I'm flabbergasted at how surreal all this is.

Since Hall and Freeland are the main attraction, the first two hours are dedicated entirely to them.

Nigel makes a very detailed presentation of the plot to assassinate the regent. He explains how the governor of the protectorate of Leeds and his second-in-command conceived of and carried out the attack. The evidence he shows using images, documents, and statements seems so real and convincing that I could easily swallow the whole story myself if I didn't know it's a hoax.

Governor Hall's case is sensational in two ways: he's not only the first governor and the first Patrician to be accused of treason since the GNIE and the Council of Governors were established, but in addition, he has been betrayed by his own family, by his son, Lucius Hall.

It baffles me that someone like Lucius, who surely has everything in life, could fall so low and become entangled with the Crowleys in this dirty maneuver to get rid of his father. What perverse motives have driven him to commit patricide? More money, more power? Couldn't he wait any longer to take his father's place?

Actually, I don't care. I don't give a damn what games of treachery and blood these corrupt Patricians want to play. But this time, their intrigues are causing our destruction.

A piercing pain runs through my body when I think about what awaits us because of these bastards.

When the accusation against Hall is over, Nigel starts praising his son.

"This honorable Patrician," he says, pointing to Lucius Hall, who sits in a prominent position in the grandstands, "has shown love and loyalty to his country through a commendable and self-less act. Therefore, Lucius Hall and his family are exonerated in advance of any responsibility for the crimes committed by his father. Due to this supreme sacrifice, the regent will personally take care of rewarding them."

"Long live Regent Crowley!" shouts an old woman in the audience after getting the go-ahead signal from one of the program's animators.

"Long live the regent!" clamors the rest of the audience after another signal from the same animator.

Seen on television, though sleek and polished, this program seems embarrassingly bogus and forced; but live in the studio, this charade is even more painfully pathetic.

It's the Defendants' Attorney's turn. This little man stands up from his desk and wanders from one end of the stage to the other while mumbling barely intelligible phrases. He tries to elaborate arguments in defense of the accused, but what he says and how he expresses himself and moves makes everyone cringe. He can't be taken seriously.

I wonder if the real reason for having this buffoon as the Defendants' Attorney is to introduce a comic element and alleviate some of the heaviness and seriousness of the three-hour program.

When it's time for the accusation against Lewis Freeland, Hall's head of government, matters become more dramatic. In his case, the immediate family has to answer for the crimes the accused is charged with. His wife and daughter are, therefore, also guilty of the actions of the husband and father. This is established by law, or by Crowley, which is the same thing.

Nigel presents Freeland as a sexually depraved person, full of vices and greedy for power, who, in his lust for an underaged

Patriot girl Hall had supposedly offered, conspired with him to overthrow the regent. He also discredits his family in a harsh and humiliating manner. During the whole segment against Freeland, the wife and daughter don't stop crying.

It's clear to everyone that like Hall, Freeland is also here to die… and who knows what horrors his family will endure.

At the end of the indictment against Freeland, the Defendants' Attorney gets up again and repeats his comic sketch of an incompetent lawyer. The audience in the bleachers let out shrieks of laughter, as is expected from them, judging by what I've seen in previous broadcasts of this program on TV. It's just despicable.

Next, Nigel introduces Michael Wallace, the guy I didn't know, who waits with his wife and two daughters in the booth to our right.

My nerves had calmed down a bit during the endless exposition against the two Patricians, but now, as our turn gets closer, I put my hands on my thighs and squeeze them tightly to keep my legs from shaking so much.

I don't pay much attention to the charges against Wallace. I only learn that they accuse him of being involved in the matter of the drones that deployed the rebel flag and then exploded near the regent.

I don't have any room left in my head to condemn the absurdity of the accusation—since everything is a hoax, a vile lie—and the terrible punishments that await not only him, but also his wife and two daughters, or even to ask myself why the Crowleys want to destroy him and his loved ones.

I'm just thinking about my family, ready for what's coming.

My mother holds my hand again and takes Lily's in the other. My father and Brian are stiff as statues.

After the required and brief comic intervention of the Defendants' Attorney, Nigel announces that the charges against the next two defendants will be presented together since both are charged with the same crimes and with a similar degree of responsibility.

I don't know if presenting the accusations against Brian and Liam together is good or not. I don't have the headspace right now to analyze it.

I bite my lower lip so hard that I soon have the sweet taste of blood in my mouth. I need to compose myself. Now our booth will become the focal point of the cameras, and we'll be the main characters.

When Nigel mentions the name "Liam Mitchell," a zoom of his frightened face appears on the screen, and then a shot from farther back shows the whole booth where he and his family are sitting. They don't look good.

The moment Nigel says "Brian Dark," I feel myself get as rigid as my brother and my father. An icy stream runs through my bones. I barely dare move my eyes for a second toward the monitor next to us, but it's enough to recognize us. We look terrible.

From this paralyzing freeze, my blood begins to warm up and then boil, shooting up my face and surrounding my skull. My heart pounds in my ears. It's as if they've covered my head with a warm helmet that only lets me hear the intense, rhythmic sound of blood flowing through my veins. I'm afraid I'll miss the details of Nigel's presentation, because, although I can see he's talking, I can barely hear him.

Control yourself, Derin, control yourself.

I force myself to inhale and exhale deeply several times to calm down.

"… these two youngsters from the Commons have strayed from the right path, with a history of rebellion and infringements against public order," says Nigel, supporting his statements with images and videos of Brian and Liam, together and separately, where they're involved in some fight, shouting insults against the Government, or staining walls with graffiti.

I'm impressed by how well they've edited these images. Some of the originals date back four or five years ago. Most were taken at our school and a public playground in our neighborhood. I even remember the one fight against those obnoxious kids who were constantly bullying the younger ones. Though the original images are real, they've been altered. The graffiti scenes are fake, and the insults against the Government are voiceovers.

"… and because of this predisposition to disobedience and revolt," he continues, "they allowed themselves to be manipulated by the deceits of defendant Michael Wallace, in order to assault security forces the afternoon of the attack and create a diversion that made it easier for the terrorists to execute their ruthless attack against the regent."

They show images of some kids fighting against the CATs, but their faces are barely visible. They've manipulated one of the kid's hair color to look like Brian's, but it's ridiculous; his clothes aren't even the same as he was wearing that day. The background is blurred and can't be recognized. The images, if real, could be from anywhere in the country. But most probably, these are directed scenes following a script.

How is it possible that he can lie so blatantly? Now it seems the story is that Wallace used my brother and Liam to distract security forces while the attack was being carried out. If the matter weren't so serious, this cartoonish plot would be laughable.

But something he said does give me some hope. He said "they allowed themselves to be manipulated" and also "they assaulted security forces." It may not mean much, but it could be our salvation. If the charges against them turn out to be less severe than previously declared, this could save them from execution.

I decide to hold on to this hope. The alternative is too painful.

Before announcing the official accusation, Nigel proceeds with the part about the defendants' families.

I take a deep breath and wait several seconds to let out the air. There's little time left until nine o'clock, the time the first day of the trial ends. I dare to hope that there's not enough time to make us look too bad.

Either way, what comes next could destroy or save my family.

He starts with the Mitchells.

To my surprise, he's quite lenient with them. He presents them as a righteous family of the Commons, honest and hardworking, who contribute to society and haven't committed any major faults, except for having failed in their son's education and upbringing.

It could have been much worse. They've barely shown images of Liam's parents and his brother Nick. They can consider themselves lucky.

Now it's our turn. My heart hammers like a machine gun.

I try to swallow, but my throat doesn't cooperate; it's stuck shut.

First, images of the CAT agents escorting us from our house to the black van appear on the screen.

This isn't starting off well, with the arrest of my family broadcasted to the whole nation, I think, resigning myself to the fact that we'll go from bad to worse.

But as Nigel continues, I calm down. He's also quite generous with us.

He presents my father as a noteworthy teacher who has contributed to the well-being of the country and is enthusiastically dedicated to the education of the future men and women of Englandom. He speaks very highly of my mother as well and describes her as a loving housewife, devoted to her family and her social work. Lily is a kind and diligent girl at school. And I, Derin Dark, the accused's older brother, am an unblemished member of the Commons, a recently graduated Army officer, and an exemplary son of Englandom.

Is it possible? Is Nigel paving the way to absolve Brian and my family?

After concluding a summary of the facts, Nigel delivers the official accusation. I prepare myself for what's coming, the crucial part. I don't know what to expect; anything could happen.

"Therefore," Nigel announces solemnly, "the nation accuses Liam Mitchell and Brian Dark of committing the crimes of public disturbance, contempt of authority, and aggression against security forces."

I can't believe it. Surely, I haven't listened closely enough. What did he say?

I repeat the charges in my mind: "public disturbance," "contempt of authority," and "aggression against security forces." I hesitate a second. I'm not sure whether I should be happy, but I decide I should be. It's good news. Of course it's good news.

No illicit associations, no conspiracy against the Government, no terrorist acts. For some reason, Nigel has decided to change the formal charges I was warned about by Captain Foster. He has lessened them, made them much milder.

For the first time since this nightmare began, I feel a slight relief. I can now start contemplating the possibility that Brian can be saved, that he won't be executed.

My whole family turns to me with confused looks. They expect me to give them a signal, positive or negative, since they're not sure what this means.

I nod very slowly, with a barely visible smile. No doubt they understand what my eyes are communicating—a spark of optimism.

Even the arguments presented by the Defendants' Attorney in favor of Brian and Liam seem more serious, more coherent, and with fewer comic elements than his previous speeches.

He points out their virtues and, above all, their families' merits. In the end, he describes them as "two poor, confused boys, who have become prey to deception and manipulation, but with no intention of causing any harm."

In short, it's a positive outcome. Sure, positive compared to the alternatives, which would have been fatal. But at least it's something.

Tonight's program is coming to an end, and Nigel insists that viewers tune in for the second part of the program tomorrow, when they must issue their verdict.

To end on a dramatic note, he steps onto the circular platform in the center of the set and, with the same fanfare as at the beginning and the applause of the audience, he disappears like an ethereal being through the hole in the floor.

—

WE'RE SITTING AT THE DINING ROOM TABLE in the Tower of Victory apartment.

At the end of the broadcast for the first part of *Trial of the People*, security agents escorted us back to our comfortable prison, where a mandatory and mouth-watering feast from Stevens awaited us. We felt exhausted after the strenuous six hours we spent in the studio: three in dressing room preparations and three during the live broadcast. However, despite the physical and mental fatigue, we have reason to be cautiously optimistic.

Besides, we're hungry, so we eagerly dig into the delicacies.

"You see, what did I promise you?" my father says jubilantly. "The generosity and the sense of justice of the regent and Commander Crowley are commendable."

He plays his role well for the hidden microphones.

"Of course, honey," my mother says. "There's never any reason to doubt the wisdom of our leaders. Even in moments of weakness, they surprise us with their benevolence. We're fortunate to have them."

She seems like another person talking like that. This is what they force us to do in order to survive.

"Then, we can go back home?" asks Lily innocently, oblivious to the revolting script that the rest of us are following perfectly.

"Let's hope so. We have to put our faith in justice," I say, smiling.

We have successfully navigated the first obstacle, but the worst is still to come.

Tomorrow's televoting will be rigged, no doubt. And even if it weren't, there's no way citizens will vote in favor of the accused.

Who would dare vote against the Prosecutor of the Nation? Who would dare challenge Nigel Crowley, knowing that every action taken on the teleCards is recorded in each citizen's digital file? That would be like signing one's own death sentence. As a Common watching the *Trial of the People* on previous occasions, I've always voted against the accused myself.

We can, therefore, assume the verdict of the people: the five defendants will be declared guilty.

What isn't yet clear is the sentences that will be given to each one of them.

The official story is that a secret guild of legal experts decides the sentences, but everyone knows that this guild doesn't exist and it's Nigel who dictates the punishments, under his father's orders.

I have no choice but to pray that tomorrow, for whatever reason, regardless of his perverse motives, Nigel will be as benevolent to us as he has been today.

Otherwise, we'll suffer in the most gruesome way imaginable.

CHAPTER 11

THE VERDICTS

I'M ABOUT TO GO TO BED when one of the security agents enters the apartment—as always, without knocking on the door. He looks around until he finds me at the kitchen counter.

"Lieutenant Dark," he says, "please come with me. Just you."

My parents, who had been resting half-asleep on the living room sofa, stand up at once. First, they turn to the agent and then to me, with surprised and quizzical looks.

"Where are we going?" I ask, frowning.

"Just come with me," he says. "Someone wants to see you."

Someone wants to see me? At this hour?

But immediately I can imagine what this is about.

Captain Foster.

He's managed to do something for us and maybe even has bribed someone to see me. To take this kind of risk, he must have something significant to communicate.

Though... the agent has spoken bluntly and doesn't seem like he wants to hide anything. Besides, they listen to us around the clock here, so on second thought, no... it must not be anything out of the ordinary. Surely, the captain has obtained a special permit to talk with me. Somehow, he's been able to intervene on our behalf. Maybe he's convinced Nigel that he owes me something for what happened years ago, and has his consent to tell me some good news.

It must be that.

I breathe a light air of optimism and can't help but smile.

"Don't worry," I tell my parents. "I think I know who wants to see me. I'll be back in a bit." I turn toward the agent. "I'm almost ready, I just need to put on my shoes."

"Take a jacket too," he says. "It's cool outside."

"We're going out?"

"Just come with me, hurry up. We can't be late."

I go into the bedroom without worrying much about making noise. Brian sleeps like a log, and it's hard to wake him up. Of all of us, he's the most exhausted and went to bed a half hour ago. It's understandable since he's in the greatest danger with this mess. Although he doesn't express it much, this nightmare has hit him hard.

I put on my shoes and look in the closet for the only jacket I brought from home.

When I return to the living room, the agent is waiting impatiently in the open doorway of the apartment. He gestures quickly with his hands, urging me to hurry up.

We go down the elevator to level eight, and when we cross the hall toward the glass doors, I understand where we're going: the rooftop park.

I'm glad the agent had the decency to mention the jacket because it's quite cold outside. I follow him to the middle of the park, near the heliport's elevated platform. He leads me to the right, toward the brick wall that surrounds the roof.

"Wait right here," he says, and without further explanation, he turns around and walks away. I follow him with my eyes as he crosses the park to the opposite side, some two hundred feet from here. He stands still, observing me from over there.

I turn around and rest my hands on the wall, leaning a little forward and trying to look in the right direction.

London is a sea of lights we're submerged in. Although I'm not high enough to see the whole city, I think I can distinguish the point where the lights of the metropolis end and the darkness outside the wall begins.

Maybe it's just my imagination, but if I squint my eyes a little, I seem to see a faint glow in the distance.

It's the Strip. Dylan is there, somewhere.

I'm amazed at how my perception of time can vary so much depending on the circumstances. It feels like it's been weeks since I last saw him, since his embrace that I clumsily didn't return, since that distant morning when I handed him the soldier figurine. Now I realize that all that happened just yesterday morning. It's as though I'm living in two parallel worlds at the same time.

In one world, I feel happy, optimistic. I enjoy a sense of bliss that I've never felt before, and I want to be close to him, to Dylan. In the other world, the one I fear is real, I'm living a nightmare in which everything I fought for my entire life falls apart. A delirium that leaves me crushed, miserable, and hopeless.

I want to go back to the world where he is.

I'm almost sure that this faint glow is the Strip. It must be.

I try to imagine what Dylan is doing right now. An irrational despair overwhelms me as I want answers to banal questions and don't get them: what did he have for dinner? How does he spend his free time? What clothes does he wear to bed? Does he think about me? I want to know everything about him, so much so that my chest hurts.

Suddenly, a muffled buzzing noise interrupts my thoughts. I turn around and look up. The pitch of the sound rises until it turns into a whistle. I see the flashing lights on the front, under the cockpit, and circles of blinking red lights that surround the cylindrical covers on the four horizontal rotors: it's a white helijet, ready to land on the heliport a few feet away.

Stirring some wind, though surprisingly quiet, the helijet descends gently on the platform. A few seconds pass by, and nobody gets off the aircraft. Out of the corner of my eye, I notice that the agent watching me from the other side of the park has turned his head toward the glass doors of the Tower of Victory.

I glance in that direction too and see three men approaching: two CAT officers escorting a shorter man with silver hair.

It can't be. It's Nigel.

Suddenly, I feel like a fool for thinking it was Captain Foster who wanted to see me. It never even crossed my mind that Nigel himself had sent for me. Because that's what's happening, right?

Maybe it's just a coincidence and Nigel is going home, or who knows where. Perhaps he won't even notice that I'm here and he'll leave without seeing me. Then the captain will come looking for me. Yes, that's probably it.

But that's not the case.

The two CATs continue toward the helijet, but Nigel turns right and walks in my direction. From where I stand, I can make out his disgusting smile.

"Commander," I exclaim when he's six feet away.

"Spare the formalities when we're alone, Derin," he says with a wave of his hand.

He's already removed his stage makeup and changed the bright blue suit for black pants and a long grey leather jacket. But it seems that he hasn't had time to shower since his hair still has that artificial silver color and that showy lock, which is undoubtedly fake.

"Well?" he continues, moving closer to me. "What did you think of the show?"

I don't know what he expects me to say. I have no clue what to say. But I'd better be careful.

"Um, you were impressive," I answer, "But I was so nervous, I was hardly aware of anything."

"My entry is spectacular, isn't it?" he says, arching his eyebrows and smiling. "Yes, of course, I know, perhaps it's a bit extravagant. But it's good for the effect."

"Yes, I guess so," I say cautiously.

"What do you think about the charges against your brother? Have I been fair?"

A lump rises in my throat. He's testing me.

"I think you've been very fair, and benevolent," I force myself to answer. I can't look him in the eyes, so I bow my head toward the ground. Then I dare to say: "I wish this was just a nightmare, and that my family and I could return to our lives without suffering any harm."

"Derin, Derin," he says, faking a gentle tone, as he grabs my chin with his right hand and lifts it up to look me in the eye. I'm disgusted by the feeling of his fingers on my face. "Of course, I've been very indulgent, more than fair. But I've done it for your family, for you. Your brother doesn't deserve it. He's not loyal to his country or the Government, you know that. He's shown his rebellious nature too many times. He's a ticking time bomb."

He caresses my cheek with his index finger. I can hardly stand it and have the urge to pull it away, but I have to control myself.

"Your brother deserved much more serious charges," he continues. "He's a danger to society. Sooner or later, he would end up joining those damn radkers." He takes his hand away from my face. "We can't let that happen, right? We must execute all traitors, otherwise, what message are we sending to the public? Our country requires a clear, firm gesture to show zero tolerance for disobedience and rebellion."

My heart sinks, and I feel like I'm falling to pieces. Nothing that happened today really matters. He's going to kill him.

"Nigel, I beg you," I say, with my voice breaking, "don't kill him, please. We'll make him change, he'll become an exemplary citizen, I swear…"

A mocking smile appears on his face. He enjoys making me beg for his help.

"Look, Derin, I don't really care about your brother. I can convince my father not to execute the two boys. We already have enough show with Hall and the others. But if I do that, it's all for you, got it? And I'm going to need something in return."

I nod wordlessly. Whatever it is, as long as he doesn't kill him.

Nigel brings his hand back to my face and rubs his thumb over my mouth, from side to side, while grinning revoltingly. My nose is filled with the pungent smell of the soap he uses, a mixture of tree bark and rotten fruit. It makes me nauseous.

"I love your begging face," he says, licking his lips. "I'm going to have a lot of fun with you."

"What should I do? What do you want me to do?" I say.

"Hmm, I haven't decided yet. But I'll let you know," he replies, suddenly changing his perverted tone for a serious one. "For now, make a better effort to look handsome. I want you nice and attractive when I send for you. You're looking disheveled and tired tonight."

He pats me twice on the cheek and turns around. He heads to the helijet and gets on board.

I stand stiff as stone, trying in vain to process what just happened as I watch the helijet rise silently and glide toward the Palace of the Governors.

I stay like this, with my mind blank, until the security agent approaches me from the other side of the park to escort me back upstairs.

Once I'm back in the apartment, I have to lie to my parents. I tell them that someone important wants to help us and has intervened on our behalf. I don't mention any name, because I don't want to cause Captain Foster any problems, but they understand I'm referring to him. In other words, I tell them what I had stupidly assumed before when the agent came to get me.

I don't have the heart or the courage to tell them the truth. I can't reveal what Nigel has told me: that the regent wants all the accused to be executed, that it doesn't matter that the charges against Brian are less serious than we first feared … that I don't know if I have convinced him not to kill my brother.

I go to bed. I want to be alone. I need to think, or at least try.

Without paying attention to what I'm doing, I wash my face with soap twice, scrubbing my lips too. I don't drink much alcohol, but I wish I had some right now to help me make the repulsive memory of Nigel's fingers disappear. They only brought us a bottle of wine with dinner. There's plenty of drinks in the kitchen, but none with alcohol.

What does he ultimately want from me? To use me to carry out his sexual fantasies? To make me his secret lover? Or is he thinking up some other Machiavellian plan to make me suffer for having rejected him?

Whatever it is, I have no choice but to accept it, if that's how I can prevent my brother from being executed. That's all that matters. The rest, we'll wait and see.

—

I SUFFER THROUGH ANOTHER DREADFUL NIGHT, WITHOUT REST. When I awake the next morning, I'm the first to get up. They've announced that we're on the same schedule as yesterday, which means long hours of terrible waiting while being confined to the apartment, plus a short break outdoors on the rooftop park and spectacular food from Stevens.

At three in the afternoon, they come to take us to the same dressing room as yesterday.

They dress my parents, Lily, and Brian in new clothes, but with the same unfortunate style, while I wear a uniform just like yesterday. At a quarter to six, Andrew Frost comes for us and escorts us to the studio. This time, we're the last ones to arrive, as the others are already sitting in the same booths as the evening before.

I've spent all day getting used to the idea that I'll accept whatever Nigel demands of me, anything. I'm resigned to doing it, in exchange for my brother's life.

However, when the thirty-second countdown begins before the start of the program, I am struck by sudden panic.

It doesn't make any difference what I agree to do. It's irrelevant. Everything is in Nigel's hands. If he decides to, he can execute Brian and still force me to do anything. He can always do a lot of damage to my parents and Lily. He has absolute power. My only hope is that there's a sliver of humanity left within him, that he's not yet wholly corrupted like his father.

This is unbearable. Every time I think I'm about to save my family, something disturbing reminds me with a blow that I haven't achieved anything.

Nigel's entrance is just as dramatic as yesterday, only today he's wearing a red robe—the color of blood—instead of a white one.

The first three-quarters of an hour are used to summarize the charges against the five defendants. Then, Nigel indicates that the time has come for citizens to make their decision and transmit their verdict.

The moment he pronounces the command—"Let the verdict of the people begin!"—, a short melody of chimes is multiplied by a thousand and echoes through the studio: the audience is receiving the activation notification on their teleCards. All citizens of the country must cast their vote.

Witnessing this sham is pathetic.

During the ten minutes of televoting, the production shows some images from yesterday's program. The dramatic voiceovers may well elevate the tension and suspense in the viewers, thus guiding them toward the show's first climax, but to us—all the defendants and their families—they mean a prelude to hell.

It seems Nigel isn't in the mood to waste time, because when exactly ten minutes are over, he stands up and goes to the center of the stage.

"The results are ready. The people have made their voices heard," he announces.

On the screen, the names of the five defendants appear under a single column, one after another. The name "Graham Hall" comes first; the last one is "Brian Dark."

"Very well," says Nigel, looking at the screen, and continuing in a dramatic tone: "In the case of the Great Nation of Imperial Englandom against Graham Hall, what is the verdict of the people? Guilty or innocent?"

From the audience bleachers, we hear the voice of an older man shouting: "Guilty!"

Nigel turns in the direction of the scream and smiles, amused, then turns around again, looking for the camera.

"Patience, fellow citizen," he says cheerfully. "Let's first see how the country has voted." He looks up again at the screen and repeats, "Graham Hall, guilty or innocent?"

To the right of Governor Hall's name, a long red bar appears with the phrase "GUILTY: 99.8%" across the middle of it.

"Guilty!" roars the audience from the bleachers, hammering the floor with their feet.

99.8%. Even for these liars, it would be too gross to show one hundred percent, I think, outraged.

Governor Hall doesn't flinch. He remains in the same droopy position he has maintained this whole time, with his head and shoulders down.

Nigel continues with the verdicts. One by one, the results appear next to each defendant's name:

Lewis Freeland. Guilty: 99.6%.

The audience roars again. His wife lets out a terrible moan and hugs her husband, crying inconsolably. The daughter is pale as a ghost and remains motionless.

Michael Wallace. Guilty: 98.7%.

There's less melodrama in his booth. His wife hugs her two little ones, who are on either side of her, and the three sob with their heads bowed. The girls don't understand what's happening, but they see their mother crying, get scared, and also cry. This time the audience seems a little moved, perhaps by the girls, and the roar of "Guilty!" is less violent than for the first two defendants.

It's Liam's and Brian's turn.

My mother squeezes my hand again, out of pure reflex, because she must know that there's only one possible result.

Liam Mitchell. Guilty: 96.8%.

Brian Dark. Guilty: 97.5%.

The roar of the audience thunders with the same force as before.

So that's it. The hoax of televoting, the sham of the verdict of the people, has concluded without surprises. All the defendants are guilty.

The tension in the studio becomes more palpable than ever. Nigel is about to pronounce the sentences. I'm covered in cold sweat and can't stop shaking.

This is the most disturbing and sadistic part of the whole program, and it saddens me that my mother and Lily have to witness what's coming.

The way they proceed with the sentences when there's more than one accused—as is usually the case—is the following: the Prosecutor of the Nation announces the sentence for the first defendant, and if he's condemned to die, his execution takes place that instant, live for the whole country. The other defendants suffer while they witness the agony of the first to be executed. They tremble fearfully in anticipation of falling prey to this same dreadful fate. It's very cruel psychological torture.

A stunning long-legged assistant hands Nigel a red envelope containing the sentence of the first defendant. He opens the envelope and pulls out a cream-colored card.

"Governor Graham Hall," he says solemnly, addressing the little man in the center booth, "stand up to hear your sentence."

Hall gets up, grabs the booth's front railing with both hands, and waits with his head down.

"The accused, Graham Hall," says Nigel, "whom the people of the Great Nation of Imperial Englandom have found guilty of the charges against him, especially conspiracy against the Government and the attack against the regent's life, is hereby sentenced to death. His execution will be carried out immediately in the Chamber of Purgation."

CHAPTER 12

THE CHAMBER OF PURGATION

FOUR SECURITY AGENTS APPROACH GOVERNOR HALL'S BOOTH. Two of them grab him by the arms, but the governor makes a signal with his hand, says something to them and, for some reason, they let him go. He stands up and lets them guide him without resistance. He has wholly resigned himself to being killed. I'm guessing he wants to die with dignity.

My stomach churns as I imagine which ruthless method of execution that I've seen in other editions of *Trial of the People* will be used on him.

The agents lead him to the circular platform in the center of the set, the same one Nigel uses for his dramatic entries and exits during the program's opening and closing. Once they're all on the circle, the agents tell the governor to look up at Nigel, who is watching from the stage.

"Graham Hall," Nigel declares, "for your betrayal to our country, you have been sentenced to death." He raises his arms with his palms facing upward and continues in the tone of a religious leader: "Prepare to receive your punishment with courage, and may God have mercy on you!"

The circular platform begins to descend, disappearing into the darkness. From now on, we'll follow Hall's path to death by watching the images on the studio's big screen and the monitor next to us.

Now we see a darkened room, with a single spotlight where the descending platform slowly appears. The image's perspective changes, showing Hall and the agents at the end of a dark tunnel that lights up in red as they walk through it—all while the Englandom anthem rings out.

This is the Path of the Traitors—the walkway to agony in the Chamber of Purgation.

When they reach the end of the tunnel, they find a thick metal door that slides to the side, within the wall. They enter another gloomy room, where nothing can be seen except a strange machine lit with powerful reflectors. It's a kind of glass cylinder, perhaps three feet in diameter and eight feet high, placed on a metal platform. Several thin tubes surround it, bending at the two-feet mark and connecting with it. At the top, the cylinder is attached to a metal chute that reaches up to the ceiling. Inside, at about mid-height, there's a black separator, a few inches thick, that divides the cylinder into a lower and an upper part.

The agents take Governor Hall to the back, where there's an access door. Suddenly, out of nowhere, two hooded figures dressed in black and wearing blank, white masks appear—the executioners. Now they'll take over, and the four agents leave.

The executioners tell Hall how to get into the cylinder. He must crouch underneath the horizontal separator, and then stand up to slide his body through an opening inside it. The opening isn't merely a hole; instead, it's attached to a vest-like suit made of dark and flexible material, like the one divers use. Hall must put his arms and head through this suit. The result is that the lower part of his body is under the separator. Above it, the vest fits him tightly from the neck to the chest—leaving arms and head uncovered—and then becomes looser, with a lot of leftover material that folds like an accordion down to the separator's opening.

I'm not sure what they'll do to the poor man—I haven't seen this machine on previous *Trials of the People*—, but I start to form some ideas. I get goose bumps, and the hairs on my arms stand on end.

The executioners attach the governor's feet to some shackles on the floor and then make him raise his arms so that they can cuff his wrists to more restraints above.

Hall begins to lose his composure as panic sets in. Drops of sweat drip from his forehead. He's got a look of terror, and he's breathing very quickly. The executioners close the rear door and withdraw. Hall is left alone and trapped inside the Chamber of Purgation, waiting for an agony that can't be wished upon anybody.

But the cruelty of Regent Crowley, perpetrated by his son, is just beginning.

"There we have him, fellow citizens," Nigel says. "The traitor Graham Hall, ready to receive his punishment. The process that will end his life and bring him before our Almighty God will give him the purifying effect of fire and water."

Now I know what's coming.

I turn my head toward my mother and lean in to get closer to her ear.

"Don't let Lily see this," I whisper.

I pray that she doesn't see anything. The screams alone will be horrifying.

"As a sublime display of loyalty to our country," Nigel continues, pointing toward the VIP area in the audience, "Lucius Hall will have the honor of activating the mechanism that will begin the purging of his father, a Traitor to the Fatherland."

There are several muffled moans among the crowd in the bleachers.

This does stun many of them. It's incredibly heinous.

Lucius Hall gets up from his seat and goes to the stage. When he arrives, Nigel greets him with outstretched arms and an exaggerated hug.

"My dear friend," he says, in a pretend sorrowful tone, "we join you in your misery. We are with you."

"Thank you, commander," replies Lucius, playing his role of the suffering son.

"We share your grief," continues Nigel. "Through your father's betrayal, you lose a loved one, but thanks to your outstanding loyalty, you win the regent's affection and admiration, as well all the people's. Is there anything you'd like to say?"

"I just want to ask for forgiveness," says Lucius. "By committing an evil act, he has stained my family's name. The man who will now receive his just punishment is no longer my father. My father died the very moment his crime was conceived. I beg the regent, I implore the citizens of Englandom: please, do not judge me and my family for his actions, please forgive this humble servant."

Lucius gets down on his knees, rests his hands on the floor, and leans forward until his forehead touches the floor as well.

"Lucius! Lucius! Lucius!" chants the audience.

"Come on, come on, get up," Nigel says, grabbing him by the arm to get him on his feet. "You must not suffer any longer. You have received your regent's forgiveness and consolation."

I can't stand this ridiculous charade. It's absolutely evil.

When praise from Nigel and the audience subsides, the same blond-haired assistant hands Lucius a small device with two antennas: the remote control to activate the Chamber of Purgation.

"Go ahead, Lucius," Nigel says. "It's time to free yourself from the filth that has soiled your good name and caused you so much suffering."

Lucius moves a switch on the remote control. Now the barbarism begins.

On the broadcast, we hear mechanical sounds and see the lights illuminating the Chamber of Purgation increase in intensity. Above the cylinder, behind Governor Hall, water begins to fall at full force. The upper half of the cylinder, above the separator, fills very quickly until the water covers his shoulders. The separator and the diver's waist-up suit must be waterproof since the lower half of the cylinder stays completely dry.

When the water level reaches the middle of his neck, the fire appears.

The tubes connecting to the cylinder work like torches. They fling thin, blue-colored flames that burn the governor's legs. The effect is immediate.

Within seconds, the fire burns his pants' fabric and scorches his skin. The governor shouts and his body shakes violently. In an instant, the skin on his legs melts and reveals raw red flesh, which then turns black.

It's a macabre spectacle.

Maybe I'm just imagining things, but I sense a putrid smell of burnt flesh. As I feel the bile rising in my throat, the cameras move away from the image of his charred legs. Now they're showing the cylinder's upper half.

I wish with all my heart that Hall dies soon. No human being deserves to suffer so cruelly. Even though the water now covers his entire head, his desperate bubbling doesn't fade. The designers of the Chamber of Purgation have thought of every last detail. Special underwater microphones transmit the governor's monstrous sounds. Now, after getting his legs burnt, he's drowning. A flash takes me back to my childhood, to Lake Windermere, to the boat... as if I'm the one who's drowning.

After several more seconds, his body finally stops shaking. Hall is dead.

I let out a long sigh and breathe deeply. I'm not sure how much time has passed since Lucius Hall activated the Chamber of Purgation, but I think I held my breath the whole time. My lungs hurt.

I don't dare to turn and look at my parents and Lily. I would have given anything to have prevented them from seeing this. Brian, in front of us, hasn't moved. I can't see his face, but I can imagine how terrible it must have been for him to witness this atrocity.

My heart beats a thousand times an hour, and panic overtakes me.

What if Nigel decides to ignore what he said last night and he executes Brian? What if he condemns him to the same diabolical death as Governor Hall?

No. I won't allow it. I have to do something.

I visualize in my mind the location of all the security agents: four behind each booth of the remaining defendants, sixteen in total; two agents at each of the rear exits, in front of the tunnels. There are thirty feet from here to the stage.

Yes, I think it's possible. It has to be possible.

When that bastard Nigel announces Brian's sentence, I'll jump over the railing and throw myself on him, before the agents reach me. I'll threaten to twist his neck if someone comes close to me. Then I'll see to it that I can get my family out of here, taking Nigel as a hostage.

That's crazy! You'll never make it, and they'll kill you all, shouts the voice of reason, but I ignore it. I won't let my brother be murdered in such a horrific way in front of my parents and my little sister. So it's decided.

Nigel's surprise announcement brings me back to reality.

The next defendant to receive his sentence won't be Lewis Freeland, Governor Hall's head of government, but Michael Wallace, the young father of the two blond girls in the booth to our right. According to the false accusations, he's the one who tricked and manipulated Brian and Liam to create a distraction by confronting security forces.

I don't understand why Nigel has changed the order of the sentences. After Governor Hall, Freeland would normally follow.

But before Nigel declares his sentence, I can think of the gruesome motive for why he's decided to wait—or, rather, needs to wait—to execute Freeland: if Regent Crowley wants Freeland to be executed in the same cruel manner as Governor Hall, then it will be necessary to remove Hall's corpse from the cylinder and to clean and prepare everything for the next victim. A practical, although very awful, reason.

This makes me think that Wallace will be executed differently.

Nigel informs Wallace of his death sentence. His wife, who during the whole previous execution had sobbed silently while embracing her daughters, can't restrain herself any longer and lets out a shrill scream. She and the two girls wrap their arms around him and don't release him until the agents arrive to escort him to the Chamber of Purgation.

It breaks my heart to think about what they'll do with the little girls, what I've heard they do if the defendant's kids are considered pretty enough. The mother will be killed, without any fanfare, and her execution will be announced later as a side note on the news. But the girls are so beautiful that it's likely they'll be sold for an astronomical amount, most probably abroad.

Wallace's journey is the same as the late Governor Hall's, except they lead him to a different Chamber of Purgation.

On the screen, we see a glass box or showcase on a metal pedestal, similar in size to the cylinder they used to execute Graham Hall, but this one is rectangular. There don't appear to be any additional devices or tubes.

The agents lead Michael Wallace into the box but don't fasten him to anything. Inside, he can move freely within the confined space.

I can't guess how they'll execute him. Maybe with some kind of gas, but I immediately discard this idea: it would be too unspectacular by Crowley standards.

"Fellow citizens," says Nigel, looking directly into the camera, "the Traitor to the Fatherland, Michael Wallace, is guilty of poisoning the minds of dozens of young people, coercing them to revolt and commit crimes against the nation. For these sins, he must experience the terrible effect of poison in his own flesh. May the traitor feel in his own body the pain and deformation that he has caused in the minds of our young people!"

Wallace desperately looks around the glass case, trying to figure out where death will come from.

Suddenly, in the box's floor, a previously unnoticeable slit opens up. A thin black line begins to emerge from it and in a matter of seconds, turns into a dark patch that gushes forth effervescently. As the image zooms in, we can see thousands of little scorpions that only know one direction: Wallace's body.

Michael Wallace frantically tries to crush the poisonous arachnids with his feet, but there are so many, thousands of them, that the task is impossible. Not even five seconds pass before the first scorpions have managed to crawl under the cuffs of his pants and insert their poisonous stings. Judging from his desperate screams and violent movements, the pain must be unbearable. The scorpions climb all over his body; some are already pricking his arms and neck. Wallace groans and writhes like a madman.

When they decide that they have stung enough, the scorpions retreat through the slit on the floor as quickly as they appeared.

High-definition cameras let us see every detail of his suffering and show us how Wallace's skin, especially his face, turns green. His veins darken until his body looks like it's covered by a cobweb of thick black threads. It doesn't take long before his flesh begins to swell, while a foul yellow liquid comes out of his nose, mouth, ears, and eyes. Wallace falls to the ground, and although his dreadful moans cease, what was once his body doesn't stop shifting.

It's incomprehensible how it has become disfigured this way. Now, it's almost unrecognizable as a human body, but the poor man hasn't died yet. At least two more minutes pass until the amorphous, pus-filled mass stops pulsating, and finally one can assume, or at least hope, that Wallace is dead.

I turn to look at his family's booth.

I only now realize that his wife has fainted and the two girls are crying inconsolably with their faces sunk into their mother's lap. Four agents approach their booth. Two of them carry the unconscious woman out of the studio through one of the back tunnels, while the other two grab the girls—now screaming in despair—and take them away through the other. It's a heart-breaking scene. I even notice some faces full of anguish and compassion among the audience in the bleachers.

My family is equally upset. My mother and Lily have tears on their faces and can barely control their sobs.

It's difficult to describe the hatred I feel at this moment toward Nigel and the entire despicable Crowley lineage. I wish that they had to suffer such brutal, diabolical torture themselves. I don't even want to think about how my parents and siblings must feel.

But we're not allowed much time to deal with our emotions. The show must go on.

Now it's Lewis Freeland's turn, Governor Hall's head of government.

When Nigel pronounces his death sentence, and the security agents approach to take him to the Chamber of Purgation, his wife goes mad and turns ferocious.

"Nooo! You bastards! Nooo!" she shouts, deranged, throwing herself over her husband and giving the agents trouble. In her hysterical attack, she manages to defend herself for longer than anyone would think until they subdue her with electric clubs and two agents drag her out of the studio. The daughter has fallen into a state of shock.

"Take a good look, people of Englandom," Nigel intervenes. "Do you see the kind of turmoil that betrayal brings about? Nothing good results from sin, only anguish and pain."

The ritual of taking Freeland into the Chamber of Purgation is the same as before. As I imagined, they lead him to the same room where Governor Hall had been taken. The glass cylinder and all the rest of the equipment are as good as new.

The executioners force and fasten Freeland inside the cylinder just as they did with Hall. Everything indicates that he will die in the same way, by fire and water.

But the Crowleys don't want to miss this opportunity to show another one of their perverse methods of torture.

I don't catch much of Nigel's preamble, only the phrases "his intention to rip apart the nation with subversive actions" and "he will suffer the pain of tearing in his own flesh."

When the Chamber of Purgation is activated, the flames don't appear to char Freeland's legs. Instead, two jets of water gush out, above and below the cylinder's middle separator, until the lower half is filled and the water in the upper half reaches up to his neck.

Suddenly, something begins to move in the cylinder's bottom.

Several small fish, about two inches long, emerge from somewhere in the floor.

They seem harmless, but obviously, they aren't. They show us a close-up of one of the fish, and we see its small mouth with two rows of tiny, sharp teeth. I've seen them and read about them in the Natural History Museum—piranhas. At first, the fish don't seem too sure what to do. Only one of them dares to nibble at Freeland's pants near his right thigh. His pants are made of Petex, but this must not be a significant obstacle for the teeth of the fish, because, after a few seconds, it tears through the cloth and begins to gnaw on his leg. Freeland, who can't see what's going on under the cylinder's separator, twists in a spasm when he feels the bites.

As the first drop of blood dissolves into the water, the rest of the little fish forget their shyness completely. The swarm throws itself onto Freeland's legs, and there's no stopping the frantic voracity for flesh. Freeland screams and writhes madly as the piranhas tear his legs apart. When blood clouds the water, the cameras focus on the top half of the cylinder, on Freeland's bestial howling.

A slot opens up in the highest part of the cylinder and begins to spit another stream of small piranhas. When they fall into the water, they don't waste any time turning on the rest of his body that remains unharmed. It's clear why Freeland's head was left out of the water: pure sadism. Not only would he have drowned too quickly and his suffering would have been less prolonged, but now that the blood has turned all the water red, the horrible grimaces on his face are the only thing that still expresses this man's cruel agony.

The piranhas must be moving very quickly over his body because soon Freeland stops screaming and contorting, and his head falls forward with his face almost touching the water. Undoubtedly, the piranhas reached a vital artery or organ, perhaps the heart, and have devoured it. Freeland is dead.

CHAPTER 13

DISLOYAL

THE LAST *TRIAL OF THE PEOPLE* I WATCHED took place about four or five months ago. In that case, the defendants were three prominent radkers, captured after a terrorist attack which derailed a train coming into London full of meat and dairy products. The incendiary bombs they used turned hundreds of tons of food into charcoal.

All three of them were executed, obviously. The ways they died in the Chamber of Purgation—all including terrible pain and prolonged suffering—seemed inhuman to me then, but what we've just witnessed far exceeds the previous level of cruelty.

Despite my psychological exhaustion after this bloodthirsty display, I can see that the Crowleys must be very nervous. The regent must feel overwhelmed by an existential danger; otherwise, I can't explain his decision to set up this extravagant hoax of a supposed attack and then publicly execute Governor Hall and the other two in such gruesome ways. It sends a threatening message to the rest of his enemies: the Crowleys have absolute power; whoever dares to question it will suffer a terrible fate.

But for my family and me, it doesn't end here. It's not just a warning. For us, it's far more personal, a matter of life or death, and the worst part is now coming. Nigel is about to pronounce Brian's sentence.

If the level of adrenaline in the human body could change one's color, the whole audience would instantly see how I'm turning red-hot right now. I can barely control my impulses. The moment Nigel announces that Brian will be executed, every fiber in my muscles will jump like a spring.

I'm ready to pounce on the stage toward his throat.

I don't care if the security agents pelt us with their machine guns. I'm not afraid that they'll kill us all with bullets. Any kind of death is preferable to what these sadistic despots could do to us. I won't let them touch my family.

Abruptly, I pull my hand away from my mother's. She doesn't want to let it go, but I must… with her hand holding mine, I would lose valuable fractions of a second.

Brian and Liam follow Nigel's instructions and stand up.

My mother can't help but grab my hand again and squeeze it with all her strength. This time, I don't pull away. I can't deny her this support, even if it means I'll be too slow when I hurl myself onto the stage.

Nigel begins to deliver their sentence, and a sudden panic seizes me.

What if my mind wants to, but my body refuses to move? I remember, terrified, the paralyzing sensation a few days back at my graduation, just seconds before Captain Foster called my name to go onto the stage. I was so nervous that I doubted if I could get up. I was frozen.

Don't think about it, Derin, focus! I shout to myself in my head.

Of course, my body won't fail me. Not now, when I can barely keep still. Every fiber of my being pushes me toward that bastard's neck. In a few seconds, I'll have him begging me not to kill him.

I focus all my senses on the words coming out of his mouth. I don't want to miss the exact moment when he announces the execution. At that moment, I must unleash my instincts.

"The defendants Brian Dark and Liam Mitchell have been found guilty of the charges," says Nigel, pointing to them with his arms outstretched. "Their crimes against the nation are repugnant and deserving of just punishment."

Say it, bastard, say it now! Here I come!

"Anywhere else in the world, in the corrupt nations beyond our borders, these misguided and traitorous young people would be punished with the maximum penalty," he continues. I can't stand the tension in my muscles anymore. "But our regent's benevolence has no limits."

The regent's official portrait appears on the screens. He smiles like a kind grandfather.

"In an act of extreme generosity," Nigel announces, "our beloved leader, my father, Eugene Crowley, pardons these two citizens from the punishment of execution."

My body flinches violently, and I know my mother does the same. She lets out a low moan, which echoes throughout the studio audience.

"Long live Regent Crowley's generosity!" shouts a woman, who is part of the animators' team. A submissive chorus replies: "Long live!"

"That's right, compatriots," Nigel says. "Our supreme leader's generosity is admirable." He turns to the massive image of his father and begins to clap.

Now the whole audience applauds and cheers enthusiastically.

Is it possible? A pardon?… He won't execute Brian. I can't believe it.

I don't remember any *Trial of the People* in which any defendants weren't executed. This would be something unprecedented.

Brian turns around and looks at me, his face pale. My parents and Lily are equally stunned. I nod slightly to indicate that yes, that's precisely what Nigel said. They're not going to execute him.

When Nigel decides that the deluge of compliments and cheers from the audience has been enough, he continues:

"Yes, my dear fellow citizens of Englandom, that's right. Our father is exemplary, without parallel. These young people have been absolved from suffering a painful death in the Chamber of Purgation. This is an extraordinary gift. But let's not forget: the crimes they committed are grave, and the culprits must assume responsibility for them."

I try to process what he's saying. I have no idea what's coming now.

"For the crimes committed against our nation and our regent," he says, reading from a card, "the defendants Brian Dark and Liam Mitchell are sentenced to work as productive prisoners in Ventus."

"Long live Ventus! Long live Englandom!" resounds from the bleachers.

So that's it. They'll be taken as slaves to Ventus, our country's main infrastructure project, on which the Crowleys' future depends a great deal.

About ten years ago, there was a period of extreme scarcity and public frustration. Our food industry still isn't able to cope with the demand of the population, and for a long time, our country hasn't produced anything that can be sold to the rest of the world to get foreign currency and buy everything we need. As a permanent solution to the problem, the Council of Governors decided to build Ventus. Considered "the most important strategic project for national security," Ventus is a huge wind farm with gigantic turbines that, when completed, will use wind energy to produce enough electricity to power the entire island. More importantly, it will create a massive surplus of clean energy that can be exported to foreign countries and fill up the State's coffers.

Since then, the colossal wind farm has been under construction in the northeast of the country, in Moray Firth, the estuary off the coast of the Highlands Protectorate, in former Scotland. In spite of the nearly impossible technical difficulties to be solved—nowhere in the world has anything of such magnitude been attempted—and the exorbitant costs and the human lives that have been lost, Ventus is about to be completed.

And that's where they're taking Brian: to break his back at the dangerous construction site.

I should feel relieved that he won't suffer in the Chamber of Purgation, the most frightening of possibilities. Even so, I know well that, in reality, his death has only been postponed. Although he won't suffer horrifically in front of an audience, Brian's sentence to Ventus amounts to a death sentence.

It's common knowledge that productive prisoners who go to Ventus never come back alive. They can survive a couple of weeks, some months or, with a bit of luck, a few years. But the extreme conditions there mean that prisoners suffer fatal accidents at a rate of almost 100%.

I must process this calmly, step by step. At least the worst has been avoided.

My parents and Lily throw themselves on Brian and squeeze him, dissolving into a sea of tears. A similar scene is repeated in the Mitchells' booth. After almost two hours of psychological torture, expecting to witness Brian's and Liam's atrocious suffering, the certainty that "they have been saved" is the only thing that counts.

I leave my musings about Ventus for later and join my family's frantic group hug.

But Nigel hasn't yet finished praising his father's remarkable generosity.

"Look at these families, dear friends," he says, pointing to us. "The regent grants them the lives of their children and, in exchange, offers them the opportunity to redeem their sins and serve the common good, our nation."

The audience doesn't fail to follow the animators' signals. They shout and cheer with the same flattering phrases used throughout the night.

"But we can't forget," Nigel continues, "that standing up to our leaders must have consequences. We are generous, but also fair, and the laws of our nation are very clear in this matter." He looks at the sentence card again and reads aloud, "According to the Compendium of Laws of the Just Society, the immediate family of the traitors shares responsibility for the crimes committed."

My pulse stops. This isn't over.

"Accordingly," he announces, "not only the defendants Brian Dark and Liam Mitchell will serve our country as productive prisoners, but also their respective fathers, Thomas Dark and Jonas Mitchell. As they are directly responsible for the unpatriotic behavior of their children, they are likewise sentenced to work at Ventus."

It can't be. They're taking away my father.

I curse Nigel. I'm sure he's punishing him like that to punish me.

"In addition," he continues, "the rest of the defendants' families are immediately stripped of their caste privileges and degraded to Disloyal. They will be banished from London and expelled to the Strip."

"Disloyal! Disloyal!" shouts a man in the audience.

I hadn't thought much about degradation. It shouldn't surprise me; it was to be expected. That's what matters least right now.

They don't give us much time to process the sentence or say proper goodbyes. We don't get a single second of privacy with my brother and my father. The four agents in our booth tell them to come along. Everything happens so fast that my mother can't even say a thing and only manages to hug them again.

"Everything will be fine, don't worry," says my father, who doesn't seem to grasp what's happening entirely. My mother just moans and sobs.

I reach out my arm and touch Brian, who looks at me, bewildered.

"You must survive! Survive!" I say to him. It's the only thing that comes out of my mouth.

I hug my mother and Lily as hard as I can, and the three of us watch as they lead Brian and my father through one of the tunnels in the back of the studio, until they disappear. Liam and his father are taken away through the other tunnel.

Before his farewell and dramatic descent into the bowels of the earth, Nigel urges the audience to follow a special live broadcast of *The Road to Banishment.*

In some key cases of degradation, the Government broadcasts the traitors' expulsion to the Strip. Of course, it's another propaganda spectacle aimed at showing how humiliating and disastrous degradation can be. This saddens me and also fills me with anger to think about what my mother and Lily will have to endure. Now we'll be the center of attention.

At the end of the program, another group of security agents escorts us back to the dressing room. Lieutenant Deacon is waiting for us there. They've brought our luggage from the Tower of Victory apartment, and there's a tray with sandwiches and drinks on the long dressing table. In the corner, I see several garments hanging on a wheeled clothes rack.

"Very well," Deacon says in a bored voice, always checking her notes to make sure she does not forget anything. "You have ten minutes to eat something. The stylists will then come to get you ready. At 9:30 sharp, I'll come for you." She turns around and leaves.

At last, we can be alone for a while. I embrace my mother and Lily.

"Don't worry, Dad and Brian are going to be fine," I say in a whisper. "Be strong, we'll make it out of this, you'll see. We must be strong for what's coming next."

They just nod.

Although the two say that they're not hungry, I force them to eat and drink something. I have no way of knowing when we'll eat again.

Suddenly, the dressing room door opens. I turn around, expecting to see Lieutenant Deacon's long, expressionless face. She's surely forgotten something.

But it's not her; it's Captain Foster.

"I don't have much time," he says in a nervous voice and with hurried gestures. "Just a minute, I shouldn't be here." He approaches my mother and Lily and hugs them. "I'm really sorry, Emma, really. I'm so sorry. Please be careful." Then he turns to me and says in an almost incomprehensible whisper: "Derin, don't trust anything or anyone. You must be very careful."

"Yes, captain," I answer in the same low voice. "Any idea what will happen to them, and us?"

"No," he says. "I must assume the announcement about Ventus is true. But you three, Derin… I don't know what Nigel Crowley's intentions are by sending you to the Strip. I don't know what he's said to you, but try to get away. Take your mother and Lily wherever you can."

"I can't leave Dad and Brian, they'll kill them."

"I know, but you have to save your mother and your sister. You have to save yourself," the captain insists.

"Do you know what Nigel wants with me?"

"No, I don't. But he's not about to leave you alone. He's plotting something. I've learned that he has to deal with a personal matter in the next few days, so maybe he'll leave you alone for a short while. But then he'll be back for you. Go far away."

"Okay, captain. I'll think about it and see what I can do."

"I'm Alan, call me Alan," he says, and then he hugs all three of us and leaves with tears in his eyes.

The stylists appear at the time indicated by Lieutenant Deacon. They rush to remove the makeup from my mother's and Lily's faces and leave their hair in a natural and simple way. They ask us to change our clothes and put on the rags hanging on the rack. They're simple garments, worn and discolored, made of very coarse Petex. I put on grey pants, a white t-shirt, and a worn dark green sweater.

Without thinking, I glance at my image in the mirror, and a sudden feeling of self-pity overwhelms me.

Just a couple of days ago, I was standing in front of another mirror, contemplating my stunning image in my shiny dress uniform, one step away from becoming an Army officer and a Patriot.

Everything seemed resolved for my family and me; our future couldn't be better. And now this. My father and my brother turned into productive prisoners; my mother, my sister, and I degraded to Disloyal, about to be banished to the Strip.

Dylan! I think suddenly, and my self-pity vanishes.

I wasn't sure I would ever see him again, but now it's very likely I will. I don't know when or where, but the mere possibility of his presence comforts me. I suppress the severe thoughts about our disastrous situation for a few seconds, excited by the fantasy of an upcoming reunion.

I don't even feel ashamed for holding on to pleasant thoughts while my family goes through this ordeal. I need to think about him. It gives me strength and courage.

At precisely half-past nine, Lieutenant Deacon appears with her entourage of security agents to escort us to what is still our home.

—

UPON ARRIVAL, WE FIND A SURREAL SCENE.

It's a dark night, with clouds hiding the moon and the stars, but our house is so illuminated that it seems like daytime. I have the impression that there are more spotlights and television cameras than a few days ago, on the morning I returned from my meeting with Dylan in the Strip when they had already come to arrest us.

But the most shocking thing is that they've filled the front garden with spectators, leaving only the path leading to our front door clear. I've never seen anything like this in previous broadcasts of the program.

We walk down the narrow path that's flanked by two rows of security agents who keep the fiery mob at bay. I recognize some of our neighbors' faces in the crowd, and I shudder when I realize that they're shouting the most vulgar insults.

Once inside, they tell us to take some things with us—in theory, whatever we want, except for electronic devices and valuables. The only condition is that we can only take what we can move ourselves, so just what my mother, Lily, and I can carry on our backs. We have little time, just a couple of minutes. I urge them to grab clothing, shoes, jackets, all the medicines in the house, and any food in the kitchen. I think about taking some blankets and pillows, though I don't know yet where to put them. They've given us few instructions on what awaits us. I act on instinct.

While we throw ourselves into the frantic task of collecting our things, the cameras follow us at all times. Apparently, the broadcast's producers want to show the viewers every detail of what we decide to take with us. I imagine the comments from the program's host, who must be speculating about—or mocking—the reasons why we choose one thing or discard another.

Luckily, they only look superficially at what we put in our bags.

When I lift up an alarm clock from my room and show it to the agent escorting me for his approval, he barely flicks his hand to indicate that I can take it with me. I put the analog alarm clock in one of the bags, and with it, the five hundred pounds I hid inside its back cover months ago, not knowing that one day I would need them so badly.

The allocated time vanishes in an instant. They tell us we must leave. We look like real vagrants carrying all the suitcases and bags that we could fill.

As we're about to leave the house, I hear the crowd outside getting more excited.

I know everything has been set up by the Government, but the roar of the outraged citizens who witness our caste degradation is intimidating. For a fraction of a second, it occurs to me that Nigel's plan is for the mob to lynch us in our garden, but I force myself to dismiss that thought.

We're about to pass through the crowd. The screams and insults they lob at us are worse than when we came in. I'm sure that if we weren't surrounded by official escorts, the enraged onlookers would at least throw stones or garbage at us. But surely the authorities have warned them, under threat of punishment, not to throw anything, as they could also hit the agents and that wouldn't look good on television.

Halfway along the path, I turn my head to the right, without thinking. For a second, my eyes meet the teary gaze of my dear friend Zara. It's just an instant, but it's long enough to see the pain and grief she feels for us. Her lips move, trying to tell me something, but I can't make it out. We go by too fast, and her face disappears in the crowd. In my head, I scold her for having taken such a risk in coming here. But at the same time, I care for her even more and thank her for this grand gesture of affection.

Just as we're leaving the front garden to get on the sidewalk, I hear an angry woman shouting:

"Damn traitors! Bitch!" she yells in a tone full of hatred, spitting into my mother's face.

It's Charlotte Harris, our neighbor.

CHAPTER 14

AFFECTION AND KINDNESS

IT'S PAST MIDNIGHT when we arrive at the dwelling they've assigned us in the Strip. From our house in London, we were taken to the exchange station for Access Point 8, where we boarded a train that brought us to the city of the Disloyal, always under the supervision of security agents. They brought us to this small apartment in a multi-level building in Sector 7, and once they gave us the last instructions, they finally left.

Everything has happened so fast that I haven't had time to reflect on our new situation. Nigel wouldn't want us to "get lost" in this vast ghetto, so I've been assigned a position as a security agent within the Strip's law enforcement units. They're not generous; they just want to control me. Although I'll receive an income, it will be in credits, not illegal paper currency, which means that my salary only serves to pay the rent on this apartment the Government has provided us. Whatever is left over, we can only use to buy food at one of the official stores.

My mother and Lily have also been assigned labor, although they won't be paid with credits, just food. This saddens me, as I suspect they'll be given the hardest tasks. Lily will have to work at least half the day, so we still don't know if she'll be able to attend school.

The apartment is located on level nine of a concrete and brick building, where all the tenants are deels who work for the

Government. It's tiny and neglected. The living room holds only a sofa, a couple of armchairs, and a small dining table with four more chairs. The floor is made of cement tiles, and the walls, which I imagine were originally white, are yellow and stained. There's a sour smell like mold mixed with vinegar. It also has a kitchenette with a sink, a stove with an oven, and a small refrigerator that seems to work.

In a separate space, there's a bedroom with two creaking old beds, a rickety wardrobe, and a tiny bathroom with a shower. The living room and the bedroom have windows overlooking a backyard surrounded by buildings similar to this one.

They gave me a teleCard for deels who work for the regime. After the amount for the apartment's rent is discounted, the few remaining credits of my salary will be transferred to the teleCard every week. My mother and Lily didn't receive any devices. I would prefer that I hadn't either since it serves as a control mechanism.

We are exhausted. We've run out of emotions and words. In silence, my mother and I start storing the food and medicines we managed to bring from our house in the kitchen's few cabinets. Lily can barely keep her eyes open and, although she tries to help, we tell her to go to bed. She falls asleep instantly.

I worry about my mother. She looks very distressed and needs to rest, but she insists on at least storing the food. We leave the task of putting away the other things—the clothes and all that—until tomorrow. She and Lily will stay in the bedroom, and I'll sleep on the not-so-promising couch in the living room. I'm so tired that I could sleep on the floor.

What a difference to the luxury apartment in the Tower of Victory! I think with an ironic humor that I can't understand myself.

We're about to go to bed when we hear a knock on the door.

We both flinch.

"What now?" my mother asks with an expression between fatigue and exasperation. "Won't they ever leave us alone?"

"Don't worry, Mom, they must have forgotten to tell us something," I say, trying to reassure her, although it occurs to me that they're doing this on purpose, to annoy us.

I open the door reluctantly and am surprised to see Mia and Dylan.

Mia throws herself on me with a hug and breaks into tears. She can't talk, just cry, but I understand everything she wants to tell me. She then turns to my mother, who has remained frozen. When Mia goes to hug her too, my mother can't hold it back anymore and breaks down in tears. It hurts me to see her like this.

I turn to Dylan, who has been standing in the doorway. I notice that his eyes are watery, but he looks as handsome as the image of him etched in my mind from the last time I saw him, when we said goodbye at the train station here in the Strip.

Without saying anything, he comes closer and hugs me, stronger than the first time.

This time, I'm not frozen stiff, and I hug him back.

It feels so good to embrace someone like this! I've never experienced this kind of sensation, and I don't want it to end. I want to stay like this forever, holding him, taking in the wonderful scent of his hair. I don't know what it smells like, but I love it.

"So good to see you," he says. "Glad you've finally arrived here. Are you okay?"

"Yes, thanks, we're okay," I answer, smiling slightly. "How did you find us?"

"As I said before, I've got contacts. We've followed your every move. Our informants have kept us up to speed."

A natural instinct makes me quickly place my right index finger over my pursed lips, signaling to him to watch his words.

"Don't worry," he says with a gentle smile before looking around the room. "Nobody's watching or listening to us here. This building has already been inspected."

"What do you mean, *inspected*? Are you talking about those mysterious 'people' of yours?" I say in a joking tone, although it intrigues me and I want more details.

"Um… yes," he says, still smiling, but maybe a little embarrassed that he can't say more.

"I see. Well, I hope you'll introduce them to me someday. They do exist, don't they?"

"Of course, they're not my imaginary friends," he replies with the same playful tone that I used. "You'll meet them soon, they're real enough."

"That's a relief! I was afraid they were ghosts."

Every second I like him more. No matter how depressed I am, when I talk to him, I'm a different person. I feel relaxed and can almost forget everything else. The only things that matter are his knowing looks and funny expressions.

My mother makes tea, and the four of us sit down at the table. Dylan inspects the disastrous apartment with a critical eye.

"Well, at least there are four walls and a roof," he says.

Out of nowhere, my mother lets out a giggle.

"I suppose so," she says. "You should've seen the pigsty where we stayed the last two days."

I don't know how he does it, but Dylan has managed, with a simple phrase, to make my mother laugh. She's even made an ironic comment. I love it.

"Yes, I know," he replies, squinting and shaking his head. "The Tower of Victory must be horrendous."

"You can't imagine," she continues the game. "Food like hogwash. At least the hosts were charming."

Wow, who would have thought? Dylan and my mother have chemistry. They've clicked immediately. I haven't seen my mother so relaxed since this hell began. I now realize it's not just me. This guy has a gift for making people feel good.

Unfortunately, we can't extend this brief return to normalcy.

"Did you see them after they were taken away?" asks Mia, struggling to keep her voice from breaking.

"No. Not even for a minute," my mother replies, shaking her head. She has to press her lips together hard to avoid letting out a sob. I take her hand and hold it tightly.

"It all happened so fast," I say. "We saw them leaving the studio. Then we were taken away too."

"They'll be okay," says Dylan. "They need strong people in Ventus. And… I know it sounds thoughtless, but… um, at least, for the moment… well… it's just that we expected the worst."

"We did too," I reply. "At least that didn't happen. Though I don't fully understand what's going on. They've never pardoned anyone before, right?"

"Not that I know of. But everything is highly unusual lately. Things are changing."

"What do you mean?" I ask.

"Well, apart from what you suffered first-hand," he says, "the mood has turned very tense here. Mass executions have significantly increased, and the presence of CATs has multiplied as well. The Government is very nervous."

We all take sips of tea in unconscious unison. The conversation stops for an awkwardly long time.

"Tomorrow I have to report to the police station for Sector 7," I say, trying to avoid the silence that makes us fall back into sadness. "They've assigned me a position within the security forces. They said it's in Area 7A West, not far from here."

"That's right," Dylan confirms. "Most police stations for each sector are located in Area A West, bordering the Transversal Corridor. They don't like going too far into Areas B, C, and D on either side," he says mockingly.

"My mother and Lily must present themselves at this sector's Administrative Council," I add. "They'll be assigned work as well."

Dylan explains to my mother how to get there. We agree that, for the moment, it's better to follow the Government's instructions to a T, without undermining them in anything. We must not expose ourselves to unnecessary punishments.

"I work the second shift today," Dylan says. "I'll be back in the Strip around seven. Should we meet at Georgie's at nine?"

"Yes, perfect," I confirm, happy to know I'll see him again later today. It's already early morning, and all of us must rest.

Mia, who hasn't talked much this whole time, turns to my mother:

"Emma, if you or Lily need anything, whatever it may be, please contact us." She then looks at Dylan and asks, "That's okay, right?"

"Yes, of course," he replies. "Just be very cautious and discreet. You can dial 7910 1920 from any phone. Ask anyone on the street where to find one. If you call, just say first names, not last names."

"Thank you, you're very kind," says my mother.

We say goodbye by exchanging hugs. At the door, when Mia has already stepped out and gotten a little ahead, I speak to Dylan in a low voice, almost a whisper.

"Seriously, I don't know how to thank you. It means so much that you've come to see us so soon, to cheer us up. It's been so good for my mom…" I say, then pause for a second before adding, "And for me."

When I say these last words, I feel a lump in my throat.

"There's nothing to thank us for," says Dylan with his usual sweet smile. He then shyly lowers his gaze toward the floor. "It's our pleasure. We do it with… a lot of affection."

A marvelous wave of soft heat spreads throughout my body and culminates in an intense, though fleeting feeling of extreme joy that makes me shiver.

With a lot of affection, that's what he said. It's incredible that a few brief words and a dreamy look can move me in such a way.

I manage to swallow, but I can't say anything intelligent, so I go ahead and decide to hug him. I surprise him a little, but he hugs me back.

"Thanks. Thanks so much," I say.

"You're welcome, Derin," he replies and then lets go of my arms. "See you later."

He gives a charming smile and follows Mia.

I want to forget the world. I want to make all our sorrows and worries disappear. I just want to hug Dylan. I want to hug him, kiss him, and never let him go. That's all I want.

IT'S BEEN A WHILE SINCE DYLAN LEFT and I still feel like I'm floating, as if my spirit has left my body, happy in a cloud, far away from what happens here. But the happiness begins to fade, and quickly. I would give anything to capture what's left of this vanishing feeling. This joy gives me the strength to overcome any obstacle. I'm terrified of losing it.

I lie down on the living room sofa, which is too short for my body, so my feet stick out into the air. Also, the seat cushions have given way at several points, so the surface feels bumpy. At least I have a pillow and blanket. What would we have done if I hadn't thought of bringing them? When we arrived here, my mother almost had a heart attack realizing she hadn't thought of it. She harshly scolded herself. I insisted that she shouldn't be so severe with herself. With the emotional stress they've subjected us to, none of us were in the right mind to think rationally. In fact, it amazes me that, despite everything, we've brought really useful things with us. I also pointed out that both she and Lily took things that didn't even cross my mind and have just as much value as blankets and pillows—like makeup and other beauty accessories that are in high demand in the Strip and can be exchanged for a lot of money.

Lying on my side, legs drawn to my chest, I pull the blanket up to my neck. The room is cold. One of the two windows facing the inner courtyard has no curtain and lets a faint light from outside creep in.

I thought I would fall asleep the second I lay down, but I was wrong. Too many thoughts bounce around my head, and too many emotions have left me feeling lucid, despite the tremendous exhaustion.

I do my best to reject the terrible images floating around my mind: the horrifying scenes of torture that we witnessed only a few hours ago.

The only thing that helps is thinking about Dylan. I try to remember what his shoulders and back felt like as we embraced. I remember his eyes, and in my mind, I play back his lips saying: "With a lot of affection." Those lips that I want to kiss so badly.

I spend a long time like this, in a violent struggle between images of terror and blood from the memory of the executions in the Chamber of Purgation, and feelings of joy and pleasure coming from everything that has to do with Dylan. I'm lucky that the latter are the thoughts I fall asleep with.

When I wake up a few hours later, drenched in sweat after a restless night of terrible nightmares, I curse humans' inability to choose their dreams. It didn't do me any good to fall asleep thinking about Dylan. My subconscious set out to give me the worst night of my life.

I don't remember everything, but what I recall is appalling. The repertoire of scenes included severed heads, dismembered bodies, and human guts taking on a life of their own and chasing me through labyrinths full of bloody traps. At some point, I even found myself inside a very distinctive Chamber of Purgation, specially dedicated to me.

I wasn't the victim in the torture room, though; I was the executioner. My mother was the first one inside the glass cylinder. A voice with incredible power whispered to me: "Now, Derin, you know what to do," and then, despite my best efforts to resist, my body moved toward the activation controls, where I started up the mechanism that tore my mother apart in the most frightful manner. I did the same with my father, Brian, Lily, Zara, Mia and, finally, Dylan. I executed all of them in this horrible way. I had no power over my movements. My mind painfully refused to follow the instructions of the voice guiding me. I fought desperately to get rid of that evil force, but it was too mighty. It was the voice of Nigel Crowley.

In another scene, I was standing in the fountain on the rooftop park of the Ministry of National Security, with the water up to my knees. Suddenly, Dylan appeared in front of me and began to hug me and kiss me, though I couldn't move. Dylan then transformed into a disgusting figure with the head of Nigel and the body of a beast, with six arms and three tails. This monstrous Nigel tore off my clothes and licked my face and my body with its long green tongue, which gave off a tremendous amount of slime, turning the pure water of the fountain into a stinking broth of blood and feces. I was petrified and unable to run away from the beast, which then put its putrid tongue into my mouth until it reached my throat, then kept sliding down my esophagus. At that moment, on the verge of vomiting, I suddenly woke up.

Immediately, I get up to chase away the terrible memory of this nightmare.

My mother, already showered and dressed, is preparing crackers and cheese for breakfast.

"Good morning, darling, did you sleep well?" she asks in a tired voice.

"Hi, Mom. So-so. And you?"

"Yes, a couple of hours maybe. Lily also rested a bit; she's taking a shower now."

I notice the dark shadows under her eyes and her drawn features. I don't believe she's slept at all. I'll have to do something to get her to sleep. She can't continue like this or she'll get sick. Maybe I can get her a strong sleeping pill.

When I stretch out my arms and let out a deep yawn, someone knocks on the door.

My mother and I look at each other without saying a word. I swear I can hear her heart's accelerated throb. These shocks aren't good for her at all.

I open the door expectantly and find two women: an elderly lady, with white hair and a round body and face, and a younger one. From the obvious resemblance, I assume they're mother and daughter. The older one smiles with a particular kindness in her face. The daughter has a more serious, almost frightened expression. Each one carries a basket.

"Good morning, I'm Mrs. Watson," says the older woman in a friendly tone, "and this is my daughter Wanda. I'm in charge of this building. We live on the fourth floor."

"Uh … good morning," I reply, still surprised and uncomfortable that they're seeing me after I've just gotten up. "Nice to meet you, I'm Derin Dark."

"Of course you are, dear," says Mrs. Watson, smiling. "We know who you are. Everyone here knows, but we just learned last night that they were bringing you to this building."

"Mother, the baskets," Wanda reminds her, in a less amiable tone.

"Yes, yes, I was getting to that," Mrs. Watson grumbles, looking at her daughter reproachfully. She then turns to me and says, "We just wanted to welcome you and bring you this."

They offer us two baskets full of food: fresh bread, eggs, ham, jelly, tea …

My mother, after introducing herself, can't find the words to thank them for their kindness and starts crying. Mrs. Watson comforts her with a hug.

"Now, now, my dear," she says. "We know you're going through hell, and this is the least we can do for you. We all help each other here, you know?"

"Thank you, thank you so much," is the only thing my mother can say between sobs.

I didn't know my maternal grandmother, and my paternal grandmother died when I was still too young, so I have few memories of her. I've only just met Mrs. Watson, but I imagine her as the grandmother I'd love to have. It would do us good to have such a sweet, wise, and good-natured elderly woman in our family.

Before she goes, Mrs. Watson tells my mother to come to her at any time if she needs anything.

We eat what the neighbors brought us for breakfast, and it tastes more delicious than the delicacies from Stevens. It's hard to believe these people's kindness. They don't even know us well, and they certainly don't have much to spare. We're deeply grateful.

After breakfast, I take a shower. I'm expected at the police station at nine o'clock.

Before leaving, I give my mother the five hundred pounds that were hidden in the alarm clock. I beg her and Lily to be very careful in the Administrative Council and warn them to be prepared for the worst. I wouldn't be surprised if they wanted to humiliate them. I also make sure they've memorized the phone number Dylan gave us.

I exit the apartment, sad to leave them alone. I wish I could accompany them.

Captain Foster's last words—Alan's last warning—don't stop echoing in my head: "Go far away… You have to save yourself." I'm sure it wouldn't be too challenging to disappear among the millions of inhabitants in the Strip. I know they wouldn't find us. But I can't do it, not yet. As long as my father and Brian are prisoners, we're trapped. We can't run away. If I defy Nigel, he won't hesitate to have them instantly killed.

Until I get them out of Ventus, he's got my hands tied.

CHAPTER 15

SECURITY AGENT

SECTOR 7'S POLICE STATION is bigger than I expected. It's a concrete and glass building, several floors high, and quite modern by the standards of the Strip. I learn that it has a permanent corps of security agents, around three hundred, who are armed to the teeth. All agents are members of the Commons and are deeply loyal to the regime. On the first six levels of the building, the precinct's activities take place, while the five upper levels contain rooms and small apartments for the agents. This is where they stay while on duty in the Strip. Every three weeks, in a staggered fashion, they get a leave of absence to go to London and see their families.

My case is exceptional. I'll be part of the security forces even though I've been degraded to Disloyal. That's why my family and I don't stay in this building's accommodations, which are by far much more comfortable and better equipped than the gloomy apartment they've given us.

I hear about all this through Bernard Johnson, the head of the police station. He's a middle-aged man with a bad temper and an ego.

"Look, Dark, let me make this very clear," Chief Johnson says in a hostile tone. "Over here, we only feel disdain for Disloyal like you. If it were up to me, I'd never assign a position of trust to someone of your kind."

No ambiguous phrases. He's a straight shooter who says exactly what he thinks.

"Unfortunately," he continues, "the order has come from high up, so I must obey it. But I warn you, I won't tolerate any mistakes or any hint of disrespect. Whatever stupidity you get yourself into will be severely punished. Bennet will make sure of that." He points to Lieutenant Julius Bennet, a young guy with a furious expression who will be my direct superior. He observes me from one side, without moving an inch. I start to wonder if he's a statue. "Do I make myself clear, Dark?"

"Yes, sir," I say in a submissive tone.

Chief Johnson finishes his sermon.

As if this cordial welcome wasn't enough, Lieutenant Bennet—who in fact does move and speak—leads me to his office to repeat the same warnings in his own very personal way.

"I'm a simple man, Dark," says Bennet in a tone full of hate. "I don't pretend to understand, nor will I ever question the political decisions of our leaders. But I will not hide my disdain toward your family of traitors and your presence among us. Here, we're loyal citizens, faithful to the fatherland and the regent. You're scum."

I'm surprisingly unaffected and even somewhat entertained by this. I wonder if all these airheads are forced to take courses on how to be assholes.

"Best thing would be to make yourself invisible," he continues. "Avoid crossing my path, and don't even think about opposing me, do you understand?"

"Yes, sir."

"Look me in the eyes when I speak to you, idiot!"

"I'm sorry, sir," I say, raising my gaze to meet his. I feel my blood starting to boil. But I must ignore his insults and threats.

It's not worth upsetting this mediocre character, who fully fits the profile of those moron extremists that come out of security agents' school and whose skills aren't good enough to get a better position in the city. He's angry with his own insignificance and channels his frustration into a visceral hatred of the entire Disloyal population. But this makes him dangerous. In a place like the Strip, such a fool with authority and weapons can be very dangerous. Better not mess with him.

Later, when I meet with the other agents that make up the unit commanded by Julius Bennet, I confirm that almost all of them are of the same deranged mold: little intelligence, frustration at having to serve in the Strip, spite and widespread hatred toward deels, passion for weapons, superiority complex due to the authority the uniform bestows them and, above all, hostility toward me. This reception doesn't bode well. But it's the least of my worries.

I keep wondering how my mother and Lily are doing. I hope they haven't been assigned work that's too hard or demeaning. I can't stop thinking about my father and Brian, either. Are they still in London, or have they already been taken to Ventus? I have no way of knowing if they're really alive, and the anguish of this uncertainty overwhelms me. It's entirely possible that Nigel had them executed yesterday after they were taken from the studio… No, that wouldn't make sense. Although lately, nothing seems to make much sense. But if he intended to kill them, Nigel would have made sure that I found out. He would have communicated it to me himself, or made me witness their executions. No, they haven't been executed. It must be true they're going to Ventus. They need them. They'll be forced to work as slaves until their bodies fall apart.

I have to get them out of there. I don't know how, but I have to get them out of there.

Andrew, one of my unit mates, who offered to be my guide when Bennet asked for a volunteer—the one who seems the least upset by my presence—shows me the locker I can use in the changing rooms.

"Look, your uniform's already here," he says, opening the little metal door. "They brought it yesterday afternoon."

"Yesterday afternoon?" I ask.

"Yes. Actually, I think it was after lunch."

"How strange," I reply ironically. "What a coincidence that someone thought of bringing a uniform in my size several hours before the sentence was given."

Andrew makes sure there's nobody around before answering.

"Here, coincidences are more common than you'd imagine," he says in a low voice.

I'm not sure why, but there's something about Andrew that reminds me of Dylan. Physically, he doesn't look anything like him, and I don't find him particularly attractive. But perhaps I see some resemblance in the way he says certain things, using sentences with double meaning. Maybe it's a way of talking that you pick up here after some time.

I can't stop thinking about Dylan. I'll see him again tonight. "Georgie's at nine," he said. There are so many hours left, and I can't wait to see him. I want to observe every inch of his face. His eyes, his nose, his lips, everything about him. I hope I can hug him again. I need to have him in my arms.

"It looks a lot like the CAT uniform, don't you think?" Andrew asks, returning me to the present. "Sure, it's a different color, but the design is almost the same."

He's right, it's very similar. Though this one is olive green with a grey bulletproof vest. The helmet is also olive green with Englandom's coat of arms in grey, and it has a reflective visor.

"What's up with the numbers?" I ask, pointing to the alphanumeric series embroidered on the left shoulder.

"Well, 7C is our unit," he explains. "All of Bennet's guys have the same number: Police Station 7, Unit C. And this one, here," he says, touching the *19* on my right shoulder, "is your personal number."

"So it goes by age, or what?" I say, squinting.

Andrew hesitates for a moment, not quite understanding my question, but then he gets it and smiles.

"No, no, if you're nineteen years old, that's pure coincidence, the real kind of coincidence. It has nothing to do with age. You don't think I'm sixteen, do you?"

I look at his right shoulder and see the number *16*. Of course he's not sixteen. I'd guess he's around twenty-five.

"Ah, well," I say smiling, "then it's not because of age."

"No, the numbers are fixed," he explains. "We're usually eighteen agents per unit. Fifteen must always be on duty, and the other three are on leave of absence in London. The numbers go from one to eighteen. So logically you would be number nineteen."

By midmorning, I'm wearing my full uniform and carrying all my equipment. I'm just another security agent of the Strip's government forces.

Our unit, commanded by Bennet, is distributed into two armored vehicles, each with a manned tower, machine gun, and grenade launcher. We have to go on a routine surveillance tour in Sector 7. Apart from the bulletproof vest, I carry with me an electric club, an automatic pistol, an automatic rifle, as well as an anti-riot shield. There are also smoke and tear gas grenades inside the vehicle.

None of this is new to me. My training at the Military Academy is far above the level of this police station, and that gives me a sense of security. But at the same time, it's a possible disadvantage, in the sense that here almost all of them resent my technical and strategic superiority. Especially Bennet, who didn't even bother to give me special instructions to familiarize myself with his methods. I assume he didn't want to expose himself and be ridiculed. He knows very well that I am—or rather was—an officer of the National Army.

This guy worries too much. The last thing to cross my mind would be to undermine or ridicule him in front of his unit. All I want is to finish this day without any problems, return to my mother and Lily and, later, meet Dylan.

I can't see much through the two small windows, but I realize that we're passing long rows of buildings that all look the same to me. I get the impression that these routine tours have the sole purpose of showing the Government's presence—in other words, intimidating the population. We've spent three-quarters of an hour driving around the streets of the sector, and we haven't stopped anywhere.

Suddenly, the driver slams on the brakes.

We hold on tightly to our seats while he performs a spontaneous maneuver to turn one hundred and eighty degrees. He accelerates again, and we head back to where we came from at high speed.

"Get ready," says Sergeant Spencer, who's in charge of our vehicle, through the helmet's intercom. "Anti-riot mission. Lieutenant Bennet has just received a call from command. Illegal demonstration in Sector 9. They've asked for a reinforcement unit from our sector and they're sending us."

"All right! We're coming for you, bastards! Some action at last!" exclaim some of my peers while making signs of approval with their fists.

It doesn't take us long to arrive, because the area in Sector 9 is only a couple of miles away and we're going at full speed.

The vehicle's tires screech as the driver brings us to a full stop.

"Everyone out! Formation!" Spencer yells.

The two agents next to the rear doors open them, and we all jump out. We stand in two rows of four next to the formation of Vehicle One, under the command of Lieutenant Bennet. He takes the lead, and Spencer stands next to him.

"Very good," Bennet says. "This is the situation: protesters from the upper sectors are heading to the prefecture. The forces of 9 and reinforcements from 8 are waiting for them one block away. We're closing up from behind. Our mission is to give these bastards a small taste of what awaits those who dare to disturb public order."

Apparently, all the agents are aware of what Bennet expects from them. The majority of them smile and nod their heads. No need for any further explanation.

"Your specific task," he continues, "after you've enjoyed yourselves a bit, is to capture at least one protester each. One per head, at least! We're leaving with a minimum of fifteen detainees, is that clear?"

"Yes, sir!" the agents roar in unison.

"Besides," he continues cheerfully, "for each additional detainee above fifteen, you'll get a pack of beers."

"Yeahhh!" roars the robotic formation.

Two by two, our unit starts to move, trotting behind Lieutenant Bennet and Sergeant Spencer. The two armored vehicles follow us at close range. We don't even make it three blocks before we see the group of demonstrators. As far as I can tell, there aren't more than fifty. They carry banners, although I can't read what they say, as I only see them from behind. Either way, there's no sign of violence. Everything points to a peaceful march.

We stop about fifty feet behind the demonstrators and quickly form a wall. They stop too. They've run into the security block put up by agents of Sector 9 and the reinforcements from 8. At least four armored vehicles and several dozens of security agents prevent them from going any farther.

Bennet gives a signal through the intercom for us to place our shields and electric clubs in counterattack position. The protesters look in all directions, sensing that something is coming toward them.

Without warning, several high-pitched whistles come from the two vehicles in our unit. The grenades land on the demonstrators with a hollow sound, hitting several of them. Immediately, the smoke begins to engulf the entire crowd. Chaos begins.

Bennet shouts the signal, "Go ahead!" and our unit throws itself at the demonstrators, who run disoriented everywhere. Our helmet visors are made of a unique material that allows us to see through the smoke, so we have no problem distinguishing the crowd's expressions of confusion and panic. Most of them are very young, stumbling with their arms groping around them.

Agents in my unit beat up the young people with their electric clubs, hitting them on the head, on the back, on the chest. Some of them fall to the ground, and the agents continue to beat them and kick them violently.

I remain frozen. I can't stand the idea of savagely attacking people who were demonstrating peacefully. I know Bennet is going to punish me, but I just can't harm these people. I'm not a monster. Some of my agent peers have already subdued and handcuffed several protestors and are taking them to the vehicles. Other demonstrators lie on the pavement, motionless.

Suddenly, a sharp blow against my back takes me by surprise.

Thanks to the protection provided by my bulletproof vest and helmet, the blow doesn't cause any damage, only disorients me a little. I turn around and find myself facing a huge kid, one head taller than me. With his face enraged like a demon's, he prepares to strike another blow with the stick he's got in both hands. Under other circumstances, I would have a lot of trouble facing this giant, but I've got the advantage. I manage to intercept his blow with the shield, and I stun him with an electric shock, though just a little. I don't want to seriously hurt him, but now that he's turned into a raging beast, I can't let him crush me either. I give him another zap and this time I think it's enough to repel his attack.

At the same second that the boy shudders from the electric shock, an agent appears from behind and bangs the boy's head with his club. He falls to the ground, unconscious.

"Dark! Help me with this one!" Spencer's voice shouts. "We're getting out of here, quickly!"

I've got no choice but to follow his instructions. Disobeying his orders now would be too evident. Anyway, this guy will be taken away, with or without my help.

I squat down and put handcuffs on him. Sergeant Spencer helps me lift him up. He's so heavy that I wouldn't be able to handle him on my own. Even between Spencer and I, we have a hard time holding and dragging him. With great effort, we make it to the vehicle being used to carry the prisoners. Two more agents are needed to help us raise this hulk and put him with the others. I take a look inside the vehicle and see that it's full of guys and some girls, all with varying degrees of blows and wounds.

"All right, we're off," says Lieutenant Bennet, and all the agents hop onto our unit's second vehicle, which soon starts up.

Along the way, several of my peers raise their visors and eagerly relive what, in their opinions, were the most exciting moments of the beating. Others speculate on where we're headed now, with almost twenty prisoners. Some think that we'll take them to the police station of Sector 9; others say we're going back to our own station. But in the end, most agree that we're going to a certain Fountain Square.

"Fountain Square?" I ask Andrew, who's sitting next to me.

"Yes, it's a big, well-known square," he says. "It's often used to carry out executions."

I remember Dylan mentioning last night that public executions have increased.

In London, we knew very little about what was happening in the Strip. Every once in a while, there was some rumor, or we learned about some dreadful story through Mia. But most of the barbarities taking place here remained beyond our knowledge. This means that I still don't have a very clear idea of the reality in the Strip.

"Are there many demonstrations?" I ask Andrew.

"More every day. Most of them come from the upper sectors, from the 15th onward," he explains, and then continues in a whisper, wrinkling his nose. "You know, the poorest and worst sectors. It's disgusting over there, it's a mess. There's almost never water or electricity, the air stinks, there are garbage hills everywhere."

"Are the protestors violent?"

"Not usually, they know who's coming for them," he says. "But things are heating up lately. We can't let them protest near Prefect Merriman's residence. He's the highest representative of the regime in the Strip. That can't be tolerated. We have to show authority the hard way. If we loosen up, they'll be all over us."

I realize that Andrew, despite being less fanatical than the others, doesn't sympathize very much with the Disloyal, nor with their problems.

It's almost noon when we arrive at Fountain Square.

We pull down our helmet visors and get out.

The first thing I notice is that the square is surrounded by armored vehicles, like the ones from our unit, and there are security agents everywhere. Furthermore, there are numerous video cameras placed on posts in several locations in the square. From our unit's vehicle, as well as from another one, security agents begin to assemble the prisoners. In the middle of the square, there's a large cement fountain. Inside it, some podiums with wooden posts are arranged in a line. Narrow planks lead from the edge of the basin to each of the podiums.

It's clear what I'm seeing. It's a firing squad line-up.

CHAPTER 16

COURAGE AND PUNISHMENT

OUR UNIT GETS IN FORMATION, about ninety feet in front of the fountain, next to the other units from Sectors 8 and 9 who aren't dealing with directing the prisoners. We all—dozens of security agents with helmets and visors covering our faces—look like a big green and grey patch, impersonal, anonymous.

A group of agents escort the first ten prisoners in a single line and lead them to the fountain. There, next to the planks connecting the lip of the basin to the podiums, ten disheveled-looking "assistants" await. No doubt they are deels, forced to perform this task. Each prisoner is made to walk along the plank, a few inches above the water, until they reach the corresponding podium. The assistants wade in, head to the podiums, and take a couple of steps up to tie the prisoners' hands behind the posts. Then they throw themselves into the water and return to the fountain's edge. They emerge soaked and move to one side of the fountain.

Bennet and the other unit chiefs discuss something with the man who must be the highest-ranking officer, the one in charge of this operation. They don't take long to come to an agreement. One of the lieutenants goes to his unit and chooses ten agents for the first firing squad.

They form a line about fifty feet from the fountain. Deeply outraged, I gaze at the terrified faces of the ten demonstrators tied to the posts. From left to right, I see four boys around my age, a middle-aged man with dark grey hair, two young women, another boy who has just entered adolescence, a red-headed woman about thirty years old—I can't help thinking about Brian—and, on the last post, I recognize the big guy who attacked me, the one I had to capture. A stream of blood from the blow Spencer dealt him runs down his neck from the back of his head.

"Ready!" exclaims the commanding officer.

The ten agents raise their automatic rifles and place them in firing position by propping the stock against their shoulders.

"Aim!"

Slight nods from the riflemen announce that each one of them already has his victim's head or chest in sight.

"Fire!"

The ten bullets go off in a single dry burst.

I close my eyes, hoping the ten agents are good shots. I don't want any of the prisoners to suffer more. It's barbaric enough what the regime is doing to these deels. Disdain and anger overwhelm me, making my blood boil.

When I open my eyes again, I realize that, indeed, the prisoners seem to have died instantly. For a fraction of a second, I look at the last one on the right, the big guy, and see with horror that his head is split in two.

The assistants jump into the fountain again. They climb to the podiums, untie the corpses, and throw them into the water, which is at once dyed with blood. The assistants, their clothes stained red, go out and retake their positions, waiting for the next group.

This macabre routine is repeated two more times. For each group of ten prisoners, a firing squad is chosen from a different unit. After a quarter of an hour, with thirty corpses bleeding below, all the water in the fountain has turned a light brown color. The clothes of the assistants are stained in scarlet.

But there's still one group of prisoners awaiting execution. The last seven of a total of thirty-seven protesters who were captured. I grow tense. This time they could choose a firing squad from my unit's agents.

Indeed, Lieutenant Bennet approaches our unit and starts calling out names.

He won't call me, he won't call me, he won't call me, I think, trying to chase away this evil possibility, but expecting the worst.

When Bennet has called six agents without shouting my name, I start to calm down.

No, he's not that stupid. He's not willing to take a chance on me. What's the point? He must know that I've never shot anyone, and he won't want to risk me missing the shot. No, he won't call me.

"Dark!" I hear. I wince, shaken to my soul.

I can't believe it. This can't be happening. It's a terrible joke.

In automatic mode, I get out of formation and walk behind my six peers to stand in line before the fountain. My mind feels numb, and I hardly realize what's happening, what I'll be forced to do. I let my shocked body be taken by some powerful puppeteer who controls my movements. I take my place, the first in the row.

As soon as I look up and see the prisoner I'm supposed to execute, my conscience suddenly wakes and jars me painfully.

My heart sinks.

The girl isn't over fifteen or sixteen years old. She's wearing grey trousers, and by the dark spot between her legs, it's obvious she's wet herself out of fear. She looks tiny on the podium, with her hands behind her back and tied to the pole. She could easily be one of Lily's schoolmates. In fact, she reminds me of those girls who used to whisper about me with my sister, flattering me with silly compliments. How am I going to shoot this innocent girl?

It's clear: I can't do it.

I think about the possible consequences for contempt of this nature. It's quite likely they'll put me up there and shoot me just like any other prisoner. Or worse, they could bring over my mother and Lily and force me to see them executed. These madmen are so sadistic that any punishment is imaginable. I can't allow my family to get hurt because of me. I have to submit. I must become a monster to protect them.

It's crazy. How am I going to kill this girl?

This conflict rips my soul in two. It mortifies me and disturbs my mind: either I choose to become despicable by savagely snatching away this innocent girl's life, or I refuse to commit such an atrocity, but with certain punishment and the risk of causing my mother and my sister terrible suffering.

In the middle of my thoughts, I notice out of the corner of my eye that Bennet is exchanging a few words with the commanding officer. Then he heads toward me.

"Dark," he says with a firm voice and a strange little smile, "take off your helmet."

"Excuse me, lieutenant?"

"Take your helmet off, at once!"

Bewildered, I obey. I place my helmet on the ground and turn to him expectantly.

Maybe he's had second thoughts or just wants to have some fun watching me suffer. I bet it's all part of a sick game and now he'll order me to go back to the unit and get someone to take my place.

"Get in position!" he shouts in a threatening tone. "Don't fail me, Dark, I'm warning you."

What the hell's wrong with this asshole? I ask myself, disturbed by his mad actions.

All of a sudden, I figure out why he wanted me to take off my helmet: the cameras.

This entire mass execution is being recorded, and undoubtedly will be broadcast later on television. Bennet wants viewers to know that I'm the one who executes this girl. My face will be recognized by the entire nation as that of the officer whose family betrayed the regime. An officer who, after degradation to Disloyal, fires on other deels, people of his new caste.

"Ready!" I hear the scream of the commanding officer.

Out of reflex, I raise my rifle and place it in firing position, as I've done hundreds of times in the Military Academy's shooting range.

"Aim!"

Through the gun-sight, I now see the girl's face closely. She has shut her eyes and is shaking uncontrollably. Tears run down her cheeks.

How am I going to kill her? How can I do this? I can't, I just can't.

In a millisecond, two images cross my mind: the face of the girl in front of me, shattered by the impact of my rifle's bullet, and the faces of my mother and Lily, disfigured by the terror and agony of some monstrous punishment.

No. I won't let them be tortured. Anything but that.

If I shoot the girl between the eyebrows, she'll die instantly and won't feel any pain. I force myself to think that I'm doing her a favor. With my bullet, I'll take her away from the regime's disgusting hands. I'll spare her any more suffering.

"Fire!"

I pull the trigger and hit my mark. Exactly where I was aiming: one inch above the girl's head, on the wooden post.

I haven't been able to kill her.

"You idiot, Dark! Out of the way!" an enraged Bennet barks, knocking me to the ground with a shove.

In less than a second, he takes out his gun, aims, and lets out two shots: one bores itself into the girl's head and the other into her chest. She dies immediately.

"Idiot, you're going to pay!" he grumbles as he kicks me in the leg. "Get up! Go back in formation!"

Limping a bit from the blow, I return to my unit.

"To the vehicles!" orders Bennet. "Back to the police station!"

Before getting on, I turn my head toward the fountain and see the deel assistants preparing to take the bodies out of the water. Among them is the big, stocky boy who attacked me, and the tiny girl I couldn't kill.

At least I haven't been used as a deadly instrument of this ruthless regime. This comforts me and makes me proud, though I immediately begin to regret what I've done, or rather, what I haven't done. Fear overtakes me as I consider Bennet's revenge. I think about my mother and Lily, about how they will be made to suffer because of me.

The trip back to the police station is a litany of insults.

"You're shit, Dark," says one of my companions, the typical show-off of the group who everybody calls Kick. "They're going to fuck us all because of you."

"Fucking traitor," adds another, whose name I don't even know. "If they take away our beer, I swear, I'll kill you."

"Aren't you supposed to be a decorated officer, bastard deel?" says a third one, who seems to be the youngest. "Decorated in what, licking commanders' asses? You've got nothing of an officer. Not even my grandma would miss that shot."

"What can you expect from a traitorous son of a bitch like this?" says Kick, now spitting from rage. "He's not even pureblood, you know? He and his degenerate family are all subhuman. They should've been annihilated ages ago."

Though it's incredibly difficult, I try to ignore their taunts. It doesn't help that I remember Kick during the attack on the demonstrators, euphoric and unrestrained. Of all the agents, he was the one who kept hitting and kicking the unconscious deels on the ground most. I suppose that violent behavior is what earned him the nickname.

Hopefully, we'll arrive soon. It won't take too long before these blockheads lose it, and no one will be able to stop them then. Even Andrew looks at me with hateful eyes. I begin to consider the idea that my own unit mates will tear me to pieces even before Bennet decides my punishment. It won't be fun, but perhaps it'll be more bearable than the torture of seeing my mother and sister suffer, so I resign myself to dying this way. It could be much worse.

When we arrive at the police station, I'm still alive.

But as the hours go by and nothing happens, I grow more restless. It's unthinkable that Bennet would let this matter go as if nothing happened. He must be up to something. Otherwise, is it possible that he thinks he made a mistake picking me for the firing squad? He could write off my "one-inch mistake" to nerves since it was the first time I had to shoot someone. Besides, any half-decent person, considering what I've been through the last few days, wouldn't find it hard to believe that my psychological state and abilities were compromised. So, maybe he'll attribute my failure to emotional instability and not necessarily conscious and willful disregard of his orders. This would be the best scenario, and I hope it's the case.

On the other hand, Bennet, and especially Chief Johnson, must be aware of my high-level military training. They must know that my physical and mental capacities had to be exceptional for me to become an officer of the National Army with the best qualifications in my class. They would know that my finesse acquired in the Military Academy wouldn't allow any psychological pressure to affect my shooting skills, especially such a basic and straightforward shot as the one I missed in Fountain Square. They must know I did it on purpose, and they'll regard it as an offense, a disrespect to their orders. A gesture of defiance against the Government.

I'm unable to decide between the two possibilities. Worst of all, they don't give me any signs one way or the other.

After lunch, we go out again to do routine surveillance in Sector 7, like we did this morning before they sent us to Sector 9. Strangely, it seems like my co-workers' anger has waned a bit, and the insults are less frequent, so the rest of the afternoon goes by without much news. I suspect they've received orders to leave me alone, though I can't imagine why. We get back to the police station shortly after five. Since my work shift ends at six today, I use the rest of the time to clean my weapons and uniform. Neither Sergeant Spencer nor Lieutenant Bennet approach me, so I begin to hope that, in fact, they have attributed my mistake to emotional imbalance.

I'm about to leave the police station, already dressed in civilian clothes, when I see Bennet at the end of the corridor. He gestures me to approach him.

"Dark," he says in a calm voice, "come with me."

All my instinct alarms go off. I follow him to his office and, when we enter, he closes the door.

"You think you're really clever, don't you?" he says as he sits at his desk chair.

"No, sir," I answer, standing and staring at the floor.

"I warned you not to undermine me. I was very clear about it," he continues, his tone of voice rising as he goes on. "You made a fool of me in front of everyone, you idiot! Because of you, Chief Johnson has questioned my decision to put you in the firing squad."

"I'm sorry, lieutenant. I don't know what happened to me." I try to answer in the most submissive and sincere way I can, but it's not convincing.

"Save your stupid shit for someone else," he replies. "The chief thinks your damn mind wasn't fit for the task, but you don't fool me, Dark."

Since I can't find anything intelligent to say in my favor, I decide to remain silent and let him continue.

"I'll find a proper way to punish you," he says. "This doesn't end here, you can be sure of that. For now, I'm canceling your salary for this week. Keep it up, and you won't have any credits to survive. Think it's funny to see your mother and little sister digging through the trash, right? Or maybe they'll be forced to sell themselves to have something to eat."

I start to burn up. If he says anything more to insult them, I don't know if I'll be able to hold myself back.

"Answer me when I talk to you, little fuck, and look me in the eyes!" Bennet yells.

"I'm sorry, sir," I force myself to respond, staring back at him. "It was a mistake, sir, I know it. It won't happen again, I swear."

"It better not," he says.

Then, changing his facial expression in a disturbing way, he gives me a feigned smile, glances at his wristwatch, picks up a remote control from his desk, and turns on the television hanging on the wall.

"Before you leave, I want you to see something you'll love," he says, still smiling.

Somehow, I have a foreboding of what's coming, and it's not good.

"You're sure to enjoy the official transmission that's about to begin," he adds. At the same time, that familiar melody sounds from the television and our teleCards. We both scan our thumbprints.

On the TV screen, a news bulletin begins reporting a violent demonstration that took place this morning in the Strip. The anchor-man explains that hundreds of rebel supporters tried to attack the prefecture headquarters and brutally confronted dozens of security agents and many others who didn't yield to the demonstrators' threats to join the riots. The altered images show a raging crowd carrying torches, rocks, and clubs embedded with nails. A mob of hooded youths throws Molotov cocktails at security agents.

It's nothing close to the peaceful demonstration that I witnessed with my own eyes. I'm surprised yet again by how shamelessly dishonest the government propaganda is.

The anchor-man indicates in a regretful tone that thirteen deels were murdered by the demonstrators, but, on a positive note, several dozen rebels among the crowd of violent criminals were captured. He then takes the opportunity to congratulate the security forces on their exemplary work, despite the enormous risk they were exposed to.

He confirms that the captured rebels were sentenced to death and that their execution by firing squad was carried out this very afternoon. Images play of the shootings in Fountain Square, focusing mainly on the bullets entering the deels' bodies and on the corpses floating in the blood-stained water. Before showing each execution, they concentrate on two or three of the prisoners tied to the poles and provide specific details, like the name of the rebel and the worst crimes he or she has committed. I'm sure all the information is fake.

At the end of the news broadcast, the host announces that he has something extraordinary to show, assuring viewers that it will be of great interest.

When I see the face of the girl tied to the post on the podium, I know this is it.

I suddenly appear on the screen, unmistakable without my helmet, pointing my rifle at the girl, who in the image they've created looks even more fragile and helpless than she is—or was. The camera zooms in on my face, while the commentator reminds the audience who I am—as if it were necessary. He explains how now that I've been degraded to Disloyal, I've found a praiseworthy task in the Strip: executing rebels.

The editing and altering of the images are truly amazing. Stupefied, I see myself, Derin Dark, a former patriotic officer and degraded brother of a traitor, cold-bloodedly executing an innocent and helpless girl. I even seem satisfied and happy after blowing out her brains. It's disgusting.

The tableau is convincing and will inevitably provoke outrage and disdain among the Disloyal population. It's not difficult to imagine that the girl's execution will generate, at least, a dislike among the members of Commons. But the millions of Disloyal who have seen the transmission will definitely hate me. Without a shadow of a doubt, they're now the ones who wish me the worst punishment.

Of course, this is the aim of the footage.

It saddens me to consider that Zara and Captain Foster have seen the broadcast. What will they think of me? I hope they know me well enough and are aware of the government propaganda team's ability to alter images. I hope they know everything's false. What if my mother and Lily have also seen the transmission? And Dylan?

I want to get out of here as soon as possible to explain everything to them. The idea of them thinking I'm a beast eats me up.

The news broadcast ends, and we both press our thumbs on our respective teleCards. Bennet turns off the television, and with a cheeky, triumphant smile on his face, says:

"Well, what did I tell you? Nice program, right?" He doesn't wait for an answer, but continues: "And now, get out! Out of my sight!"

IT'S PAST SIX IN THE EVENING, and there are many people in the street. I try to cover my face with my hand, pretending to scratch my forehead. In my terrible shame, I don't want anyone to recognize me. Maybe I just imagine it, but it seems to me that everyone is looking at me with suspicion, trying to identify my features.

I get off the bus at the station closest to our apartment and continue on my way over narrow streets and alleys. A short distance from my destination, I turn into an alley that I must go down to get to the thoroughfare in front of the building where we now live. Halfway along the alley, I notice two guys leaning against the wall on the right; they mutter something to each other when they see me.

Instinct makes me stop abruptly and turn to go back the way I came, but my reaction comes too late: three other guys are coming in my direction, their faces covered with masks.

It's an ambush.

I turn again and run at full speed toward the end of the alley, but the two guys leaning against the wall intercept me. Though I knock one of them down with a sharp blow to the face, the other manages to hold me long enough for the other three to arrive.

I have no chance against five.

While the rest of them hold me down with all their might, two hit me with their fists and feet until I can't resist anymore. Completely undone by the pain, I run out of air, and everything around me turns dark. I fall to the ground. All I can do is try to cover my face with my arms while they continue to kick me.

Before I pass out, I hear the voice of one of the thugs saying in my ear:

"Best regards from Julius Bennet."

CHAPTER 17

UNEXPECTED ALLY

WHEN I OPEN MY EYES, I'm startled to see the face of a middle-aged woman I don't recognize. I'm lying on a bed, with my upper body exposed. This unknown woman is applying an ointment to my ribs and sides. Something cold burns my skin. I make a grimace of protest and let out a moan when I sense the intense waves of pain coming from different parts of my body.

"I'm sorry," the woman says. "I know it hurts, but I have to put this on so you can get better. You'll be okay. You don't have any fractures."

"Where am I? What happened?" I ask in a faint voice.

"Relax, rest a bit," she replies while arranging cold compresses on several parts of my torso and on my forehead. "Don't worry, you're safe. In a minute, Taddeus will tell you everything you want to know."

I turn my head carefully to the side and see a thick man with a round face and shoulder-length, straight grey hair sitting in a chair.

"Hi, Derin. My name's Taddeus," he says with a smile. "Let Lisa finish tending to your injuries. We'll talk soon."

I obey and let the woman continue her work.

After a while, she asks if I think I can sit on the edge of the bed. I respond in the affirmative, and both she and the man called Taddeus help me get up.

"Slowly, slowly," she says. "There's no hurry. You got a good blow to the head and better avoid sudden movements if you don't want to get dizzy."

I manage to sit up without too much trouble, and then Lisa starts to roll a wide bandage around my torso, from my abdomen to my chest. When she's satisfied with her work, she takes a step back and studies me carefully. Then she nods.

"Excellent, you're ready," she announces in a friendly tone. "Take this ointment with you and apply it to the bruised areas three times a day. Then put the bandage back on. Let someone help you, okay?"

I nod to her instructions. She grabs my chin with one hand and, very delicately, turns my head from side to side.

"You were lucky the blows to your face weren't too severe," she continues. "You've got bruises, and you're swollen, but with the mask I put on you earlier, inflammation has already gone down a lot. You'll have your handsome face back again in a couple of days, good as new."

I feel myself blushing when she says that.

She then hands me a bag with two masks soaked in a solution I'm not familiar with, but which smells like wood and something citrusy.

"If you've got a refrigerator, it's best to keep them there. Place one on your face tonight and let it take effect for at least half an hour. Do the same thing tomorrow night, that should do the trick."

"Thanks," I answer.

Lisa says goodbye with a smile and a gentle pat on my cheek.

"You'll be fine, Derin, you'll see. It's not as bad as it seems."

As I watch Lisa leave the room and close the door behind her, I wonder how she knows my name. But I suddenly remember my special teleCard, and now it seems obvious how they've figured out who I am.

The chubby man brings his chair closer to the bed. He's dressed like a typical deel, with frayed and worn Petex clothing, although there's something in his demeanor that doesn't quite fit this place.

"So," he begins. "I imagine you want to know how you ended up here, right?"

"Yeah, what happened? I remember the thugs hitting me, but I can't remember anything else. What is this place?"

"You were lucky," he continues, the smile remaining on his face. "A group of boys went into the alley where they were hitting you, and the other bastards ran away like chickens. They picked you up and brought you here. 'Here' is Lisa's home. She's one of the best nurses I know. Sometimes I trust her more than doctors. She called me, and I came over as soon as I could."

"I see," I reply, still quite confused. "Thanks for that. But where is this place? And who are you?"

"We're in a safe area. Don't worry, we'll take you to your family as soon as you get dressed. Let me introduce myself: I'm Taddeus Green… Let's say that I hold a 'certain position' here in the Strip. I know a lot of good people who are always willing to help."

I don't understand anything he says, but they've treated me well. I may even owe it to him that I'm still alive, so I decide to trust him.

"I'm Derin. Derin Dark," I reply to his introduction.

Taddeus lets out a laugh that resonates within the walls of the small room.

"I know, my boy," he says brightly. "I know perfectly well who you are."

"You know who I am?" I ask, narrowing my eyes. He seems to enjoy my amazement.

"Of course, Derin. We've followed your family's misfortunes closely. It's shameful what those bastard Crowleys have done to you. But don't worry. Rest assured you have friends here. We're going to help you."

"Help me? Um, I'm sorry… I… I don't understand what you mean."

The veins in my head are throbbing, and I start to feel dizzy.

"Let's see, let's see," he replies, standing up. "Let me help you put on your shirt and jacket and then I'll take you home. You don't want your mother to worry, right? We'll talk more on the way there, and I'll answer your questions."

Taddeus Green drives his car himself. It's an old model typical of the Strip, one that runs on a combustion engine. I'm sitting in the passenger's seat next to him, and we're accompanied by two stout, stern-faced men in the backseat who haven't said a word. They look like bodyguards. I'm positive they're armed.

"It's a big change from London, don't you think?" says Taddeus, making a wide movement with his left hand to indicate the surroundings. "For me, the worst part is the smell and the smog, but you get used to it over time."

"You're also from London?" I ask.

"No, no, I'm not. I spent long periods in the city during my youth, but I'm from a little farther north."

"But then, you were also degra…" I start, but he doesn't let me finish the sentence.

"Yes, yes, son, me too," he says. "I was degraded too. Though my degradation wasn't as spectacular as yours."

I knew he wasn't a Disloyal by birth. I can't explain why just yet, but I knew it.

"And what caste did you belong to before?"

"The Commons, like you and many others," he answers without hesitation, though he hastens to change the subject. "But my background isn't that fascinating. Let's talk about you and your situation, which I imagine will interest you more."

I nod.

"Perfect. Look, Derin," he begins, replacing his relaxed and casual tone with a soberer and more focused one, "I know I can trust you, so I've decided to reveal some confidential information. I want you to know who I am and what I do. I'm not wrong in trusting you, am I?"

"No, of course not," I rush to answer. "You can trust me."

"Fabulous," he replies, showing his huge smile again. "Well, then, I'll cut to the chase. No need to get bored with unnecessary details. My name is Taddeus Green, as you know, and I lead the most important insurgent forces in the Strip—in the entire country, in fact. We've infiltrated even the highest levels of the Government."

I'm speechless. I had suspected that Taddeus was a good-natured neighborhood boss with some power and influence, but I never thought he was a rebel leader.

"How much do you know about the true situation in our country?" he asks, turning away from the heavy traffic for a second to look me in the eye. "I'm referring to the regime's precarious situation, not the propaganda that even children don't believe anymore."

"To be honest," I say, a bit embarrassed, "I don't think I'm aware of much. I've heard rumors, of course, and I deduce certain things by intuition, but that's about it."

"No matter," says Taddeus. "Let me fill you in with a simple summary." He pauses as he maneuvers the car through a tangled intersection of streets, and then continues. "The regime is teetering like never before. More and more influential voices throughout Englandom are speaking out for radical change in the Government. In addition, the insurgency's strategic and military power is reaching a point where overthrowing the regent is no longer a distant possibility, but rather an approaching reality. Crowley's desperate actions in recent days attest to the imminent danger he feels. He's shitting with fear. Do you follow?"

"You mean Governor Hall's execution?" I ask, eager to hear more.

"Yes. There are other things as well, but the arrest and execution of Hall and Freeland have been the most dramatic," Taddeus explains. "Hall was one of those influential official voices fed up with the abuses and the disastrous direction the country is headed in. He decided to take action, making an alliance with us, with the insurgency. Unfortunately, his idiotic son, Lucius, betrayed him and turned him over to the Crowleys. This fact has complicated things."

"So it's true, then, that Hall turned against the regent?" I ask. "I mean, according to the rumors I heard, the whole terrorist attack was a charade."

"Ah, you're already aware of that, good," Taddeus replies, showing no interest in knowing how I've found out. "Yes, Hall was on our side. Just a handful of governors remain faithful to Crowley, but Hall was the first one who dared to challenge him directly. Yet the attack was a hoax, as you know. Another one of those little games the regent enjoys staging to get attention. Unfortunately for you and your family, your brother Brian had the terrible luck of becoming a figurant in the Crowleys' theater."

"Figurant?" I ask, raising my eyebrows.

"Yes, a performer who isn't involved directly in the plot. Someone used as filler, to improve the setting and staging."

"Then you know that my family and I aren't guilty of anything."

"Of course I know that," he replies in a more compassionate tone. "I've kept track of your family since I learned that your brother would be judged in the *Trial of the People*."

"Why have you been following us?"

"Because it's not normal for the Crowleys to waste time and resources on—forgive me—two insignificant kids from the Commons. If they wanted to get rid of them, they could have done so at any time without the big fuss. There was something else there. I immediately got interested in them and their families… in your family, or rather, in you."

"Interested in me?" I say incredulously.

"Yes, in you," Taddeus replies with an absolute naturalness as if it were the most obvious thing in the world. "The big toad—sorry, that's how I like to refer to the regent—just wanted to kill Hall and Freeland, so the other three must have been there because of the tadpole."

"The tadpole?"

"Yes, yes, the tadpole. That's what I affectionately call the thick-head, Nigel Crowley," he explains mockingly. "Anyway, we know Michael Wallace was the tadpole's former lover. For some reason we still haven't discovered, he wanted to punish him publicly."

This last piece of news leaves me stunned. Michael Wallace, the father of the two blond girls, had an intimate relationship with Nigel? If Taddeus knows all this, what else does he know?

"But, what about my brother and Liam Mitchell?" I ask, and then add, fearing that he's aware of everything: "And your interest in me?"

"We haven't yet tied up loose ends regarding the Mitchell boy," Taddeus replies. "But we do know that the tadpole exposed your brother and your family like this because he has his eyes set on you. I want to find out everything about this."

He catches me off guard. I don't know what to say. Somehow, he knows there's something between Nigel and me. And he wants me to tell him everything.

"Don't worry about that for the time being," he says, noticing that I've become nervous. "I won't mortify you about this right now. We'll find a chance to talk later. Look, we're almost there. The Blakes will let you know when I want to meet with you again. You'll be glad to know that maybe we can do something for you and your family."

I freeze.

What did he just say? The Blakes? This is a trap. He has me here to get to them and destroy Dylan, Mia, and their parents. I'm an idiot.

"Oh, sorry," he hurries to say. "I think I've scared you. I know the Blakes very well, and I know of your close relationship with them. But don't just trust what I say. I know you have your suspicions, but ask them about me, they'll confirm everything I've said to you."

I don't answer, just nod, feeling insecure and confused about all this.

"Well, we've arrived," he says, stopping his vehicle in front of the building where I live. "I trust you will follow Lisa's instructions to take care of your injuries, yes? It was fortunate that my boys found you at the right moment. Otherwise, who knows what would have happened."

"The guys who helped me were *your* people?" I say, bewildered.

"Of course they were. In fact, they were on their way to bring you to me. It was about time we met." Taddeus turns to one of the bodyguards in the back seat and says, "Give him back his teleCard."

The gorilla-faced guy disconnects my teleCard from a handheld device it had been connected to this whole time and hands it to me.

"That device modifies the tracking signal," explains Taddeus. "Your movements and location have been altered since they found you in the alley."

We say goodbye with a handshake. I get out of the car and wait for him to leave, then watch the car until it turns the corner and disappears. I stand there for several seconds without moving, on the curb of the sidewalk, with lost eyes and confused thoughts.

This unexpected encounter with Taddeus Green, a supposed rebel leader, has left me with a lot to digest in a couple of minutes. I think about Dylan. It's not long until I see him. I need to tell him about this and hear his opinion. I need to be with him.

It's already past eight when I enter the apartment.

I feel tremendously happy to see my mother and Lily, healthy and safe, preparing dinner. Though my mother doesn't feel the same way when she sees my beaten face.

"Derin! Darling, what happened to you?"

She runs toward me. She's about to grab my face with both hands, but stops a few inches before touching me, afraid of hurting me.

"It's nothing, Mom," I say quietly. "A small disagreement with another agent who wasn't happy with my presence at the police station. You should see his face."

I don't sound very convincing, but it seems I've managed to persuade both her and Lily that it was nothing serious, that I've been taken care of at the police station's infirmary.

To my great relief, they don't mention anything related to the executions and my star appearance in the official news broadcast. I relax. They haven't seen the images. Now I realize that it wasn't a given that they would see the transmission—unless they were near a public television—since they no longer have teleCards. I have to leave soon, so I decide not to reveal what happened at the moment, though I'll have to tell them eventually.

While I hurriedly eat some bread with cheese, the two of them tell me that things have gone better than expected. They were treated with kindness by the Administrative Council and were assigned tasks as part of the cleaning team in charge of this very building's maintenance. It occurs to me that maybe Taddeus Green also had something to do with this. If so, I wouldn't know how to thank him. I can't even begin to understand why he's helping us.

Visibly happy, they tell me that Mrs. Watson, the friendly neighbor who brought us baskets of food this morning with her daughter, is the maintenance manager, so they'll work with her. The work is demanding, but bearable. And Mrs. Watson is "a sweetheart."

"We finished today at about six o'clock," says my mother, "and then Mrs. Watson gave us directions to a well-stocked store around the corner. We were able to buy some things at very good prices. I hardly spent twenty pounds!"

I gather Mrs. Watson didn't see me on TV either, but I wonder if she's learned about it all by now. I must figure out a way to tell my mother the truth before somebody else does.

"That's excellent news, Mom!" I reply. Then I get out of my chair. "I need to clean up a bit before going out to meet Dylan."

I stand in front of the bathroom mirror and see my bruised and still somewhat swollen face for the first time. Lisa's mask is exceptional, but it hasn't worked a miracle. I feel a sudden hatred toward Bennet and his henchmen. Not because of the pain they caused me, but because I don't want Dylan to see me like this.

⁓

I RECKON IT'S PAST NINE O'CLOCK when I turn onto Down the River Alley. I hope I'm not delayed more than a couple of minutes; I would hate to arrive late to my *date* with Dylan. I don't know the exact time since my wristwatch was also a victim of today's beating and rendered useless, and, obviously, I didn't take my teleCard with me. The tracking device will record that I spent a quiet night inside the apartment.

I enter the pub, leaving my jacket's hood on. I dread being recognized by anyone. But nobody seems to care about me, and I'm surprised by how busy and cheerful the place is. There are people at almost every table. The bar is overflowing, and an intense but pleasant hubbub fills the atmosphere: a nice mixture of laughter, carefree conversations, and music that I've never heard before.

I stop and gaze around the room, looking for Dylan, and locate him immediately.

He's at the back of the pub, in the same booth overlooking the canal where we were a few days ago. He stands up and beckons me with his hand.

My heart races and I'm filled with joy, but also with fear.

I walk toward him, and he smiles at me, which is a good sign. But as I get just a few steps from him, his expression changes abruptly.

"Derin! What happened to you?" he asks, alarmed.

"It's nothing, don't worry," I answer, ashamed to be seen like this, but more ashamed of what he might think of me if he saw me on the broadcast. "I'll tell you everything in a moment."

We sit face to face. There's a jug of beer and two glasses on the table. Dylan serves us both, and I take a big sip. The cold beer tastes delicious and sits well with me. Next, I begin my account of recent events.

He listens attentively, without interrupting, as I tell him everything from the moment I went to the police station in Sector 7 this morning. I can't avoid the strange fascination I have with observing the different emotions dancing across his face according to the part of the story we're in: surprise, disturbance, indignation, curiosity, compassion, pain… All bewitch me; there isn't one that I don't like. I can't stop staring at him.

His eyes and lips make me feel an unfamiliar weakness.

I have to make an effort not to lose the thread of our conversation, or look like a fool since I'm drooling. I'm afraid he'll notice how nervous I get when we're alone. I'm an idiot! But I manage to concentrate. I even think I give a pretty decent account of the day.

When I get to the shootings, to the moment they called me to join the firing squad, I stop. Inside, I'm dying of shame and sadness. He understands the reason for my hesitation and says:

"I know. I saw it. I know everything is fake. It's disgusting how they edited the images to portray you like that as if you were a bloodthirsty monster, the total opposite of what you are in reality. I'm so sorry."

My heart melts when I realize that he never doubted my innocence.

"What happened, really?" he asks.

I continue my report, telling him what actually happened in Fountain Square. I explain how Bennet set everything up to make me look like a depraved asshole.

When I start explaining that my injuries are from bullies sent by Bennet, I avoid giving too many details. I don't want to look like a victim, nor do I want him to feel sorry for me. In fact, I'm ashamed to confess that they left me unconscious and I couldn't defend myself, even though it would be absurd to imagine that I could've done anything against five attackers.

"They're animals," he says. "I'm so sorry they did that to you."

I notice with excitement that his hand is moving inch by inch toward mine.

For a brief moment, I'm convinced he'll touch me. But when our hands are on the verge of meeting, he stops, as if unsure of whether to continue. For my part, I can't overcome my own insecurity to grab his hand. So it remains a frustrated moment, one that could have been, at least for me, something wonderful.

I scold myself for my lack of courage.

Am I reading too much into this? Am I giving these little moments deeper meaning than they really have? Is it possible that Dylan's interest in me is based solely on friendship and his kind nature, nothing else?

It wrecks me to consider the possibility that I've fallen in love like a fool, that my hope that he feels the same way is based on illusion. But his signals have been clear, haven't they? The hugs, the way he talks and looks at me when we're alone, his evident interest in my life and everything that concerns me… I don't know what's happening to me.

Maybe he's as shy as I am in these matters. Perhaps it's up to me to take the first step, but I'm terrified to do something that isn't reciprocated and could instead make him uncomfortable. It would be so embarrassing to expose myself like that and realize he doesn't feel the same way.

After everything else that's happened today, rejection would be too humiliating. It would tear me apart.

CHAPTER 18

TOO MUCH SHYNESS

WHEN I MENTION HOW I WOKE IN AN UNKNOWN ROOM, where I had been taken, unconscious, to be treated, Dylan straightens up and then leans even more onto the table, his eyebrows raised and his eyes wide open in amazement. I talk about Lisa and describe in detail the mysterious character of Taddeus Green.

I sense in his reaction that he knows who I'm talking about.

"So he's already gotten in touch with you," he says. "Though I find it strange that Taddeus allowed this to happen, for you to be beaten like that. His men were supposed to follow you."

"How do you know that?" I say, before rushing to ask the question that interests me most: "How do you know Taddeus Green?"

I'm not surprised to hear his explanations.

Since our first conversation in this place, before my family was arrested, I gathered that Dylan had a very close link with the radkers. It wasn't difficult to imagine that many young deels were sympathizers and even active members of the rebel groups. It seemed logical to me, in light of the repression and injustices they suffer under the regime.

Besides, given Dylan's extraordinary technical skills, which both Mia and Brian praised on many occasions, and his superior intelligence and maturity as I witnessed myself, I've thought he would be valuable to the enemies of the Government. So, I'm not astonished to hear what he confesses next.

"I've been an active member of NATFOR," he explains, "the National Forces of the Resistance, since I was fifteen years old. I'm part of the special technology and systems team, headed by my uncle Jonathan."

"So your uncle, too?" I ask, eager for answers.

"Yes. He got into this first after they killed my parents."

He says this casually, but I'm sure he's hiding the pain. I long to hold his hand, but it would seem forced now. I was a moron before when I let the chance pass. It's too late. His hands are interlaced at the edge of the table, close to his body, terribly far away from me; the magical moment has passed.

"How were they killed?" I dare to ask.

"They were murdered by counterterrorism troops," Dylan replies calmly. "Their names were Jeff and Susan Blake. They weren't part of the rebel movement, but they were captured along with other innocent people and executed to intimidate the population, as the Crowley regime's oppressive strategy has always been. I was two."

"I'm so sorry, I can hardly imagine how much you must miss them," I say.

"Sometimes I also have to *imagine* how I miss them," he replies innocently. "I mean, I force myself to miss them. In reality, I barely remember them. But I'm furious that they were taken from me before I could even get to know them properly."

"I think I get what you mean. So you've lived with your aunt and uncle since then?"

"Yes. They took care of me and welcomed me as their own child," he says. "Even though I call them aunt and uncle, they're really like my parents."

"Your father was your uncle Jonathan's brother?"

"That's right. He was the younger of the two; they were very close. When they killed him and my mother, my uncle swore he wouldn't rest until he got revenge. From then on, he devoted all his efforts to the insurgent cause and fought to end the Crowley regime. Over the last ten years, he's become a prominent figure. His technological contributions have been invaluable for many of the rebels' most significant strikes."

I always imagined that the Blakes were a simple family from the Strip. I couldn't have been more wrong.

"And your aunt?" I say next. "I suppose she and Mia are aware of everything, right?

"Of course," he replies with a charming smile. "My aunt Belinda is a doctor at a hospital in Sector 4, but she also runs a clandestine clinic where they treat wounded rebels returning from missions against government forces. Mia also knows; we have no secrets at home."

Suddenly it occurs to me that perhaps Brian was aware of all this, but Dylan is one step ahead of my thoughts.

"Your brother didn't know a thing," he says. "I'm sure it never even crossed his mind to suspect anything. We're very careful about this."

"I can imagine," I reply, realizing for the first time that Dylan and his entire family belong to those who, until very recently, I was supposed to consider "enemies of the people," and therefore also my enemies. It's amazing how the perspective on things can change so radically.

I smile at him, and we both pause briefly to drink our beers. When I put my glass back on the table, I feel a sudden pang in my side that makes me wince.

"You're not well. My aunt has to see you," Dylan says, frowning and shaking his head. "You must let her examine you."

"It's not necessary," I answer, flattered that he's showing concern for my wellbeing. "Lisa treated me wonderfully, and she's given me something great for the pain, I promise."

"That's all well and good, but I insist that my aunt see you, she's the best," he repeats in a sweet but firm tone.

How can I refuse when he asks so charmingly?

"Besides," he adds, "my aunt Belinda is eager to meet you. Plus, it's best you meet my uncle as soon as possible. We live nearby, and I've come on my scooter, so we'll arrive in no time."

"All right, let's drink up and then go, though it's really not necessary. But I do want to meet them."

While we finish the rest of the beer, I try to process everything he's told me. Suddenly, a disturbing thought regarding my brother's capture explodes in my mind, and I can't stop myself from sharing it with him.

"Dylan, wait!" I say in an alarmed tone. "What if the state intelligence discovered that your family is involved with the rebels, and that's why they captured Brian? Perhaps they made inquiries about your uncle's inner circle and discovered Brian and Mia's relationship. They might have captured him to get information about your uncle, and who knows what else."

The instant I say such stupidity, I feel ashamed, aware of how irrational I must have sounded. If the Government knew anything about the Blake family's relationship with the insurgents, the CATs would have captured Mia and Dylan that same day, since they were in the same place as Brian. I know that my brother's capture was a coincidence, an unfortunate turn of fate, although of course a welcome surprise for Nigel, who unexpectedly encountered me again and took the opportunity to make me suffer; or to force me to do something, though I'm not sure yet what.

Dylan gives me a compassionate look and says patiently:

"No, Derin, that's not it. We're pretty sure the Government doesn't know about us yet. Believe me, Brian had no idea about all this."

"I know, I know," I say, feeling like a child scolded by an adult. "Forgive me, it's so silly. It's just that… maybe that blow to my head left my mind a bit dazed."

"All the more reason for my aunt to examine you," he replies, with the most adorable look I can imagine.

I return his smile and lower my gaze, still somewhat embarrassed. I look at his interlaced hands, and it occurs to me that they're perfect, neither too small nor too big. It hurts to think that I could have had them between mine a moment ago.

As I try to find a way to vindicate myself for such a foolish comment, something pops up in my mind, and this time it's something intelligent and appropriate.

"But in any case," I say, looking him in the eye, "Brian's situation does put you in danger. Even though the attack was a charade and Brian had nothing to do with it, we can't rule out that an overenthusiastic investigator, acting on his own initiative, might look into Brian's life more thoroughly. His relationship with Mia will raise some red flags, and could put you and your uncle at risk."

"You're right about that," he says. "Of course, we've considered that possibility from the start. That's why Mia won't be going back to London. She sent a message to the family she works for, saying that she caught a virus and doesn't want to spread it to the children. We don't think they'll be suspicious for at least another two or three weeks. As for me," he continues after a brief hesitation, "I can't miss work. It's… important."

"Really? Why?"

"It's a bit complicated. I'll tell you another day, okay?"

"Sure, no problem," I say, though I can't help but feel slightly disappointed that he doesn't tell me now.

Then I consider whether to tell him about my relationship with Nigel Crowley and the last encounters I had with him, but I decide it's better to wait until I meet his uncle. It's important that he also listens to what I have to share on that subject.

We enjoy the last sips of beer while we chat about the music blasting throughout the pub. It's coming from the colorfully illuminated jukebox, which had caught my attention the other day I was here. I don't know any of the songs, but I like the melodies, the sounds, and the voices.

"It's pre-war music," Dylan explains. "Popular at the time, but banned by the regime when they decided to close the borders."

"That's what I thought," I reply. "It's difficult to find this banned stuff in London."

"My uncle and I repaired this jukebox for Georgie, you know," he says, and I notice a flash of pride in his voice and expression. "It turned out pretty good. I also have an electronic device with hours of 'forbidden' music at home. If you're interested, I could play you some of my favorite songs."

"Of course I'm interested," I let out excitedly. "I'd love to hear them."

He nods and smiles, satisfied, as he takes the final sip of his beer. I can't wait for him to share the songs he likes most with me. It would be something special, something intimate. I would also like to share many things about me: what I like, what I detest, funny situations from my childhood, my dreams, my goals. Anything, as long as I can be alone with him and forget this nightmare surrounding us.

When we finish our beers, we get up, put on our jackets, and make our way through the lively crowd. We try to find Georgie, but there are so many people at the bar that we decide to leave without saying goodbye. Fine with me; I'm still afraid someone might recognize me, even with the jacket's hood over my head.

I shiver when we step outside and wish I had put on a thicker jacket. Dylan's motor scooter stands about thirty feet from the pub, fastened with a thick chain and padlock to a power line post.

"Better to be safe than sorry," he explains as he removes the chain. "It took me two years to get all the missing spare parts to repair Nancy."

"You call your scooter *Nancy*?" I ask, raising my eyebrows and smiling.

"I know, it sounds a bit silly, but she was my parents', one of the few things they left me, and they used to call her that, I don't know why. My uncle kept her for me until I was older. All this time, she stood unused in a corner of my uncle's workshop, and we always referred to her as Nancy. When I finished repairing her, I kept calling her that. She's beautiful, isn't she?"

Each and every one of his musings is enchanting. He's so cute that I'd love to hug him right now and never let him go.

Dylan gets on Nancy and slides forward so I can get onto the remaining seat space behind him. He puts on his helmet and, before switching on the engine, turns his head back and says:

"Um… you don't have your teleCard on you, right?"

"No, of course not," I reply with a hint of reproach. "I left it in the apartment."

His question wounds my pride a bit. It would never cross my mind to put him in danger by letting the teleCard register where I was tonight. But I can't blame him for wanting total certainty. The risk is too high.

I'm not wearing a helmet, so the icy air lashes my injured face as we drive through the streets of Sectors 5 and 4. Under different circumstances, the journey would be extremely uncomfortable—every bump in the road shoots a twinge of pain all over my bruised body—but being close to Dylan and holding on to his hips, I feel such freedom and joy that I beg the universe to never make us reach our destination. I'd love to wrap my arms around him and rest my chin on his shoulder. But I don't dare.

The trip is too short. In less than ten minutes, we arrive at the Blakes'. Their apartment is located on a block formed by several buildings about ten or twelve levels high, all with grim appearances in different shades of grey—like most buildings I've seen in the Strip. As we go up in the elevator, Dylan explains that it's not very common for these types of buildings to have lifts or any technical infrastructure. But in some, neighbors have organized themselves and together repaired or installed central heating, drinking water, and other amenities. He also tells me that all the buildings in this block communicate with each other, and, besides residences, they contain other things like small businesses and offices. His uncle, for example, has an electromechanical workshop—his "official" occupation—on the ground floor and basement of the corner building. His aunt's clinic also operates nearby.

We arrive at the Blakes' apartment on the top level.

We go in, and the first thing I notice is its spaciousness and welcoming atmosphere. At first glance, I see nothing luxurious—the furniture and accessories seem simple and, in many cases, restored and remodeled—but everything is tasteful, neat, and clean. The space immediately feels like a home. Though lacking great comforts, they've managed to build a more than decent place to live.

Mia's the first one to come out and meet us.

"Derin, what a surprise!" she gushes, but she notices my injuries at once, as expected. "My God! What happened?"

"It's nothing, don't worry, I just…" I begin to explain, but her parents also come into the living room, and I stop.

"Aunt, Uncle, this is Derin," says Dylan, and I don't miss the huge smile he shoots at his aunt, Belinda.

I instantly realize that the Blakes are lovely people. Jonathan is taller than me and older than I imagined, but I remember that Brian once mentioned Mia's father was several years older than her mother. He has a stern face and wears glasses, but smiles with great kindness.

Belinda Blake catches me by surprise. She reminds me of Mia, partly because she's so young—she could pass as her sister. But while Mia has a rather sweet, shy, and vulnerable personality, her mother is a bundle of energy and joviality. She speaks loudly and quickly, like a machine gun, with a cheerful and determined tone. I've only been at the Blakes' for a few seconds, and I already know Belinda's the one who runs things around here.

"Good Lord, honey! What happened to you?" she exclaims, her eyes widening like saucers as she notices my injured face.

"Those bastards gave him a beating for what happened this afternoon," says Dylan, answering on my behalf. There's no doubt they know exactly what he's talking about. "Aunt, you must examine him."

"Absolutely, right away," Belinda replies as she grabs my arm. "Come with me, Derin. Let's see what they've done to you."

She leads me to a separate room, which I'm guessing is a study or guest room. The others stay behind in the living room. I hear Dylan telling his uncle and Mia the news he's learned from me.

Belinda asks me to undress, keeping only my underwear on, and sit on the bed. I follow her instructions without hesitation and try to answer all her questions accurately. In particular, she wants precise answers to her inquiries about who treated my injuries and how. I'm relieved that the others stayed back, as it would have been quite uncomfortable for everyone to look at me, almost naked, while the doctor examined me.

Belinda is entirely satisfied with what she hears and sees. She approves of Lisa's treatment and confirms her diagnosis: the blows are superficial, no serious damage, no broken bones or anything. I'll be fine. She also approves of the masks and ointment that Lisa gave me, and she only hands me a few extra pills. She says they'll help a lot with the swelling and will relieve the pain even more.

CHAPTER 19

HOPE AND MANIPULATION

BACK IN THE LIVING ROOM, we join the rest of the Blakes, and Jonathan asks us to sit down. Someone has set tea and cookies on the coffee table. As if we had all unconsciously agreed, Jonathan and Belinda sit down on the three-seat sofa, while Dylan and I take the two-seater. I don't miss the expression on Belinda's face as she gazes at Dylan and me sitting side by side; she looks at him with a knowing smile. I turn my head a little to the right, toward Dylan, trying to make out his reaction. I could swear he stares back at his aunt with reproach. He seems to blush.

It's probably just my imagination because I'd love for it to be true, but I have the feeling that he and his aunt share secrets and confidences, some of which have to do with me. When she turns her eyes toward me with the same expression she showed to Dylan, I'm sure about my conclusions. I immediately look away from her glance and feel my cheeks heating.

Has he talked to her about me in a particular way? Has he hinted that he's interested in me? Or is she so perceptive that she realizes on her own the intense attraction between us? I deliberate, unable to decide whether I feel pleased or embarrassed. Meanwhile, Mia does the honors of serving us tea and then sits down on one of the two armchairs in front of us.

"You don't know how sorry we are that your family has to go through this," Belinda says. Jonathan expresses the same compassion, though with far fewer words, only nodding at what his wife says. "And, of course, we share your pain," she adds, looking at Mia, who nods sadly. "What they've done to your father and Brian is awful, I can't imagine how your mother is feeling. You should know that we love Brian, and his situation affects us greatly."

"Thank you very much," is the only thing I can think of saying.

I always assumed that Brian visited Mia's home, but because of the rift between us, I never knew for sure, until now. For a second, I'm alarmed—perhaps he wasn't careful enough in his visits to the Strip. He might have risked travel using his teleCard and thus left a trail. That would further endanger Mia and her family. However, I dismiss that fear. Brian may be careless in many things, but I'm sure he was always cautious about this and paid bribes at the access point to enter and exit without a trace.

"How are your mother and your sister coping?" Jonathan asks.

"Well, they're very affected by all this," I reply. "But so far, I'm surprised by their strength. Everything's been so unexpected and violent, and it's happened so quickly. Sometimes it's hard for us to believe that it's really happening."

"Yes, of course, it's terrible," he says. "We were thinking that maybe Belinda could go to see them tomorrow and offer them some support."

"I'd appreciate that," I say, turning to Belinda. "I'm sure your visit would do them lots of good."

"Of course, honey," she replies. "It's the least I can do."

After this brief exchange of courtesies, Jonathan recaps what Dylan told him while Belinda was examining me. He asks me to add details to some parts he has questions about and to confirm that everything he repeats is correct. He's a very meticulous person who wants to be certain about every aspect. As for my meeting with the rebel leader, he explains that he knew Taddeus would contact me, although, like Dylan, he too seems surprised by the way things have turned out.

"I don't understand how he let them hurt you," he says, frowning. "I'm guessing you weren't aware of it, but Taddeus has had people watching you ever since you got here. Naturally, they couldn't intervene in the unpleasant matter at Fountain Square, but I'm pretty sure the beating could've been prevented."

"Well, don't worry." I shrug my shoulders slightly and shake my head in an attempt to downplay the issue. "At least they arrived when they did, it could've been worse." I pause and then add, "What I don't quite understand are Taddeus' intentions. Why is he so interested in me?"

"That's a bit complicated," says Jonathan, and hesitates for a moment. I sense he's deliberating what he can and can't tell me. Then he continues, "Look, I don't know every detail and motive of Taddeus' plans, but what I do know is that his interest in you and your family is based on two issues: first, the strange relationship between you and Nigel Crowley, and second, the risk to a very important insurgent mission caused by the unfortunate capture of your brother. We can assume these issues are related, can't we?"

Wow, he goes straight to the point. His knowledge about what's between Nigel and me takes me by surprise. I wasn't ready to talk about this so soon.

"Well… um…" I start stuttering and notice Dylan's inquisitive expression. "It's true, I know Nigel Crowley personally," I go on. "He was one of my instructors at the Military Academy several years ago. I went to see him and try to intervene on Brian's behalf after he was captured. I suppose my pleas to help Brian had something to do with his pardon, especially considering that he was innocent and the attack was a charade and all that. But his capture was a coincidence, I don't think it had anything to do with him being my brother. It was simply bad luck."

"Are you sure about that?" Jonathan insists.

"I can't explain it otherwise."

"That's fine," he says. "But Taddeus will want to know everything about it. You must be prepared to answer him without omitting details."

This is so embarrassing. Now I'm sure that Jonathan is aware of everything. In his own discreet way, he's made that clear to me. I thank him in my mind for not insisting more on this matter. It would be too awkward to talk about it in front of everyone, and besides, I want to tell the most intimate details of my relationship with Nigel to Dylan first.

"But what did you say about an important mission?" I ask, both because I want to hear the answer and also divert the conversation from the topic of Nigel and Derin. "A mission is at risk due to Brian's capture?"

"That's right," Jonathan replies. "His capture, for whatever reason it happened, has meant an unforeseen risk for us, with possibly disastrous consequences." He gestures to his family with one hand. "By this point, you're probably aware of how closely we're linked to the rebel cause. If some bureaucrats snooped around Brian's background—let's say to show off to Commander Crowley—they would immediately find Mia and Dylan and all of us."

"That's exactly what I was saying to Dylan recently!" I exclaim, trying to meet Dylan's eyes. "You're in great danger because of this mess."

"Yes, well, we're aware of that and have taken necessary precautions," Jonathan replies. "But what really worries Taddeus is that if they keep track of Mia, they'll immediately find Dylan. And if something happens to Dylan, the rebel operation collapses."

Speechless, I turn my head toward Dylan. He shrugs his shoulders and cracks a mischievous smile.

"What do you mean?" I ask, burning with curiosity. "Are you saying the rebel operation depends on Dylan?"

"That's right," Jonathan replies and throws a proud glance at his nephew. "He's the mission's master key, so to speak. But let's not get ahead of ourselves. You'll find out everything in due course.

I want you to come to a very special event tomorrow evening, a meeting of several insurgent leaders. There will be many people from all over the country, and Taddeus will make a very illuminating presentation. You must come. We'll talk to him then."

"Of course!" I answer, quick as a bullet. I now have an incredible thirst to know as much as possible about the rebels and their plans, especially concerning Dylan.

Jonathan pauses for a long time as if trying to decide whether or not to tell me what's on his mind. Finally, he continues:

"There's something I can tell you to cheer you up, but I must ask you not to raise your hopes too much," he says in a serious tone. "Taddeus' plan, which I referred to earlier, might also include the possibility of rescuing Brian and your father."

This truly stuns me.

"What? What are you saying?"

"That it's possible we'll rescue Brian and your father," repeats Jonathan.

Just hearing about a possible rescue fills me with hope.

"But… what are you talking about? Is this for real?" I notice slight smiles and glimmers of hope in Belinda's eyes and especially in Mia's, which confirm that Jonathan is serious about this. "But how? When? How can I help? I'll do anything you ask me, as long as we get them out of there," I say in an almost euphoric state.

"Be patient, you must wait a little longer," Jonathan answers. "You'll soon know everything. I can confirm that they're well; they've arrived at Ventus and are already working."

A comforting sense of optimism fills my soul. They're alive. And there's a possibility of rescuing them. Now everything seems possible.

"Liam and his father are at the same location and also doing well," he adds.

The Mitchells! I've been so absorbed in my own misfortune that it hadn't occurred to me to think about their whereabouts. I feel ashamed because their misery is equal to ours.

"That's good," I answer. "Do you know anything about Catherine and Nick Mitchell, Liam's mother and brother?"

"Yes, they've arrived in the Strip," he says, "They're fine, somewhere in Sector 11, but they haven't been contacted yet. If this matter regarding the rescue of Brian and your father goes ahead, we'll try to rescue the Mitchells as well."

It's almost midnight when Jonathan offers to take me back to the apartment in Sector 7. Dylan immediately objects and announces that he'll take me on his scooter, and I pray that this will happen.

"No, Dylan, better not," Jonathan replies. "Remember you have the early shift tomorrow. You can't risk being late and getting unnecessary attention, much less now."

Dylan agrees, albeit reluctantly.

Just as I was beginning to think Jonathan was a nice guy who I could be friends with, I curse him for depriving me of the pleasure of traveling several miles embracing his nephew's body on his scooter. But he vindicates himself a bit by proposing that Dylan and I meet at Georgie's tomorrow evening at seven and go together to the rebel event. At least I get this comfort: the assurance that I'll see him tomorrow. I have the impression he's disappointed because I didn't talk to him earlier and he had to find out through his uncle that there was something between Nigel and me.

During the ride in his car, Jonathan is very strict about his decision to continue our conversation about the rebels until tomorrow, when we meet with Taddeus.

He does talk about Dylan and his parents, though. He shares how close he and his brother were, the appreciation he had for his sister-in-law and how much he suffered when they were murdered. He emphasizes how much he, Belinda, and Mia love Dylan. He mentions that what matters most to him in the world is the well-being and happiness of his two children—yes, he refers to Dylan as his son. I can't help but feel that when he announces that he won't allow anyone to hurt them, he's hinting at something.

Is he referring to me? Has he also noticed my interest in Dylan and doesn't approve of it? I think, discouraged and somewhat fearful.

—

I ENTER THE APARTMENT QUIETLY, trying not to wake anyone. But I find my mother waiting for me.

"Mom, what are you doing up?" I say disapprovingly, and feeling guilty as well. "You must rest, you need it."

She says nothing, just stands up, comes toward me, and hugs me, relieved.

I should have expected that she wouldn't go to bed until I was back, safe and sound. I should have tried to come back sooner.

I tell her briefly about my meeting with the Blakes, but I don't mention anything about the possibility of rescuing my father and Brian. Before anything else, I have to find out for myself what the rebel plan is all about. I must convince myself that it's a real and feasible option. I couldn't be so cruel to give her high hopes that crumble as quickly as they're raised.

But I still feel electrified thinking of a possible rescue.

Though I almost don't dare to believe it's true, I give in to the fantasy and fall asleep making plans.

With Brian and my father returned to us, I imagine disappearing forever in the unknown depths of the Strip. I see Dylan and me together, in a stable and loving relationship. I get excited thinking about a possible escape for both families, the Darks and the Blakes, to Ireland, where we'll live in peace until the end of our lives. Everything will be happiness and joy.

I wake up cheerful, with the feeling that today will be a great day. During breakfast, my spirits lift even more when I notice that my optimism radiates around me and manages to infect my mother and Lily, who for no apparent reason smile more and, in general, seem less disturbed.

I arrive early at the police station, still in a good mood, but with the unsettling expectation of encountering Bennet. I wonder what his thugs reported to him after beating me up. I hope that after he sees the result of the attack with his own eyes, he'll leave me alone, at least for a while. But I don't see him all morning.

My unit, without Bennet and under Sergeant Spencer's command, goes out again to do surveillance rounds through Sector 7. We return at noon after an uneventful morning. I'm surprised that none of my colleagues, not even Andrew, has said anything about my injuries. In fact, they ignore me and act as if I didn't exist. I wonder if any of them were among the three masked thugs. It doesn't seem too crazy to me; it's even quite probable. Maybe Bennet ordered them to leave me alone for the moment, or perhaps he'll have another surprise waiting for me.

I should be alarmed, but I'm not. The expectation of seeing Dylan again this evening and meeting Taddeus Green to find out about the possible rescue of Brian and my father takes up most of my thoughts.

The afternoon goes by in a similar way to the morning: routine surveillance through the sector, without major news. Even the ominous dark clouds that gather for a while refuse to break into rain. When we return to the police station around five, I'm genuinely relieved. My second day in the security forces has gone by with an almost suspicious calm. It's nothing compared to the traumatic day yesterday, with the shootings and the beating ordered by Bennet, who still has yet to be seen.

However, shortly after our return to the police station, a change becomes evident. I've been in the locker room for a quarter of an hour, cleaning my boots and my uniform, when I notice that something isn't right. First, one of my peers comes in and looks at me very strangely. Then, two others also enter, watching me out of the corner of their eyes and approaching the first one who came in. They discuss something in low voices. The three of them look back at me, but when they realize I'm watching them, they turn around and leave.

When I get out of the locker room, several groups of agents are in the hallway whispering nervously. They follow me with their eyes when I pass in front of them. The atmosphere feels tense and charged. I know that they're talking about me and my senses are on high alert. I turn into a hallway and see Bennet leaving Chief Johnson's office.

Our eyes meet for a moment, but he turns around and walks in the opposite direction. Something weird is going on, and it doesn't bode well.

As I pass by the closed door of Johnson's office, a voice on the other end of the hall calls me:

"Dark, wait!" It's the agent who works as Johnson's assistant and personal secretary. "The chief wants to see you. Right now."

"Chief Johnson?"

"What other chief is there?" he replies, annoyed. "Yes. Now. Go in, he's waiting for you."

I don't have much time to deliberate; I'm already a few steps past his door. I turn one hundred and eighty degrees, go back three steps, knock twice, and go in.

"Dark, come in," Johnson says from behind his desk.

As I come closer, I spot out of the corner of my eye that the wall monitor is on, although the distorted image on the screen is frozen, paused, a grey background with some unintelligible blue squiggles.

"Sit down, I have to talk to you," he adds in a much less aggressive tone than yesterday when he "welcomed" me and made his displeasure at my presence here known.

I sit down and nervously await what he has to say to me.

"Do you always carry your teleCard with you?" he inquires first.

I didn't expect that question at all, but I respond immediately, trying to imagine where he's going with this.

"Yes, of course. I always carry it with me."

Now it dawns on me. I'm in trouble. Somehow, they've figured out that my teleCard has been manipulated by Taddeus' men.

"Have you noticed it acting strange? Have you received any unusual messages?" he continues, while I desperately try to come up with some reasonable argument to explain what happened with my teleCard.

"Um… no, no sir, what do you mean?"

If I don't find a convincing explanation, soon they'll use torture to get the truth out of me: that I've had contact with a rebel leader. I decide that my only option is to inform him of the beating I received yesterday and say that my teleCard must have gotten damaged during it. After all, my wristwatch was wrecked too. Yes, that's what I'll tell him.

But, instead of continuing with the teleCard issue, he starts talking about the beating on his own accord.

"Those injuries." He points to my face with his index finger. "Tell me what happened to you. I'm warning you, I want the truth."

I wasn't expecting this. For a moment, I consider not saying anything about the ambush in the alley and inventing another story instead, like falling down the stairs. But my instinct tells me that he already knows what happened and wants to hear about it from me. So I tell him everything exactly as it happened, until the moment they knocked me unconscious on the pavement. Then I change the story. I tell him that some boys found me, and carried me to my house, where my mother took care of me. I explain that we brought some medicines and a first-aid kit from London.

"Do you have any idea who the thugs were, or who sent them?"

He realizes my hesitation.

"I already told you, I want the truth," he says. "You have nothing to fear."

Something in his tone of voice and behavior tells me that, rather than wanting to intimidate me, he is nervous and disturbed himself. As if he had gotten a scare.

"Well… um," I say, trying to select the right words. "I didn't see the three masked faces, obviously. And I had never seen the other two before. However… um." I clear my throat. "One of them said something so that I'd understand who had sent them. Though I have no way of knowing if it's true or not."

"What did he say?"

"That the order to beat me up came from Lieutenant Bennet."

Chief Johnson nods and doesn't say anything more about it. Instead, he grabs a remote control from his desk and points it toward the wall monitor to play the video that had been paused.

"This is an illegal propaganda message, broadcasted a moment ago by the insurgents, by the enemies of Englandom," he explains. "They managed to infiltrate the government transmission signal. There must be a glitch in your teleCard, which is why you didn't get the message."

So that's why he was asking about my teleCard. Not because he knew it had been tampered with, but because I didn't receive a transmission. I calm down a bit, but it doesn't last long.

When the video on the monitor resumes, I first see the silver-grey background with the blue rose, surrounded by the well-known slogan of the radkers. Then the deep voice of a man describes what appears on the screen next.

They present a collage of images showing government forces, both CAT and security agents of the Strip, violently attacking various groups of deels, including children, women, and the elderly. These images are interspersed with others of Regent Crowley talking about the successes and benefits of his regime. Another series of images shows ragged groups of deel children—apparently from the most impoverished and neglected sectors—scrabbling among mountains of garbage in search of food, while the regent appears praising the wellbeing of the inhabitants of Englandom, who are happy to live in the fair and equitable society of the castes. Next, I see footage from yesterday's demonstration in front of the

Strip's prefecture, showing the security forces brutally attacking the peaceful protesters. The narrator explains that Dictator Crowley intimidates everyone who dares to ask for a little justice, and contrasts the real images of the demonstration with the altered images the Government used for the official transmission.

I realize the rebels have television technicians just as good as the government's because the propaganda spot is of excellent quality. The message is set up well. It's compelling.

When I see the first images of Fountain Square and the shootings, my pulse accelerates.

The narrator describes the bloodbath with horror. In an ardent tone, he reminds the members of the Disloyal caste that all they can ever expect from the criminal, authoritarian regime of Eugene Crowley is oppression, injustice, scarcity, hunger, torture, and death.

But then, to my surprise, he also talks to the Commons caste, and my heart stops when I hear my name.

"Pay close attention, dear members of the Commons, and see what these bastards do to brave Derin Dark, the way they manipulate his courage to punish him even more as if it wasn't enough what they've already done to him and his family."

The unedited images leave me stupefied: there's Bennet calling me for the firing squad … now he asks me to take off my helmet … there's the girl tied to the post and … the moment I missed the shot, obviously on purpose, and then Bennet pushing me down on the pavement and murdering the innocent girl. The narrator says it's not necessary to explain who I am, because the whole country knows, but nevertheless reminds viewers of recent events.

He describes me as an exemplary, honest, kind, and decent citizen, someone with such an untarnished concept of justice that even under threat of punishment, I haven't given in to orders to execute a girl. I'm an admirable son of the nation, banished and harassed unfairly. I represent all those praiseworthy virtues that the oppressive regime of the Crowleys detests and intends to eliminate.

As if it weren't enough to be presented to the country in such a heroic way, now they've set out to paint me as little less than a martyr.

I'm stunned to see footage of the five men beating me in the alley. They leave me lying there, half dead. It blows my mind how violent the beating apparently was. I don't understand how the rebels got hold of those shots. They're so clear and professional—it's impossible not to recognize me. I have to rule out that these images are a product of mere chance. But what impresses me most are close-ups of my face and my body, beaten and bloodied. It's me, motionless on the pavement. No doubt they took those shots before bringing me to Lisa's house. But the blood... is fake. I never had open wounds, only bruises.

This is a lot to take in. I'm disoriented, and my head hurts. What's Taddeus playing at, exposing me and using me this way? Because there's no other explanation; I don't doubt for a second that he's behind this. He's used me for a smear campaign against the Government. He's put me at the center of a message that ridicules and humiliates the regime and the regent. I fear the consequences.

Maybe it's the price I have to pay for the rescue of my father and Brian, but at least they could've warned me.

The rebel's propaganda message ends with a clear incitement to reject Crowley's oppression and join the insurgent cause to bring true justice and freedom to the country.

Johnson turns off the television and fixes his eyes on mine with an indecipherable expression. When he moves his hand toward his desk drawer, I'm sure he'll grab a gun and shoot me in the forehead.

CHAPTER 20

REBELS

BUT CHIEF JOHNSON doesn't grab any gun and doesn't try to kill me either. Instead, he takes out a bottle of pills and swallows three. Then he gives me a rehearsed and repetitive speech ranting about the "scandalous" propaganda video from the insurgents. His attempt at expressing outrage at the way "they've manipulated the images to discredit the Government" is so disastrous that, under other circumstances, the blunt irony of his comments would have been comical. But his reaction makes me cringe, and I almost feel sorry for him. Both his lofty verbal attack against rebel propaganda and his flattering praise of the regime sound ridiculous.

However, I'm still surprised by the profound change in the way he's addressing me: yesterday, he was arrogant and offensive; today, cautious and … frightened.

Although he pretends to be tough, his nerves give him away. Bennet's stupid action has made him look incompetent. He understands that my unnecessary exposure to the cameras—used by the rebels to deliver a humiliating media blitz against the regime—will have serious consequences. I'm sure Nigel Crowley himself has conveyed his anger directly to him.

I don't know what will have provoked Nigel's anger more: the fact that I was beaten up and left half-dead without his consent—I remember how he demanded that I take care of my appearance—or the foolish action of an insignificant lieutenant that allowed the rebels to obtain such compromising images. Images showing me as the good guy, which were then used to expose and unmask the Government's own propaganda in a shameful and highly explosive way.

Chief Johnson orders me to go to the police station's infirmary at once to be examined and to make sure there's no significant damage. Afterward, he wants me to go home. He also orders me to see him again tomorrow morning as soon as I arrive at the police station. His sudden concern for my wellbeing confirms that a higher authority has contacted and reprimanded him, or rather, threatened him.

The unnecessary medical examination doesn't take too long. They confirm everything I've already heard twice, first from Lisa and then from Belinda Blake. They prescribe and give me the same medicines and ointments that I already have.

On my way home, with my head full of anxieties bouncing in all directions, I try to make sense of the events that occurred in Johnson's office. I have so many questions to ask Taddeus that I wouldn't know where to start.

When I enter the apartment building, I run into my mother and Lily, who are waiting for the elevator. Lily appears calm, but my mother's acting disturbed. I immediately know what's happened. I don't need to ask if they've seen it live or if they've been informed by others. They've learned about the rebel broadcast.

"Is all that true, Derin?" asks my mother.

Maybe I shouldn't have waited to tell her what happened yesterday, but, in my defense, I could have never predicted the rebels would use me to launch a propaganda counterattack. In less than twenty-four hours, I've been exposed before the eyes of the whole country again. This time, however, in much more favorable terms.

"We'll talk about it, Mom," I answer. "Let's go up to the apartment first, I'll explain everything there."

They didn't see the broadcast, but they were told about it in great detail by Mrs. Watson, who also commented that everybody's talking about the surprising action of Derin Dark. As my mother raises her tone of voice, scolding me for not having told the truth, her anxiety and nervousness become more intense too.

"Mom, listen to me," I say firmly, but with a soothing tone of voice, "you can't fall apart now."

"Derin, how am I not supposed to fall apart? I just can't take it anymore. I'm going crazy. Not a day goes by without some horrible shock. I can't hold it together any longer! I'd rather they kill us in one fell swoop so that this nightmare ends!"

She's so upset that I'm afraid she's about to suffer a nervous breakdown. I try my best to reassure her, but nothing I say works. Aware that I don't have much time, since I must leave soon for Georgie's to meet Dylan, I decide to mention the one thing I would have preferred to hold back until I was absolutely sure.

"Mom," I say, taking her hand and looking into her eyes. "There are reasons to be optimistic, believe me. There's a chance we'll rescue Dad and Brian."

My mother's eyes half-close in a skeptical expression.

"And when we get them back, we'll disappear forever," I add.

"But, Derin, what are you saying? What are you talking about?"

I've piqued her interest. I can see a glimmer of hope in her eyes.

"It's true, Mom. I've met the leader of the insurgency, and he's told me himself that they'll help us rescue them."

I tell her the short version of my meeting with Taddeus Green and the conversation I had with Jonathan Blake about the possible rescue of Brian and my father. I insist that I'll get more details after my next meeting with them tonight. I beg her not to raise her hopes too high, but my pleas to contain her enthusiasm are in vain. She and Lily embrace me and embrace each other, alternating between nervous giggles and tears.

I hope I won't regret telling her this, but I had to do something to lift her spirits. Lily amazes me again with her display of strength. Even though she also breaks down a bit when she sees my mother crying, in general, she gives an impression of serenity and resistance that I've never seen in her before.

The anticipation of an early reunion with my father and Brian, which my mother already takes for granted, is more powerful than the fears generated by my involuntary involvement in the insurgent video. And not even the danger of my imminent meeting with the rebels, now voluntary and desired, is intimidating enough to ruin this moment of joy and hope.

So, apart from her pleas that I be extremely careful, my mother isn't at all opposed to me going out again tonight to take part in the rebel event.

Once again, I'm overcome with a guilty conscience for leaving them alone, but a second before I leave the apartment, Belinda Blake shows up at our doorstep. I remember suddenly that last night she offered to come over.

"Belinda, you're so kind!" I say gratefully. "It's so generous of you to come and see them."

"Oh, it's nothing, darling, it's the least I could do," she says, then turns to my mother and my sister. "Nice to meet you, Emma. And you, Lily, are even more beautiful than Mia described."

Belinda is once again a bundle of positive energy, releasing her words like a machine gun. Her comforting effect on my mother and Lily is immediate and undeniable.

This woman may be somewhat fast-paced, but any flaw in this is more than compensated by her contagious enthusiasm.

"Mia and Jonathan left for the meeting together," she says. Then, with a wink of her right eye, she adds: "Dylan must be at Georgie's already, no doubt eager to see you, so go on, honey. Go, I'm staying here with these girls."

I'm paralyzed. Did she really say that? Eager to see me?

Belinda turns to my mother, smiles at her and, with another exaggerated wink, continues:

"Aren't our boys cute?"

I want to sink into the ground. I can't believe what she's doing. My mother isn't sure how to react and only smiles back. She avoids looking me in the eye.

By saying that Dylan is "eager" to see me and that we're both "cute"—along the lines of "a cute couple"—Belinda's left no room for doubt. She's insinuating that there's something between us. She must assume that my mother and Lily are aware of this, or she doesn't give a damn that they find out now in such an embarrassing way.

Before the blushing on my face becomes too noticeable, I say goodbye quickly and leave. I'm consumed with nerves and shame as I imagine that later tonight my mother will want to ask me about what Belinda said. Or worse, they're talking about what's going on between Dylan and me right now.

I'm thankful to Belinda with all my heart for her kindness, but there was really no need to expose me like that. Now I have no choice but to sit down and talk to my mother about this issue, however uncomfortable. Because I know her. Though she has always avoided talking about personal matters with me, she's made a point on more than one occasion that she would like me to be able to discuss anything with her.

Belinda's comments have been so blunt that my mother isn't going to wait for me to start the conversation. She'll ask me directly.

—

I ARRIVE AT GEORGIE'S EARLIER THAN AGREED, and I'm glad that I'm not late this time around. I see "Nancy" chained to the same electricity pole as last night, and I can't help but smile as a wave of blissful expectation runs through my body. I enter the pub just when it starts to rain. I could see it coming all afternoon, judging from the dark clouds covering more and more of the sky. I'm sure to get soaked on the way to the insurgent event since my jacket isn't waterproof.

I locate Dylan as soon as I come in. He's at the bar, talking animatedly with Georgie. She sees me first and gives Dylan a funny signal to tell him to look toward the entrance. He turns his head and welcomes me with the most charming smile, opening his eyes like a child who's excited to get a surprise. I smile back and eat him up with my eyes.

"Derin, how are you? Everything okay?" he says with his velvety voice as I approach him. I know he's referring to the rebel video.

"Hi. Well, what can I say?" I reply. "Surprised? Perplexed? I'm not sure."

I hadn't planned on it, but we spontaneously half hug each other, from just one side, because Dylan's afraid of hurting me. Even though the embrace isn't like the intimate interlocked grip from the night I arrived in the Strip, I enjoy it just as much. I catch a hint of his scent. I would like to get drunk on his smell; it drives me crazy.

"I can imagine," he says. "I haven't seen it yet, but I've been told about it. I'm surprised they didn't warn you beforehand… because you didn't know anything, did you?"

"No, of course not, that's why I was so confused."

Two things draw my attention: Dylan didn't know anything about the rebel propaganda video, and he didn't get the transmission on his special teleCard either.

Georgie, who did watch the broadcast, spares no praise for my "heroic behavior," and repeats three times that she's never met someone so brave and noble.

"It's disgusting what those beasts did to you," she says in an outraged tone before leaving us to tend to other customers.

Dylan says it's getting late and we better leave now.

"Wait a second," I say, holding him back by the arm. "I want to tell you something. I mean, I want to offer you an explanation, to apologize."

"Apologize? What for?" he says, frowning. "What are you talking about?"

"The business with Nigel Crowley, what's between us… I'm sorry I didn't tell you before. I wanted you to be the first to know, but I couldn't find the right moment."

Dylan cracks his unique smile, the one I've begun to adore, that he uses to express a peculiar mixture of innocence, compassion, and mischief.

"Derin," he says, "It's all right, you don't have to apologize for anything. How could you think I'd get angry about something like that? Look, we have to go now, but you can tell me when you think it's a good time, okay?"

"Okay, it's a deal," I reply.

I wasn't wrong about the rain. It's not a heavy curtain of water like a summer storm, but it's coming down enough to get through to my skin. I feel cold even to my bones, but I don't care. Lava and ash could be falling from the sky, and I'd still be happy, so close to Dylan, holding him by the waist, daring to tighten my arms a little more around him.

The journey takes us a half hour. Judging by the direction we're going and the areas we're crossing, I guess we're headed to somewhere in Sector 13 or 14. We move through a very dense block, changing directions so many times on different streets and alleys, which all look the same, that it would be impossible for me to find my way back again. It's like entering a labyrinth made from an endless sequence of concrete buildings. The lack of lighting and street signs don't help matters either.

Dylan begins to slow down. Without turning off the scooter's engine, he stops in front of a metal gate and knocks on it several times with his fist. He waits a moment and, getting no response, knocks again, louder.

After a while, we hear a metallic screech and a small wicket opens up in the middle of the gate, revealing a bearded face with an angry expression.

"What do you want?"

"I'm looking for Mrs. Robinson," Dylan replies in a clear voice, looking into the man's eyes. "I have a package from her daughter."

"Is it the fish?" says the man with the same grumpy tone as before.

"No, it's the cheese."

The man doesn't answer. He directs his penetrating gaze toward me, inspects me with suspicion, and closes the door again. We hear another series of metallic squeaks and clicks, and then the gate slides to the side, allowing us to enter a passageway. When we ride into it, I turn my head to the left and see the bad-tempered man who guards the entrance. He's not alone. Several other men are inside a small room next to the gate. Everyone appears to be armed.

"You know where, right?" the guard asks Dylan, this time in a less gruff tone.

"Yeah, thanks."

We pass through the short tunnel and find ourselves in the open again. We're in a large courtyard surrounded by concrete buildings of seven or eight levels and dotted with wooden sheds. I see bicycles everywhere, several scooters similar to Nancy, and some vehicles. I think I recognize Jonathan's car, but before I can ask Dylan, he's already one step ahead of me:

"They're here, Mia and my uncle," he says, pointing to the grey-green car.

Then he notices a projection on the side of one shed and decides it's an excellent place to park Nancy. We stop next to an iron gate. As he starts to fasten the scooter to the fence with the chain, he turns and looks at me with narrowed eyes and a funny expression on his face: a mixture between adult caution and child shrewdness.

"The rebels all fight for the same noble cause," he says in an earnest tone, "but not everyone is equally honest. A scooter like Nancy could be too much temptation for many of them."

I let out a laugh, which he answers with a playful smile. He's adorable.

He's got such a peculiar way of expressing himself that whatever he says is captivating to me. I could contemplate all his movements, gestures, and expressions for hours. At any given moment, he seems carefree, innocent, somewhat timid, though street-smart and mischievous, but the next instant he turns into a handsome young adult who is serious, mature, intelligent, perhaps too cautious and too responsible for his age. I've never met someone like him. Nobody has ever made me feel this way nor has ever managed to seduce me so intensely without intending to. He has me enchanted.

I can't stand this silent adoration within me for much longer. I have to confess how I feel about him, how much I like him, that I love him. I don't care anymore if I make a fool of myself, and I don't even fear the risk of rejection. I have to tell him that I need him and that it hurts every time I have to be away from him.

We enter one of the buildings, and I follow him through an endless series of corridors. We walk along a long hall, climb a level up on a dark staircase, zigzag through other hallways, and go down two levels. All doors are closed, and we don't see a soul.

"This place has several entrances," he explains while we move along, "and here we're going through a secondary one. Almost nobody knows them all, but I do."

I quickly realize that he knows this place like the back of his hand. He doesn't hesitate even once on our way.

He continues with his explanations. "This is the insurgency's operation center, NATFOR's central command. It's spread across several hidden rooms within this group of buildings. It doesn't look like it, but it has quite sophisticated surveillance tech, protection, and defense systems."

I listen carefully to what he says, but it occurs to me that it wouldn't be a good idea to get lost in this place. I would starve to death here before finding the way out. As we approach a side door at the end of a narrow corridor, I begin to hear a swarm of unintelligible voices.

"We're here," he says, smiling as he stops in front of the door.

When we open it, we're suddenly greeted by the cheerful hubbub of a crowd and a pleasant wave of heat. We go through another corridor and, although we still don't see anyone yet, the increasing volume of the human noises makes it evident that we're getting close.

"This is a big space in the basement that used to be a machinery room or something like that," he explains. "They've transformed it into a multipurpose room, a kind of theater, auditorium, event hall. Well, you'll see."

We continue walking until we find a heavy curtain. Dylan pushes it aside, goes through, and then holds it back so that I can come in too. I drop it behind me and stop for a moment to appreciate what I see.

We're in the gallery or back balcony of a theater, I reckon on the second or third level, from what I can see. The venue is brimming with people. If it was ever a classic theater full of carved wood details, cushioned seats, thick carpets, and luxurious lamps, it's been stripped of all the decoration and comforts, with only the basics left over: a coarse structure of cement, steel, and lumber. There are no chairs or stalls, but wooden bleachers with two levels. I approach the edge of the balcony. On the main level, below, there are no chairs either. A multitude of people talks animatedly, standing in a cramped huddle on the parquet floor.

"Come on," Dylan calls me, gesturing for me to follow him. "I hope Mia has set aside some space in our favorite spot."

When we make our way among the people—mostly teenagers—many of them look at us with curiosity, some of them smiling. We find Mia sitting together with other young people in the bleachers located at the corner, just where the theater's rear gallery bends into the side gallery. She gets up when she sees us and greets me with a big hug. I wince.

"Oh, sorry, Derin!" she exclaims in distress.

"It's nothing, I'm fine," I say, smiling, although, it did hurt a bit.

She introduces me to her friends. As everyone greets me, I realize that I'm not a stranger. Everyone knows who I am. Everyone makes comments that make me feel like they've known me for years, even though I've never seen them before. Other people in the stands are also pointing to the enthusiastic little group around me, or rather, they point to me.

Suddenly, someone touches my back. I turn around and see a girl with short curly hair who can't be much older than my sister Lily.

"Excuse me, you're Derin Dark, right?" she asks, not beating around the bush.

"Um… yes… I'm Derin," I stammer.

"I just wanted to say that you're really brave and we're glad you're here," says the girl, very sure of herself.

"Err… I… thank you," I reply like a fool. She's caught me off guard.

Smiling triumphantly, the girl returns to her group, where her friends receive her with nervous giggles. Dylan comes closer to me and says in a low voice, "Looks like you've got plenty of admirers."

I've been too slow in processing the situation.

What image do the rebels have of Derin Dark? Most likely, all these kids followed the horrible spectacle of the *Trial of the People*. They've been able to get to know my family, they've witnessed the sentence against Brian and my father, and they've seen our caste degradation and banishment. Then later on—yesterday—they saw me as a bloodthirsty monster in the manipulated images of the execution. And today, just a couple of hours ago, they've seen me again in the rebel video, where I was used to unmask the government propaganda and to inspire deels and citizens to join the rebellion against the Crowleys.

My name has been vindicated dramatically. I've been presented as a victim of the regime's cruelty, and as a hero.

I suppose this is how they see me now.

CHAPTER 21

INTERTWINED

I CAN'T THINK OF ANYTHING BETTER TO DO than to smile shyly and thank everybody for their appreciation and solidarity. Not expecting this situation, I wasn't ready to react appropriately to the girl's words. But now that I start analyzing the events of recent days objectively, I can see what's happening more and more clearly.

Without a doubt, the admiration and support I'm receiving are the product of one of the two following alternatives:

On the one hand, if the deels didn't swallow the hoax attack against the regent for a second—as they're so accustomed to the Crowleys' manipulative propaganda—then they'll understand that my family and I are innocent victims of a cruel and blood-thirsty charade. Therefore, they'll see their own pain and anguish suffered under the regime reflected in our suffering. They'll feel compassion and sympathy for us.

On the other hand, if they believe that the attack was real, that is, an actual rebel attack against the dictator, then they must feel ecstatic and grateful to the supposed agents of such a heroic attempt to end repression. They consider us heroes of the insurgent cause, heroes of the Disloyal. Their heroes.

In either case, my family and I will receive a lot of sympathy from the deels, especially among the rebels. Becoming aware of this produces a strange sensation within me, a mixture of pride and gratitude: we're not alone, there are people out there who support and admire us.

There's some movement on the stage at the front of the theater, and the buzz of the audience begins to quiet down. The official part of the rally is about to start. We're sitting on the top row of the stands, and now I understand why Dylan mentioned that Mia would save us places in their favorite spot: from here, we have an unobstructed view. But what's even better is that, just behind our backs, on the wall, there's a heating radiator that works great. Since I'm still chilled to the bone, and Dylan and I are soaking wet, its proximity is a delightful surprise.

Mia bends down to reach for a large bag on the floor and pulls out a blanket.

"I knew I hadn't brought it for nothing," she says triumphantly. "I was sure the two of you would show up sopping wet. You're going to catch a cold."

"My dear cousin, always so thoughtful and far-sighted!" exclaims Dylan playfully, "Thank you! You're an angel."

"But you must take off your soaked clothes; otherwise it's no good." Smiling, Mia hands us the blanket. She adds in an authoritative but maternal tone, "Come on! At least jackets and shirts. Hang them behind you on the radiator, so they get dry."

I don't know if she's serious or just kidding. Does she really want us to take off our clothes? I turn to Dylan, unsure, but he smiles at me, arching his eyebrows and pursing his lips in a funny grimace, then shrugging his shoulders.

"We must obey her," he says. "Take my word, you don't want to face an enraged Mia."

Right off the bat, Dylan begins to take off his jacket, hoodie, and then his shirt, until he's bare-chested. I try to hide it the best I can, but I'm drooling when I see him. He's perfect: thin, athletic, and very defined, but without being too ripped; his skin is immaculate, with a light amber color, the kind that turns a golden shade in summer. Out of the corner of my eye, I see a drop of water trickling down his wet hair, falling on his shoulders, and sliding over his chest and then down his abdomen.

I'd die to be that drop of water! I think, stunned, though I would also consider the more than acceptable alternative of receiving that drop of water with my tongue.

Dylan grabs his clothes, turns to the wall, and spreads them out over the radiator. Now I can see his delicious wet back, which reflects the room's dim light and casts small flashes while he moves. I follow the path from his neck, along his slightly muscular shoulders, to his narrow waist. As he turns a little toward me, I see him in profile. I place my gaze on his hips and discover a thin strip of underwear peeking out from his waistline. When my eyes follow the pronounced, firm curvatures at the end of his back, a sudden chill runs through my body and shakes me. He's perfect.

I have to control myself, otherwise…

I realize how obvious I've been when I turn to Mia and see her smile, which says it all. She's delighted to notice how I enjoy Dylan's beauty. For the second time tonight, I want the earth to swallow me. How embarrassing to be caught this way!

"Hey, come on, Derin, you too," she insists in a roguish tone, still smiling.

"Yes, yes, I'll do it, don't worry," I say without daring to look her in the eyes. I get up, take off my clothes, put them over the free space Dylan has left on the radiator, and sit down again as fast as I can beside him.

I'm so ashamed that Mia has caught me drooling over her cousin's body that I didn't even check as I was undressing to see whether he was watching me. I hope he was. Though I'm not as naked as he is since I've got bandages wrapped around my torso.

Sitting to my right, Dylan takes the blanket and throws it over his shoulders. He gives me one end, and I cover myself too. Now we're both under the blanket, which is big enough to wrap us from our shoulders to our knees. He then throws the remaining end of his side of the blanket over me, so that we're completely covered, with only our heads free.

"Is it okay like this?" he asks me with a hint of shyness.

I'm not sure if it's due to the dim light, but I think he's blushing.

"Perfect," I reply, trying to sound natural.

It's more than perfect. It is divinely exciting. Under the blanket, sitting shoulder to shoulder, thigh to thigh, every little movement of his arm, brushing mine, bristles my skin. I place my hand on my right thigh, the one that comes in direct contact with him. I'm about to move my fingers to brush his leg for an innocent, casual first contact, but I stop short.

Coward!

I feel an intense tingling in my belly, and my hand is paralyzed. I can't take the first step. I just can't.

Damn coward! I repeat to myself, enraged.

Suddenly, I notice Dylan rearranging his arm. He puts his hand on his left thigh, at the same height as my hand.

It's almost imperceptible, like the delicate touch of a butterfly's wing: I feel how he moves his little finger cautiously toward mine, touches it, and caresses it twice with a slight movement from top to bottom. It's a tender motion, soft as the brush of a feather. But since it's intentional and repetitive, it can't be confused with accidental contact. He did it on purpose, sending me a signal.

It's all the incentive I need.

I move my hand and grab his, sure he won't reject it.

And he doesn't. On the contrary, he intertwines his fingers with mine and rubs my hand with his thumb. I do the same, and I melt. I never imagined that caressing someone's hand could feel this way and cause this degree of excitement. The tickling of my belly now runs throughout my body, generating heat and happiness. It's the most sensual and rewarding experience I've ever had in my life. And to think that this is only the beginning! I'm not sure I'll be able to withstand everything that's to come.

The dim lights of the theater darken even more for the beginning of the rally. Dylan and I look at each other for a second, directly in the eyes, both smiling shyly. No need to say anything; everything is clear. I'm happy.

To euphoric applause, whistles, and cheers, Taddeus Green enters the stage.

He's joined by a dozen people, undoubtedly important leaders of the insurgent cause, including Jonathan Blake. It strikes me that more than half of those with him are women. In fact, at least half of the audience—of some two or three hundred people—is made up by women. The public is quite varied in age, from teenagers to older people, although I would say that the largest group consists of young people between sixteen and twenty-five years old.

"Good evening, dear friends!" Taddeus greets the audience. "Are we ready to take the big toad down from his throne of shit?"

"Yeahhh!" the rebels roar.

Taddeus proceeds to deliver a powerful motivational speech to his audience. I don't doubt that he has prepared and rehearsed his words meticulously, but he pronounces them with such ease and spontaneity that it's difficult not to fall prey to his charm. I now realize that my first impression of him wasn't entirely correct. His disheveled appearance and his somewhat clumsy behavior are, without a doubt, a facade, a kind of disguise. This guy is clearly brilliant. He's a talented speaker and actor as well.

His charisma is undeniable.

While Taddeus speaks, the part of my brain responsible for rationality and logic strives to listen carefully and process what he says. Meanwhile, the other area, the one in charge of emotions and pleasure, is still enjoying the sweet sensation caused by Dylan's hand intertwined with mine.

Without exchanging words, we have agreed on an alternating rhythm, which consists of him caressing my hand, then me stroking his. We pause without letting go, and after a while, we start all over. I know it's a foolish thing, but sharing this sweet intimacy, surrounded by so many people but hidden under a blanket, creates a sense of novelty, the excitement of which only grows.

I don't want it to ever end.

In the first part of his speech, after a sweeping introduction to warm up the audience, Taddeus presents a summary of the latest and most significant rebel attacks. Everything I hear in this respect impresses me. If what he says is credible, the Crowley regime stands on a much shakier foundation than I previously thought. In addition to heavy blows aimed at weakening the infrastructure that provides essential services to the cities of the upper castes, attacks have also been carried out against strategic military points and industrial complexes for sophisticated weaponry.

The chokehold grip of the Crowley lineage is threatened like never before on three different fronts: first, the insurgent uprising that flourishes among millions of Disloyal people fed up with repression; second, the unsustainable economic situation of the island, resulting from terrible management by a corrupt government; finally, and according to Taddeus, the issue that has Regent Crowley in a permanent state of anxiety and paranoia, the fact that more and more members of the Commons, Patriots, and even Patricians are joining the insurgency's reform movement.

After telling a couple of jokes ridiculing the regent—which the audience responds to with loud laughter and shouts of "Fatgul!" "Shitty toad!" and "Fucking bastard!"—Taddeus doesn't miss the opportunity to praise the most recent rebel victory, this time of a psychological nature.

Dylan holds my hand tighter.

"I figured they'd show it," he says softly, almost in a whisper, tilting his head toward me.

"I think I expected it too," I reply. "Whatever. Do you think they'll show the whole thing again?"

"I don't know, but I guess so."

The rebel video is projected onto a cinema screen at the back of the stage. Taddeus comments on the most relevant points, although he doesn't need to. The video is so well done that it doesn't require further explanation. Furthermore, judging by the murmuring around me, I assume most of the audience has already seen the broadcast or at least is aware of it.

When the scene of me with the firing squad in Fountain Square appears, Dylan squeezes my hand.

"Damn bastards…" he curses when he sees Bennet ordering me to take off my helmet.

"I thought he just wanted to fuck around with me for a while," I say, "but he had something else in mind."

After emphasizing the repugnance of executing innocent young people, Taddeus starts talking about me. He reminds the audience how the regime has made my family suffer and how they manipulated my image to make me look like a vengeful instrument of the oppressive forces.

For the second time today, I see my deliberate failure at the shot, in clear defiance of the orders received, and Bennet pushing me to the ground and then shooting the girl himself.

"Really, you were so brave!" Dylan whispers in my ear, his fingers moving warmly over mine.

"It was nothing special," I say, shaking my head. "Any decent person would have done the same."

"That's not true. Not just anybody. Besides, you're not just *anybody*, you're a very special person."

"You don't really believe that," I say. "I do have my flaws."

"We'll see," says Dylan in an enigmatic tone, cracking a half-smile.

"But they're so stupid that their game backfired," Taddeus exclaims in a voice animated with triumph. "They didn't count on the righteousness, the strength, and the courage of Derin Dark!"

Several enthusiastic voices from the audience shout, "Bravo!"

"And that's not all," continues Taddeus, now in a sterner voice. "The lowlifes then attacked Derin in the regime's usual cowardly manner: five against one, in a dark alley. They wanted to beat him to death."

Dylan's hand and mine are still entwined on top of his leg, but when the images of Bennet's thugs beating me up appear, he lifts his hand and puts it on my leg; he immediately begins to stroke my thigh with his thumb. It's the most moving way he could communicate his pain and compassion as he sees for the first time how they hurt me.

"Luckily, some of our young rebels entered the alley at the right moment, surprising and scaring away those monsters," says Taddeus. "Otherwise, our brave Derin Dark would have been lost to this atrocious attack."

Please, stop there. Please, don't go on, I pray in my head, fearing what may come next.

"But, Derin Dark is safe and sound!" he exclaims, returning to his animated tone. "He hasn't allowed the Crowleys to destroy him! He has raised himself against repression and injustice! and…"

No, please. Don't!

"… he's here tonight, among us!"

My heart starts beating like crazy.

With a general murmuring, the people on the parquet floor turn their heads in all directions, trying to find me. Those around us, who were already aware of my presence, turn, smiling and expectant, in my direction.

"Where are you, Derin? Let us see you!" Taddeus shouts, grinning from ear to ear.

"Derin! Derin! Derin!" the audience starts cheering.

"Come on, boy, where are you? Just make a sign so we can see you. We won't make you come up here, I promise."

All of Mia's friends encourage me to get up. They demand it, and I feel like dying of shame.

"I don't think you have a choice," says Dylan, shrugging and smiling.

"But I'm shirtless."

"So what? They'll love it."

Resigned, I shake my head slightly, take off the blanket, and stand up on the bleachers. Immediately, the heat of the spotlight from a powerful reflector wraps around me. Blinded by the glare, I feel like an exposed statue, half-naked, observed by hundreds of eyes.

"So, there we have him!" exclaims Taddeus. "Apparently, we'll have to get a shirt for the poor boy," he adds in an amused tone. "Or would you rather he stays shirtless? Because the boy is handsome, isn't he?"

"Derin! Derin! Derin!" the rebels cheer with a roar of applause that floods the premises.

I stand there, just nodding a couple of times shyly to indicate my gratitude. I know I look like an idiot.

Taddeus lets the audience express their enthusiasm for about twenty or thirty seconds, which never seem to end. When, at last, he says, "Thank you, Derin!" and they move the reflector light off me, the audience calms down and turns their attention again to the rebel leader. I feel immense relief. I turn to get my clothes from the radiator; they're almost completely dry. As I start to get dressed, I notice that Dylan is watching me, smiling.

"Clothes are dry," I say, returning the smile.

He stands up and begins to dress too.

"I'm sorry they made you do that," he says in a tone of mock compassion, with the corresponding ironic facial expression. I think he's amused by the embarrassing moment they've put me through.

I don't say anything, just smile and move my head from side to side, signaling disapproval. We understand each other perfectly. I want to get out of here and kiss him.

Meanwhile, Taddeus is ending his speech and announces that very soon, there will be several decisive events to advance the insurgent cause. He thanks the audience for their presence and, above all, for their invaluable contribution to the struggle to recover justice and freedom. He also wishes them fun at the party that will take place afterward, where there will be drinks and music. He recommends they not miss the special performance of a surprise guest, who will surely enchant everyone.

Under a storm of ecstatic screams, the blue rose on a silver-grey background is projected onto the screen where earlier we saw the propaganda video.

"Pride! Justice! Freedom!" shouts Taddeus as a goodbye, and the crowd responds with a resounding roar: "Stop oppression now!"

CHAPTER 22

DON QUIXOTE

EVERYBODY SEATED STANDS UP in a single motion, as if coordinated in advance. The rebels, with their spirits high in the sky after Taddeus' energetic speech, still have more to look forward to. Dylan has warned me that parties like the one that awaits this night's audience are always "intense and unforgettable."

But my case is different. Instead of feeling more cheerful, my enthusiasm has fallen to the floor. The end of Taddeus' speech has also marked an abrupt and cruel end to the magical intimacy that Dylan and I shared under the blanket. Even though I'm fully aware of how childish—even ridiculous—this is, I can't help but blame Taddeus for daring to finish his presentation. I'm disheartened and spiteful, overwhelmed by an irrational sense of anger toward the rebel leader for pulling me down from cloud nine.

I force myself to reject this nonsense. If the people around me could hear my thoughts, they would think I'm a pathetic loser.

"We've got to meet Taddeus now," Dylan says, "but I want to show you something first."

"What?"

"Wait, you'll see."

We make our way through the crowd, back to the other end of the gallery and to the entry with the heavy curtain that we came through earlier. We leave the theater and go back down the corridor we used before.

"Come on, hurry, we don't have much time," Dylan says urgently as he speeds up his pace.

"Where are we going?"

"It's not far, you'll see, just wait."

I follow him through a new labyrinth of corridors. We reach some stairs and go up four levels without stopping for a second. He doesn't seem fatigued at all from running up this many stories. In general, I wouldn't have any problems myself, since my physical condition is excellent, but Dylan forgets that I got a hard beating just yesterday and a good part of my body is still bruised and sore. I put up with the pain because I don't want him to think I'm a weakling.

At the top of the stairs, we find a metal door, which rattles in a scandalous way when he opens it. After my body had regained a comfortable temperature under the blanket and near the radiator, the cold of the night hits me like a stabbing chill that runs down my spine when we get out onto the building's rooftop. At least the rain has stopped.

"What are we doing here?" I ask, squinting.

"Come on," he replies with a smile and a glow of enthusiasm in his eyes. He grabs my hand and leads me to one side. We stop at the low wall marking the edge of the roof.

"Look," he says, stretching out his arm and pointing toward the horizon.

We're definitely in an area very close to the western edge of the Strip. Dark countryside stretches before us. Several miles away, we can make out a long bright line that gives off a tenuous but visible halo: the city of London.

"Cool, right?" he says.

It looks truly fascinating from here, as if it were a distant and enchanted place. I've never before had this impression of the city, which was my home until a few days ago. Or maybe it's just that, when I'm with Dylan, I see everything differently. Everything is more beautiful, more exciting.

"These last few nights I've come up here several times," he continues in a soft, almost melancholic voice. "When I'd gaze at the lights of London… well… um… I was thinking of you."

Without letting go of my hand, he turns and looks into my eyes with the most beautiful expression he's ever shown me. How can I not surrender to his charms? I place my right hand on his cheek, which I trace tenderly with my thumb, and then I slide my hand until my fingers brush against his ear and tangle in the silky hair at the back of his head. In a firm but delicate way, I pull him closer to me. I put my lips on his, and we merge in a kiss that makes me feel like the happiest man on the face of the earth.

I can't understand how I've survived this whole time without the sweet and intoxicating taste of his delicious lips. I feel like my entire life I've had an inescapable and inexplicable thirst that I've only now managed to quench. Time and the world around me disappear. Nothing else matters. It's just him and me. Only our caresses and kisses.

I would sell my soul to prolong this moment for all eternity. I feel complete, but after a while, it's Dylan who takes on the tough responsibility of returning us to reality. He says goodbye to my lips by pursing his and giving me one more small, tender kiss.

"We have to go down," he says with a sigh.

"I know," I reply in a similar lamenting way as I touch his cheek again.

I don't want to go anywhere. I want to stay here and keep drinking from his lips, but he's right. I console myself with the thought that it won't be long before I can taste them again.

We leave the rooftop and head down the same staircase.

When we've gone down three flights of stairs, Dylan stops at the next landing. He leans slightly over the handrail and looks down the air shaft to see if anyone's coming up. Nobody is, so he turns around, grabs me by the waist, and kisses me passionately.

"Sorry," he says when his lips separate from mine. "I had to. I wanted to kiss you one last time before going down."

I give him the widest smile I can, my eyes set on his caramel gaze. I grab his face between my hands and bring it so close to mine that the tips of our noses touch. Speaking the words right over his lips, I say, "Don't be sorry. Kissing you is the best thing in the world."

We melt into a last, amazing kiss that's even more intense than the ones on the rooftop. It's heavenly.

—

WE MEET TADDEUS AND JONATHAN in a large room which holds a big conference table surrounded by several rows of desks with computers, monitors, and other devices. Besides us, two women and another man take part in the meeting.

Taddeus makes the introductions.

The eldest of the two women, who's in her early forties and has short blond hair and a cheerful expression, is Commander Scott, leader of the insurgency in the Highlands—the northernmost of the fourteen protectorates. The other woman, perhaps in her mid-twenties, is Commander Anderson, from the Glasgow Protectorate, also in the north. Her dark hair is very short, almost shaved, and her big, deep eyes have a stern expression. She's small and thin-built, but judging by her muscular forearms and her upright and confident posture, she's clearly an athletic woman.

"I've asked Commanders Anderson and Scott to join us," Taddeus explains, "because the matter we'll discuss next concerns them directly. And, as I mentioned already, it includes the possible rescue of your father and brother."

I nod. He now has my full attention.

The tall, well-built, and dark-skinned man is about thirty years old. It's evident that he's a restless person, since he can't keep his hands still for a second: either he's finger-tapping on the table, or picking up a pen and oscillating it vigorously between two fingers, or resting his elbows on the table with his hands together and his fingertips making nervous and accelerated movements. One can see his military bearing at once, and I wonder if he's a former army officer who's also been degraded, or whether he's one of the "traitor" Patriots who's decided to join the rebels. I'm inclined to think that he's a degraded officer, like me.

"Commander Will Burke is in charge of Operation Don Quixote," Taddeus explains.

"Operation *Don Quixote*?" I ask, raising my eyebrows.

"We'll explain everything to you. Just hold on, be patient," Taddeus replies, raising his hand.

I nod without saying anything.

"Very well, first of all," he continues, "how are you feeling? I mean, since the beating. A bit better?"

For the last twenty minutes, when I was on the rooftop with Dylan, I hadn't thought about the beating at all. Every unpleasant thing had been forgotten under the overwhelming feeling of his kisses. Without thinking, I slide the tip of my tongue over my lips. I don't want to lose his flavor.

"Yes, much better, thanks," I answer, smiling.

"I'm glad to hear that. You must get better soon."

The images of the rebel broadcast where Bennet's thugs beat me up in the alley come to mind.

"About the video…" I start, trying not to sound reproachful, but Taddeus is one step ahead of me.

"Yes, yes, you'll have to forgive us." He makes a strange grimace as if smiling but pressing his lips together and tilting his head a little. "We should've warned you, but unfortunately there was no time. You'll understand that in matters of intelligence and strategy, sometimes you have to make decisions very quickly to achieve the optimal result."

It irritates me how he tries to rationalize a decision that could have caused—and still could cause—a lot of damage to my family and me.

"We had to act immediately," he adds, sensing that his first explanation wasn't enough to convince me. "We hacked the Fountain Square images from the official network and the others we got by a stroke of luck. It was an invaluable opportunity to counteract Crowley's propaganda and make the regime look ridiculous. But we had to act quickly to get the maximum effect."

I feel a twinge in my stomach when he says "stroke of luck." That stroke of luck was the beating I got. Personally, it doesn't seem like luck was on my side.

"Jonathan and his people did an extraordinary job," he says, turning to smile at him.

Jonathan was involved in this? And he didn't mention anything about it last night when we talked? I didn't expect that. Did Dylan know too? I gaze at Jonathan first, looking for the expression in his eyes, but I can't see them. He has his hands together in front of his body, keeping his gaze fixed on a dead spot on the table. I immediately turn to Dylan with a questioning look. His eyes leave no doubt: he didn't know. He's as surprised as I am.

"You may not be fully aware of it," Taddeus continues, still smiling, "but the broadcast's success has far exceeded our highest expectations. It's the first time we've achieved full coverage in the entire territory, and we owe it to the technological maneuvers of Jonathan's group." He turns his head toward Jonathan, who nods.

"According to our most recent reports," Commander Scott intervenes in a pedagogical tone, "outrage among the Disloyal population and their predisposition to rebellion has risen to levels never seen before. In addition, discontent and the desire for radical change among the Commons caste is increasingly evident and palpable. We have good reason to be optimistic."

Taddeus nods and smiles at the commander in a very brief and artificial way. It seems he doesn't like to be interrupted.

"Thus, we're at a major crossroads in this fight," he states with an air of significance. "We believe the time is right to launch a high-impact insurgent campaign to overthrow Eugene Crowley's regime."

Any action that aims to topple Nigel, his detestable father, and all the poisonous Crowley kin, has my full sympathy. But right now, what matters most to me is my family's wellbeing and future.

"I understand, but… how can you help me rescue Brian and my father?" I ask, trying not to seem too impatient.

"Well, that depends to a large extent on you and your contribution to our cause," he replies.

"What do you mean? In what sense?"

"This is where Operation Don Quixote comes into play," he says, and then he turns to the dark-skinned man. "Burke, please."

"Operation Don Quixote involves an attack of high strategic value that the insurgency has been preparing for months," explains Burke. "We hadn't planned to launch the attack until well into winter, but the events of the last two weeks have turned our plans upside down and forced us to reassess them. I'm referring specifically to the sham surrounding the false attack against the regent, the execution of Governor Hall, and your brother's capture."

"Brian's capture? I don't understand, what does his capture have to do with the insurgency's plans?" I ask, narrowing my eyes.

Somewhere in my mind, I begin to remember what Jonathan mentioned yesterday. He said that Taddeus is interested in my family because of my relationship with Nigel, but above all because Brian's arrest represented a danger to an important rebel plan where Dylan plays a key role. Burke is undoubtedly referring to that.

"Take it easy," says Taddeus, faking a smile. "Let Burke finish talking and then ask whatever you want, okay?"

I obey, biting my lip to avoid interrupting.

In short, Burke explains that Operation Don Quixote is a massive attack plan to destroy Ventus. The Crowleys impatiently await the project's completion. They intend to export all renewable energy produced there, as they urgently need the money.

Destroying Ventus would mean to take away the most significant source of wealth that they could use to hold on to power. It means striking a highly debilitating blow to an already wounded and wobbly beast.

Suddenly, I understand with amusement the meaning of the operation's code name: Don Quixote, the insane gentleman in Spanish literature who centuries ago fought against monsters that were actually windmills. I can't deny that Taddeus has a unique sense of humor since there's no doubt the operation's name is a result of his wit.

"But something unexpected happened," Taddeus says, taking over the discussion again, "which has put the entire plan at risk. By an unlucky turn of fate, your brother Brian was accused of participating in the fake attack. The choice was random; they could've captured any other young man, it really didn't matter who. Unfortunately, it turned out to be your brother. The consequent public exposure of your family has come to complicate matters and has put everyone working on Operation Don Quixote in a state of alarm."

"You mean the danger to the operation if they get Dylan?" I say, unable to suppress my curiosity and impatience any longer.

Taddeus is visibly surprised and throws an inquisitive glance at Jonathan, who hasn't taken his eyes off the table and seems immutable.

"Ah, I wasn't informed he was already aware of that," Taddeus says reproachfully to Jonathan.

"Actually, I don't know much about it," I answer quickly. "I've only been told that Dylan plays an important role in a special mission, but apart from that, I don't know anything."

"No matter," says Taddeus, still in an annoyed tone. Then he softens his facial expression, looks at Dylan, and continues to speak in the same enthusiastic tone as before. "It's true. It's up to our little genius to carry out a vital and risky mission, which we're sure he'll successfully complete, won't he?"

"Of course." Dylan nods. Then he turns to me and grimaces slightly with a brief shrug. "No problem, a piece of cake."

Then I learn for the first time that Dylan works in the Ministry of Public Services and Utilities. Thanks to his technological genius, he will hack a control system and then extract a series of codes that are essential for destroying Ventus. These codes allow access to the program that regulates the operation of the wind turbines.

"After your brother Brian's capture," Taddeus explains, "the danger became imminent. It's child's play for the Government to establish a link between him and Jonathan's daughter. From there, it would be only a small leap to Dylan. Let's hope our bad luck doesn't continue. His position in the ministry wouldn't go unnoticed, and a squeamish bureaucrat could possibly remove him. That would ruin everything. We don't have anyone else in a similarly privileged position. Without those codes, the plan doesn't work. So we've been forced to move up the attack."

Now that I've learned about Dylan's central role in all this, I understand the danger he's exposed to if he falls into Nigel's hands. Taddeus fears that they'll remove Dylan from the ministry, but I know that Nigel wouldn't just settle for that. It wouldn't be hard for him to find out how much I care for Dylan, that I love him. He wouldn't hesitate for a second to use him to hurt me.

I try not to think about that now.

In a matter of minutes, I've been able to tie up loose ends and see everything much more clearly. I roughly understand the insurgent plan to sabotage Ventus. I'm also clear about the urgent situation caused for Operation Don Quixote by the unfortunate capture of my brother. I know about Dylan's valuable role, and I'm terrified of the danger he's exposed to.

Now I just need to know how Taddeus can help me rescue my father and my brother, and what he's going to ask from me in return.

INVOLUNTARY HERO

ONE OF THE MOST VALUABLE TACTICS to increase our mission's chances of success is to avoid falling into despair in the face of sudden, unforeseen obstacles. Moreover, we must consider them an opportunity to adapt our plans; to improve them. It's also necessary, more often than not, to be attentive to whimsical changes in luck, which tend to appear with opposite effects—good and bad—like two sides of the same coin. Even though we might not realize it at first.

This, at least, is the opinion of Taddeus Green, who takes on a philosophical attitude and shares his wisdom.

"The best example of this truth," he says, smiling and pointing to me, "is you, Derin."

I think he notices the confusion and disbelief in my eyes. He raises the corners of his lips even more until they almost reach his ears, drawing a smile that, for lack of a better analogy, reminds me of a clown.

"Yes, yes, Derin, I mean you," he continues. "Let's see, let's imagine the current stage of our fight as the plot in a play. In the first act, your brother's capture shook up our plans and turned them upside down, as I've explained. But in the second act, you appeared in an unexpected and extraordinary way: as the revitalizing element that could inject the enthusiasm needed to finally finish this exhausting struggle of so many years. Now, it's up to us to take advantage of this twist of fate to successfully carry out the third act."

Now I'm convinced that Taddeus has lost his mind.

"You still don't get it, right?" He seems to enjoy my bewilderment. "Well, I'll explain it to you more clearly."

I don't know whether to believe what he says next or if I should dismiss everything as crazy talk. But even though I find it absurd at first, I slowly notice expressions of assent from the other three commanders and I realize that Jonathan also agrees. This makes me wonder if Taddeus' wild expectations regarding me aren't that farfetched after all.

Dylan seems as confused as I am, but I get the impression that he finds it easier to imagine the version of me that Taddeus paints.

In short, Taddeus explains that to get the Disloyal population to fully join in the revolutionary struggle, the only incentive they need is a clear and convincing sign that overthrowing the Crowleys is a close and tangible reality; an assurance that any sacrifice will have been worth it. The strategic and military triumphs that the rebels hope to obtain soon will take care of that.

On the other hand, despite general discontent and desperation over shortages and lack of prospects, despite the desire for radical change, millions of citizens of the Commons and thousands of Patriots don't dare to rise up against the regime. They're too scared. To stand up to their fear, they need a guide to show them that change is possible, a leader from their own ranks who dares to speak for them and who confronts the Crowleys head-on; someone who gives back their lost illusions and dreams, who instils certainty that it's possible to deprive the Crowleys of their power and make them pay for the evils they've committed over three decades; an emblematic figure that for millions will become a symbol of the insurgency, of the just cause and of hope… The face of all the good things that are to come. That face, they've decided, is me.

They want me to be the face and the voice of all just citizens, of all those who long to live in peace and freedom, without the threat of an authoritarian and repressive regime; they want me to become a hero of Englandom.

"We must thank the idiot who exposed you so stupidly in front of the cameras," Taddeus adds sarcastically. "Thanks to his ineptitude, and of course your integrity and courage, you're already a recognized and admired figure throughout the country. Now we just have to further develop and guide your image to become the face of all young citizens who are fed up with Crowley."

So that's what he wants from me. In exchange for my father's and Brian's rescue, which will be carried out as part of Operation Don Quixote, Taddeus demands that I join the insurgent cause, support the rebel operatives with my military training, and accept becoming the emblematic face of the people's revolution.

I don't fully understand what this all really means at this point, but I have no choice but to accept all his conditions, without any objections. There's nothing I wouldn't be willing to do to secure the release of Brian and my father, to have my whole family reunited again. All I ask additionally is that they guarantee the protection of my mother and Lily and that the Mitchells are also rescued. Taddeus has no problem with that.

"When will the operation take place?" I ask.

"In forty-eight hours, at midnight and in the morning hours of the day after tomorrow," he replies while looking at the other commanders, who nod in confirmation.

"The day after tomorrow?" I repeat, a sudden rush of energy filling me with vitality. I didn't expect it so soon, but the sooner, the better.

"That's right," Taddeus confirms. "Will you be ready? Physically and mentally?"

"Of course."

The final minutes of the meeting are used to coordinate details regarding my mother and Lily, as well as the Blakes. They'll need to hide once the operation starts, otherwise, they'll be easy prey for Nigel's revenge. Liam's mother and brother will be informed tonight about their relatives' rescue, and they'll also be provided shelter.

Taddeus ends the meeting, and the commanders say goodbye and leave. When Jonathan, Dylan, and I are about to leave the conference room, Taddeus stops me, holding back my arm.

"Wait a moment, Derin, I want to ask you something else."

Jonathan and Dylan understand Taddeus is seeking a private conversation.

"I'll wait for you out here, okay?" says Dylan, smiling. I nod and smile back. He and Jonathan leave the room.

When Taddeus and I are alone, he continues:

"Derin, I need you to explain the exact nature of your relationship with Nigel Crowley."

There he goes, catching me off guard again.

My intuition tells me that he's already aware of all the details and only wants to test my character and frankness. I decide to tell him the full story and not just the more superficial version I told Jonathan Blake. Taddeus isn't surprised by anything I confess regarding Nigel, including the last two times I saw him since Brian's capture. I find it unnerving to speak about these intimate aspects. Like it or not, those details expose me too, and I'm not sure how he'll take it, or how it'll influence his perception of me. In the end, he doesn't seem to attach much importance to any of this.

"And what did he demand in exchange for your brother's life?" he asks bluntly.

"I'm not entirely sure," I answer without hesitation, although I feel my cheeks burning. "I mean, he made it clear he would want something in return, something personal … something intimate. But he didn't say what, or when."

"I see. All right. Thanks for your sincerity."

I nod and get ready to leave, but Taddeus raises his index finger, signaling me to wait.

"One more thing," he says. "What's going on between Dylan Blake and you?"

Now I'm really blushing. What the hell does it matter what's between him and me? I can't imagine why Taddeus asks me this question, which in my opinion is very personal, even more so than the Nigel issue. It has nothing to do with what we're dealing with today. But, despite his brazenness, I decide I have nothing to hide or anything to be ashamed of. On the contrary, being with Dylan fills me with pride.

"I… I love him… and he loves me," I try to say in a firm voice, but it breaks at the end.

It's done. I said it. Yes, I love him. Any problem?

"I thought as much," he replies without altering his casual tone of voice. "He's an excellent boy, very skillful, a genius. But what's between you and him won't cause any problem to the important mission we have before us, will it?"

"No, of course not."

"Very well, I'm glad to hear it. Thank you."

He doesn't want to know anything else. He smiles and makes a sign to indicate that I can leave.

Dylan is waiting for me outside. I'm surprised to see that Jonathan has also stayed behind.

"Derin," Jonathan says, "I want you to know that it's true my team and I were in charge of the video's technical aspects, but I assure you that I was convinced it wouldn't be broadcast before they warned you. I'm sorry it happened this way, I really am."

"I know, Jonathan, don't worry," I answer, not doubting a word of what he says. Then I lie to lessen his sense of responsibility: "Taddeus just confirmed it to me, and he apologized again. Well, what's done is done. We now have more important issues to deal with, right?"

"Yes, that's right, but I thought it was important that I tell you personally. I wouldn't want you to think that I consciously exposed you to more danger, which is what I've told Dylan as well."

"I know, Jonathan. Thank you. Seriously, there's no problem."
He feels genuinely sorry for what happened.

To divert the conversation to a different matter, I bring up an issue that I wanted to discuss with him anyway, in case Chief Johnson insisted on the subject.

"By the way," I say, "why didn't I get the broadcast of the insurgent video on my teleCard? Dylan didn't get it either, right?" I add, turning to Dylan, who shakes his head. "There wasn't any problem with the official news broadcast yesterday, with the altered images."

"Oh, that," Jonathan says. "None of the special teleCards for deels received the signal. All of them, which by the way aren't many, are connected to a different network and, well, it's already quite complicated and expensive to infiltrate the official signal. The key goal was to hack the TVs and the millions of regular teleCards, so Taddeus decided that it wasn't worth the cost to send the signal to the others as well."

"I see," I reply, without questioning his explanation.

THE THEATER COMPOUND has become a hotbed of young rebels dancing and jumping ecstatically to the rhythm of the strident music coming from a group of powerful loudspeakers. Alcohol runs freely, and everyone seems to enjoy the best moment of their lives.

I'm stunned and delighted to witness such a display of carefree freedom, exalting joy, lack of worry, and naturalness in public displays of affection. Couples are dancing and kissing everywhere, boys with girls, boys with boys, and girls with girls… Nobody seems to pay too much attention to what others do. Meanwhile, the sheer number of human bodies has brought up the temperature quite a bit. Many of the boys and young men have taken off their shirts, and several girls are wearing only a bra or a thin tank top.

We find Mia and her friends near the center of the parquet floor, where people crowd the most. When she sees Dylan and

I holding hands, she lets out a charming smile; she hugs Dylan and says something in his ear, which I can't hear because of the noise. Then she turns to me and, without altering her cheerful smile, also hugs me.

"I'm so happy for you," she says. Though I barely hear her, her joy for us is genuine and fills me with pleasure. I return her smile. She seems cheerful and animated, but I know she's making a tremendous effort to overcome the grief of Brian's absence.

We get something to drink and start to chat with the others. After a while, some kids led by a middle-aged woman begin to set up the stage for the special artist's performance. I can barely hear what Dylan tells me—we have to shout into each other's ears to understand—but I manage to decipher that the singer is a young man from the Strip whose fame has begun to skyrocket, especially since his music was banned by the regime. It's considered explosive, radical, and anti-system. I'm intrigued to see him and listen to his music.

When the woman acting as the official party hostess grabs the stage's microphone and announces Riley Pearson's entry, the audience explodes in a roar of screams and applause.

I feel compassion for the thin, shy-looking boy who enters the stage nervously, visibly overwhelmed by this shrill reception. He has with him a guitar on a strap that hangs diagonally at the front. He's more or less my age, perhaps a little older, but his thin build and insecure bearing make him look younger. The lights of the theater darken and a single spotlight, projected from a reflector in the background, illuminates the performer.

"Good evening," Riley says into the microphone, his voice soft. "This is dedicated to all of you, to all your sacrifices, to all your struggles… to our struggle."

Riley begins to play a simple and tender melody. But when the chords and the cadence of his music intensify, and his incredible voice floods the theater, he leaves us all hypnotized. It's absolutely amazing how a guy with an introverted and subdued appearance can produce such a powerful voice. In his song, he speaks of twin souls, of tortuous roads full of obstacles, of shadows and light, and also of nightmares and dreams come true. To me, it doesn't sound radical at all, nor does it seem to incite a revolution. What I can say is that his music has a captivating effect on the masses, I'm convinced of that. I love it.

Dylan is standing in front of me. I put my arms around him and hold him tightly against my body. We stay to listen to two more songs by Riley Pearson, until the third one, which, by the audience's enthusiasm, seems to be the best known and requested of his repertoire. At the end of this melancholic ballad, we decide it's time to leave.

Now that we've taken the fantastic first step, I no longer hold on to his hips insecurely while we ride on his scooter; now I put my arms around him and cling to him. I'm filled with an exciting sensation of freedom.

But once again, the journey is too short; we arrive sooner than I'd hoped.

"Be honest, how risky is that business with the codes?" I ask after he's taken off his helmet. This matter has been whirling in my head this whole time, and I've been burning to discuss it with him.

"Actually, not so much," he replies. "I mean, just the act of breaking into the system and extracting the codes doesn't worry me too much. I can do it. The problem is that there's a protection program within the system that makes a 'surveillance tour' four times a day, every six hours. During that control protocol, the infiltration and extraction of the codes will come to light. When that happens, I better be far away from there."

"And you'll be able to leave on time?"

"Yes… if nothing unforeseen happens," he says nonchalantly.

As far as I've managed to understand—despite my limited technological knowledge—Dylan has to get the codes right after the control protocol ends. From that moment on, the rebel forces involved in the sabotage operation on Ventus will have less than six hours before the following protocol will discover the hacking and theft of the codes, after which the intelligence forces will go code red and warn of a possible attack. To guarantee the operation's success, everything must happen within five hours: Dylan must leave the ministry with the codes, flee from London, and meet our command in the Strip, led by Commander Burke. From there, we all leave for Moray Firth, the estuary in the north, using helijets the rebels have obtained from I don't know where. When we get to Moray Firth, we'll launch the rescue operation of my father and Brian, while the rest of the rebel forces, already in position in the northern protectorates, will be in charge of carrying out Operation Don Quixote.

It sounds clear and straightforward, but in reality, the plan involves a high degree of risk. Despite the most thorough and exhaustive preparation, an infinity of unforeseen factors may arise. We're aware of the danger: we know that there's a real possibility that we'll all end up dead. But it's a risk so worth taking that it doesn't scare us too much.

"See you tomorrow," Dylan says when he lets go, after kissing and hugging me for a long time. "Dream about me," he adds, winking.

"Of course, who else would I dream about?" I reply, smiling and stroking his jaw.

I wait outside the building until I see his scooter disappear in the distance.

—

I FIND MY MOTHER ASLEEP on the living room sofa, the one I use as a bed; she has left the lamp on the side table lit. No doubt she wanted to wait up for me but gave in to fatigue. She gets up immediately upon hearing me enter.

"Everything okay, darling?" she says, suppressing a yawn.

"Yes, Mom, everything's great."

When I confirm that the rebels have committed to carrying out a rescue mission to free my father and Brian, she starts crying in my arms. They're tears of joy, but also of anguish. On the one hand, she's full of happiness at the prospect of reuniting with Brian and my father again, ignoring how risky it will be for everyone to stay hidden after their rescue. On the other hand, upon learning that I'm going to participate in the dangerous mission, she shudders at the thought that, at the end of it, both they and I could end up dead.

Without mentioning the operation to destroy Ventus—she doesn't need to know that—I explain that Dylan will also play a vital role in the rescue mission.

"You can tell he's an excellent boy," she says. "They're all very good people, Mia, Belinda, Dylan, and I imagine Mia's father is too."

"Mom," I say in a nervous voice. After a second of hesitation, I decide to cut to the chase: "I'm in love with Dylan… I really love him."

She looks me in the eyes, smiles, and hugs me.

"I know," she replies, holding my face with both her hands, like a small child. "I'm glad you found someone. I just want you to be happy."

"I am, Mom. I feel really happy."

How relieved I am! It was much easier than I expected. My mother knows that I'm in love with Dylan, and she approves. She's happy for me.

I spend a night of heavenly rest, the first time in a long time. My subconscious must be feeling generous with me, or simply wanted to fulfill Dylan's request since it decides to gift me sweet dreams where he and I are the protagonists of our incredible love story. Given the adventurous mission upon us, it wouldn't be too farfetched for terrible nightmares to harass me throughout the night, making me wake up soaked in sweat and with an accelerated pulse. But I only feel joy.

—

I ENTER THE POLICE STATION early at the start of the workday and go straight to Chief Johnson's office. I have instructions from Taddeus to follow my superiors' orders point-blank, so as not to draw any attention to myself. I must avoid raising any suspicion. Considering that in less than two days I'll be out of this place and far from these zombie slaves of the dictatorship, I don't mind putting up with them for a while longer.

Just before I knock on Chief Johnson's office door, his assistant yells at me from his desk across the hall:

"Hey, Dark, have you heard the news?"

"What news?" I ask in return with a frown.

"Bennet. He shot himself in the head last night."

I freeze.

"What did you say? Bennet shot himself? Is he dead?"

"What do you think?" he replies sarcastically. "In what universe do people shoot themselves in the head and are alive and kicking? Of course he's dead, man. Get in there now, the chief is waiting for you."

This isn't good news. Bennet was an idiot, a cruel and dangerous fanatic. But he wasn't one to shoot himself in the head. Bennet has been killed.

Chief Johnson is more nervous than he was yesterday afternoon. The anxiety is noticeable in his pale face, and the dark shadows under his eyes show that he's had a bad night. I notice the glass of water on his desk and several open packages of headache pills.

"Dark," he says without much preamble and without asking me to take a seat. "Things have changed. Your situation has changed."

My instinct warns me that something has gone very wrong.

"What do you mean, chief?"

"I've gotten orders from above," he replies. "They've decided you can't stay here. Go back to your place, get some rest, and pack your things."

"What do you mean? Pack my things?"

"Yes. Commander Crowley's agents will pick you up tonight. You're going back to London."

CHAPTER 24

IMMINENT ATTACK

MY HEART STOPS, FALLS OUT OF MY CHEST, and drops to the ground like a stone. I feel the roof crashing over me, and sudden paralysis prevents me from running away to avoid being crushed like an insect. But even if I could move, there would be nowhere to escape; everything around me seems to collapse.

What Johnson tells me can't be true. It has to be a mistake.

"I'm sorry, chief, what did you say?" I manage to babble as my heartbeat returns violently, threatening to make my chest explode. "They're taking me back to London?"

"That's right. That idiot Bennet's stupidity has ridiculed the regime. Commander Crowley is furious and has decided to get you out of here. He wants you under his direct control."

"I don't understand," I say, shaking my head with my eyes closed in an attempt to clear my mind of the blur of thoughts obscuring it. "But, um… how?… Err, why?… My mother and my sister?"

"The orders only concern you. You're going. Your mother and your sister stay here."

I leave the police station, dragging my feet like a wandering ghost.

It is as if a foreign body that looks like me, with my head, arms, and legs, walks in automatic mode without will or direction, pulling my stunned consciousness, which is unable to formulate coherent thoughts. I remain in this disturbed state, surrendered and impassive, until the image of my mother and Lily helpless in the Strip makes me flinch.

It doesn't take me long to find them in the apartment building. They're busy with their cleaning chores on the third level and are surprised to see me show up.

"No time for explanations," I say urgently. "Let's go up to the apartment. We have to leave now."

"Derin, what's wrong?" my mother asks with a puzzled expression.

"Something has come up," I answer. "We must get away earlier than expected."

We quickly pack some clothes and our personal belongings. I put my teleCard inside a drawer in the kitchen. Everything else is left as is. We stop by Mrs. Watson's apartment and slip a note signed by my mother in the slot between the frame and the door leaf. In it, my mother explains that there's been an emergency and they had to go out but will return as soon as possible.

Relieved not to encounter any more shocks along the way, we arrive at Georgie's.

I couldn't think of anywhere better to go, but I'm sure it's not the worst place. It seems Georgie always spends her mornings dealing with the administrative aspects of her business because, once again, I find her behind the bar, busy with a pile of papers and folders. There's nobody else in the pub.

"Hey Derin, hello handsome! What a surprise!" she exclaims with her singular cheerful, shrill voice as she sees me enter. At the same time, she looks curiously at my mother and Lily.

I don't have time for formalities or politeness, so I introduce them without much pomp and circumstance and get straight to the point.

"There's been an emergency," I say. "I have to get hold of the Blakes right away. Can I use your phone?"

"Sure, honey," she replies, somewhat alarmed.

She leads me to the room just behind the bar, where there's a telephone. I dial the Blakes' contact number and hear the ringtone three times, until someone answers. It's Jonathan. I inform him of what happened in a concise manner.

"You did well," he says, his voice as always unruffled. "Don't go out. I'll be there right away."

While we wait, Georgie offers us tea and entertains my mother and Lily with pleasant, though irrelevant conversation. I try to take part in it, but in my mind, I'm impatiently counting the minutes. After a quarter of an hour, Jonathan appears.

"You must be Emma," he says, greeting my mother politely. "Belinda has already expressed how much we regret what's happened to Brian and your husband, but we have reason to be optimistic, right?" He looks at me, and I nod, confirming that my mother is aware of the rescue.

Jonathan's carefree attitude helps calm down my nerves. He takes all the time in the world to introduce himself properly to my mother and Lily, and he chats for a while with them in a friendly way, without showing any signs of urgency. Death itself could appear before him, and he still wouldn't change his calm, reflective, almost laid-back bearing.

Under other circumstances, he might be considered a dull and boring man, but his personality is now very comforting. Oddly enough, his apparent impassivity gives me courage. A nervous and restless person wouldn't help at all now.

"I spoke to Taddeus," he then says, turning to me. "He has summoned us to an emergency meeting. He's already making inquiries. Let's go over there."

Then he turns to Georgie and asks, "The rooms are ready, right?"

"Yes, of course, everything's ready," she answers.

"Perfect. We're all moving in today."

Jonathan explains that several rooms have been prepared in a building not far from here, stocked with everything needed to lodge us. That's where we'll remain hidden as long as necessary. Georgie will take care of bringing my mother and Lily there, and Belinda and Mia will also arrive right away. I have no doubt that they're in good hands. I still don't understand what role Georgie plays in all this, but I'm increasingly aware that her participation goes beyond what I had previously supposed.

On the way to meet Taddeus, Jonathan lets out a hint of uneasiness. He confesses that this unexpected turn of events complicates things, and he admits to feeling worried. He thinks Nigel's decision to take me back to London could be due to many reasons, some perhaps more insignificant than others. Nevertheless, it puts the entire operation at risk. He dares to suggest that it might be necessary to move up the start of the operation again, maybe by twenty-four hours. Dylan could try to obtain the codes today, but Taddeus and his commanders have the final word.

—

WE FIND THE REBEL LEADER in the same place where we met him yesterday, inside the tangled and concealed group of buildings that houses the NATFOR headquarters. This time, the room and the whole area are overflowing with people.

With all the lights on, I realize the room's bigger than I thought. All the computers and monitors are on, with respective specialists intensely focused on the information flashing on their screens. There's a continuous and half-chaotic flow of people coming and going, bringing and carrying messages. Everyone seems to be very concentrated on their tasks, despite the intense bustle dominating the place. This is obviously the command center of a military operation.

Taddeus stands in one corner of the room, together with three other people, around a table with an illuminated surface. I know what it is since I had a technical class in the academy that exclusively dealt with the handling of this type of military strategy device: a digital module that serves to make projections of territorial maps, plans, troop movements. They're preparing an attack.

When he sees us come in, Taddeus raises his arm and signals us to approach him.

"We'll continue later," he tells his three companions when we arrive, then he turns to us and says: "Come on, over here."

We follow him into a small adjacent room that holds only one oval table with six chairs and some monitors on one of the walls. With the door closed, the noises from the main hall are barely noticeable.

"See what I was talking about yesterday?" he says, smiling as always. "What did I say about bad luck? Luck is giving us a hard time, right? But we're not going to let it have its way." He lets out a laugh, throwing his head back. "The stupid tadpole is as pathetic as his vermin father," he continues in a mocking tone. Addressing me, he adds, "So he wants you back at his side, huh? It seems he can't stand being away from you."

His comment seems entirely unnecessary and out of place. I don't find it funny that he tries to crack a joke at my expense, even when he makes it clear that he detests Nigel as much as his father.

"You did well, Derin. The right thing was to get out of there immediately and get in touch with us." Now he changes to a more serious tone. "All right, this is what we'll do."

No, Taddeus doesn't intend to move the start of operation forward. It's not possible.

At this very moment, Commanders Scott and Anderson are leading the deployment of their troops into lurk positions in Moray Firth, the estuary where Ventus is located. They won't be ready until tomorrow at noon. Due to the complexity involved in mobilizing all the military equipment, vehicles, and troops in camouflage, it's impossible to speed things up without being discovered. Besides, Dylan has already left for his job at the ministry. Although there are ways to communicate with him, it would be too risky to rush him into getting the codes today. So the previous times agreed upon with the regional command for the start of Don Quixote are now set in stone.

But since Taddeus is a shrewd strategist, he's already got a solution for the obstacle Nigel has put in our way. The rebels' informants haven't found out yet what Nigel plans to do with me, but they confirm he'll be quite busy all day with a large foreign delegation. They don't think he'll have time to deal with "my business" until tonight. Without a doubt, a group of agents has orders to take me to his office in the Tower of Victory. They'll come to pick me up tonight at nine o'clock, in the apartment in Sector 7. Once they've realized I've fled, they'll immediately launch a search and capture operation.

Among the various options Taddeus' experts have considered, they suggest that the most convenient thing is to create a false trail regarding my whereabouts. Just enough to keep Nigel's bloodhounds busy, at least until the start of the Ventus sabotage operation. They'll have them believe that, after learning I'd be taken back to London, I panicked, thinking Nigel had changed his mind and now wanted to kill me, my mother, and my sister. A fake trail pointing to an escape attempt to Ireland will be laid out.

This idea doesn't seem too farfetched. In fact, at some point, I had considered the option of fleeing to Ireland as an alternative, and I would have tried if it weren't for the fact that I'd leave my family members to certain death… have to abandon Dylan.

"But what about my father and my brother?" I ask Taddeus. "The second Nigel finds out I've escaped, he'll want revenge and have them killed."

"I'll be honest, Derin," he says, putting his elbows on the table and resting his chin on his fists. "We can't dismiss this possibility one hundred percent. Unfortunately, it's a risk we can't eliminate. But my people trust that Nigel won't waste time or energy arranging for them to be killed so long as he's not sure of what's happened to you."

"I really don't think so," I reply, shaking my head. "I know Nigel. He's impulsive and proud and loathes being mocked. He'll want revenge, and he'll want it soon."

"I'm sorry, Derin," Taddeus continues, "but there's no better option. If you accept and follow our plan, your mother and sister will be safe. Besides, there's a high probability that you'll find yourself back with your father and your brother, safe and sound, the day after tomorrow. But, if you think it's best to let yourself be captured again by Crowley, you can forget about the rescue mission, and who knows what that miserable man has in mind for you and for them."

He's right. There's no other alternative. I must go ahead with his plan and trust that his experts won't be wrong.

—

I SPEND THE REST OF THE MORNING and all afternoon in intense preparatory sessions with Lieutenant Greg Nelson, chief of the small special rescue team that Commander Burke has put together. I've been granted the rank of lieutenant in the National Forces of the Resistance. I can't help noticing, with an air of wry amusement, that just a week ago I became an officer of the National Army of Englandom. Now I'm an officer of the rebel forces.

Though I don't fall short compared to Greg Nelson in my skills, preparation, and capacities, Commander Burke has decided that he, not I, should be the one to lead our rescue group. Greg is only one or two years older than me, but he has much more experience on the "battlefield." Besides, he knows the troops, lines of command, and rebel strategies much better. So it's he who will lead us in the liberation of the "strategic prisoners," which is what they call the quartet formed by my father, Brian, Liam, and Jonas Mitchell. I think it's a wise decision and I'm not against it.

In addition to Lieutenant Nelson and myself, Second Lieutenant Marvin and Sergeant Davis are with us. I'll meet the rest of the unit tomorrow. Between the four of us, we analyze over and over the intelligence information that high command has placed at our disposal. First, we spend hours putting plans together, then we discard them, put them back together with modifications, and finally agree on the primary and contingency shock strategies that we deem most appropriate. We present our final plan to Commander Burke, and he approves it with a few alterations to coordinate better with the rest of the operation.

By dinnertime, I know the geographical details of Ventus like the back of my hand. I've memorized the number of wind turbines and their position within the extensive wind farm; I know the exact location of the operations center; I can locate and describe the different electrical substations on land and sea; I can draw the map of the prison camp where my father, Brian, and the Mitchells are being held, and know their presumed location inside the compound; and I know how many guards are in the camp, and where they're stationed.

I'm so deeply immersed in the mission's preparations that, from time to time, I have to pinch myself to remind me that all this is real. It's not a strategic training at the Military Academy. In a few hours, I'll find myself smack in the middle of a real battle against government forces. If everything goes well, we'll have Brian and my father back in little more than a day… If everything goes well.

Dylan appears in the cafeteria of the rebel headquarters shortly after I've fetched my dinner tray and taken a seat at a large table along with members of our rescue command. I see him as soon as he enters, even though the dining hall is crowded with hungry rebels. I make a sign with my hand, and he locates me. He smiles, waves, and signals that he's going to grab something to eat and then he'll join us. For a moment, I forget everything and dream of his kisses.

When he approaches our table with his tray, I'm surprised as he greets Nelson, Marvin, and Davis by their first names, calling them Greg, Helen, and Alex. I have the impression that everyone here knows Dylan, something I really don't like at all. This is especially true because I'm sure I don't imagine the somewhat clumsy and tense way he and Davis greet each other, as if they know each other better, but are trying to hide it. Even worse, the obvious tell-tale glances that Alex Davis throws at Dylan don't escape me; he must think nobody else notices, but I do. I understand too well what this kind of look means, and I can't help but feel furious and filled with jealousy.

Dylan takes a seat next to me and gives me a mouth-watering smile.

"Hi," he says somewhat self-consciously. "My uncle already told me what happened."

The sparkle in his eyes, that of someone in love, immediately eclipses my jealousy. I read in them the same desire and impatience that I feel to take him in my arms and kiss him.

"Yeah, what a mess, right?" I answer, smiling but shaking my head. "What the heck, we just had to get out earlier than expected, that's all."

I'm dying to at least hold his hand, or caress his cheek, but we're both aware that our displays of affection would be quite out of place in this military environment. There's a clear difference between the spree of celebration, freedom, and exaltation last night in the theater and the calmer, more introspective and anxious spirit that's now perceptible before the imminent battle. We must contain our impulses until later.

After our meal, Dylan and I go to meet Taddeus, Burke, and Jonathan. On the way to the meeting room, the thoughts I had during dinner come back, perhaps this time more out of curiosity than jealousy.

"Do you and Alex Davis know each other well?" I ask, trying not to sound too interested.

"Err… well, more or less, I suppose," he says. "We grew up in the same neighborhood and went to the same school, but he was two years ahead of me."

I wasn't wrong, then. They know each other. But judging by Davis' behavior, I suspect there's more, so I insist, "But the two of you don't get along, or something? He looks at you in a … penetrating way."

Dylan looks at me, smiling and squinting. "Don't tell me you're jealous," he replies mockingly.

"Should I be?" I return the question in the same tone.

"Of course not!" he exclaims, amused. Then he comes closer to my ear and whispers, "I only have eyes for you."

I can't resist his sweetness! If there weren't so many people in these corridors, I would devour him with kisses.

"But, if you really want to know," he continues, "Alex confessed that he had a crush on me about a year ago. I told him I didn't feel the same way and that I could only be his friend. He accepted, though I must admit that since then, whenever we see each other, the situation is somewhat uncomfortable."

I knew there was something more between them, and I can't help feeling jealous. But the candor and innocence that Dylan shows in telling me this makes me feel very safe. I stop thinking about it, at least for the moment.

During the discussion with Taddeus, Dylan confirms that everything is going smoothly. No one suspects anything, and he's begun to introduce small support programs into the ministry system so tomorrow he can obtain the codes required for Operation Don Quixote without a problem.

Everything seems to be going according to plan: five minutes past six in the evening, after the ministry's security program has completed its control protocol, Dylan will extract the Ventus codes. He'll then leave his job as usual and go to the interchange station at Access Point 13 to take the train back to the Strip. His estimated time of arrival at the operation's meeting point—where we'll be waiting with helijets to take us to Moray Firth—is shortly before eight o'clock. As soon as he shows up, we'll head north.

IT'S NINE O'CLOCK AT NIGHT when Jonathan, Dylan, and I arrive at the hideout where our families will remain. I get a little uneasy when I remember that, at this time, Nigel's people will be discovering my disappearance and looking for me. I hope with all my heart that they've swallowed the story of our escape to Ireland.

I hadn't stopped to think about what our hideaway would look like, though I would have certainly imagined it as a dark nook located in the cold, damp basement of some ruined building. But the rooms of our "secret lair" positively surprise me. Mia, Lily, and Nick Mitchell accompany us on the preliminary tour of the place.

We're on the sixth level of a seven-story building that borders the canal. It's kind of an additional level, like a mezzanine, that's been inserted between two original stories. Therefore, the ceilings are unusually low, but apart from that, it's a reasonably spacious place. Access is complicated since, to get to the apartment, you have to go through a series of secret passageways and stairs that start from the second level. But once inside, it's like being in a comfortable home. There's a well-equipped kitchen, a dining room with three tables and six chairs each, a large living room, at least seven or eight bedrooms with bunk beds, and two large full bathrooms.

The apartment occupies the entire half of the added mezzanine that overlooks the canal, and we even have some windows on that side. From a cellar behind the kitchen, a narrow spiral staircase secretly crosses through the floor above ours and goes up to the attic. Dylan explains that there, under the roof, there's a well-concealed little room, his "refuge." From what I gather, it's a room where he's installed all his technological gadgets, his personal things, and I don't know what else.

"I'll show it to you later, okay?" he says casually.

I have the impression that he doesn't want others to go up too.

"Sure, definitely," I reply in the same almost disinterested tone. But I can't wait until it's "later."

My mother is already at home in a room where there are two bunk beds and a closet; she, Lily, and I will share that room. The Blakes have taken two bedrooms, and the Mitchells, who were brought here only a couple of hours ago, as I was told, are also staying in one like ours, with two bunk beds. Anyway, we have enough space for everyone, even for when my father, Brian, Liam, and Jonas come here.

I know it's not the proper time to think about this, but since there are at least two free bedrooms, I let myself dream for a moment and enjoy imagining that at some point, later on, Dylan and I could share one of them.

CHAPTER 25

HEAVEN ON EARTH

THE NIGHT BEFORE OPERATION DON QUIXOTE and the rescue mission, we share our first dinner together in this peculiar hideaway. Nerves and anxiety overtake all members of the three families, though each one of us in a different way and for various reasons.

My mother and Lily waver between the intense joy of an upcoming reunion with Brian and my father and the dreadful possibility that the operation fails and ends with both them and me dead.

The Blakes fear the danger Dylan will be exposed to during his mission to obtain the secret codes. What's more, Belinda doesn't hide her nervousness for what comes afterward, since Jonathan and Dylan will travel with Commander Burke to Ventus as indispensable members of Don Quixote's technical group. Mia shares her mother's fears, and as far as Brian is concerned, she also shares my mother's and Lily's alternating feelings.

Catherine Mitchell wasn't coping very well with the emotional pressure and had to take a sedative before retiring to her room, while Nick Mitchell, instead of being nervous, is furious. He wasn't allowed to take part in the rescue operation. Burke decided that since he lacks any type of military training, he'd be more of a hindrance than a help.

At sixteen years old, he's quite smart and almost as big and stocky as his brother Liam, but he still gives in to too many spontaneous and thoughtless actions. His sudden mood swings would not only put him in grave danger but also disrupt the mission. Lily has taken up the task of comforting him and making him see reason, and Nick seems to like the attention he receives from my sister. I'd rather she didn't show so much interest in him, though. She's still too young to be thinking about such things.

Immutable as ever, Jonathan hides his nerves very well.

More than anything, both Dylan and I feel—despite undeniable anxiety about the upcoming events—impatient for the others to retire to their rooms so we can finally be alone.

It's nearly eleven when, besides us, only Lily and Nick remain in the living room. They're so entertained by their conversation that they show no signs of going to bed anytime soon, so I decide to take matters into my own hands.

"Don't stay up too late," I say to Lily as I get up. "Tomorrow will be an intense day for everyone. Dylan and I still need to discuss some things. We'll be upstairs in the attic. Goodnight."

Dylan looks at me, smiling and grateful. He springs to his feet and also says goodnight. We manage to hold back our impulses until we reach the middle of the spiral staircase up to the attic. There, wrapped in the safety of darkness, we can't resist any longer: we devour each other with kisses of such voracity that we forget to breathe. Our embrace is so passionate that for a moment, we're about to lose our balance on the thin triangular steps.

"Sorry," Dylan says, between gasps. "I simply couldn't stand another second without kissing you… I just had to… I've spent all day thinking about this moment."

"I told you, don't apologize. I wanted it more than you."

We repeat the sequence of kisses, hugs, and caresses until I begin to feel some discomfort from my healing bruises and the uncomfortable position we're standing in. It's necessary to resist the urge to continue just to catch my breath.

"Come on," says Dylan, taking my hand.

We enter his "refuge" through a trapdoor at the end of the stairs. It's a small room, with one of the walls—the one facing the canal—inclined along the slope of the roof. It also has a pivoting window at waist height. Although the walls have been covered by wooden boards—and I imagine some insulating material too—it's much colder up here than in the rooms below. I'm pleased to see an electric radiator. I hope it works.

There are two long desks, one on each side of the window, and they're packed with computers and electronic devices, as well as numerous cables, tiny pieces, and tools that I don't recognize. There are two shelves full of books and strange gadgets. Several posters of film artists and musicians hang from the walls—similar to those at Georgie's. I'm surprised to see in a corner, over a base of wooden pallets, a thick mattress with several colored cushions and a quilt.

"What's with the bed? You'll sleep here?" I ask. "I thought you'd be sharing a room with Mia."

"No, I'm better off up here. Well, what do you think?" he then says expectantly, turning on the radiator. It works. We won't freeze.

"I like your refuge," I say, nodding in approval. "It's a bit like you: full of little surprises and mysteries to be discovered."

By the time I realize how corny that sounded, it's too late. But he smiles in delight and doesn't seem repulsed by my non-sense. He comes closer to the bedside table and picks up a tiny device with a digital screen. The delicate gadget is connected through a thin cable to a black box, which in turn is attached to two small speakers.

"Well, here's one of those surprises," he says, sliding his finger with short, quick movements over the device's display. "Do you remember me saying I have a collection of illegal music? I've got both foreign tunes and those from here, but before the war, when we were still the United Kingdom. I wanted you to listen to some songs I like best."

"Oh, great! I didn't think you'd bring them here with you."

"Of course, why not?" he replies. "It helps me relax when I'm stressed. Besides, I said I wanted you to listen to them."

From the speakers, at a low but sufficient volume, an electronic melody of rhythms and percussions emerge. I find it somewhat unusual. The emotional singing voice of a young man leaves no doubt that he's in love.

"This one's called 'Let Me Love You,'" he says, avoiding looking me in the eye.

I approach him and embrace him from behind. I lean my head on his shoulder, place my lips on the nape of his neck, and trace a path of tender kisses until I reach his earlobe.

"I love you," I whisper into his ear.

He turns around, grabs me by the back of my neck with both hands, and looks at me with the most beautiful eyes I've ever seen in my life: deep honey eyes that I could lose myself in forever.

"And I love you."

My lips merge with his, and we share the most intimate kiss of all so far, savoring every little second of joy that ripples through our bodies. It's our first declaration of love.

I grab his t-shirt by the hem in the back and slide it up slowly. I lift it over his head and outstretched arms until I remove it completely, and let it fall to the ground. He does the same with me: he takes off my t-shirt and then carefully removes the bandage wrapped around my torso.

While the boy's voice coming out of the speakers promises that he'll never disappoint his love, my hands and lips caress every corner of Dylan's perfect body: his shoulders, his arms, his chest, his sides, his abs… everything is so delicious that, when I just start discovering a new spot, I want to return to the previous one… and continue with the next… and go back again to the one before…

I'm fascinated by the smoothness of his skin over a body that's both firm and exceptionally soft. His exquisite scent makes me drunk. I take a deep breath through my nose to enjoy all the scents of his skin, and then I store them in a safe place in my memory. In a trance, my fingers, lips, and tongue traverse the landscape of muscular hills and valleys covered with honey skin and charming paths of fine golden hair: my new favorite landscape.

But Dylan interrupts this fabulous journey. I'm involuntarily forced to pause my expedition of paradise because he's anxious to undertake his own adventure. He signals his intentions, separating me from his naked torso to discover mine. The sensation of his hands and mouth exploring my body with zigzag movements, from my chest to my abdomen, drives me crazy. I don't know what I prefer: the rapturous delight I experience in discovering and enjoying his body, or the maddening excitement of him enjoying mine.

Fortunately, I don't have to choose between the two pleasures. I'm lucky I can enjoy them both.

The first song—about the boy in love—has ended, but its passionate phrases repeat in my head, and I decide that song was made for us.

I unbuckle his belt, unbutton his pants, and slide them over his beautiful thighs. I help him take off his shoes and socks and then lay him with his back on the bed. I grab his pants by the ends and, with two pulls, remove them entirely. I let them fall to the floor next to the rest of our clothes.

While I undo my pants, I contemplate with delight the body of a young Greek god lying on the bed. He's placed his hands behind his head, which makes his biceps stand out, and he's raised his left leg at an angle, with his foot resting on the quilt, showing his well-defined and delicious thigh. His dark grey boxer shorts fit him like a glove, though they can no longer disguise his arousal.

I lie carefully on top of him, going directly to his eyes and mouth, and we merge in an intricate and rhythmic dance of kisses and caresses. It's a symphony of extraordinary sensations:

our accelerated breathing and heart rates, the tension of all the muscles in our bodies, and the mutual stimulation of our most erogenous zones.

By the time the singer of the fourth or fifth song declares his true feelings in his ardent and harsh voice, we've both taken off our underwear and have become one body, overwhelmed with love and passion, accelerating our intense choreography until we reach the maximum point of ecstasy and fullness. I'm in heaven… and I've become one with the most beautiful angel in the sky.

Now everything makes sense. My whole body and soul are filled with joy.

Without the slightest exaggeration, I can say that I've enjoyed the most extraordinary experience of my life. If I die tomorrow, I'll die with the satisfaction of having lived this heavenly moment.

We remain a long time in silence, totally exhausted.

Dylan rests his head sideways on my chest, and I wrap him with my arms. I feel so good that I've almost stopped feeling the pain of my injuries. I trace his silky hair with my left-hand fingers, and with the other hand, I stroke his shoulder and back.

It's all I need to be happy.

When the last song ends, I turn my head toward the bedside table and notice, next to one of the speakers, the soldier figurine that I gave him that first time I came to see him before they captured my family and me. Thanks to that silly gift, he hugged me for the first time. I'll never forget that day.

"You have it here!" I exclaim. "I hadn't noticed it before."

Dylan raises his head and sits up. When he sees the little figure I'm pointing to, he smiles.

"Yes… I also had it on my nightstand in my bedroom," he says, reaching over to grab it. "You know, that day you gave it to me, on the train platform… I think that was the moment I fell in love with you."

I smile at him, grab his hand holding the "little tin soldier," and kiss it. Then I kiss him on the lips.

"I remember that day perfectly," I reply. "I had already fallen in love with you. When the train started moving, I watched you stay behind, and my heart shattered. I was sure I'd never see you again."

Now he kisses me.

"How did you come up with that nickname, the little tin soldier?" I ask him later, talking playfully. "Were you making fun of me before you realized I wasn't a complete idiot?"

"Of course not! How could you think that?" He hastens to clarify things. "The truth is, I liked you from the start. But to be honest, you seemed a bit stuck-up and indifferent. It never occurred to me that you could like me."

I can't help laughing, delighted by his candor. He doesn't mince his words.

"I'm really shy about these things, as you know," I say, stroking his lips. "It's always been difficult for me to show my true feelings. When I met you, I was terrified that you or someone else would notice how much I liked you. So I foolishly tried to disguise it." He cracks a sweet smile and nods. Then, I insist: "But what about the nickname?"

"Oh, that…" he says. "It was spontaneous, a spur of the moment thing. When I saw you that morning after your graduation, glowing in your dress uniform, I thought you should be a model for all soldiers. There was no one more handsome or sexy than you. For some reason, the little tin soldier popped into my head. I don't know why since he has nothing to do with you."

"Maybe he does," I say in a silly tone. "Because I too have fallen madly in love… though not with a paper ballerina."

"Don't be so sure about that, you still haven't seen me dance," he says, winking.

I let out a loud laugh. He's precious.

After another round of caresses, kisses, and whispers, we fall asleep with our bodies entwined.

It's about five in the morning when I wake up. Without opening my eyes, I smile at the scent and warmth of Dylan's body next to mine. I don't remember when we got into a "spooning" position, but it's lovely. We're both lying on our sides, facing the wall, with his back touching my chest and my arm wrapped around him.

I stroke his hand, and he reacts by intertwining his fingers with mine.

"Are you awake?" he asks in a low voice.

I open my eyes, move my head closer to his, and kiss him on the shoulder.

"Hi, good morning. Did you sleep well?" I say, also in a very soft voice. It's still dark outside, so no light comes through the window. But the numerous little lights from his devices and gadgets give the room a faint glow. I turn toward his delicious earlobe and bite it softly.

Dylan sits up, arches back his shoulders, and lets out a slight moan. Then he lies down again but in the opposite position. Now he's looking straight into my eyes and kisses me.

"Yes, I slept like a log, and you?"

"Better than ever," I answer, returning his kiss with three of my own: one on the tip of his nose and two little kisses on his lips.

Then, he brings his hand to my face and runs his thumb over my left eyebrow.

"What happened to you here?" he asks, referring for the first time to the scar that divides my brow in two.

I tell him the story of the boat on the lake when I was a child and fell into the water and almost drowned after Brian hit me with the oar.

I feel very comfortable and relaxed talking about my secrets with him. Apart from Zara, Dylan is now the only person I've opened up to like this. Not even my parents know the truth about my scar and the distance between Brian and me. That day at the lake, they accepted the ridiculous version without suspicion: that I hit my forehead against the crossbar of the upper bunk bed. I've always been sure they attributed the permanent conflict between

Brian and me to our opposite personalities, which became more evident as we got older. Sharing these complicated feelings with Dylan is very intimate. It makes me feel close to another human being like never before.

We have to get up now, but we're so happy that we decide to indulge ourselves with a few more minutes. We want to delay our return to reality as long as possible. But after a while, too short a time, it's me who brings us back to earth.

"I don't want you to be alone in the ministry, putting yourself at risk that way," I say, looking into his eyes and stroking his cheek. "I must find a way to be there and protect you. Something unforeseen could come up, something may go wrong. I can't let anything happen to you."

Before answering, Dylan kisses me.

"Derin, nothing's going to happen to me," he says confidently. "Everything will be fine, you'll see. Besides, how dare you consider putting yourself at risk like that, going to London? They're already looking for you everywhere. The chance of you being captured puts me in even greater danger. You could make the whole operation fail."

I know he's right, but I can't stand the thought of leaving him alone.

"To be perfectly honest," he continues, "I'm much more nervous about what comes after, in Moray Firth. I know the situation there will be much more intense."

He's right again. Both the rescue operation I'll be a part of and the mission he and Jonathan must complete at Ventus headquarters involve extremely high risks. Dylan's invaluable contribution to the success of Operation Don Quixote doesn't end with the extraction of the secret codes. He and Jonathan will be a part of a special unit, led by Commander Burke himself, tasked with setting in motion the most significant element of the sabotage operation.

The rebel forces led by Commanders Scott and Anderson will launch a massive attack on the giant turbine towers. The main objective of this attack is to distract the regime's military forces stationed on the coast of the estuary and keep them occupied. Although the estimated damage from conventional weapons such as explosives and guided missiles is considerable, the real death blow will be technological.

The codes Dylan will obtain from the Ministry of Public Utilities and Services will give us access to Ventus' central operating system, which is located in the control room on the coast of the Moray estuary. In addition, they're needed to modify the parameters that regulate the function of the wind turbines. The experts in Jonathan's group discovered a technical failure in the design. The success of the operation is based on this Achilles' heel.

According to the brief explanation I got from Jonathan, the regime's engineers, either due to lack of resources or pure negligence, didn't correctly dimension the automatic braking systems of the wind turbines. They didn't include a support system in case of an emergency if ever the turbines exceeded the maximum speed allowed. The discovery of this defect was the spark that led to Taddeus' plan, which, simply put, consists of the following:

While the attack troops distract government forces at high sea, Burke's unit will burst into the Ventus control room. That's where Dylan, with the codes he's obtained, will infiltrate the operating system. Next, he will alter the parameters that regulate the maximum speed allowed for the turbine blades, making them rotate without resistance to the mighty north wind. According to calculations by Jonathan's team, with the brake system disabled, the relentless wind force will spin the blades at such speeds that the turbines, unable to withstand the intense overheating, will explode. In a matter of minutes, this will wreak massive devastation, unmatched even by weeks of constant attacks using conventional weapons.

Over the last two days, I've become tired of asking why Dylan must be the one to alter the operating parameters. The risk he's taking by stealing the codes is bad enough. But again and again, I've received the same answer: Dylan's the safest bet to guarantee the plan's success. Taddeus and his people are convinced that only he, with his genius and in-depth knowledge of the ministry's systems, is capable of resolving any unforeseen event in a matter of seconds once he's inside Ventus' operational program.

I make a tremendous effort to break away from my angel and get up.

"Do you think the others have realized that we slept together?" I ask him.

"Derin," he says in an amused tone, after letting out a chuckle, "I'm sure everyone's been thinking for a while that we've done lots of 'nice stuff' together."

I'm surprised because I don't think we're that obvious, although maybe he's right. I turn around, smiling and shaking my head, and bend down to give him another kiss.

"You're such a cheeky rogue."

I leave Dylan in the attic and go down the metal stairs. With each step, I feel that the fantastic world in Dylan's arms is becoming more and more distant and, instead, the unsettling reality of the events before us is quickly coming closer. I'm glad I don't run into anyone, either in the kitchen or the hallway. Even if Dylan is right, I want to avoid being seen before I've showered and dressed.

I tiptoe into the room where my mother and Lily are still sleeping and quietly take out my clean clothes. I don't find anyone in the bathroom either. I shower, shave, brush my teeth, and get dressed in less than fifteen minutes. Clean, I might be presentable to face any challenge, but the invigorating shower also left me with the unpleasant sensation of having rinsed away Dylan's delicious smell. I never thought that one day I would come to hate water and soap so much.

We all have breakfast together: Jonathan and Belinda, Mia, Dylan, me, Lily, my mother, and Catherine and Nick Mitchell.

Although we try to have a pleasant and casual conversation, our nerves are on edge, and the tension is palpable.

The first farewell takes place at a quarter to seven.

Taddeus' men wait in the street to escort Dylan to the station, where he'll take his usual train to London. From there, he'll be alone, though they'll be watching him from a distance. When he leaves the ministry's building, shortly after six o'clock this evening, they'll also be waiting to make sure he returns without mishap.

Dylan says goodbye to everyone. Although Belinda and Mia can't hold back their tears, he remains firm and calm, assuring them again and again that everything will turn out fine. They won't see him again until we've all returned from the operation, because when he comes back from London with the codes, we'll immediately leave for Moray Firth.

I go down with him and Jonathan to one of the building's side doors.

"Uncle, can you tell them I'm coming?" he asks Jonathan.

Jonathan smiles, gives a friendly nod, pats him on the cheek, and leaves the building to meet Taddeus' people. He's understood what his nephew wants, and I thank him silently.

We only have a few seconds. We embrace each other as hard as we can so that they'll never be able to break us apart.

"Be careful, please," I beg, emphasizing each word. "Be careful."

"Don't worry, I'll be fine. See you later, okay?"

We kiss one last time, and I have to force myself to let go of him. He turns around and walks out of sight.

When the door closes behind him, I feel my heart tearing apart.

CHAPTER 26

THE CHIPMUNK AND THE NUTS

SHORTLY AFTER, I HAVE TO SAY GOODBYE to my mother and Lily too, as another group of guards comes to take Jonathan and me to the command center. As we bid each other farewell, I try hard to push away the dreadful visions of them helpless and alone. I can't stand to imagine what will happen to them if the rescue mission is a failure and I end up dead in the attempt.

To my amazement, they both are calm and peaceful. I'm not surprised anymore by Lily's composure, but my mother is clearly making a superhuman effort to avoid overwhelming me even more than I already am. She must be aware that now I need, more than anything, concentration and serenity. Though it's also possible that the psychological burden of the past week has consumed her so much that it's left her in a state of lucid sedation, a kind of forced resignation where she accepts that nothing now is in her hands.

I hug both of them, assuring them that I'll be back with Brian and my father in a few hours. I don't look behind me when I step out the door, but I sense that they're struggling to hold back tears as I leave.

—

THE MORNING FLIES BY. Fortunately, I'm too busy at first with our rescue mission's final preparations to think about other matters.

But as time goes on, anxiety takes over with increasing intensity. I can't sit still for a second.

After lunch, Belinda and Mia show up at the command center. They'll be part of the medical unit that will treat rebel soldiers who return wounded. Belinda is one of the doctors in charge, and Mia, though without formal medical training, has enough knowledge and practical experience to be useful to her mother. The nursing unit plans to be stationed in the designated place two hours before our return from Ventus. They will set up a field hospital there. My mother, Lily, Catherine, and Nick Mitchell will also be transferred there to help the doctors and nurses with whatever they can.

The countdown to the start of Operation Don Quixote begins at five o'clock in the afternoon. By this time, Commanders Scott and Anderson's rebel forces are already hidden in the bays and peninsulas protected by the rocky formations of the cliffs along the Caithness coastline, in front of the rough waters of Moray Firth.

In one of the inner courtyards of NATFOR's command center complex, Taddeus directs his last words of motivation to our two units.

"Don't forget," he says effusively, "you'll be our mission's heroes! In a few hours, you will have dealt the hardest blow to the dictatorship yet, and opened the path to final victory! Be brave, we're all with you!"

I know his message is directed to Burke's unit, the one in charge of destroying Ventus, and not really my rescue command. Nevertheless, I let myself get excited by his words.

The members of Unit 1, led by Commander Burke, board the first vehicle. Jonathan, Dylan, and several soldiers and technical experts belong to that unit. It's the command that will execute Operation High Speed, which consists of breaking into the Ventus control center, infiltrating the program that regulates the function of the wind turbines, altering their rotation speed parameters, and causing their destruction. The members of my unit—Unit 2—under the command of Lieutenant Nelson, board the second vehicle. Our unit also includes Second Lieutenant Marvin, six soldiers with specialized training in rescue missions, and Alex Davis, the sergeant whose mere presence makes me feel jealous—I'm sure he still has a crush on Dylan. Operation Liberation consists of breaking into the prison camp, subduing the guards, locating the "strategic prisoners"—my father, Brian, and Liam and Jonas Mitchell—, and freeing them.

After a long journey winding through streets and alleys in the densest sectors of the Strip, we arrive at the starting and return point for our operations. We're in Sector 17, in the central part of a block formed by hundreds of shabby brick and concrete buildings between five and ten stories high.

"From Sectors 15 to 23," Nelson says, "almost all blocks are equal to this one in density and appearance. We have hordes of enthusiastic snipers stationed on the rooftops. Their only task is to engage in hunting."

"Hunting?" I say, squinting my eyes.

"Yes, that's what we call the task of shooting down flocks of surveillance drones that the Government deploys throughout the Strip. They're idiots, it's useless trying to control an uncontrollable zone. But their arrogance plays to our advantage."

"What do you mean?"

"Most of the drones aren't destroyed," he continues. "Those that suffer slight damage are repaired and reconditioned, and become part of our own military infrastructure."

Nelson makes a sign to indicate that we're arriving. The vehicles go down a ramp, which then becomes a tunnel, and stop after entering an enormous industrial building. Because of the infinite concrete pillars that support the roof, it vaguely reminds me of a forest. I'm amazed by the sheer amount of military weaponry stored on this site, including dozens of armored vehicles and several military helijets. Among them are the two helijets assigned to our operations. The crews are waiting for us.

It's ten minutes to six, and I'm on edge. Soon, Dylan will extract the Ventus codes. I despair at not being able to be at his side, protect him, and make sure he gets out of there without problems.

Jonathan, usually very composed, can't hide his anxiety either. He seems to be trying to distract himself by giving me technical explanations of all the security devices and camouflage measures available in this compound, which is also an armory and military hangar.

"The whole roof is covered with grass, shrubs, and trees," he says, his arm extended toward the ceiling and pointing with twirling motions. "There's even a basketball court up there. From the air, you see nothing but a park."

I nod, trying to seem interested in his comments. But the truth is that I'm not interested at all. Right now, I'm just thinking about Dylan, and I'm sure Jonathan is too.

At five minutes to six, Commander Burke sits in front of the radio transmitter on his unit's helijet. It's time to get in touch with Taddeus' agents, who await Dylan's departure from the ministry. Jonathan and I, tense as steel beams, stand nearby.

"Big Bad Wolf, this is Falcon One. Over," Burke says into the microphone. He waits a couple of seconds and repeats: "Big Bad Wolf, this is Falcon One. Over."

"Falcon One, this is Big Bad Wolf. Copy. Over," answers a voice through the radio's speakers.

"Big Bad Wolf, this is Falcon One. Confirm position waiting for Chipmunk. Over."

"Falcon One, this is Big Bad Wolf. I confirm position. Waiting for Chipmunk to leave the tree with the nuts. Over."

"Big Bad Wolf, Falcon One here. Roger. I await news. Over."

So far, so good. They're waiting for Dylan outside the ministry. As soon as he comes out, they'll be ready to escort him back to Access Point 13. Despite the tension, I grin inside when I hear the codename they've assigned Dylan: the Chipmunk. In my opinion, it's very fitting; chipmunks look cute, but they're very astute, agile, fast, and extremely smart. It suits him.

While my ears listen carefully for any sound from the radio, I don't look away from the military watch I'm wearing on my left wrist: three minutes after six. Dylan is about to infiltrate the system. I close my eyes for a moment and pray that he has no difficulties.

At ten past six, Jonathan can't stand the wait anymore.

"What time are they supposed to confirm Dylan's departure?" he asks Burke in an impatient voice, though he knows the plan and timetable by heart.

"Within the next few minutes," Burke replies dryly.

The next few minutes turn into five. But nothing happens.

At six-twenty, Jonathan has lost his cool composure and can no longer stand still. He drums nervously on the metal surface of the radio dashboard with all his fingers and changes the foot supporting his body weight time and again. It baffles me to see him so restless, and he infects me with his anxiety.

Six twenty-five. Nothing. No news. Absolute silence.

Dylan, get out now… Dylan, get out of there… Dylan, get out now… I repeat in my mind as if evoking a spell to keep away bad luck.

Burke also begins to get impatient. He contacts the agents once more.

"Big Bad Wolf, this is Falcon One. Situation report. Over."

"Falcon Once, this is Big Bad Wolf. Nothing to report. No sign of Chipmunk. Over."

Something isn't right. This can't be happening. No sign of Dylan. Something's gone wrong; he should have left a while ago. What's going on? A dark abyss opens beneath my feet. It's the terrible sensation you feel when you realize your greatest fear, the worst possible outcome, is becoming reality.

Dylan, please, get out of there! I'm begging you…

Six thirty. Nothing.

Six thirty-five. Silence. No sign of Dylan.

It's over. The worst has happened. They've discovered him. That must be it… We've failed. I've failed him. Everything inside of me crumbles like a house of cards. Everything has been in vain. I've lost him forever. Dylan!

How could I have let him go alone? I should have been there with him, I knew I had to, I knew it.

"Big Bad Wolf, this is Falcon One. What's going on, damn it?!" I hear Burke shout into the radio with an exasperated tone.

"Falcon One, this is Big Bad Wolf. Err… still no sign of Chipmunk. Err… we don't know what's going on. What should we do? Ov—wait!"

Jonathan and I jump in unison and lean over Burke, sticking our ears next to the radio speakers.

"Falcon One, this is Big Bad Wolf. Chipmunk leaving the tree. I repeat, Chipmunk leaving the tree. Over."

Dylan! You're safe! Thank you, thank you…

"Big Bad Wolf, this Falcon One," Burke replies, after letting out a long sigh of relief. "Confirm contact with Chipmunk. I repeat, confirm contact with Chipmunk. Over."

Several seconds of unbearable silence pass.

"Falcon One, this is Big Bad Wolf," we hear at last. "I confirm. Contact with Chipmunk. Chipmunk has left the tree and has the nuts. Coming back to the burrow. Over."

The frightful tension from just a few minutes ago magically vanishes and is replaced by a euphoric feeling of bliss and triumph.

You did it, my love, you did it. Now come back to my arms.

But his unexpected and lengthy delay scrambles the operation's itinerary. We must leave here at eight o'clock, and as things are, Dylan won't arrive on time. Taddeus Green, who's been following the operation's progress live through the command center's sophisticated communication system, contacts Burke. From what I gather, we will need to have left behind a certain point along the route before nine. There, an infiltrated radar operator will ensure that we pass undetected through the most radar-heavy stretch, but he has limited time. We can't risk being late, so Taddeus decides to send a private helijet to get Dylan.

"Won't that be too dangerous?" I ask Burke.

"It's not child's play to fly in and out of London without the authorization of air traffic controllers. But that special helijet's radar signal deflector systems, as well as the rest of its technological gadgets, are very sophisticated; actually, the private helijet is even more advanced than the military ones we are using for our mission. It'll do the trick."

I meet Jonathan's gaze. He nods and smiles slightly, in his usual state of serenity. To me, that's the most reliable sign that he agrees with Burke.

While we wait for Dylan's arrival, the nursing unit appears. They show up long before the scheduled time, accompanied by Belinda and Mia.

"Where's Dylan? Is he back? Is he all right?" Belinda asks impatiently, addressing Jonathan.

"He's about to arrive," he replies, smiling. "Everything went well."

She gives him a hug and sighs in relief.

Jonathan does the right thing by not upsetting her unnecessarily. There's no need to tell her about the minutes we endured during Dylan's delay. The important thing is that he's fulfilled the first part of his mission and he's on his way.

Belinda explains that they've come earlier on Taddeus' orders. He decided it would be better to have the field hospital ready as soon as possible, with plenty of time to prepare everything. After all, there was no reason for them to wait until later.

At seven forty, Burke announces that the helijet with Dylan on board is about to arrive.

A muffled mechanical sound makes me look up, and I see two large surfaces on the roof slowly slide in opposite directions, leaving a wide opening that shows the night sky. A few seconds later, with an almost imperceptible hum, a shiny silver helijet appears and descends like a feather. From one of the rear windows, Dylan smiles and gives us the thumbs-up to signal his mission's success.

When he gets off the helijet, he raises his arm and holds up a small gadget in his hand with the most radiant expression of triumph on his face. It's surely a memory device where he's stored the codes.

I let Belinda, Mia, and Jonathan go forward to welcome him, and then I approach him too. Without saying a word, and forgetting that everyone is watching us, I hug him so hard that I could be about to break him.

"I'm okay," is the only thing he says. "I'm okay."

I don't answer. I just want to hug him and never let go.

Burke immediately approaches and says in his typical military tone, devoid of emotion:

"Well done, Blake. Make the backup copies right away. I await your report. We leave in fifteen minutes."

I let go of Dylan, and he explains to all of us what happened: everything was going smoothly. At six minutes past six, he had obtained the codes without any problem and was about to leave the ministry. But then, his supervisor called him and ordered him into his office. He had changed next week's work schedule to allocate more time for his birthday celebration—to which Dylan, as the only deel in the team, was not invited. He wanted to assign him additional shifts so that all other team members could join the party. Dylan didn't have any other choice but to follow instructions; anything else would have been too suspicious. He knew it wouldn't take more than fifteen or twenty minutes, so he decided to act as if he had all the time in the world.

His delay made us suffer in hell, but there's no doubt he acted most prudently.

Ten minutes before our departure, Belinda and Mia say goodbye and go to the annex building where the small field hospital is being set up. They don't want to see us leave; they just beg us to come back safe and sound.

Before getting on my unit's helijet, I rush to take Dylan behind a tall pile of ammo boxes, the one closest to us.

"Don't ever scare me like that again," I manage to say in a sigh, before smothering him with kisses.

"Sorry, I didn't want you to worry about me," he says, panting from emotion and lack of air. "Now I want *you* to be very careful."

"Don't worry about me, focus on what you still have to do." Then I insist: "Dylan, this isn't over yet. Please stay close to Burke and don't do anything foolish, do you swear?"

"Yes, I swear… but only if you promise me something in return."

"What?" I say, narrowing my eyes.

"If everything goes well, promise me that we'll fly back together in the same helijet, and you'll kiss me in front of everyone exactly as you kissed me last night."

I laugh while he gazes at me, amused.

"My cheeky rogue, the things you come up with… okay, I promise."

We kiss and hug each other without stopping until we hear Burke's shouts.

The time has come to leave. Unit 1's helijet, carrying Burke's team with Jonathan and Dylan, takes off first; then Unit 2's helijet, with me onboard, follows immediately afterward. Our military helijet has room for many more people than the number of elements in our rescue team, so we have plenty of space to spread out. We must use the trip to focus our minds on the mission awaiting us in a few hours.

After about twenty minutes in flight, Lieutenant Nelson receives a message from the command center. Since he has his headphones on, I don't catch what they say on the other side. I just hear his answer:

"Blue Nest, this is Falcon Two. Did you say here, in our wings? Please confirm. Over."

Nelson nods silently as he hears the response. "Blue Nest, this is Falcon Two. Roger. Initiating search. Please wait. Over," he says into the microphone. He takes off his headphones and gets up.

With a contemplative gaze, he examines the inside of the helijet, trying to find something. Then he approaches a storage area in the service module that separates the pilot's cabin from the rest of the aircraft, opens one of the doors, and discovers the stowaway.

"Get out of there now!" he says in an angry tone.

I can't believe my eyes when I see Mia tumbling out of the narrow cabinet.

After Nelson's harsh reprimand for her "childish stupidity," Mia explains to me why she's done it.

"I had to come, Derin. I had to be here to help however I can with Brian's rescue. I couldn't stand waiting from so far away."

"It was a stupid thing to do, Mia, I'm almost as angry as Nelson," I reply. "But I understand. If you love Brian half as much as I love Dylan, you had no choice."

She beams delightedly.

"You really love him then, don't you?" she says. I confirm by nodding and smiling from ear to ear. Then she adds, "I'm glad because he's crazy about you."

"I would give my life for him."

After confirming to central command that Mia is indeed on board, and requesting that Belinda be informed—she was the one who alerted Taddeus since Mia left her an explanatory note—Nelson has Mia promise that she'll remain inside the helijet during the entire operation. On the other helijet, Jonathan and Dylan have already found out about her situation from Burke.

The flight route is quite complicated. We can't head directly to Moray Firth but have to fly low, following a winding, zigzag course that sometimes even requires us to head in the opposite direction of our destination. The route takes us through "safe corridors" by flying over protectorates more sympathetic to the insurgent cause and, where possible, avoiding those that are loyal to the regime.

We cross the unavoidable stretch with the densest radar coverage without incidents. The rebel infiltrator has done his job well. From here on, our aircrafts' deflectors and defense systems will guarantee that we remain invisible for the rest of our journey.

The next hour and a half of flight go by quite calmly, but as we enter the Highlands Protectorate—the country's northernmost area—and especially when we head toward the coast to go over Moray Firth's waters, strong turbulence causes the helijet to wobble and jump violently. There's a storm over the estuary, and the relentless wind is already shouting out who's in charge of these lands.

CHAPTER 27

VENTUS

THE FINAL MINUTES OF FLIGHT make my stomach rise to my throat. The helijet starts shaking so intensely that we must cling to the seats' armrests; our faces have turned pale and tense. For my taste, we're traveling on too risky a route, although the aircraft's pilot doesn't seem to flinch at all.

To our left, at a menacingly short distance, we can glimpse the impressive sandstone cliffs of the east coast of Caithness County. To our right, a few feet below us, the rough waves of Moray Firth advance like unstoppable furies until they crash against the rock formations.

I feel nauseated as my imagination mocks me with ironic images of us crashing into this rock face and falling into the dark abyss of the relentless waters, which would engulf us like insects before our dangerous mission even begins.

The past also wants to play with me and bombards me with flashes of my family's summer trip to Lake Windermere, when I was twelve years old. I see myself fighting with Brian on the boat, that night when we sneaked out of the cabin to fish alone. I run my fingers over the scar on my left eyebrow as I remember the blow Brian dealt me with the oar, and shudder as I feel surrounded by the cold, black water, about to drown.

No. I can't allow this damn hydrophobia to take hold of me right now. I can't afford the distraction.

I close my eyes and try to meditate. I take measured, deep breaths, and let out the air in my lungs with the same slowness. I search my mind for memories that make me happiest… and I find them. There are the cozy Christmases with my family, full of laughter, carols, good food, and gifts. I also see those Saturday afternoons in the park where my father, Brian, and I used to play with Cinnamon, our beloved beagle, while my mother and baby Lily kept the ants away from our picnic spread on a blanket, under the shade of my father's favorite oak. I visualize my mother's gleaming face and her tears of joy the day I was accepted at the Military Academy and promised her I would become an Army officer and make us all Patriots. I try to recreate every moment of the heavenly night I spent yesterday in Dylan's arms.

Dylan… I say to myself, smiling, and let out a happy sigh. It's probably just my imagination, but under the dominant odor of electronic devices and military equipment here, I can still smell his delicious scent, and I feel the sweet and addictive taste of his lips on mine.

A few miles from our destination, we abandon the route along the cliffs and head in above the mainland, still flying at a very low altitude. The aircraft's stealth technology will now be really put to the test. If the radar detects us, everything will be over before it even begins.

The helijet traces a fairly wide curve, which first takes us away from the coast and then returns and leads us from the north to our final destination. We begin the descent maneuver toward the landing point, a narrow clearing within a copse of trees on high ground behind the Ventus operations center. Nelson gives the orders to start our final preparations. We put on the rest of our equipment, helmets and bulletproof vests, and prepare our weapons.

As we descend vertically, I see the set of buildings that make up the control center and the prison camp—our two objectives—through the window. Everything is still and quiet. Apparently, they haven't detected us.

The Ventus operations complex is located within a crescent-shaped bay, on a short section of beach between endless miles of cliffs. The narrow stretch of sand and rocks is divided in two by a river that flows into the sea. The control center, a massive and well-lit concrete building, is located in the western section, protected from the sea by a breakwater that also acts as a pier. A concrete bridge over the river is the only connection that exists between the control center and the prison camp, which is located on the eastern section, facing the water.

The camp is composed of several low buildings arranged in a grid within a rectangular enclosure. It's surrounded by an electric fence and topped by spirals of barbed wire. A watchtower with an armed guard stands at each of the four corners of the fence. It seems incredible to me that nobody is aware of our arrival from such a short distance, but the technical marvels of these helijets have made our undetected descent possible.

I say goodbye to Mia with a hug before leaving the helijet using the motorized ramp at the rear. Our unit immediately lines up next to Unit 1, which landed before us and is already in formation.

"Mia?" says Jonathan when he sees me.

"Back inside the helijet. She's okay, she'll stay in there."

Dylan and I exchange a smile and hold each other's hands for a moment.

It's strange to see him and Jonathan in the same military uniform the rest of us are wearing; I'm only able to recognize them because we still have our helmet visors up. They're dressed like this for their own safety, of course. The uniform and helmets provide additional protection and give them access to the unit's intercom system.

Burke gives our final instructions and confirms that the attack on the wind turbine towers began the moment our helijets started to descend. The government forces have been deployed and are already in direct confrontation with ours.

We come out of the forest and direct our gaze toward the horizon. From our elevated position, it's unmistakable: several miles out at sea, in the black curtain of night, we can make out small glimmers and illuminated traces. These are explosions caused by grenades and missiles launched by the hydrojets and helijets of NATFOR's revolutionary army, as well as the counterattack by the regime's forces.

Below us, at the end of the slope and on the other side of the access road, is the main entrance to the Ventus control center. About six hundred feet to the east, on the other side of the bridge, lies the prison camp. My skin bristles as I identify the gable-roofed building where, according to our reports, my father and Brian are detained at night.

Commander Burke gives the order to advance.

I put my right arm behind Dylan's neck and pull him close to me.

"I'll see you in a while," I say, looking him in the eyes. He's very anxious, just like me, but impatient to fulfill the second part of his mission. "Be careful… and tear them to pieces!"

"I will," he replies triumphantly. Before letting go, he adds in a whisper, "You be careful, too. I love you."

Nelson and I take the head of our command and lead Second Lieutenant Marvin, Sergeant Alex Davis, and soldiers Miller, Stanley, Brown, Parker, Evans, and Hill toward our objective. We descend quickly but stealthily down to the riverbank. The current isn't very strong, but it's too deep to cross on foot.

"Evans, Parker, the boats," Nelson orders.

The two soldiers carrying oars take off their backpacks and place them on the shore. They pull tightly on small hoops linked to the bags by a cord and, in a matter of seconds, the backpacks are transformed into surprisingly large inflatable boats. Nelson boards one of them with Sergeant Davis and three of the soldiers, and I board the other one with Second Lieutenant Marvin and the rest of the team. I get the creeps as the current growls below us like a mad dog ready to bite.

We cross the river without much difficulty, charting a diagonal path. Lucky for me, no one seems to have noticed the anguish on my face. Evans and Parker make another quick maneuver to deflate the boats and fix them to the ground with anchors, next to the oars. There'll be no danger of them scattering in the wind.

The electric fence surrounding the camp is three hundred feet away. From our angle and position, we can clearly see three of the four watchtowers using our night vision binoculars. Miller, Brown, and Hill arm a high tripod in seconds; it's a long-range sniper rifle with anesthetic darts as ammo.

"Ready at your command," Karen Miller announces, aiming through the scope.

By radio, Nelson coordinates with Burke, who waits with his unit to break into the control center. Upon receiving a response, Nelson gives the order:

"Go ahead, shoot. Don't miss."

We can barely hear the muffled whistle of the first projectile as it is fired; it sticks in the right shoulder of the first watchtower's guard. In my binoculars, I watch the guard flinch when he feels the prick. Then he moves his left hand toward his shoulder to grab whatever has been jabbed into his body, and suddenly loses consciousness and collapses.

In a matter of seconds, Miller rotates the rifle's position and fires twice more; she hits the target both times. The three guards in watchtowers one, two, and three won't wake up for another couple of hours. The guard in tower four, which we can't see from here, is the only one who in theory remains at his post.

"Towers one, two, and three disabled," Nelson indicates to Burke by radio.

Almost instantly, we see flashes on the dock in front of the control center, and a fraction of a second later, we hear the loud explosions. Burke's unit has begun its assault by detonating grenades on the dock. They intend to divert the guards' attention in that direction, while they break into the control center through the primary access.

"Let's move it, quickly!" says Nelson when he hears the next explosion.

We advance at full speed to the nearest point in the fence. Nelson stops ten feet in front of it, aims with the compact grenade launcher he's holding waist-high and fires a "termite" grenade. Upon impact, the chemicals inside the device activate and form a small incandescent ring that eats up the metal wire and expands in all directions; the orange ring fades a few seconds later and leaves a gap at least six feet high and six feet wide.

From the other side of the river, at the control center, we hear several bursts of automatic weapons. It's impossible to know if they're coming from Burke's command or the guards, though it's most likely from both. I have to force myself to dismiss my anguished concern for Dylan. Now I must focus all my attention on the rescue mission. I have to trust Burke's ability and his unit to keep him safe.

We burst into the prison camp and move swiftly, passing the numerous buildings that contain the prisoners' dormitories. We go straight to Building 5, near the main structure that houses the kitchen, cafeteria, control room, and guards' rooms. The guards on duty at the camp's entrance gate will already have noticed that something is wrong with three of the watchtowers guards; they've surely tried to communicate with them without response. They also must have noticed the interruption in the electric fence's energy flow. They'll show up at any moment if they haven't gone to support their colleagues on the other side of the river.

We arrive at Building 5.

My father and Brian, and the Mitchells are all being held here. My adrenaline rises to maximum levels. In a second, I'll have them with me.

Brown sticks a few tiny termite grenades with a time detonator to the right edge of the door and activates them. Three short and flashing explosions immediately destroy the hinges.

I can't take it anymore. I kick down the door violently, and it collapses under the sole of my boot without difficulty. Nelson, Evans, Brown, and I burst into the bedroom while the others stay back, guarding the entrance.

The first thing I see are two long rows of bunks on either side of the corridor in front of us. Despite the darkness, the night vision viewer allows me to see that some of the prisoners have sat up in their beds, looking stunned.

I'm about to light and throw a flare into the center of the room, but one of my unit members has found the switch and turns on the lamps hanging from the gable roof.

"Dad! Brian!" I shout with all my strength, after lifting my helmet's visor.

Dozens of confused and frightened eyes gaze at me.

"Dad! Brian!" I exclaim again, not receiving a response.

I hear several shots outside. They've discovered us.

Nelson orders Evans and Brown to go out and support the other six.

"Thomas Dark! Brian Dark!" he then yells with his shrill voice.

"Dad! Brian!" I shout again, my patience fraying.

"Derin?" says a hesitant voice behind me; I recognize it.

I turn around and see Liam Mitchell standing by the side of a bunk. His father, Jonas, has sat up on the bottom bed and looks at me with unbelieving eyes.

"Derin, is that you?" says Liam.

"Liam!" I exclaim. "Get up! We're leaving, quick!"

I turn my head everywhere, inspecting the two rows of bunks, trying to find Brian and my father.

"Dad! Brian!" I scream again, overwhelmed with exasperation. There are several more shots outside. "Liam! Where are Brian and my father?"

"Err… Derin… they're not here," he answers, still trying to process the situation. "They've taken them away."

My heavy heart sinks to the ground.

"What do you mean, they're not here?" I exclaim desperately. "Where are they?"

"They took them away after dinner. Err… they were chosen to work on some unexpected repairs on one of the platforms."

"Where? Which one?"

"I don't know," he says in a stricken voice. "One of the sea substations, but there are several, I don't know which one they took them to."

I turn to Nelson. "I'm going to get a guard," I say sharply. "I'll beat the information out of him if I have to."

"Dark, three minutes," Nelson replies. "We're leaving in three minutes."

I run to the door and look out carefully.

"Everything under control. Two dead guards and one wounded," says Marvin, very sure of herself. Then she points to her left and says, "Evans got a scratch on his forearm, but he's okay. Stanley's taking care of him."

For a moment, I glance at Julie Stanley bandaging Evans' wound, but I immediately turn back to Marvin.

"Where's the wounded guard?" I ask. At the same moment, I see Parker and Miller pointing their guns at a guard sitting ten feet to my right with his back against the dormitory wall.

I reach the wounded guard in two strides and grab him by the neck.

"Brian and Thomas Dark! Where are they?" I shout, shaking him forcefully.

"At 2, Substation 2," he lets out at once, with a grimace of pain. "They're working over there all night."

Still holding him by the neck with my right hand, I point directly at his eyes with my left hand's index finger.

"If you're lying to me, I swear I'll kill you," I warn him. "If what you're saying isn't true, I'll throw you into the middle of the ocean, do you understand?"

"It's true, I swear, they're at Substation 2," he replies without hesitation.

I don't have any other option. I have to believe him. There's no time to verify his words.

Nelson comes out of the dormitory building with Liam and Jonas. They just had time to put on shoes.

"Dark?" he shouts impatiently, raising his eyebrows with an expectant expression.

"They're in Marine Substation 2," I say and add decisively, "I must go after them, Nelson. It's very close to here."

Nelson quickly consults his device holding interactive maps and plans.

"It's four miles offshore," he says, studying the details appearing on the display. "It has a wide landing platform, but the whole thing is too risky. It's full of enemy ships out there."

"Nelson, this is what we came here for. We must get them out of there," I reply bluntly.

Nelson looks at Second Lieutenant Marvin, who nods without saying anything, indicating that she's in favor.

"Helijet on the way, arriving now!" Nelson says, pointing to the open space on the side of the kitchen building. "Everybody ready to evacuate! Rescue mission continues at Marine Substation 2."

"This one's coming with us," I say, picking up the injured guard. "If he's lied to me, I'll throw him into the sea from the air."

Once the helijet is over our heads and descending, Nelson receives a radio transmission from Unit 1. He gives a thumbs-up and repeats what he hears over his headset:

"Operation High Speed concluded successfully. Function parameters of wind turbines have been modified. Blades are accelerating rotating speed. The turbine's maximum resistance limit is about to be reached. Destruction imminent. Evacuation of Unit 1 in progress… Two casualties."

Two casualties.

My breathing and pulse suddenly stop.

The frightful black abyss begins to break open under my feet, ready to swallow me, but I reject it with all my strength.

No… it's not him; Dylan is still alive. I know he is.

The rear ramp of our helijet opens downward, and we all get in. The aircraft ascends quickly while the ramp is just starting to close.

Mia, in the middle of the cabin, is looking everywhere like crazy, not finding what she's searching for until she locates me.

"Derin!" she lets out, looking at me with an expression of anguish. "Where's Brian?"

"We're going to get him now, Mia. He wasn't here. They're in an offshore substation."

We glide over the prison camp in the direction of the ocean. From my right-side window, I catch a glimpse of the control center and see Unit 1's helijet descending to evacuate our people. From this height, everyone looks the same. In their rebel forces uniforms, it's impossible to distinguish one from the other or to identify the two bodies being carried by some of the others.

Mia, watching from the same window as me, anticipates my thoughts:

"No, Derin, it's not them. Dad and Dylan are fine. I heard it on the radio when Burke communicated with Falcon One's pilot."

I knew he was safe… I felt it inside me, I think, relieved.

The very instant we fly over the beach and head out over the water, the visual spectacle of Ventus' destruction begins. The rest of the unit rushes to the right-side windows to see the pyrotechnic show of the wind turbines several miles away exploding on the dark horizon. It's like watching giant popcorn bursting over the ocean: first a few kernels, and then more and more, until the sky lights up in a frantic swarm of flashes and bursts.

I imagine the expression on Taddeus' face. He must be overwhelmed with joy as he learns of his plan's resounding success.

But my plan, my personal operation, hasn't yet ended. I still haven't rescued Brian and my father, and the operation has become complicated.

It doesn't take us more than five minutes to reach Marine Substation 2, one of the closest to the coast. When our helijet's pilot descends in a semicircle to the landing platform, I see the large, brightly lit number 2 painted in yellow on one side of the structure.

I know Dylan's fine, but for some stupid reason, the substation's number triggers a pair of simple but sinister words in my head: "Two casualties."

CHAPTER 28

SEA OF DARKNESS

WE LAND ON THE LARGE HELIPORT on the marine substation's upper level. Nelson and I have figured out that there may be two or three guards, as well as several technicians, possibly armed as well. No big deal. The highest risk is from the Army forces, but we're encouraged thinking that they'll be too busy in their vain attempt to save Ventus.

We get off the helijet. The only ones staying behind are the pilot, Mia, the Mitchells, the two injured—Evans and the camp guard—and Julie Stanley, the army nurse.

The wind force here is fierce. It takes great effort to move forward and avoid being thrown over. So far, there's no sign of anyone.

We descend in a single file through the narrow metal staircase that connects all levels on one side of the structure. I lead the group. Nelson follows behind me, consulting the interactive map of Ventus on his digital device. The wind is so strong that there's no way to take a step down without holding on to the handrail. I try not to pay too much attention to the roar of the rough sea's menacing waves beneath us, but it's impossible to ignore. I fight my fear of these stormy waters with all my strength, though I feel it's about to paralyze me. One false step, one slip, and I'll fall over the railing and into the bowels of this hungry ocean, which won't hesitate to devour me.

"It's here," Nelson says when we reach the lower level. The wounded guard had told us, under a new death threat, that my father and Brian would surely be on this level.

This is the substation's base platform, supported by colossal steel columns that are submerged in the ocean about thirty feet below us.

Nelson stops for a moment and signals us to wait. He's receiving a message from Burke.

"Falcon One is on its way," he announces. "Two government aircraft are heading toward us. Falcon Two is going to intercept them while Falcon One arrives."

"Will Burke get the civilians off first?" I ask.

"I don't think there will be enough time. But our people are getting out now."

He communicates with our helijet's pilot and orders him to get everyone out, take off, and follow Falcon One's command to coordinate an interception maneuver against the enemy aircraft.

We continue advancing through the lower level. It's a tangled mechanical forest, full of loud machines, pipes, and gigantic electrical power transformers. The machines' roar, together with the shrill whistle of wind gusts slipping through all the corridors and corners, is deafening. As if I weren't already laboring under the threat of a hydrophobia attack, much of the platform's floor is made of metal grids. The powerful reflectors illuminating the columns that support the substation clearly show the seething ocean beneath our feet. When I look down, I blink, trying not to panic.

I turn right into a corridor and see a small booth with a window. I cautiously approach. There inside, a man in a green and orange uniform sits behind a small desk, but turned sideways, with his legs resting on a chair. He's watching a movie on a monitor against the side wall. I gesture to Nelson and the others that there's only one man, grab my gun and open the door.

"Don't move!" I shout when he turns and looks at me, dazed. "Now put your hands up, slowly. Behind your head!"

I step aside and let in Parker, who ties the man's hands behind his back.

"Where are the prisoners they brought in tonight?" I ask him, placing my gun's barrel against his temple.

"Err… what… err…" he mumbles. Apparently, he's the night shift supervisor on duty. He seems harmless enough.

"We won't do anything to you if you stay still and tell me what I want to know," I assure him in a less harsh tone of voice, withdrawing the gun from his head. "Understood?" He nods. "Let's try again. Where are Brian and Thomas Dark, father and son, the prisoners who arrived from the camp tonight?"

"Err… here," he starts, with a clearer but still faltering voice, "they're here… err… finishing some repairs on transformer eight."

"How many guards are there? Where are they now?"

"Err… two… they must be upstairs in the cafeteria… or sleeping."

It's incredible, but nobody here has noticed the massive attack taking place just a couple of miles away. At least not yet.

"Stand up," I order. "Take us to the prisoners Brian and Thomas Dark."

We exit the booth. I retake the lead with the technician showing us the way, and Nelson and the others follow a few steps behind.

We barely advance a couple of feet when Nelson stops us. Another message from Burke.

"Falcon One has arrived. They've let off the whole unit onto the platform. They'll try to shoot down the regime's aircraft."

They've let them off. Good! I think with relief. I'm grateful to Burke for not taking Dylan into air combat.

We continue on our way through the labyrinth of corridors, floored with those see-through grids.

"It's over here, right this way," the supervisor says.

Suddenly, a shrill alarm goes off, accompanied by the flickering signal of red lamps.

"What's that?" I scream at the handcuffed supervisor, but he shrugs, shakes his head, and looks at me with a disoriented expression. He's just as surprised as I am.

"They've detected our aircraft," Nelson explains. "The government's fighter jets must have communicated with the substation to warn of an imminent attack. They've put them on alert. Come on, hurry up!"

We pick up our pace, turn left, then turn right and go out again, onto a wide corridor that runs along the edge of the platform. A metal railing, with bars too far apart for my taste, is the only thing between us and a free fall into the stormy sea. Suddenly, a bright glow illuminates the sky on the opposite side of the substation, followed by a powerful explosion.

"That was one of them," Nelson says, giving a thumbs-up. "Falcon One has knocked it down."

Nelson hasn't yet finished his sentence when one of our helijets passes like thunder a few feet from the railing. Just as it turns left and disappears behind the corner of the substation, the government's helijet—one of the newest models—also whizzes by, chasing it.

An instant later, our second aircraft shows up. We barely manage to see the daredevil maneuver it performs: it passes horizontally next to us, rises almost vertically, rotates on its own axis, twists and crosses above the substation in an upside-down position, and disappears over our heads.

We hear a new explosion, but this time the whole platform shakes, and we must hold on to anything we can find to avoid falling into the sea.

"Enemy missile has been diverted… but has hit the substation," says Nelson, always in communication with Burke. "Get moving! There's no time to lose. This whole thing could fall apart!"

We're about to continue when the rattle of footsteps on the metallic surface behind us makes me flinch. We all turn around, aiming our guns, ready to fire. But I let out a sigh of relief as I see several soldiers from Unit 1 come out onto the exterior corridor.

One of them lets up his visor, and I recognize him immediately. Dylan raises his hand to greet me and smiles, so casual and unconcerned that, for a moment, I forget the explosive situation we're in.

"Nelson, we're here to back you up," says Lieutenant Rees after sliding up his visor too. "The others stayed behind with the civilians and the injured. We must hurry; the missile impacted the substation's north side and has caused a fire that's expanding rapidly. There's possible structural damage."

I don't have time to exchange words with Dylan, who's in the middle of the group of soldiers. I only indicate with signs and grimaces that he must remain in his group, surrounded by rebels with military training. He nods and shows me a thumbs-up.

We run to the end of the outer corridor and turn left, to go inside the substation again. We continue for another thirty feet, but a few steps before we can turn into the passage to the right, the roaring explosion of the next missile impact makes us stop abruptly. This time, the platform's structure shakes much more violently. I feel a shuddering sensation to my very core. The floor, once horizontal, starts to slant, grinding menacingly. We're momentarily flustered, listening to the terrible screech of twisting metal when the flames appear at the end of the corridor. The fire sprinkler system is activated, and water begins to soak us.

"Falcon One has destroyed the enemy!" Nelson shouts. "But the regime's aircraft has crashed into the platform's supporting columns. Come on! Let's go!"

I turn to the right, look ahead toward the end of the corridor, and feel my heart jump with violence when I see them coming swiftly in our direction.

"Dad!" I scream.

Brian is two feet behind him, hauling an unconscious, wounded worker with the help of another prisoner.

The two freeze when they see me, stunned expressions on their faces.

"Dad! Brian! Hurry!" I shout again. "We have to go! We're getting out of here!"

We meet halfway, and I throw myself onto my father with a hug.

"Derin, son, what's going on?" he stammers.

"Dad, are you okay?" is the first thing out of my mouth. "We're leaving, we've come to rescue you." I turn to Brian, who's also looking at me with incredulous eyes. "Brian, everything okay?" He just nods his head. My father looks a bit worn-down, but Brian seems to be in good physical condition. "Okay, come on, hurry up, this thing is about to collapse."

I hold up my father with one arm and help him walk. Two soldiers from Unit 1 take charge of the wounded prisoner, but after a quick examination, one of them announces:

"This one's dead. What happened?"

"Electrical discharge," Brian replies. "I think he had a heart attack. We thought we could save him."

We leave the deceased prisoner and start returning along the same path we came. Nelson confirms with Burke and our pilot that we have my family and that we're heading back to the heliport.

We've barely made it back to the outside corridor when two tremendous explosions shake us. Without a doubt, it's the transformers bursting. The vibrations are now constant, and the entire structure of the substation creaks and grinds. This doesn't look good. We must get out of here immediately.

We reach the accessway that we came through before to get to the outside corridor, but as we're about to enter, Brian exclaims:

"No, we should go straight ahead! It's faster. We'll get to a staircase at the end of this corridor, it leads to the upper level."

Nelson and I look at each other for a second. Then I turn to Brian. "Are you sure?" I ask.

"Yes, totally. Besides, there are lots of machines back there. If we take that way, it's possible the fire will block our way."

"Maybe he's right," Nelson says, uncertain as he looks at his interactive map. Then he turns to Brian. "Okay, take the lead, show us the way out."

As Nelson says those words, the next explosion throws us to the floor. This time, the hot, expansive wave hits us from very nearby, directly from the path we would have taken a few seconds ago. Everything wobbles around us. I look behind us and see flames. Brian was right, we barely escaped that one.

We run along the outer corridor until we reach the end. Here, the corridor becomes wider and is more like a terrace. Brian points to a metal door.

"It's over there," he says. He goes to the door and moves the handle, but nothing happens. The door is locked.

"Brown!" Nelson shouts.

Brown pulls out a pair of small termite grenades from his backpack. He places them on the metal door's hinges, activates the detonators, and moves away. We see the flashes of the chemical reaction immediately eating up the metal. Brown and I kick the door, and it gives way without much resistance.

Brian leads us to the back of a room that looks like a warehouse. We find another door, but unlike the first, it's not locked. We go out onto another open space and see the staircase that leads up to the heliport.

We move quickly, holding tightly onto the handrails, which are wet and slippery. Above us, I hear the metallic clicking of some loose part hitting against the side of the substation. The whole staircase seems very unstable.

"Move faster! Come on!" Nelson shouts. "This shit isn't going to stand much longer."

Suddenly, he pauses to listen to a message entering his earpiece.

"Stop!" he orders with an alarmed face. "We must go back. The helipad's platform has tilted too far and is threatening to collapse. The helijets can't land. The others are coming down now."

I raise my head and see a group of people stumbling down the stairs. It's Mia, Jonathan, the Mitchells, and everyone else who was waiting on the top level.

"Mia!" Brian exclaims when he recognizes his girlfriend.

He rushes toward her like a madman, slipping halfway but soon regaining his balance. He reaches Mia and wraps her with his arms. She hugs and kisses him with abandon.

"Everyone, get back, fast! The helijets will approach the edge of the platform," says Nelson, pointing to the open space that we left a while ago, at the end of the outer corridor. "The rear doors will be let down to evacuate us. Come on, hurry!"

We turn around and start coming down. We reach the bottom of the steps, cross the short open corridor, and go into the warehouse. We head through it quickly and go outside again, to the terrace where the helijets will pick us up. There, we gather in a semicircle and Nelson takes a headcount to make sure no one is missing.

I'm still holding on to my father, who leans on my shoulder. He pants intensely and seems exhausted.

"How are you feeling, Dad?" I ask in a worried tone. "Hang on there, we're leaving soon."

He doesn't have the strength to speak. He just nods and gives me a shadow of a smile. His face is ashen. He's in worse condition than I'd thought.

"Lean on here for a while, rest a bit," I say as I help him lean against the railing. He has difficulty breathing.

I immediately look away from the violent waves below us. I turn around and lean on the railing too, with my back facing the sea. Just a few more seconds and we'll be out of here. I know everything will be fine, but a gloomy feeling overwhelms me for a fraction of a second until I notice Dylan's beautiful smile coming toward me.

I step ahead and hug him tightly. Although he keeps smiling, I notice the anxiety in his eyes. The explosions continue, and each time they feel closer.

"Is your dad okay?" he asks.

"He's exhausted. He needs a doctor," I reply. Then I smile at him and pat him on the cheek. "You did it, huh? You blew it to pieces."

Dylan's eyes shine again.

"Yes… It got a little tense, but we did it in the end. I'm dying to tell you everything if we get out of here alive."

I grab him by the shoulders and bring him close to me, against my chest.

"We're leaving now, don't worry."

At this very instant, our helijets appear and begin to turn smoothly so that the rear doors can descend and lie on the platform's railing.

"You see? We're leaving now," I say, hugging him harder, but I feel the floor grids below vibrate with such intensity that I fear they'll break free from the structure before we can get on the aircraft.

I close my eyes for a moment, begging for the platform not to yield so soon, and open them again. Then, over Dylan's shoulder, I see the two guards.

They come running toward us on the outer corridor, wielding their weapons.

As I grab my gun with my right hand, I jerk Dylan hard with my left arm, trying to throw him to the floor and get him out of the line of fire. But I don't manage to knock him down. Dylan remains standing, confused, six feet beside me, in the exact direction that the first guard's gun is pointing.

I shoot, and the bullet hits the guard's chest and kills him, but it's a thousandth of a second too late. He's already fired.

From the corner of my eye, as if in slow motion, I see someone pouncing on Dylan. The two fall to the ground while I hear shots from the other guard, who is still running toward us.

I feel a terrible twinge when one of the projectiles hits me on the left shoulder, but despite the intense pain, I know it has struck the bulletproof vest that runs a few inches over my arm. I'm sure it hasn't penetrated it. I release three shots that hit the guard's arm and torso. His gun goes flying to one side, and he collapses, his body sliding several feet over the floor's slippery metal surface.

A quick look at my shoulder confirms that I'm not hurt, though the throbbing pain continues. I throw myself to my knees next to Dylan, who now sits up.

"Are you okay?" I shout, examining him and frantically feeling his whole body, looking for injuries—but I don't find any.

"Yes, I think so," he replies, somewhat stunned.

I turn to the soldier who received the bullet aimed at Dylan. He writhes in pain on the ground next to us. It's Alex Davis, my unit's sergeant, who cared so much for Dylan. The bullet hit his leg, and he's bleeding a lot. He must be taken care of right away.

But then I hear Brian's deranged cry, which shakes my soul: "Daaad!"

I turn to the platform's railing, where my father had been leaning on to rest, and see him too.

My father is stretched back over the railing, with both hands over his blood-stained chest.

I jump like an animal to grab him, but I can only see the faint smile on his face and the placid look he gives me as his body slides over the metal railing and falls into the ocean.

"Dad!" I cry desperately.

Everything happens like in a dream, as if I weren't really here and someone else took charge of my body.

In a millisecond, I take off my bulletproof vest, climb on the railing, and throw myself into the abyss. As I fall into the raging waters, I know I won't make it out of this alive, but I don't care. The only thing I regret is not turning around to see Dylan one last time, to look into his beautiful eyes and tell him that I love him … that I will love him forever.

I drop like a stone into the sea and submerge several feet, but somehow I manage to break the surface. Trying not to swallow water, I turn my head in all directions, hoping to find my father, but I'm overwhelmed by the certainty that the ocean has swallowed him. I'm amazed at how well I can see. The substation's reflectors illuminate the ocean around me as if it were daytime. In a small corner of my mind, I notice the fire burning at the bottom of the platform.

I keep swimming around frantically.

I'm about to give up, and I'm reaching the limit of my strength, when I finally see something.

It's my father, floating unconscious a few feet to my right. I swim toward him, making an enormous effort to fight against the waves pushing me in the opposite direction. Finally, I manage to reach him. I hold him from behind, placing my arm over his neck.

"Hold on, Dad, please hold on," I beg.

I hear the hum of the helijet's engines right above us. I raise my head and spot Burke and Brian on the open rear ramp. They shout something I can't understand. The pilot brings down the aircraft until the ramp almost touches the water.

I only need to swim a short stretch. I can do it.

"Hold on, Dad, we're almost there. Hold on. Mom and Lily are waiting for us."

With my last remaining energy, I reach the helijet's platform.

Burke and Brian take my father out of the water and pull him into the aircraft. I cling to the edge and let out a deep sigh of relief before I start to climb up, panting from the effort and lack of air.

When half of my body is already onto the helijet's ramp, one of the soldiers leans down to help me. I recognize Dylan's face before a huge wave appears out of nowhere and crashes over me.

Totally exhausted, I don't have a drop of strength left. I resign myself to the inevitable and let the wall of water engulf me and drag me down with it.

The force and weight of the wave instantly pull me down into a deep place, where cold and darkness surround me.

This is it. This is how I die, I think, amazed at the serenity I feel.

The hydrophobia tries to make me despair, to panic, but I reject it indifferently. Yes, my life ends here, but I will die calm and content. I've done what I could. I've rescued my father and my brother, and they'll get back to my mother and Lily. Promise fulfilled. They will take care of them, and with the help of Taddeus and the Blakes, they'll be able to flee the country. They'll be safe.

Dylan, my love… you made me so happy, I will love you forever. Don't forget me.

I love you all. Goodbye.

I'm about to open my mouth to swallow water and end this once and for all, but a hand grabs me by my uniform's collar and pulls me hard, bringing me to the surface. In my half-unconscious state, I can barely make out the blurred image of my brother Brian's face before everything goes dark.

—

WHEN I OPEN MY EYES AGAIN, with my back on the hard floor of the helijet, I see out-of-focus faces and lights. Someone turns me over to throw up the water I've swallowed. A while later, when I've recovered enough strength and can breathe without too much difficulty, I sit up slowly.

I see my father lying on a stretcher, next to one of the helijet's outer walls. Brian is squatting beside him, holding his hand with both of his. He turns to me with eyes full of tears.

He doesn't need to say anything. I know.

A terrible emptiness enters my heart and gives way to heart-rending pain that seizes my whole being.

Our father is dead.

CHAPTER 29

FACE OF THE INSURGENCY

THE HARDEST MOMENT OF MY LIFE, to live through and to forget, was when I walked out of the helijet's rear ramp and had to break my mother's and Lily's hearts by announcing that I was bringing my father's corpse with me.

Three days have passed, and I still can't process that my father is gone forever.

I just can't believe it's true. I'm moved by the serenity with which my mother and Lily have faced this tragedy, though. After the initial blow of the news and their tears, their emotional strength hasn't ceased to amaze me. Of course, Brian's return, the relief of having him back among us, also helps them cope with the loss. But I don't understand why I'm the one in our family with the most problems accepting my father's death.

There are times when I feel that I'm going crazy with despair, tormented by remorse for failing to save his life. We were so close. A few more seconds and we would have boarded the helijets. We would all be back safe and sound.

In my mind, I review every second that we were on the marine substation's platform until I'm exhausted. I look for any indication, something that says I could have acted better, but I don't find anything conclusive to help me accept the facts and begin the process of emotional healing. I always end up with extreme alternatives:

either there was nothing I could have done differently to prevent my father from dying, and I'm, therefore, free of all guilt; or everything I did that night was wrong, and his death is due solely and exclusively to my negligence and clumsiness.

Neither of these two options satisfies me.

Why couldn't I see those bastards sooner? I ask myself again and again, but my inner voices can't agree on whether that would have made a difference.

Everyone has been trying hard to cheer me up, to convince me of my courage and heroism. Even Brian, who until recently spared no criticism of my actions, is now the most enthusiastic voice of praise and admiration in my favor. He never tires of thanking me for coming to rescue them, and he doesn't stop repeating how proud he is of having me as a brother. He insists that nothing I could have done otherwise would have prevented our father's death. But what's the use of all the courage, heroism, and brotherly pride in the world, if, in the end, I couldn't bring back my father alive?

The only one who seems to understand what's happening inside of me—better than everyone—is Dylan.

He's the only one who doesn't overwhelm me with continuous and exhausting—although well-intentioned—attempts at consolation. He's just there with me, embraces me, loves me and, for brief moments, makes me forget everything.

He wanted to accompany me to my father's farewell, but Taddeus objected outright. It was already too risky, as well as horribly costly, to allow us to come here to scatter his ashes. "Of all the places in the world," he said, "you couldn't have chosen a worse place." But we insisted that he provide us with some way to come to London, to the park near our house, so we could place my father's remains under the big oak tree that witnessed some of the happiest moments of our family: those Saturdays when we played with our beagle, Cinnamon, and later enjoyed my mother's delicious sandwiches under the branches' welcoming shadows.

My father would have wanted us to say goodbye to him here, in his favorite corner of the world.

In the end, Taddeus agreed to our request, no doubt thanks to the overflowing euphoria brought about by his great strategic strike.

"The Crowleys won't think we're so stupid as to let Derin Dark and his family go right into the lion's den," he finally concluded with a sarcastic smile, before arranging to get us fake teleCards, convincing disguises, and a first-rate escort.

Our bodyguards have been sitting on a bench on the paved sidewalk behind us. They play their role well as a loving couple enjoying the picnic from their basket, which, in addition to some sandwiches and drinks, is packed with lethal weapons.

It's a beautiful autumn afternoon, fresh but sunny. The foliage on the trees has begun to fall, predicting the upcoming winter leaf by leaf. But our beloved oak is still a huge sphere of yellow and orange, like a ball of fire in the middle of the park. It's an image of autumnal beauty and tranquility that invites us to forget the sad reason why we're here. It also belies the state of chaos that the regime—in fact, the whole country—is facing since the attack on Ventus.

We spread the blanket on the lawn, near the thick trunk, and sit in a circle looking toward the center. From the basket, we take out the small containers with my father's ashes, one for each of us. After silently checking our surroundings, we say a few words one by one and scatter the contents of our little boxes discreetly among the oak's roots. My mother is first, then Lily and Brian follow. I'm the last one.

"Dad… thanks for everything," I start in a weak, trembling voice. Then, I can't hold back the tears any longer, and all my repressed emotions overflow. "Forgive me, Dad… please forgive me…" I stutter between choked sobs.

My mother takes my hand, and Brian puts his hand on my shoulder, while Lily, in front of me, wipes the tears from her cheeks. I turn around, and with three quick shakes, I let the ashes drop to the ground.

"Goodbye, Dad…"

It's done. He's gone forever.

At least we've been able to say goodbye to him intimately, at his favorite place. At least in this matter, I haven't failed him.

Suddenly, perplexed, I realize that the simple act of scattering his ashes under "his oak" has had an almost magical effect on me. I can't say that the pain and remorse of not being able to save him have vanished. That's not it; they're still there, intense as ever. I know the grief and emptiness that his death has left behind will follow me for the rest of my life. But something has changed inside me: I begin to accept that I'm not the one responsible for his death, nor for the suffering of my mother and siblings.

It was foolish of me to think so.

There's only one cause of all the misfortunes that have shaken my family. There's only one reason why millions of people have to suffer so unjustly and cruelly. It's a devilish disease that has corrupted our society at its roots, and that only destroys lives. It's an evil that must be annihilated, and the sooner, the better.

It's the despicable lineage of the Crowleys.

—

WE RETURN TO THE STRIP before sunset without any major incident. In our hideaway, we get rid of the disguises that gave us new identities for several hours, and then we're escorted by a large security deployment to NATFOR's headquarters.

Today is the official celebration of the victory of Operation Don Quixote, and Taddeus has insisted that we be there. There will be a recognition for all those killed in the operation and, of course, my father will be honored too. The insurgency's new propaganda video, in which I play a starring role, will also be broadcast live to the whole country tonight.

The first thing I do when I get there is to search for Dylan. I need to hug him.

I find him in the infirmary, sitting in a chair next to the hospital bed where Alex Davis lies, recovering from the bullet wound in his left thigh. Upon returning from our operation, he had to undergo a complicated surgery that lasted several hours, but fortunately, everything went well. They managed to save his leg, and doctors say that, with the right therapy, he won't have any significant issues. I'm glad to see that Mia is also with them because I don't like the two of them being alone together.

I'm aware that I'm an idiot for feeling jealous. After all, I should feel forever grateful to Alex for standing between Dylan and the bullet. I don't even want to imagine the horror of the double loss that would now torment me if that bullet had reached him. But, for some stupid reason, I feel that if someone had to throw himself in front of Dylan to protect him, it should have been me. And it wasn't… It was Alex. Exactly the one guy who doesn't hide his feelings for Dylan.

"How are you doing, Alex?" I ask, struggling to sound genuine.

"Hi, Derin. Great, thanks. I barely feel any pain now," he replies.

I approach Dylan, who has stood up, and greet him with a big hug and a kiss, which he responds to with a sweet smile and a stroke on my cheek.

"How did it go?" he asks with a sad expression in his eyes.

"Well… all good. I'll tell you later, okay?"

Mia greets me with a hug too and immediately goes looking for Brian.

Dylan and I stay with Alex for another five minutes, awkwardly exchanging a few sentences about the weather and the latest news reports. When we finally leave for the theater for Taddeus' victory speech, I feel relieved.

The theater is even more crowded than a few days ago. I don't know how they've managed to fit more people in here. The atmosphere is euphoric. This time, instead of witnessing the event from the gallery in the back, Dylan and I take our seats in a group of chairs on the stage. Apart from the Blakes, my mother, Lily, and Brian, the places of honor are occupied by Commander Burke, Commanders Scott and Anderson of the Northern Forces, and several other insurgent leaders. The members of our special command units are in the front row, right by the stage. I see Lieutenant Nelson, Second Lieutenant Marvin, and all the others, including those who were slightly injured. Liam Mitchell and his family are also close to the stage.

Taddeus makes his triumphant entry by pounding the air with his fist in victory, under a deafening roar of applause and cheers. He immediately turns to our side of the stage. He motions to us with both arms outstretched and then applauds effusively, nodding with total conviction. He encourages the audience to join his applause in our honor.

When the ovations drop in intensity after several minutes, Taddeus goes to the microphone at the podium.

"Dear friends," he exclaims enthusiastically, "we're facing a historic milestone in our country. We've started the final race toward the most desired victory of all: the overthrow of the dictatorship!"

He raises his fist in the air, and the audience explodes madly.

"That's right! Ventus has been completely destroyed," Taddeus confirms. "The big toad Crowley can find the remains of his flagship project on the ocean floor. There it lies in thousands of pieces!"

"Yeaahhh!" the audience roars. Now Taddeus tosses both fists into the air.

"We've eliminated the largest source of future government resources," he continues, "we've cut off their arteries, and…" The audience roars again, but Taddeus signals for them to wait a little, and continues, "in addition, the rebel forces from the north carried out devastating attacks on government military installations, greatly weakening the regime's military capacity in that half of the country. The north is ours!"

"Yeaahhh!" The elated cry of the rebels is repeated.

I'm surprised to hear this announcement from Taddeus since I wasn't aware of that part of the operation.

"We can't honor enough the ability and leadership of Commanders Scott and Anderson," Taddeus says, pointing to the two and beckoning them to rise while the audience cheers and calls them by their names. "Yes, friends, these brave women have struck our enemy's military power hard and sent him to his knees. Let's learn from them! Let's follow their example!"

Ana Scott and Lina Anderson greet and thank the audience, the first with jubilant gestures, the latter just nodding, visibly uncomfortable.

Next, Taddeus proceeds to honor the "masterminds" that made this cunning plan possible.

"Come on, guys, stand up!" Taddeus requests. "Here they are, friends: Jonathan and Dylan Blake! Our geniuses, our best minds."

When the two stand up to receive enthusiastic applause and thanks, I look at Dylan with admiration and pride. He waves shyly to the audience. I can't help but smile from ear to ear.

The most difficult part of the speech for my family and me is when Taddeus pays homage to those who lost their lives in the insurgent operation.

"They all are…" he exclaims, forcing tears, "they all are our heroes. Those who gave their lives in the struggle for justice and freedom. We owe them and their families the greatest gratitude and respect for such a sacrifice."

When he makes special mention of my father, his photograph is projected onto the big screen at the back of the stage. My mother, Lily, Brian, and I stand up to thunderous applause, and I have to make a considerable effort to prevent tears from flowing.

I feel much more comfortable when Taddeus concludes the emotional part of his speech and moves on, with the same enthusiasm from before, to what must be his favorite part.

"We're stronger than ever!" he exclaims. "More and more protectorates dare to speak out against Crowley. I assure you, dear compatriots, it won't be long before most of the governors in the Council join our just revolution!"

The whole theater reverberates with victorious shouts and exclamations, so much so that for a few moments, I'm afraid the entire structure will collapse on us.

Taddeus ends his speech by announcing that next, we'll watch the new video from the insurgency, which will be broadcast live to the whole country thanks to the technological mastery of the revolutionary forces.

"It's a very personal message," he explains, "and it's especially directed at the members of the Commons, to convince them once and for all to join this fight." He then turns to me and continues, smiling broadly: "And who's more suitable and convincing to deliver this message than our steadfast and brave Derin Dark?"

"Derin! Derin! Derin!" The crowd begins to chant my name, even without Taddeus' instruction.

Hot blood rises to my cheeks and ears. I'll never get used to this.

A few seconds later, the video broadcast starts.

It's a strange feeling to hear my own voice address the nation, accompanied by a persuasive compilation of images. I almost don't recognize myself as the person speaking so fluently and confidently, but I know it's me. Yesterday, I spent several hours in the recording studio until I was exhausted, repeating the script they'd prepared for me again and again. We had to record it dozens of times until finally, the propaganda director and Taddeus were satisfied.

I know it by heart, and now that I hear my voice uttering the phrases I recorded for the world, I repeat them in silence, almost as if encouraging the speaker in the video, so he doesn't make any mistakes and end up embarrassing me.

I address the millions of citizens of the Commons as one of them. My image hasn't appeared yet, but I state at the beginning of the video that it's me, Derin Dark, speaking to them. I start by narrating, using authentic and simple words, the ways my family and I, as well as millions of others, have been honest, hard-working, and loyal citizens of our country. I explain, in a very personal tone, my own challenges, the obstacles I've had to overcome, and the great effort that my training at the Military Academy demanded, where I graduated with honors, always with the intention of humbly serving my country.

Then I make a brief summary of the extraordinary events during the last two weeks, beginning with the charade of the attack on the regent. Convincingly, I outline the elements that expose the supposed rebel attack as a Machiavellian plot orchestrated by Regent Crowley himself. I point out the cruel reason for that farce: to have another excuse to further increase the oppression of the country's citizens and to publicly and theatrically get rid of some of the regent's bitterest enemies, such as Governor Hall, who had dared to speak out against crimes committed by the regime.

The scriptwriters did well to include a scathing appeal to public memory regarding the two events that changed our country's history during the war, and which were key to the Crowley's grabbing total power: the destruction of Blackpool with a nuclear device and the attack on Westminster, which burnt the old parliament to ashes and took the lives of most of its members.

I explain to the population that those inhumane acts were also perpetrated by the Crowleys, and not by the separatists who fought against the Government three decades ago. I warn that the Crowleys have no regard for the limits of human decency and that they won't hesitate to commit any atrocity that contributes to keeping them in power.

Next, I describe the horrors the regime has made my family suffer.

In this part of the message, I speak directly to Nigel Crowley.

When my voice begins explaining the reason why my brother Brian was selected for that cruel show, I start to blush.

Taddeus insisted that I mention the harassment I suffered from Nigel at the Military Academy, suggesting that his anger and spite, provoked by the humiliation of my rejection, was the reason why he wanted to take revenge on me.

My story makes him look ridiculous. I present the regent's son, the Prosecutor of the Nation, the head of the counterterrorist forces, as intoxicated with power and willing to destroy anyone who stands in his way or refuses to give in to all his whims and wishes.

Before concluding, I list the main elements of the operation to destroy Ventus, accompanied by impressive images of the wind turbines exploding in a spectacular display of bursts and lights. I make clear to the viewers that the wind farm wasn't going to bring any benefit to the people, and that their sole purpose was to generate energy to sell abroad, so that the Crowleys and their henchmen would become richer and more powerful than they already are, while most of the country would have to continue accepting crumbs.

During the video's final seconds, my face appears for the first time, filling the entire screen and looking directly into the eyes of each of the millions of viewers.

"You look super handsome," Dylan whispers in my ear as he grabs my hand. I smile and stroke his thumb.

My blown-up image assures the members of the Commons that life in the Crowley's chokehold will never get better. It will get worse and worse until everyone becomes a slave to the dictator. I urge them not to be afraid, to rise up against the ruthless regime, and to join the insurgent struggle to restore freedom and justice for all.

At the end of the video, my face fades out and, in its place, a graphic, stylized representation appears, showing half of my nose, my left eye, and my eyebrow split in two by the scar. The three supreme virtues of Englandom and the insurgency's revolutionary motto appear beneath it: "PRIDE, JUSTICE, AND FREEDOM." "END OPPRESSION NOW!"

AT THE FIRST OPPORTUNITY, Dylan and I slip away from the celebratory party in the theater. We don't even have to say anything. With discreet looks and signals, we agree and run up the stairs, competing to see who arrives first. We stop twice on the way to hug and kiss each other and then race again to the rooftop.

As I'm winning, just before I reach the creaky door at the top of the stairs, Dylan grabs me from behind and tickles me on the sides. I stop in my tracks.

With a charming, triumphant smile on his face, he swiftly moves past me, opens the door, and crosses the finish line. I go after him with the clear intention of disputing his tricky victory, and catch up with him at the exact spot where we shared our first kiss.

But, instead of admonishing him, I embrace him, and we melt again into a symphony of kisses, caresses, and hugs.

"You know, we could get out of here, right?" he says, looking into the distance at the lights of London as we stand side by side, our arms around each other's shoulders and waists. "We could get away if we wanted to… Escape to Ireland. I know some people have done it, and I'm sure we could convince Taddeus to help us. He owes us."

I hug him harder and then turn him to face me. I kiss him on the lips.

"I know… and it would be wonderful," I reply softly. "There's nothing I want more in the world than to put all this madness behind us, to be with you somewhere where we're left in peace. But… you know we can't just leave. At least, not yet. My family… and yours."

"Yes, I know," he says, returning the tender kiss. "But I can still dream, right?"

We embrace each other, enjoying this moment just between the two of us. For a brief time, we can almost forget the chaos around us and the hard road ahead.

The truth is that I have no choice.

My body and my spirit will be restless until I've made sure my family is safe.

I won't be satisfied until I avenge my father's death.

I can't think about being happy until I've done everything I can to liberate my country from dictatorship.

—

END OF BOOK ONE

AUTHOR'S NOTES

Dear reader,

First of all, I'd like to thank you for taking the time to read *Heroes of Englandom*. I hope you enjoyed the first part of Derin and Dylan's story. If you liked the book, I'd genuinely appreciate it if you could write a review on the shopping platform where you bought it, even if it's just a sentence or two. Every review is important and helps other readers discover the book. Also, your opinion represents invaluable support for me as an author.

On the other hand, Derin and Dylan's adventure is just beginning. If you don't want to miss the release of the second book of the Englandom series, please subscribe to the VIP list at www.erikjacobsbooks.com. Your email will be handled with total confidentiality, and you can unsubscribe at any time.

Thanks a lot for your support!

Erik

ABOUT THE AUTHOR

ERIK JACOBS wrote *Heroes of Englandom*—the first book in a trilogy—eager to introduce a young gay protagonist as the hero of a YA-dystopian novel.

After a successful career in design, finance, and e-commerce, Erik rediscovered that his true passion is writing stories that entertain and even motivate readers—through their characters, with their virtues and flaws—to have a more positive view of the world and their own mission in life.

Erik feels at home in different countries, but he spends most of his time very close to the Pacific Ocean.

More about Erik at www.erikjacobsbooks.com